SEARCHING FOR A KILLER

"Anybody can kill," Lang argued. "And Catherine seems to be a woman of rigid rules."

"If Cat is really a member of the Colony, and she took a lover and became pregnant, that might certainly stir up some strong emotions in Catherine, but I don't think it would set her on a path of murder. Either the baby, Cat, or even this Rafe."

"Then why won't she even talk to me?" Lang asked.

"You haven't given her a clue what it's about."

"She knows Cat left. She has to be worried about it. But for some reason she doesn't want to face it, and why would that be? Because she's at fault in there somewhere. Maybe criminally at fault."

"You're trying to force facts to fit your own theory."

"Why are you so dead set on defending a woman you don't even know?" Lang demanded. "You don't think a woman could be diabolical enough to chase them down and knife them to death?"

"Oh, yes, I do. Women can surprise you with their strength, fury, and commitment," Claire said. "I just think you're totally off base with Catherine. You're focused on her and it's taking you away from the real killer . . ."

Books by Nancy Bush

CANDY APPLE RED

ELECTRIC BLUE

ULTRAVIOLET

UNSEEN

BLIND SPOT

Published by Kensington Publishing Corporation

Blind Spot

NANCY BUSH

ZEBRA BOOKS
KENSINGTON PUBLISHING CORP.
http://www.kensingtonbooks.com

ZEBRA BOOKS are published by

Kensington Publishing Corp.
119 West 40th Street
New York, NY 10018

All Kensington titles, imprints, and distributed lines are available at special quantity discounts for bulk purchases for sales promotion, premiums, fund-raising, educational, or institutional use.

Special book excerpts or customized printings can also be created to fit specific needs. For details, write or phone the office of the Kensington Special Sales Manager: Attn.: Special Sales Department. Kensington Publishing Corp., 119 West 40th Street, New York, NY 10018. Phone: 1-800-221-2647.

Zebra and the Z logo Reg. U.S. Pat. & TM Off.

ISBN-13: 978-1-4201-0341-0
ISBN-10: 1-4201-0341-5

First Printing: July 2010
10 9 8 7 6 5 4 3 2 1

Printed in the United States of America

AUTHOR'S NOTE

This is a work of fiction. Yes, there is a Tillamook County Sheriff's Department but in my novel all the members of the department are fictional, and I've relocated the department itself to the center of town, rather than on Long Prairie Road, where you would actually find it if you were looking. All of the other characters in this book are fictional as well, and though some of the places are real, I've futzed with the geography enough to make driving from Portland to the coast more like a trip on a superhighway than the two lane, unlit road over several mountain passes that it mostly is. Anyone who's traveled Highway 26 at night, in the rain or snow or whatever, will know what I'm talking about. And for the purposes of keeping the characters doing something other than driving, I've made the state of Oregon just a little smaller.

Prologue

A blast of wind slammed against the old pickup and nearly wrenched the wheel from Rafe's hands. He muttered under his breath and with an effort kept the vehicle bouncing hard down the road. Night was thick and black, and the keening wail of the wind kept his senses on high alert.

He glanced down at the crown of the blond angel snuggled up next to him. She was older than he was by six months, but she was so fragile that he felt manly and protective around her. He wanted to put an arm over her shoulders but needed both hands to wrangle this miserable old Chevy truck down the highway.

They were running away. Running away together. It scared him and thrilled him at the same time.

He saw her slide a hand over her protruding belly, and it made him feel warm inside. His baby. Their baby. He wanted to crow with delight.

They'd gotten away!

But there was still danger.

She was silent as they continued to rattle and shake down the road. He hoped to hell the rough ride didn't hurt the baby. They were going for a new start, a new life.

Damn! It felt *good*!

Rafe gazed through the inky blackness and saw tree limbs bend toward the vehicle as he passed, as if they were trying to stop them. Nothing could stop them. He wouldn't let it.

A dozen more miles passed beneath the tires and he mused into the silence, "You know they found that woman's body. The whore that everyone kinda called a witch? She'd been dead a while. Nothing but bones, really."

Rafe was better at being a dope in love than a conversationalist; he just didn't know it. The girl beside him listened quietly, neither encouraging nor discouraging him.

"I told you about the Blackburns, right?" he went on. "I do some work for them sometimes? That old couple who hide behind their curtains in their big house and spy on other houses? They saw the fire across their field a few years back and thought the witch died then. Maybe she did. But the cops and stuff dug all around and didn't find her. Guess he hid her. But they found her now. Just a bag of bones."

They drove on for a while. The crying wind rose to a shriek as they passed through the mountains. The Coast Range. Rafe was taking them away from the beach and toward Portland, though he didn't have the foggiest idea what they would do when they reached the city. But Tasha had wanted to get far away, and so the biggest city in Oregon was where they were heading.

They passed a rest stop, one lonely light shining through the cold night air. Rafe had been feeling his bladder and, with a grimace, stepped on the brakes and swung the truck back around.

"What are you doing?" she demanded sharply.

"Gotta drain the lizard, hon. I'm quick. You know how quick I am."

"Hurry."

He dared to touch her silken hair, comforting her. But she was tense and her blue eyes were shadowed and haunted as they looked up at him.

Rafe drove into the rest stop and parked in the handicap spot closest to the restrooms. The men's and women's signs were visible under the yellow light by the doors.

He started to get out and Tasha scrambled after him. Lovingly looking down at her awkward form, he asked, "What are you doing outta the truck?"

"I have to go, too," she said.

"You're peeing for two." He grinned in the darkness, his dark hair flying around his face. "Pretty soon that little bugger's gonna be here."

He helped her toward the door and made sure the women's room was unlocked, then whistled as he strode toward the men's room. He couldn't believe his good fortune. She loved him. Loved. Him. They'd only made love a half a dozen times or so, all under the cover of secrecy because she would be in deep, deep shit if anyone at the house found out. Once they'd gone out to the graveyard and made love right on top of one of her dead relatives. Cold as a witch's tit, and he'd felt guilty and strange, but she'd been so beautiful. White skin, blond hair, a kind of smile that made him want to throw her down and screw the hell out of her. Brand her as his. And he had, too. God, it had been something. She'd had to clap her hand over his mouth 'cause he'd wanted to howl and scream that he'd claimed her.

Another time they'd made love standing up—their usual way, 'cause of the weather—under her bedroom window. It had been a lot colder, and they'd had to be quicker. The danger was heightening. He'd come so fast he'd been a little embarrassed but she'd said it was okay. Had to be that way. Only way they could be together.

And then the people in the house had started to guess

what was going on. They'd gotten stricter with her. He'd had trouble seeing her alone. But she loved him. She told him she loved him over and over again. And he loved her just as much.

They'd had a heck of a time seeing each other. Stolen moments here and there. And then they'd learned she was pregnant. She'd whispered it to him when they were outside, under a cold spring night. He'd been scared shitless at first. Then thrilled. He'd begged her to run away with him and she'd said yes.

So here they were, months later, fulfilling their dream. Their destiny.

Zipping up, Rafe strolled out of the bathroom. She wasn't out yet. Women never were. He glanced at a small field surrounded by the waving firs and decided to walk over and have a smoke.

Tasha leaned against the side of the stall, feeling cumbersome and fat. Her eyes were closed and she was mumbling encouragement to herself. She had set them on this path and now it was just a matter of timing.

A curtain of darkness was descending inside her head. Nothing new. She'd had the same trouble since she could remember. An affliction, she'd been told. Well, they were never going to tell her that again!

She heard the rumble of another vehicle pulling into the rest stop, the noise just barely discernible over the keening of the wind. Her heart clutched. She waited and then footsteps headed into the women's room, carefully measured treads.

Tasha's eyes flew open and her lips parted. The saliva dried in her mouth.

The footsteps slapped against the concrete floor, pausing a moment by Tasha's door. She was glad for the dim illumination; the lightbulbs barely worked at all. She dug her fingernails into her palms.

They didn't even bother going into another stall. Just turned around and headed back outside without using the facilities.

Carefully, Tasha slipped her lock, peeked out, then tiptoed toward the outside door. She would be seen under the yellow light if she made a break for the pickup. Yet she had no choice.

Silently cursing her ungainly shape, she drew a long breath, then hurried as best she could into the night and to the passenger door. It was open and she clutched it like a lifeline. But there was no Rafe inside. Where was he?

Sidestepping the door, she slipped around the rear of the pickup. The newly arrived vehicle was three spots over, a dark sedan. She gave it a long, hard look. The driver was nowhere to be seen.

Then she thought she heard voices. A snatch on the wind.

". . . baby . . ."

". . . wasn't supposed . . ."

". . . get . . . away . . ."

". . . you can't . . . !"

Tasha moved from the rear of the Chevy back to the side, keeping the pickup between her and the grassy area where the voices seemed to be coming from. She couldn't discern who was talking. But they were talking about a baby. They were talking about *her*.

Clenching her fists, she waited, counting her breaths. Minutes passed. Eternities, it seemed.

She finally dared to leave the security of the pickup, but when her feet hit the muddy field grass she slipped and went down on one knee. She glanced around anxiously but there was no one. Nothing but the shrieking wind and rattling limbs and wet slap of water that flew off the branches.

She opened her mouth. "Rafe?" she called softly, sliding one clenched hand inside her coat pocket. "Rafe?"

No sound. But then . . . something . . . near?

The knife came swiftly. Slicing down on her. Cutting through her coat and piercing the skin of her left shoulder. Tasha screamed. Shocked. The blade was pulled back, then stabbed again. She jerked herself away and stumbled into the field.

"Rafe!" she screamed and she heard him crashing toward her.

"Tasha?"

But then her attacker was on her again and she went down, rolling with them in the mud, frantically trying to stop the blade. Rolling and rolling. Fighting.

Then Tasha was on her back, the knife blade held high above her, glinting in the yellow security light. She recognized the figure looming over her as the devil himself.

The devil herself.

Long-haul trucker Denny Ewell had to take a whiz really bad. Damn motherfuckin' coffee. Went through you like you had no pipes. He pulled into the rest stop as the faintest sign of daylight, more like just a lifting of darkness, started moving over the hills.

He pulled his rig into a spot designed for RVs and big semis and leaped from the cab, racewalking to the men's room. He was peeing by the time he got the damn zipper down and he let out a huge sigh of relief.

Finished, he looked at his reflection and ran a hand through his thinning hair. "Fuckin' A," he said to his receding hairline. Making a face at his craggy mug, he headed back outside. A little lighter. Little better. He'd be in Astoria in an hour or so, depending on the snowpack in the Coast Range.

He was just about back to his rig when he heard something. Something like a groan. He glanced around. There was a beat-up Chevy pickup in the lot and he realized its passenger door was ajar.

"Hey," he called.

No answer.

Squinting at his watch, he went to the opened door and pulled it wider. No one there.

The groan was louder. Coming from beyond the pickup. Circling the vehicle, he checked the field opposite. Something there. Movement of sorts.

"Hey," he called again as he walked cautiously toward it. Wouldn't do to run into some kind of wild animal searching for food scraps. He could do without that encounter.

Something on the ground.

Something with clothes on . . .

And then it rose to its feet, a bloodied figure, towering over the prone body still lying on the wet grass.

Denny's heart nearly exploded from his chest. "Holy shit!"

"The baby," it said, clutching its chest.

Denny stepped back—he couldn't help himself—as the figure before him staggered toward him, then fell to its knees. A man. Twisting to bend over the limp mound on the ground.

"Hey. Hey, man," Denny said, reaching out a hand.

The mound on the muddy grass turned out to be human. A woman, pregnant, her belly exposed like a white mound with black marks across its crest. Bloody marks. From knife wounds scored across her taut skin.

"Oh, Jesus." Denny pushed the bending man away, not sure what he intended. He fell over without resistance, his eyes staring at the sky, blood dampening his chest.

Horrified, Denny dragged his gaze back to the woman. She was breathing shallowly. Alive. Barely.

And the baby? Whoever had tried to cut the poor little thing out had not succeeded.

Sending a prayer to the man upstairs, he ran for his truck and cell phone.

Chapter 1

"Get over here," Leesha said. "You need to meet our new patient. Someone tried to cut her baby out!"

Dr. Claire Norris wheeled into Laurelton General's parking lot and peremptorily nosed her car into another doctor's designated spot. She wasn't affiliated with Laurelton General. She was a psychiatrist at Halo Valley Security Hospital, a facility located some fifty miles south of Laurelton for patients with mental problems. But today, on her day off, she'd gotten the call from Leesha, a friend and associate, who believed this patient would be transferred to Halo Valley as soon as her physical ailments were addressed.

Damn near catatonic. Knifed across her shoulders and abdomen. Not deep enough to cut to the baby, but Jesus, Joseph, and Mary . . .

Claire drew a steadying breath. She'd seen the damage a knife could do to human flesh. In her office. Directly in front of her. A knife slashing through a woman's throat, the last awful sounds as the victim lost her life and the murderer turned his attention on Claire . . .

As she had since the beginning, she pushed the memory aside with an almost physical effort as she switched off the

ignition. But, like always, it nagged at her. Wouldn't let her
go. The killer had been one of her patients. Heyward Marsdon III. A paranoid schizophrenic who suffered from hallucinations and delusions. He hadn't meant to kill his
girlfriend, Melody Stone. He hadn't known what he was
doing. He'd dragged Melody to see Claire and then been
overrun with visions of ghoulish zombielike creatures who
he believed were trying to attack Claire. He'd grabbed
Melody, no longer his girlfriend but an evil being out for
blood, and threatened to kill her. Claire begged him to
stop. *Begged* him. Cajoled and reasoned and expected re-
sults. Heyward hesitated briefly, just long enough for
Melody to whisper *"Do it!"* to him, as if she were under
the spell of some rapture, and then he slit her throat. Just
like that. Slaying the woman he believed to be a soulless
monster in one stroke.

Claire screamed. Shock ran through her like an electric
current. But then Heyward was on her, the knife to Claire's
throat, determined to kill her—or, more accurately, the
evil being Claire had become. He pressed the knife's edge
to her throat, his hand quivering. Claire told him over and
over that she was his doctor, that she meant him no harm.
She asked quietly if she could get help for Melody and
somehow her words finally penetrated his brain and he
allowed her to call in Wade, one of the hospital guards.
But Melody Stone was long gone before help arrived.
Only Claire survived.

Six months ago. As real a nightmare now as it had been
then. Claire had been in her own kind of therapy ever since
it had happened. A memory that wouldn't go away. Ever.
She could only hope she could put it aside a bit with time.

Now, glancing through the windshield and spotting rain,
her gaze extended to the sprawling gray concrete-and-stone
hospital that was Laurelton General. She probably shouldn't
be here. Was doubtlessly overstepping her limits. By all

rights she should leave this to the higher-ups at Halo Valley who had so uncaringly thrown her to the wolves after the incident with Heyward Marsdon. That's what they'd reduced Melody Stone's death to: *the incident.* And though Claire's life had been threatened, too, they let her take the fall alone.

In the time since the incident Claire had been seen by a barrage of other psychologists and psychiatrists and varying concerned hospital administrators and investors who'd rubbed their chins and offered antidepressants, which she'd refused, and then tentatively, finally pronounced her mentally good to go. Everyone professed great relief for her well-being, but all they really wanted was to dust their hands of her: the sole witness to a murder on hospital grounds.

Ironically, after Heyward Marsdon, delusional and hallucinating, was pulled away from Claire, wrestled to the ground, and taken away, he was eventually incarcerated at Halo Valley Security Hospital himself, on the side of the hospital reserved for the criminally insane.

Claire had dutifully followed through with her own therapy, but it had yet to make so much as a dent in her lingering feelings of horror and inadequacy. She had someone else for that. Another friend who understood human emotions and treated Claire with compassion. Dinah Smythe lived at the coast and was Claire's closest neighbor. Dinah was the only person who seemed to truly understand the long road Claire was traveling for her own mental health.

Thank God for her, Claire thought passionately.

Now, climbing out of her black Passat, she hit the remote lock and listened for the beep. Fall guy or not, today she'd answered Leesha Franklin's call and was going to meet the comatose, pregnant patient on her own time. Before the tragedy Claire had been considered top in her field. She still was in the larger world, but within the inner circles at Halo Valley there was a definite cover-your-ass mentality overriding common sense, and Claire had lost value because of it. No one wanted the taint of the consequences to stick to them. *Let Claire Norris take the hit. She's the one who witnessed the murder. She's the one who couldn't stop it. It was her fault. Yes, her fault! No one else's.*

Claire felt a simmering anger as she thought of it, followed by a sense of inadequacy that she couldn't help Melody. She could recall every moment, every syllable, everything: the bright yellow tulips in a bouquet on her desk splashed with equally bright red blood; the soft cadence of Melody Stone's voice as she goaded Heyward to *do it*; the rustle of clothing as he pulled her closer; the metallic scent of blood; the resonating terror of her own voice in her ears; the slam of the door as Wade burst into the room; the shriek of sirens as the ambulance screamed up the long lane to Halo Valley hospital and medical offices.

She shook the memory free, fighting its grip. No amount of dwelling and soul-searching was going to help now. She needed to keep putting one foot in front of the other, moving forward, learning to forget.

A sharp wind whipped up as Claire headed for the hospital, yanking her hair from its restraining clip at her nape. Dark brown strands snapped in front of her eyes and she bent her head and trudged on, seeing the toes of her brown pumps march rapidly toward the sliding glass doors of the main entrance. She heard the sound of an approaching engine and glanced around to see a news van turn into the lot. "Vultures," she muttered aloud, aware that soon this particular patient's story would be blasted across the airwaves. Claire had had her fill of newspeople types. She'd been the object of their bristling mics and pointed questions enough times to become disillusioned with the lot of them.

The hospital's main entrance doors slid open and she was inside, moving rapidly toward the elevators that led to the upper floors. Laurelton General was positioned on a sharp incline resulting in the two west-side floors being on the lower hillside and therefore below the main entrance. This explained why the main floor sign declared in big block letters: FLOOR THREE.

Claire finger-combed her hair, smoothing it behind her ears. She chafed at the delay of the elevator and practically slammed into a doctor hurrying into the elevator as she tried to exit on floor five.

He made a disgruntled sound, which she ignored. Departing elevator riders had priority and she was clearly in the right. He could just bite it.

"Well, there you are!" Leesha called when she saw her. At five feet four and a hundred and sixty-five pounds, Leesha was a solid wall of a woman, built like a square, by her own admission. Her skin was a warm coffee color and her black hair was lined in cornrows that looked tight enough to cause a migraine. Leesha was as cranky as she was empathetic—cranky to imbeciles who got in her way and whined; empathetic toward her patients. She couldn't bear indecision and finger-pointing and she knew enough about Melody Stone's death and Claire's recent problems to be thoroughly pissed off at all the people trying to scuttle away and leave Claire standing alone to take the heat.

But today there was underlying panic on Leesha's face. The horror of the attack on the Jane Doe was inescapable.

"C'mon this way." She motioned for Claire to follow her, then moved quickly to the end of the hall and into a room already occupied by at least one other doctor and a nurse.

"Been like that since she was brought in this morning, poor child," Leesha said in an aside as Claire gazed down at the woman in the bed who was attached to an IV and a heart rate monitor for both her and the baby. Her hair was a soft yellow shade, her skin smooth and unlined. She appeared to be sleeping but there was something deeper in her manner.

"No head injury," Leesha added, reading Claire's thoughts. "Coma, maybe emotionally induced? If she doesn't come to, she'll be heading your way for sure."

"I'll try to make her my patient," Claire said.

"You better. My girl here needs the best."

"Just know it might not happen."

Claire's success rate in treating patients with psychological disorders was the best at Halo Valley; Heyward Marsdon the notable exception, although she'd warned everyone from the hospital administrator on down that he was a danger to himself and to others. But Heyward Marsdon III's family didn't agree and threatened to cut off their hospital funding, and so she'd been ignored. When the incident happened, she was in the process of finalizing her recommendation letter concerning Heyward and suggesting he be held on a seventy-two-hour watch, but it became a moot point. She'd been removed as his psychiatrist, and though she did try to defend herself, explaining about her recommended course of treatment, no one cared. It was too late. The damage too severe. No one was about to throw Claire a life raft when they were all scrambling to keep from drowning.

"Excuse me, who are you?" The doctor who had tried to ignore them now gazed at Claire authoritatively. His bushy gray brows were all over the place, one side looking as if it were trying to crawl to the other. He wore the requisite white jacket and had a habit of dropping his chin and looking through the tops of his eyes, a disciplinarian's unconscious body language. His name tag read Dr. Franco Blount.

"This is Dr. Claire Norris from Halo Valley," Leesha answered. "I called her."

"This woman is our patient," he said frostily to the nurse.

Leesha pointed to the blond girl in the bed. "*This* woman was attacked by someone trying to take her baby. When she comes to, y'think she might need psych?"

Blount glared darkly at her but Leesha held his gaze. She didn't scare easily, if at all, and she knew what she knew. The other nurse in the room, however, must have decided it was high time to get out as she muttered some excuse and scurried from the room.

"When did the patient arrive?" Claire asked.

"A trucker found her around six A.M. She was brought in about seven thirty," Leesha answered.

"Closer to eight," Blount corrected her.

"Unconscious the whole time?" Claire asked.

Blount opened his mouth but Leesha beat him to a response. "ER said her eyes were open when she arrived but she never spoke. She didn't respond to their questions."

"And the baby?"

"So far, so good." She raised crossed fingers.

"Considering this." Blount pulled back the covers and lifted the hospital gown. The woman's protruding abdomen was scored with knife wounds that crisscrossed both above and below her navel. Dried blood could be seen, and the yellowish orange swab of antiseptic. The cuts hadn't been bandaged yet.

"Those wounds as superficial as they look?" Claire asked neutrally, but it took an effort. Her throat felt completely void of liquid.

"They are," Leesha said, but before she could go on, Blount tried to wrest back control.

"The police have been here," he said. "It appears someone sliced at her wildly. No method. They never got close to actually taking the baby."

"There are some wounds on her shoulders," Leesha said. "Like she was attacked there first and then overtaken."

"That's what the police said?" Claire asked.

"More or less."

"Did they say anything else?"

"Are you planning to investigate, too?" Dr. Blount broke

in scathingly. He twitched the hospital gown back into place, then lightly tossed the blankets back over the unconscious girl.

"There was a second victim. A man. DOA," Leesha said.

"From knife wounds?"

"Uh-huh." Leesha nodded.

"So they were both attacked by the same person."

"Looks that way."

"If you both plan to be amateur sleuths, perhaps you should seek different employment," Blount stated flatly. "Dr. Norris, calling you was premature. When we've made a full examination of the patient, decisions will be made."

He tried to hustle them out of the room but Leesha was a blockade. They had a brief standoff where Leesha tried to step aside and make way for the doctor to leave and he stood in lockjawed annoyance. Claire decided to alleviate the small drama by heading into the hall herself, but as she gave a last glance back at the patient she saw the pretty blond woman's face contort with pain.

"The patient," she declared, pushing back into the room past Blount, who still maintained his stance. Leesha was on her heels as Claire jerked back the covers as the Jane Doe moaned and thrashed. "Is she in labor?" Claire asked, seeing the contraction.

"Hope not." Leesha pressed the call button, then hustled into the hall for additional help.

Claire looked to Blount, who hesitated, then swept after Leesha. As Claire leaned down to the patient, Jane Doe's eyes slowly opened. Cornflower blue. Confused. Full of pain.

"You're all right," Claire told her. "You're in a hospital."

Her pupils seemed to dilate, then retract.

A team of medical personnel suddenly rushed into the room. "Excuse me," one of the nurses said sharply and Claire was pushed aside. Reluctantly she moved to the door. There was nothing she could do but get in the way. They needed room to move. Drugs to inhibit the contractions. Prayers that they could keep the baby from coming too early.

Too early . . .

Leesha was in the hall. They looked at each other and Leesha came over and gave Claire a pat on her arm. *Too early.* Claire knew what that was like as well. Life was full of unexpected pitfalls, and today Claire was revisiting all of hers.

"Dr. Norris?"

The tight male voice was familiar. Claire's stomach tightened as she turned and faced the frowning visage of the insufferable Dr. Freeson as he made his way toward them. One of the psychiatrists at Halo Valley. Her immediate superior, in some ways, though he thought he was in all ways.

"What are you doing here?" he demanded.

"I called her," Leesha jumped in. "She was good enough to come on her day off."

"Well, you're not needed." He gazed at Claire hard. "I was in a meeting with Avanti, or I would have been here earlier," he said primly, his Vandyck beard bristling. Forty-something with sandy-colored hair and eyes and a blotchy complexion, he wasn't exactly God's gift but he sure thought he was. He'd made a casual pass at Claire when she'd first joined Halo Valley and when she didn't jump for joy, he'd been irked and somewhat embarrassed. It hadn't helped their working relationship.

"I'm already here." Claire forced a faint smile. It was better to treat Freeson like she was impervious, but sometimes she just wanted to smack his smug, supercilious face.

"Tomorrow, when you're back at work, Avanti wants to talk to you."

So what else was new? Dr. Paolo Avanti, Freeson's immediate superior, loved giving daily lectures about anything and everything. He was at least as much of a prick as

Freeson, though he had better social skills in front of the public. But neither Freeson nor Avanti had come to Claire's defense when she really needed them, and they would both prostrate themselves in front of the head hospital administrator, Dr. Emile Radke, if they thought it would help their positions at the hospital.

"Okay," Claire said neutrally.

"Where is this patient?" Freeson demanded.

"The staff's in with her now," Leesha answered. "You'll have to wait."

He eyed her frostily from head to toe. He was a fairly slight man and Leesha's stolid form seemed to nonplus him a bit. He wasn't used to being thwarted, wasn't used to anything but complete capitulation. "Then I'll wait."

Claire knew Freeson didn't give a damn about the patient. This was all about jockeying for position within the hospital, and this patient provided media attention, something Freeson went after like a heat-seeking missile. He seemed to also have made it his personal mission to keep Claire in line.

It was such utter bullshit. A means for everyone to believe that they were doing everything possible to rectify the fact that Melody Stone had been attacked on their hallowed grounds, in front of one of their own doctors, by another patient whose wealthy parents had coerced his release from those selfsame doctors and therefore helped set up the very events that led to Melody's death.

Why was she the only one who saw it?

She answered her own question: hospital politics and money.

The nightmare scene of Melody's death tried to play across Claire's mind again, but this time she resolutely stuck it inside a box in her mind and tied it tightly. Not now. Not today. She knew grief and shock took their own sweet time in relinquishing their grip, and so she was trying to let nature take its course and heal her. She'd made good strides and was beginning to understand and process Melody's death. She was also almost managing to forgive Heyward, knowing he was at the mercy of his own disease, though that was happening much slower.

The team of nurses and Dr. Blount came out of Jane Doe's room and Leesha hurried over for a quick consult. Freeson breezed past them and entered the room. Claire felt compelled to follow him as he stood over the now peacefully resting patient.

"Not labor," Leesha said near her ear. "Some other pain. Maybe mental."

"She was attacked," Claire reminded her.

They were all silent for a few moments, then all left together. Claire said to Leesha, "Keep me informed."

"She's not your patient," Freeson told her, but Claire ignored him as she walked rapidly down the hall in the opposite direction that she'd arrived. By design she'd chosen a different exit. She had no interest in speaking to Freeson any more than she had to, and since he was likely to leave by the front, she would hit a side door. If he wanted her to wait for him, he could just go ahead and be pissed off that she'd avoided him.

"Hey!" He called after her before she could turn the corner.

Claire increased the length of her strides, pretending she didn't know he was calling for her. She hit the stairs and hurried down the steps, pushing through a door to a small walkway that circled the building. Turning toward the front of the hospital and the parking lot, she bent her head to the chilly, drizzling rain. The Passat was still parked in a reserved spot. The hovering newspeople barely gave her a passing glance as she climbed into the car. She hadn't left by the main entrance. She wasn't wearing a lab coat.

They couldn't connect her to the patient and didn't know who she was.

Good.

She'd had enough of them six months earlier. Oh, brother, had she! As she backed out, she glanced through the window at their news van and the smattering of people milling around. She could see the dark, slickly combed head of Pauline Kirby.

Claire made a growling sound as she twisted the ignition. That woman had been particularly invasive. Between her insinuations, the accusations from Melody Stone's family, and the abandonment of her colleagues, Claire had been under lethal assault.

And when she thought about it—really thought about it without all the underlying sorrow and horror—it really kind of pissed her off.

Turning the wipers on, she wheeled the Passat out of the lot. The interior was warm and she could smell her own body scent, dampened by rain. Lavender Mist. The body gel she'd washed with that morning in the shower. Today's flavor, after lemon, apricot, and that horrible sea foam, was a fresh, almost minty scent that had been as ineffective as all the rest. Nothing could wash away the feeling of guilt, though she knew rationally she had nothing to feel guilty about.

In her rearview she saw Freeson step from the vapor-locked portico in front of the hospital. His gaze searched the parking lot, the impatience on his face a tight mask. But he didn't focus on her car as the news horde bore down on him.

"Pretend you know something, Freeson," she muttered, turning onto the main road. "Like you pretended to know what drove Heyward Marsdon to kill Melody Stone."

"Heyward Marsdon killed my sister and nobody did a damn thing about it," Langdon Stone stated flatly as he tipped up a longnecked beer. He swallowed a third of the bottle, wiped the back of his hand across his mouth, and added, "I'm not coming back to the department. I'm not doing a damn thing until that sick, privileged bastard is behind bars. Prison bars."

"We know," was the long-suffering response. His ex-partner, Detective Trey Curtis, dark-haired, lean, gruff, and still at the Portland Police Department, waved for the bartender to send over two more longnecks. "I'm not trying to get you to come back. Everything's been better since you left."

Lang snorted.

"Celek's been doing a helluva job. I couldn't ask for a better partner. And he's better-looking than you are. Gets all the chicks. They swoon."

Curtis almost made Lang smile. Almost. He knew Curtis's new partner, Joshua Celek: a chubby, freckled thirty-year-old with a sunny disposition and a belief in human nature that couldn't be hammered out of him no matter how much depravity he encountered on the job. He looked and acted like a kid out of a fifties sitcom. He'd been elevated from robbery to homicide after Lang unceremoniously walked away from the job he'd worked for nearly a decade.

"Swoon," Lang repeated.

"Yeah, swoon."

"Well, that's good, then, 'cause I'm not coming back."

"Who says there's a job waiting for you? You're out. The chief . . . the captain . . . Lieutenant Drano . . . they're all glad your pain-in-the-butt attitude is gone."

"Drano called me yesterday. Offered me more money and a new partner if I had problems with you."

"Drano's on vacation in Mallorca."

"Yeah, he got back last night and phoned me as soon as he touched down at PDX."

"You're lying. Good one, though."

Lang did smile now, and Curtis reached over and knocked Lang's baseball cap off his head. They locked their arms around each other's necks, alarming their waiter, who'd already seemed to want to comment on their choice of beer with breakfast. It was a long-standing rule with Lang and Curtis: whenever they met, whichever one saw the other first, that one would buy the first beer. Lang had spotted Curtis and had ordered two Budweisers and they'd been enjoying them with bacon and eggs.

Curtis shoved Lang away from him and said to the waiter, "You don't have to call the cops. I got a badge. Just off duty and trying to knock some sense into my friend here." The waiter nodded slowly but the consternation on his face didn't quite leave. "Really," Curtis said.

"Okay. Can I get you anything else?"

Lang said, "Scotch and water, hold the water."

"No. Thanks." Curtis waved the waiter off. "Not until after nine thirty." As the waiter turned away, he admitted to Lang, "Okay, butthead, Drano does want you back. We all do."

Lieutenant Draden was called Drano because his craggy, world-weary face and dispirited manner made him seem drained of life. He was, in fact, savvy, smart, and surprisingly full of ideas, but you had to get to know him a while to see the man behind the persona. So far Celek hadn't clued in. Curtis had told Lang a story about the newbie homicide detective and his penchant for keeping the gory details from Draden, as if it might somehow spiral him over the edge, that almost made Lang chuckle. Almost.

"Celek thinks if he tells Drano anything but sunshine and lollipops that Drano will jump off a bridge."

"Tough to keep details from your lieutenant."

"Oh, he writes up these bang-up reports—way better than yours, except for spelling and punctuation, your specialty—"

"Thank you."

"—and then he tries to make me turn them in. Like Drano won't see his name at the bottom. Celek's got all kinds of weirdness. Nicety-nice stuff that takes up so much time and energy that you want to knock him sideways."

"You've controlled yourself so far?"

"No thanks to you. When are you coming back?"

"I told you: I'm not." Lang shoved back his chair. "Let's go somewhere with a pool table."

"Too early. Besides, you got enough money off me last time we played." Curtis threw some cash on the table and said, "My treat." Lang threw the same amount down and walked away. Swearing, Curtis picked up Lang's cash and followed him onto the street and into a pouring rain, surprisingly chilly for September. "I'm giving this to charity," he said, waving Lang's bills at him.

"To the Neglected Children of Strippers Named Taffy or Sugar or Cinnamon."

"Only if they're my kids," Curtis agreed, playing along. Their relationship was long and deep. "When are you going to give up the vendetta? Marsdon's behind bars."

Lang frowned and shook his head, rainwater collecting on his black hair. "That facility is a hospital, not a prison."

"Damn near a prison. And at the risk of getting my head bit off, the man's sick."

"Sure, he's sick. But he killed my sister. And now he gets to stay at the very hospital where he slit her throat? Why not send him to a five-star hotel?"

"He's in the lockdown section. With all the other super crazies who are incapable of standing trial."

"He should be in prison," Lang insisted, his jaw tightening.

"Not according to the courts and the doctors," Curtis reminded him quietly. They were getting into dangerous territory, and even being the good friends that they were,

Trey Curtis was completely aware of the depth of his friend's anger, misery, and need for retribution. He didn't want to get in the way.

"Doctors," Lang sneered. "She's dead because of them. Because of *her*."

"I'm not going to argue with you."

"You're sure as hell doing a good job of it."

"I'm just lobbing out little facts. Doesn't mean I like any of it." He lifted his hands in surrender.

"He could stand trial," Lang insisted again. "Heyward Marsdon the Third is at Halo Valley because of his grand-dad's money."

"He's a paranoid schizophrenic, Lang. He's probably where he should be." Lang looked ready to argue. He certainly wasn't going to capitulate, so Curtis went on, "You're too good a man, too good a cop, to let this define your entire life. Do what you can in the matter, but do it on the job. Drano wants you back. I want you back. Hell, even Celek wants you back." He paused, then added, "No matter what you think, Halo Valley ain't no summer camp."

"I want him dead," Lang said then.

"So do I, man," Curtis agreed. "For you. I wish he'd hang himself, or throw himself in front of freeway traffic, or put the barrel of a forty-four in his mouth. But it's not gonna happen, and neither you nor I is going to make it happen. So, let's move on."

"Move on," Lang repeated, his eyes taking on a far-away look as he gazed over Portland city center's morning traffic. "I got a job offer from the Tillamook County Sheriff's Department."

"Which you haven't taken yet, either." They were standing under a narrow awning and had been speaking in fierce, if partially hushed, tones. "So, okay, I got a different job for you," Curtis said. "Something I want you to look into."

"What, am I your personal gofer now?"

"A body was found at a rest stop on the outskirts of Winslow County. The guy was stabbed to death, and someone tried to cut out the baby from his pregnant companion. Didn't succeed, as far as I know. She's at Laurelton General. He's at the county morgue."

"I saw it on the morning news," Lang said, then, "Not your jurisdiction."

"That's why I want you to look into it."

"And piss off a lot of people who might think I should mind my own business."

"I hear the county's swamped and would like some help," Curtis said mildly.

"You're full of it."

"Call the sheriff and see if I am."

With that Curtis gave him a light punch on the upper arm and bent his head to the falling rain. Lang watched him walk up the street. He wasn't going to call Winslow County's Sheriff Nunce, a man who'd been reelected the fall before though it was rumored he had been reluctant to run again, had been, in fact, expected to retire. Lang had met Nunce a few times over the years when their cases overlapped and had found the sheriff congenial and able to share investigative work, but that didn't mean Nunce would be looking for Lang to stick his nose in where it didn't really belong.

"Celek doesn't want me back," he said aloud, though Curtis was long out of earshot.

He bent his head to the rain as he headed toward his gray Dodge truck, yanking open the stubborn driver's door, ducking inside. Slamming the door shut with an effort, he reminded himself he needed to take the truck in and have the door fixed. He just didn't ever seem to have the energy or initiative. He'd been that way for months, ever since his sister's death.

Now, running a hand through his wet hair, he stared through the windshield. He'd found parking only a block and a half away from Dooley's, the breakfast/lunch pub where he'd met Curtis in downtown Portland, not far from the station. Curtis was walking back to work and Lang, though he refused to admit it, felt a faint twinge of regret or envy or a mixture of both. He didn't want his old job back. He didn't want a new one, either. He'd been unable to concentrate on it after Melody's death. He wanted Heyward Marsdon's neck in a noose, and that's all he wanted. Not exactly the kind of attitude conducive to good police work.

And Marsdon's damn family. Wealthy. Arrogant. Above the law. Unable to believe in their son's culpability though it was understood all around that Heyward III had indeed committed the unthinkable crime. Of course the asshole had feigned remorse. Had actually shed tears. And there had been a lot of psycho mumbo jumbo about schizophrenia and illness and an inability to truly understand his own feelings and actions.

Yeah, yeah, yeah.

The guy was sick, all right. Sick in the head. But someone to be *pitied*? Lang simply did not have it in his heart. Heyward Marsdon had killed his sister and he had to pay for it along with the rest of that supercilious hospital staff. Heyward's doctor, Claire Norris, being at the top of Lang's hit list.

Throwing the truck into gear, he rumbled into traffic and was cut off by a guy in a black Ferrari on his cell phone who nearly got his rear end crunched by Lang's truck. Lang was half amused, half irked when the driver flipped him off. He pulled up on the left side of the asshole and rolled his right window down. The driver looked up and threw him a cold look.

Lang signaled for the man to hang up and the bastard released the bird a second time, pointing at him with that same middle finger, making deep, stabbing motions. For half a second Lang thought about continuing the insanity. He felt an almost overpowering need to drag the guy out of the car and beat the hell out of him. Transference? The need to release pent-up aggression? You bet. With an effort he turned his eyes forward, set his jaw, thought about Dr. Claire Norris, and wondered if he could have just one meeting with her. He'd been advised against it by a passel of lawyers. He was too personally involved. It wouldn't do any good. She wasn't completely responsible. Marsdon had killed Melody, not anyone from the hospital. He wasn't thinking clearly.

The Ferrari jumped ahead, then screeched to a halt at a light where a gaggle of teenage girls were trying to cross the street. They stared at him in collective horror, then broke into the filthiest language and gestures Lang had ever seen from a group their age. Lang pulled up on the driver's left again and smiled over at him. He could practically see the steam pouring from the guy's ears. The girls became truly obnoxious. Standing directly in front of his car and not moving, dangerously, until Lang worried for them as the light was about to turn green.

But they sauntered away, arms crossed behind their backs, middle fingers sticking up for the Ferrari asshole's uninhibited view.

As ye sow, so shall ye reap.

Lang wasn't much for religion, but a few key phrases sometimes popped into his head from time to time, a gift from his sister, who'd flitted from religion to religion like a butterfly to a flower.

His sister. Beautiful. Fresh. Intelligent. Deeply flawed.

Lang shook his head. Couldn't think of her. Instead he concentrated on the other woman who haunted his thoughts: Dr. Claire Norris. The reason Heyward Marsdon III had been outside hospital walls looking for whatever his sick, twisted brain considered its next need. Dr. Claire Norris. She'd probably been the conduit for Melody and Heyward to meet. The good doctor, introducing one homicidal sicko to a sweet but slightly twisted woman with delusions and hallucinations of her own, probably putting them together in some kind of therapy class.

Claire Norris. Lang had seen her from afar, a slim, dark-haired, prettier-than-average woman with a strained look on her face. She had witnessed something horrific; he could give her that. His own mind shied away from what must have happened in that room. But Dr. Norris was the one who had okayed Marsdon's release into society. It was her name on the form. She was the one with the ultimate responsibility for Melody's death. She was the one who *allowed* Marsdon to cut his sister's throat.

He'd said as much a number of times, to anyone who would listen. He'd been told his thinking was convoluted. He was just looking for someone to blame. He needed antidepressants and therapy. He needed help.

Drugs? That kind of help? From the psychiatric community? Like he was going to listen to anything those head-shrinkers from Halo Valley had to say. Quacks, every one. Self-serving quacks.

He was driving out Sunset Highway through a misting rain, leaving the Portland skyline in his rearview mirror, passing through the tunnel and headed west into the sunset. Except today the horizon was all gray and dreary. No sun in sight. Two weeks ago it had been blazing hot. Early September. Not much change from August. Then *bam*. They'd been hit with an early storm and now this rain.

Well, the rain suited his mood.

He exited the freeway on the outskirts of Laurelton, still within the western edge of the Portland city limits. He'd bought the property as soon as he'd scratched up enough money for a down payment, and after their parents died in a fiery crash on I-5, he had Melody move in with him. She'd been seventeen and he'd been twenty-three. Now he was thirty-seven and she would have been thirty-one this past May if not for Heyward Marsdon.

She'd been in and out of rehab more times than he liked to recall. She was crazy without medication. She hated taking medication. She took the wrong kind of medication. She crashed. She went to rehab. Got clean. Got crazy again.

But . . . she was such a sweet, funny person when everything was in line. Slightly ironic, slightly off-kilter, slightly acerbic. He loved her. And now she was gone.

He'd quit the force shortly after Melody's death, though Drano had told him the job was open whenever he felt like stepping back in. Lang supposed he should have felt grateful, but all his energies were directed somewhere else and he didn't honestly give a damn.

Now when he walked into his house, he had the peculiar notion that Melody was there. Something in the air. A left-over scent. But it was an illusion. He'd identified her body in the morgue. There was no question it was her. No question she was dead. No question where the responsibility lay. It was just sometimes—rarely—Lang wanted her back so badly that he almost made himself believe it could happen.

Nutty behavior. Grief taking over the sane part of his mind from time to time.

Walking onto the small back deck outside the kitchen, he was impervious to the shivering drizzle that seemed to have gripped the area in a firm hand. The deck was about three feet off the ground and he'd been building steps to it from the backyard, more for something to do than any serious interest in home improvement. Now he tested the wooden rail and wondered if he should change them out to wrought iron. He could do the work himself.

Trying to come up with something to fill your time?

Back inside, he poured cold coffee from the pot into a mug and heated it in the microwave. He thought about Claire Norris some more. He'd seen her on television, mostly; in person he'd had to keep his distance and he didn't want to be too near her anyway. Self-preservation. He didn't want to do anything rash.

So, he'd watched her on television with an intensity that was undoubtedly obsessive. He'd DVR'd her only interview with the press and kept it still. She was about five-eight with sexy legs and small feet encased in sensible black pumps. She wore a lab coat over a skirt or dress, mostly. Her hair was chin length, and she had a tendency to tuck it behind her ears when she was speaking, an unconscious focusing act. She was good-looking, her teeth white, her waist slim, her chin slightly pointy. She appeared . . . honest, he could admit. But then, that was Halo Valley's prime disguise.

Now Lang threw himself in a chair in front of the television. Clicking around, he found nothing but game shows, talk shows, and daytime dramas. He stared out the sliding glass door to the rain-soaked cedar boards of his deck. Then, like an addict, he accessed his DVR interview of Claire Norris. Dr. Claire Norris.

She only said a few words, and Lang knew them by heart.

Pauline Kirby: *Would you have done things differently, knowing what you do now?*

Claire: *Heyward Marsdon the Third is under continuing psychiatric care.*

Pauline: *But shouldn't he have been locked up? Shouldn't you have known?*

Claire seemed to struggle a bit when a man with a goatee jumped forward and practically shoved her aside.

Dr. Freeson: *I'm Dr. James Freeson with Halo Valley Security Hospital. We always strive to give each of our patients individual care. Dr. Norris has been Mr.*

Marsdon's primary psychiatric physician for several years and is highly competent.

Blah, blah, blah.

Lang rewound and watched it again. Funny, how Freeson initially sounded like he was defending Claire Norris, but after hearing his tone a thousand times and seeing his face, Lang suspected the man was trying to distance himself from the woman who'd brought this destruction to the hospital.

He watched it again and then froze the picture on Claire Norris's face.

"You're obsessed," he said a few minutes later, never taking his eyes from the screen. "It's dangerous."

I got a job for you. Something I want you to look into.

Curtis was worried about him. Maybe he was right. Maybe Lang was starting down that nutty lane his sister had traversed most of her adult life.

With a feeling of inevitability, he picked up the phone and asked for the Winslow County Sheriff's Department.

Maybe it was time to talk to Sheriff Nunce and see if there was something he could do.

Chapter 2

Summer tried to return with a burst of heat that steamed the tarmac and pushed through the gray clouds. It lasted about two days, the time it took Laurelton General to feel confident Jane Doe was fit to be discharged. Claire was eyeing the weather and snatching up her jacket on the way out of her house when she got the call from Leesha.

"I'm on my way to work," Claire told her without waiting for Leesha to speak. "Don't worry. I'll meet the transport car. She won't be alone."

"No hurry. Your Dr. Freeson's meeting her," Leesha said. "She's his patient."

Leesha humphed. "You look out for her, Claire. Don't let this become some political bullshit."

"I'll do what I can."

Claire's bungalow sat on a knoll in a small neighborhood of homes that had been built on a sloping hillside above the town of Deception Bay. Through her pane windows she had a peekaboo view of the Pacific Ocean, and now she glanced out angrily, blind to the sunbursts arrowing through the silvery cloud cover, shimmering on the ruffling waves.

Damn Freeson and the whole Marsdon family. They all

wanted to keep her under their thumbs. They wanted her capitulation. They wanted her to write a favorable report on Heyward III and get him moved to the less restricted side of Halo Valley. Their money was grease to the axle that ran the hospital, and therefore they had a certain amount of control on who was a patient and who wasn't. The Marsdons wanted Heyward's case reviewed and Claire's testimony would go a long way to the good, and Freeson and Avanti were more than willing to help.

Locking the side door, she headed to her Passat, seeing huge drops of rain plop onto its shiny black hood. The staghorn sumac, whose green leaves had turned to orange and fiery red, began to shiver from an onslaught of water. Claire tucked herself into her car and backed down her drive. From along a side gravel lane, which connected her bungalow to the other homes that meandered down the hill, she caught sight of Dinah standing on her deck in a long caftan, her face turned up to the heavens. Dinah lifted her arms and smiled at the skies, her long blondish hair waving around her head like a golden aureole.

Claire thought about her as she drove the twenty-plus miles inland to the hospital. Dinah had grown up in the area and she had a list of clients, much like Claire, whom she treated with homeopathic remedies and exercise in the form of yoga and her own kind of tai chi. She was also a sometime foster parent to a young boy named Toby, whenever Toby's mother fell back into her pattern of choosing abusive partners, and she was far more grounded than Claire had originally thought. Claire used her as a sounding board, and Dinah was both a good listener and advisor. And, as she wasn't totally against alcohol, she would occasionally share a glass of wine with Claire and some good conversation.

But if Freeson or Avanti—who'd both now been all over Claire about her trip to Laurelton General to see the patient without asking—knew she was friends with an herbalist and even listened to her advice, they would probably try to have Claire's license yanked. The irony of that made Claire perversely happy. Maybe some of her interest in Dinah was merely a way to thumb her nose at the Halo Valley politicos. Whatever the case, it worked for her. Her own "homeopathic" medicine.

By the time she drove up the winding two-lane drive to the hospital, she'd gone from annoyed and angry to taut and determined. She wasn't going to let Freeson have his way with Jane Doe. She wasn't going to let the Marsdons work their influence on her. She wasn't.

She parked in the lot and strode into the concrete-and-redwood side building that housed the medical offices of the hospital doctors, taking the elevator to the second floor. After hours she used a keycard and code, like the hospital, but before seven P.M. the medical offices were accessible and open and anyone could just walk in.

Inside the office building the hallway was carpeted in commercial grade brown-speckled carpet with halogen can lights offering pools of illumination along its length. Light oak doors with sturdy brushed chrome levers marched down both sides. Claire's new office was now around a turn and toward the skyway that led to the hospital. She'd been located at the far end previously, but by mutual decision between her and hospital administration, she'd moved.

Healthier for everybody.

Today she hung her jacket and purse in the closet, shrugged into her lab coat, then locked the closet with a small key that she pinned into her coat pocket. She didn't have an immediate appointment, so she headed for the hospital proper.

Halo Valley Security Hospital was an experimental model, designed more like assisted living quarters. The second floor of the office building led through a skyway and door to the hospital itself, and when Claire inserted her keycard and punched in the code, she could enter the second floor of the hospital itself. Side A. The less restrictive side. A separate, older, brick building stood behind the newer Side A and had been nicknamed Side B—the place where the more disturbed patients, ones who were a danger to themselves and/or others, were housed.

As Claire pushed open the access door to the hospital, she could hear wailing as loud as a siren.

Gibby, she thought. *In Side A's morning room.* She picked up her pace but didn't run. There was no running in the hospital. Running panicked the patients. Besides, Gibby had a tendency to scream when nothing was wrong, and Claire knew Darlene, one of the day nurses, was more than capable.

She walked across the gallery above the morning room—the central meeting area of Halo Valley hospital—and saw, past the main foyer, Balfour Transport arrive, a van service for patients, which could be converted to carry a gurney or a wheelchair, or basic seats. She headed down the curving stairway to the first level and glass front doors as outside a wheelchair was hydraulically lowered to the ground with Jane Doe sitting quietly in its seat. Her hands were folded across her lap and she wore a robe over hospital garb. Wind snatched at her blond locks but she didn't respond, just stared straight ahead.

Claire stepped outside to meet them, and the driver, a Hispanic man who couldn't have been more than five-six but with a weightlifter's muscles, thrust a clipboard at her. She signed and he looked at the name and asked, "Dr. Freeman?"

"Freeson. He's here, somewhere."

"I need his signature."

Claire turned her attention to the patient. "Let me take

you inside," she said, ignoring the driver, who was looking past her, hoping for Freeson to appear.

"I can't leave till I have his signature."

"He'll be here." She pushed the wheelchair inside and was met by Fran from administration, who did all the paperwork for this side of the hospital. Claire signaled back toward the driver and Fran collected the papers Laurelton General had sent over on the patient.

Freeson appeared at that moment, racewalking toward them. "I'll take her from here," he told Claire brusquely.

Claire looked past him and saw that Dr. Paolo Avanti had chosen to join Freeson in this venture. His dark hair was smoothly combed to his head, and he wore it a little longish, not too much, just enough to appear more youthful. He was in his middle forties but wanted people to believe he was still in his thirties. He could almost pull it off with his swarthy good looks and quiet, commanding style, but Claire knew him too well. Behind a practiced smile lurked a man whose narcissism surpassed Freeson's. Avanti liked conquests. In sports. In debate. In women. He wasn't shy, but he was cagey. Like Freeson, he'd circled Claire early on, though she'd given him no indication she was interested in him at all. Avanti had stepped back, smarter than Freeson, parrying the rejection before it came. But he hadn't given up entirely. He was biding his time, waiting for a more perfect opening, one that Claire steadfastly refused to give. How he expected this after the way he'd abandoned her in her hour of need, Claire couldn't fathom. Male ego. Who knew?

"So, this is our new arrival," he said, examining Jane Doe with a frown. "She's young."

"Old enough to have a baby," Freeson observed.

Claire gave him a look, wondering if that comment had deeper meaning. "We don't know anything about her."

"Pauline Kirby wants to do a follow-up story," Avanti said,

not taking his eyes off the patient. "No one's come forward since they aired her picture, so I think it's a good idea."

"The news crew's coming here?" Freeson asked casually, as if he didn't care.

Claire schooled her expression. They both wanted the publicity and notoriety. An attractive young woman who would garner empathy by her very looks was perfect for their purposes.

"You're not letting them film her, are you?" Claire asked.

"No, no. Just the outside of the hospital. And a still frame of her face." Avanti's dark, liquid eyes bored into Claire. "You do want her to find her people, don't you, Dr. Norris?"

"Yes."

Nurse Darlene, a tall woman with blunt-cut brown bangs and hair and an attitude to match, fresh from taking care of Gibby, reached them at that moment. "Her room's ready. Right down the hall."

Freeson's goatee quivered and he looked ready to wrestle Darlene for the patient, but when Claire pretended to lose interest and headed toward the morning room, he simply followed after Darlene, close enough to damn near give her a flat tire. Darlene threw him a look and he backed off while Avanti sauntered off in another direction.

Determined to check in on Jane Doe as soon as Freeson stopped circling the area and went back to his own office—where he spent most of his time, as his people skills were practically nil and he was best forming speeches and pontificating at hospital fund-raisers—Claire looked for Bradford Gibson, Gibby, a twenty-eight-year-old mentally handicapped patient with the mind and intellect of a five-year-old. In the morning room she saw that he was working on an art project of some kind. His tongue was buried in his cheek as he concentrated. His hair was buzz cut as he had a tendency to rip it out by the roots. He was a little on the heavy side with eyes so round and unblinking that he looked eerily like an owl sometimes. But he was sweet and generally satisfied, unless thwarted in his routine.

One of the aides, Alison, slim, with a mop of unruly dark hair, said, "He thought Thomas wanted his picture," as way of explanation for the outburst.

"Ah." Claire headed back to her office. She had a ten o'clock appointment with a regular outpatient. She would check on Jane Doe later.

The morning room was a misnomer at Halo Valley Security Hospital, as it was used all day and it was a patient gathering area with tables, chairs, bookshelves, and a television. The walls were painted yellow and patient artwork was displayed in a haphazard fashion, placed there by the artists themselves. Gibby carefully taped his latest spaceship onto the wall and looked on in satisfaction. It was blue and red and silver flames shooted into the sky. He glanced around and surreptitiously took Maribel's horse picture down to make room. Maribel was stupid, anyway. She never remembered nothing. Gibby was pretty sure she had that Zimer's disease. At least she wasn't really, really crazy like those guys in the other building.

Shivering, Gibby glanced out the window on the back side of the morning room. They tried to hide it with trees and stuff, but there was a really mean fence over there with curly wire on top, the kind he'd seen on that show about criminals that he wasn't supposed to watch. Every time he turned on the TV without permission, one of those nurse people came. Greg was okay, but Darlene was a witch with a capital B. That's what his mom always said. A witch with a capital B, and that meant she was really, really bad.

But the morning room was a great place. He was safe

here. The halls were scary with creatures popping their heads out of rooms. Everyone told Gibby he was just imagining them, that the rooms held people, either patients or hospital personnel, but Gibby knew better. They just weren't able to see. But here, they never bothered him. Once he got inside the morning room sliding doors, he was safe. He always wanted to close the doors, but it was against the rules. This bothered Gibby, but since the creatures couldn't cross into this space without burning up from the inside out, he could live with it. And if he was in his special chair, he was really, really safe. If someone was sitting in his chair like Maribel, though, anything could happen, but today the chair was free so Gibby grabbed it and sat down hard. The nurse people had brought in another chair, not as good as Gibby's but it was blue, which was his favorite color, and it looked not hard like those wood ones. Darlene was helping a lady with yellow hair into it.

Greg, one of the big nurse guys, looked at the lady and said, "She okay to be here?"

Darlene stood up and walked away and Greg followed. Gibby heard her say, "Dr. Freeson wants her to have lots of stimuli."

Gibby thought that maybe Darlene didn't think that was the thing to do, but then Darlene was mean. The yellow-haired lady was staring at the TV though the TV wasn't on.

Shooting a look at Darlene and Greg, Gibby said in a whisper to the woman, "You have to ast. They won't turn it on unless you ast."

She didn't respond. Didn't even move. Gibby saw her belly and wondered why she was hiding a ball under her clothes. "They'll do it for free if you ast," he told her conspiratorially. "You just have to ast."

Maribel cruised by, then turned around and sat down right on Gibby's lap. He started yelling at the top of his lungs and Darlene came over and helped Maribel off. Gibby watched as Maribel wandered away, touching everything as she went.

"You have pretty hair," Gibby told the woman in the chair. "What's your name?"

"She doesn't have a name," Darlene said crushingly, making Gibby jump the way she creeped up on him. She was mean, oh, she was mean! He stared at the lady in horrified wonder. No name? "She hast to have a name!"

But Darlene was heading out of the room. Good. Gibby didn't like her. She smelled like an ashtray. That's what his mom always said. She smelled like an ashtray.

"You have yellow hair like the morning room," Gibby said, pleased with himself. The lady's lips moved. He looked closer but wasn't quite sure if they did. Was she trying to talk to him? "I hope you don't have Zimer's disease," he said. "I want to talk to you."

"I want to talk to you, too," she said.

Gibby was even more pleased. But her lips didn't move, did they? He wasn't sure. He was pretty sure she'd talked, though. Pretty sure . . . He wished she would turn her head and look at him but she stared straight ahead. He finally got up from his chair and stood in front of her. He had to squeeze down and squat to see into her eyes. They were blue. His favorite color! She didn't look like she saw him, though. She kinda looked empty. A little like Maribel.

And just like that Maribel sat down in his chair and started laughing.

Gibby threw back his head and screamed and lunged for her.

Claire missed Gibby's second bout of screaming as she was listening to Jamie Lou Breene's account of her latest escapades. An outpatient, she suffered from narcissism in a severe form, complicated by a bipolar disorder. When she was "up," she went on crazy sprees that had landed her a number of stints at the hospital. When she was down, she was almost suicidal. The only thing saving her was, ironically, her own narcissism. She couldn't take her own life.

She was also incapable of accepting blame or consequence and had run through a number of psychiatrists before being placed with Claire.

"I woke up in Salem at some place. Don't remember how I got there," Jamie was saying with a hint of pride, lifting her chin. She'd been pretty; she still was. But at thirty-three, with years of wild behavior and hard living behind her, she was showing signs of wear. Sometimes, on her meds, she could keep herself under control. Most times she just let herself ricochet from one disaster to the other.

Claire tried hard to keep her from hurting herself and others, but the woman was a ticking time bomb. She wouldn't stay on her meds. She hated the dulled feeling that robbed her of herself.

"What kind of place?" Claire asked.

"Some guy's apartment," she said with a shrug. "He was nice enough, I guess. I mighta had sex with him. Pretty sure I did."

"Did you use precautions?"

"I doubt it."

"Dangerous behavior, Jamie."

Her family, an ex-husband, a seven-year-old son, and a sometime alcoholic father, had all tried to help but they were falling away from a problem that wouldn't, maybe couldn't, be corrected.

"I'll get the tests again," she said. "I'll . . . get on my meds."

"You have to mean it. You have to follow through."

"I know, I know. I'm going to change."

There was no conviction in her voice. Or maybe there

was, but Claire couldn't hear it any longer. "It's not easy to completely change your life, Jamie. Changes are incremental. This isn't a dress rehearsal. We've talked about this."

"I said I was going to change."

Claire wrote a number down on a piece of paper. "If you get in a situation like this last one again and you need help, call me."

Jamie took the paper and stared down at it. "You don't believe me."

"I want you to be safe. Everyone should have someone they can call." And Jamie had just about run out of those kind of friends.

She left about twenty minutes later, promising to change, promising that she was definitely better this time, promising she wouldn't need to call, promising, promising, promising.

Incremental changes. . . . Claire just hoped those changes were in the positive direction.

She glanced at the clock. She dealt with outpatients like Jamie, mostly, but she was also familiar with the live-ins who resided on this side of Halo Valley, like Bradford Gibson. Side B was a different story and out of Claire's field of work. She'd only crossed to it twice in the three years she'd been at the facility; once as an initial introduction, and once when Heyward Marsdon III had been taken there kicking and screaming and demanding she be with him, much to his family's disgust.

Claire had wanted nothing to do with Heyward, either. But she had been his therapist and she had been part of the incident. One moment he was saying how much he loved Melody, then he was threatening to kill her and Claire was trying to talk him down, then he pulled a knife from his pocket and slit Melody's throat in one smooth movement. So fast. So horrifyingly fast.

Do it, Melody had said, and Heyward had complied.

Later, Heyward had screamed for both Melody and Claire. He couldn't quite fathom that Melody was gone, let alone at his own hand. He'd begged for Claire, too, though his family did their best to keep her away from him. Not that she was anxious to be with him, either. She stayed away until the day he was moved from the jail cell where they'd first thrown him to his more permanent home at Side B. Crossing from Side A to Side B had been like being forced down a gangplank. Her steps were slow as she headed down one of the two skyways that led to the back building, through the guard's station with its security cameras and deadlocks. When she reached the room where Heyward was detained, he stared at her beseechingly and begged to see Melody. Claire had quietly told him Melody was gone. He shook his head in denial. He didn't remember any of it. His family all eyed her with suspicion, and his grandfather, Heyward Marsdon Sr., glared down at her from icy eyes beneath white, bushy eyebrows. Heyward Marsdon Jr., fifty-ish, whose distaste of the hospital showed on his face though he tried very hard to be neutral, was less interested in Claire and more in his son, the way it should be. He wanted Heyward III out of Side B. Period. There was no real interest in helping his son cope; he only cared how Heyward III's incarceration would affect the family name.

Claire hadn't felt really secure until she was back past the guard's station. She knew the histories of some of Side B's inmates and she knew very well that she would never be equipped to treat them in any way. They were seen by professionals who thrived with those kind of patients: the irredeemable, in Claire's opinion. Monsters that they were, they were treated humanely. Sometimes it even helped a little, most times it didn't.

Did Heyward Marsdon III fit in there? Claire wasn't really quite sure. He was a danger, definitely. A schizophrenic, plagued by visions, acting on the crazed counsel of the demons within his own mind. In his lucid moments, he understood right and wrong, life and death. In the throes of his disease he was a maniac. But everyone save Claire had believed he was on his meds and in control enough for outpatient treatment. Claire had worried about that; she'd wanted him admitted into Side A where she and the rest of the staff could monitor him. But, as ever, the Marsdon family had pressured the administration and they, in turn, had pressured Claire. When she'd waffled about whether he should be admitted, a momentary indecision that she'd rescinded almost immediately, she'd been brushed aside and Heyward had been released. No, she hadn't sanctioned it, but nobody wanted to remember that now.

And for a while Heyward had stayed on his meds and managed a fairly productive life, going the charity rounds with his well-connected family, who swept his "little problem" under the rug, as if it had been cured, or more likely, never existed. But then Heyward met Melody Stone, who was young, beautiful, and completely screwed up. Claire had continued to see Heyward professionally, a condition of his release from Side A, and Heyward had brought her Melody, who viewed Claire as an interference between her and her boyfriend. Melody was not Claire's patient, merely another piece of the Heyward Marsdon family/friend picture. But Claire saw that Melody needed help. She had a complete disaffect: she was unable to relate to anyone, even Heyward.

Claire told Freeson, Avanti, and others about Melody, but since she wasn't a Halo Valley patient, she wasn't their concern, and the powers that be advised Claire to treat Heyward III and forget about his messed-up girlfriend.

Do it . . .

It was a recipe for disaster. That last night that Heyward brought Melody to Claire's office he swore his love for Melody, but his eyes were deep hollows, staring somewhere past Claire's ear to a distance beyond what Claire could see. Melody was passive at first. But she was uncomfortable, scratching her arms, moaning a little. Claire suspected she was high on something.

Suddenly Heyward said, "I hear them! They found us!"

"It's just us, Heyward," Claire said, aware he was fighting a delusion.

"They're here."

His voice was hushed. He was holding Melody tightly. She wriggled a little in his arms, but her eyes were stretched wide, as if she were also looking for the evil beings pursuing them.

Claire said calmly, "I'm going to call a friend to join us."

"No."

"Would you like to speak to someone from your family?" She let her hand move toward the phone.

"No!"

"Are you sure?"

"They want me to die. I embarrass them."

"They don't want you to die, Heyward."

"Shhh!" A harsh whisper. "They're coming!"

Melody leaned into him, singing a little tune, her eyes closing. A lullaby, Claire realized much later.

Claire's fingers touched the receiver. "Heyward, it's late. I was just on my way home. I'm calling a good friend of mine."

"You're calling the police!"

"No."

Melody's lashes fluttered and she opened her eyes. She fixed her gaze on Heyward, looking at his profile.

Heyward trembled violently. A look of intense fear crossed his face. "You!" he shrieked. "You!" He was looking at Melody in horror.

"Don't," Claire said, holding out a hand, sensing true danger.

"Do it," Melody whispered into his ear.

And Heyward Marsdon III ripped a knife from his pocket, slit Melody Stone's throat, and came for Claire.

Tragedy. Disaster. Horror.

The news hit the airwaves and the hospital scrambled to cover its ass. All the right words were uttered. All the careful platitudes of sorrow and regret mouthed over and over again. Heyward was a killer, but a victim of his disease, too. The Marsdons didn't like that angle, but that's how Pauline Kirby and her news crew played it, along with a healthy dose of all the personal tragedy that had plagued the Marsdon family for generations. It made good television. It placed the hospital in the background and the unlucky Marsdons in front. It worked.

And Melody Stone?

Apart from Langdon Stone, Melody's hotheaded brother, no one seemed to care too much about Melody herself. She was just the woman Heyward Marsdon III killed. Almost nameless.

Do it.

In the first few moments after her rescue, in a stream of nearly incoherent words, Claire related to Wade from security what had transpired in her office. She told him what Melody said. She told him everything. But much later, when she was asked for her account of the incident, she couldn't make herself reveal Melody's last words to Freeson and Avanti. It seemed . . . unfair and unnecessary at the time. Still, that reckoning was yet to come, because Melody's illness was part of the whole unfortunate series of events that led to her death.

"Claire?" a voice called from the hallway, breaking into her thoughts. She glanced up to see Alison duck her head inside the room. "Jane Doe is in the middle of a fracas in the morning room. Gibby's mad at Maribel for taking his chair, and Jane's chair got pushed out of the way with her in it."

"What's she doing in the morning room?" Claire jumped to her feet. "Is she all right?"

"Dr. Freeson told Darlene to take her there. She didn't fall out of the chair. She just hung on to the sides, so she's okay. Just thought you should know."

"Thank you." Claire was already on her way out the door. She glanced at her watch. Another appointment in thirty minutes.

She hung on to the sides.

Even though Freeson had put the patient in a situation she might not have been ready for, Jane Doe had sensed danger and had recognized what to do to save herself. A great sign that maybe she was coming out of her catatonia. Encouraging, even if it galled Claire to admit that Freeson might not have been completely wrong.

The morning room looked deceptively serene when she reached it. Lester, an octogenarian with dementia, was rocking on his feet in the corner and looking out the window toward Side B, mumbling softly. Maribel, an Alzheimer's patient who was wily and intuitive, was sitting at a table, clutching a doll, but her eyes were sliding back and forth, as if she were looking for some kind of opening to make mischief. Two older women were seated in wheelchairs and talking quietly. They were Mrs. Merle and Mrs. Tanaway, and they enjoyed taking imaginary tea together. Thomas McAvoy, a borderline personality, glared at the two of them as if they were plotting against him, but he always looked that way. Gibby was seated in his favorite chair, and beside him, in the chair she apparently had grabbed onto, Jane Doe was staring silently toward the television.

Greg Fanning, one of the orderlies, asked Claire, "You here to see Cat?"

"Cat?"

He shot a look toward Jane Doe. "Cat Atonic," he deadpanned. "Better name than Jane Doe."

Claire was noncommital, as she didn't want to encourage Greg, who took things to the nth degree sometimes. But he was good with the patients, and that was the most important thing.

"Hello," Claire greeted the new patient. "My name's Claire."

"I'm Bradford," Gibby interrupted. "Don't you has a name?"

"Call her Cat," Greg said.

"Cat," Gibby repeated.

The woman in question stared straight ahead. Her hair was blond, straight, and hung down to lie just past her shoulders. Her eyes were a crystal blue. Brilliant. Icelandic. Claire wondered who her people were, her family, her friends. It had been over a week since she'd been found, so where were they?

"You're safe here. Your room is down the hall," Claire reminded her. "Would you like to watch television?"

"She don't talk," Gibby said. He was gripped onto the sides of his special chair as if expecting someone to steal it from him, which happened at least once or twice every day.

"Dr. Norris . . ."

Claire looked up at the familiar voice. "Hi, Donald," she said to the approaching man in khakis and a pressed shirt. He smiled effortlessly through blindingly white teeth. If he'd had a sweater he would have hooked it with one thumb and thrown it over his shoulder.

"Who's our new friend, here?" he asked.

"We don't know her name yet," she said, shooting a quelling glance at Greg, who ignored her and said, "Cat."

"She looks like a Marlene," Donald responded.

He walked away. Claire's eyes followed him for a moment, then she glanced back at the blond woman. There was a glimmer in her eyes, as if she'd reacted to some stimulus. Donald? Claire yanked her attention to Donald's retreating back and thought of calling him over again, but he was chatting with Big Jenny, who was staring at him as if she'd like to eat him alive. Claire knew Don Inman well enough to know he wouldn't be any help to her in the way she hoped. He wasn't interested. Neither was he part of the staff, but he acted like it sometimes.

Turning back to the blond woman, who seemed to have tensed up, Claire said, "Your baby's doing fine. So are you. If you'd like to talk sometime, I'd like to listen."

There was no response.

Claire waited for a few moments, then smiled encouragingly and told her that she'd be back to see her later.

Gibby twisted to watch Claire leave, then turned back to his new friend. "She's nice," he said conspiratorially. "Some of 'em aren't as nice."

The blond woman gazed blankly at the television. Gibby reached over and patted her hand.

Tasha faded in and out of a strange reality. She could sense the danger. It was chasing her. Breathing down her neck. She was trapped . . . trapped . . . and they were coming for her. Always coming for her. There were bindings at her wrists. Leather straps that cruelly bit into her flesh. They tied her up rather than leave her alone. They were evil. Evil! They never let her be.

She had to get out! Had to find a way.

They were coming for her. They were just outside the door. She had to tell someone. Warn them!

Help me! Help me! Please! PLEASE!

* * *

Gibby gazed at the blond woman with concern. She was squeezing the arms of her chair and softly moaning. Gibby fretted. His friend was having a problem. She was staring at the TV. Eyes wide.

"Could we get the TV on!" he yelled, looking around, flailing his arms. "The TV. *Damn it!*"

Darlene cruised over, her eyes hard. "Hold your horses," she muttered, breathing smoke onto him.

"You smell like an ashtray," he declared.

Darlene walked to the television and pressed the button for the power switch. She changed the channel until she found a game show and Gibby, who felt pressure building, beat at his own head. "There," Darlene said.

"Stop it! Stop it! Stop it!" Gibby screamed.

Darlene came back in a flash, leaning into his right ear. "If you want the TV on, you have to be quiet."

"Nooo!"

"Yes."

"I don't want the TV. I don't care about the *damn* TV." He threw a hand in his companion's direction. "She wants the TV. I don't give a *damn*."

"She doesn't care about the TV," Darlene said. "She doesn't know whether it's on or not."

"She does! She said so."

"She doesn't speak."

"She does! She does!"

"Gibby, if you don't calm down, you're going back to your room."

He grabbed onto his chair and started rocking. *"No!"*

"It's up to you. TV time. Or back to your room."

"She wants the TV. *She* does. She said so."

Darlene motioned to Greg, and Gibby knew he was going to be hauled away from his new friend. He gazed at his blond friend wildly. She gazed back at him. Her eyes were blue, blue, blue.

"Go ahead," she said. "I'll be right here waiting for you."

"I'll be back! I'll be back!" Greg and one of the other big guys who yanked Gibby around whenever he got upset walked toward him, but Gibby shot out of his chair. "Okay. I'll go. Okay. I'll go."

Darlene folded her arms and gazed at him in that mean way. Gibby shuffled off toward his room but glanced back just before he turned the corner. The blond woman's eyes were sending out blue laser beams. She was saying something, wasn't she?

"I'll miss you," Gibby yelled at her. "You're my friend!"

She didn't respond, but then Darlene got in the way and he couldn't see the laser beams any longer. Darlene was looking down at her hard, like she thought she was lying or something. She always thought Gibby was lying to her but he never was.

Help me. . . . Tasha thought again, but the words floated away slowly. She could see the words. They were black. Right in the air in front of her. But they were leaving, and after a while she couldn't see them anymore. Couldn't remember what they'd said. She wanted to reach out a hand and grab them, but her hands were tied with leather thongs.

Time passed . . . it grew darker. They moved her to her room, fed her, left her alone.

But they always kept her tied. She had to get away. She had to escape.

When? How?

They were coming. She could hear the death knell of their footsteps.

Coming for her.

Coming for *her*.

She tried to scream. The scream was in her throat but it was caught there. As caught as she was by them. She heard their steps on the floorboards and smelled the scent of seawater.

The ocean . . . so near and yet so far.

She had to get away. Get away. Get away. . . .

Somewhere outside her world, a woman's voice: "Look at her. Get Dr. Norris."

"You mean Dr. Freeson?" a man's voice questioned.

"Norris! I don't give a damn about Freeson!"

"I'll go." A younger woman.

"Hurry," the first woman urged. "I think she's coming out of it."

Chapter 3

The coroner's office was painted green and smelled of antiseptic with a faint underlying metallic scent that Lang recognized as blood. An autopsy was taking place in an adjoining room, and as Lang watched, the door to that room opened and the medical examiner stepped through in bloodstained scrubs. Seeing Lang, he brushed by and growled, "Who are you? You're in the wrong place."

"I came to see the body that was found at the rest stop."

He was tall and stooped and had a tendency to glare. He glared at Lang, who returned his gaze blandly. "On whose authority?"

"Sheriff Nunce," Lang lied. He hadn't heard back from Nunce yet. The man was on vacation and Lang, surprising even himself, had been bitten by the need to do something and had moved forward as if he were the homicide detective assigned to the case.

"Nunce didn't call me."

Lang shrugged. "Yeah, well. I'm Detective Langdon Stone. Portland P.D. We're helping County on this one."

"Winslow County," the man said suspiciously. "Not Multnomah."

"They're short on manpower," Lang went on, freewheeling. "Call Nunce and check it out."

"I don't have time to entertain you or the sheriff." He pushed through another door, Lang right on his heels.

"Show me the body and I'll leave you alone."

"When Nunce calls me, then we'll talk."

"You want it that way? Sure, I'll just sit down over here." Lang grabbed a rolling stool with a Naugahyde top and plopped down on it. He glanced at a tray of utensils sitting on the counter and reached a hand in to pull up a scalpel.

"Pain in the ass," the doctor snarled, then threw up one hand in a gesture for Lang to follow. Lang jumped up and strode to catch up with the man, who turned right and pushed through swinging doors into another green room, this one with a bank of stainless steel drawers, the kind that held bodies. Lang unconsciously held his breath against the odor of death, though there was none. He'd seen his share of dead bodies but it always gave him a moment's pause; his own particular need for solemnity and the passing of a human spirit.

The drawer ran back with a loud rattle, evidence of his guide's impatience. Inside was a young man with dark hair, olive skin, and a body slashed and stabbed with knife wounds. An autopsy had been performed to determine cause of death, and the Y of the incision stood out against his sallow pallor.

"Stab wound to the heart did it," the doctor told him dispassionately. "Not the first wound, but it was the C.O.D."

Cause of death.

"Anything else?" Lang asked.

"No defensive wounds."

Lang glanced again at the corpse. A young man. Muscular. He leaned down and looked at his palms. Nothing.

"He was either unconscious or he didn't want to fight back. He's got a contusion near his temple. Maybe that incapacitated him and then whoever had the knife just started slashing."

"Age?"

"Around twenty."

"And no one's come forward with any information?"

"Missing persons isn't looking for this guy. Not a word. He's off the grid, or no one cares."

He thought about that as the doctor waited with studied patience. "Got a picture?" Lang asked.

"You're such good friends with Nunce, get it from him." He stomped off and Lang was alone. He stared down at the man's face a long time, memorizing it. Angular cheeks. Black hair, longish.

Young.

Carefully, sensing the quiet of the room, the sharp scents, the feeling of a deep, impersonal institution—exactly what it was—Lang closed the drawer. Even with his effort of quiet, it seemed to clang and reverberate, a harsh metallic sound that spoke of the finality of death.

"Dr. Norris! Jane Doe. Cat . . . she might be coming to."

Claire glanced at Alison, then at her office clock. It was almost five. "What's happening?"

"She's tense. Gripping her chair. Gibby says she's talking."

Claire and the aide shared a look. "I'll be right there," she said and Alison nodded and hurried away. It was early, but she might be able to leave after she checked on Cat. There was no pressing reason to stay late, and she'd already spent far too many hours on the job.

Grabbing her coat and tossing her purse strap over her shoulder, she walked briskly down the hall toward the skyway that led to the main hospital and the gallery above the morning room. Descending the steps, she could smell the scents of cooked carrots and potatoes and chicken. The kitchen was preparing the evening meal and tables were being arranged in the morning room. Patients could eat in their rooms or one of several dining rooms, or the morning room, if there were seats available. Claire frowned and headed down the hall toward room 113, Jane Doe—Cat's—room. Side A of the hospital had three floors; Side B, which housed the criminally insane, sported four floors and two subterranean levels as well.

The door to room 113 was open. Dr. Freeson was staring down at the patient, whose blank face stared right back.

"Alison said she might be coming to," Claire said.

"Well, you can see that's not true. Why did Alison go to you?"

"What happened?"

Freeson fluttered a hand. "That Gibson boy was bothering her, so we took them both back to their rooms. Actually, I was just about to call you, so it's just as well you're here." He frowned at the sight of her coat and purse. "There's a meeting tomorrow morning with the Marsdon family concerning Heyward's incarceration. I want to make sure you're available."

"I'm not available," she said tightly. "I have patients."

"Well, rearrange them, for God's sake," he said. "This matters, Claire. Eleven o'clock. Avanti will be there, and Neumann, and of course Dr. Radke."

As hospital administrator, Radke was the big cheese and was also the man in bed professionally with the Marsdons.

"I'm no longer Heyward's doctor," she said.

"In Heyward's mind, you are," Freeson replied. "I'm not asking, Claire."

"You never do."

"You want to take this up with Avanti, be my guest." Color swept up his neck and his voice tightened. "The

Marsdons will be there, too, and the team from Side B: Zellman . . . Prior . . ."

Claire could see the pressure was going to be on her to agree to Heyward's release from Side B to Side A. "Maybe someone from the lockdown section will argue that Heyward should remain with them."

Freeson looked at her as if she were dense. "Just be there."

Feeling someone else's eyes on her, she glanced back and saw that Cat had turned her head and was staring at her. Claire stared back and a frisson slid up her arms in spite of herself. Was there any chance she understood their words? "Hello," she said.

But the girl's gaze was in the middle distance. Not on Claire. After a few minutes, she turned back to stare toward the blank television on the wall across from her bed. Claire turned the set on and put the remote near Cat's right hand, next to the call button. Then she headed out of the room and to the side exit where her car was parked.

Lang sat in his truck, his head against the headrest, eyes closed, ears filled with the *pitter, pitter* of rain and then sloppy plops when it started pounding in earnest. He opened his eyes. He was in the lot of the Winslow County Sheriff's Department, parked in a visitor's spot, nose out. He'd been there an hour. If he stayed much longer he suspected someone would come and knock on his window and demand to know what the hell he was doing. He would, if he worked there.

But he didn't want to move. He was caught in a funky inertia, the same one he'd battled since Melody's death. Sometimes he won, sometimes he lost. It had a strong grip that had lessened a bit over time, but still held on hard. He had no family now. He was alone, and a voice in his head kept asking him, *What now? What's next? What's the point?*

Shifting in the seat, he sighed, a sound somewhere between a snort and a groan. He supposed he suffered from depression, although it didn't completely immobilize him. In fact, given the slightest chance to get Heyward Marsdon a guilty verdict and send him to the big house, he'd be sprinting down the halls to do that.

He glanced toward the sheriff department's front doors. He'd called for the sheriff again, but had been told the man was out. Lang figured Nunce must still be on vacation, because he was never in. He was asked, again, if he wanted to speak with someone else, but Lang had once again declined. Going to see the medical examiner, pretending that he'd talked to the sheriff, that maybe hadn't been wise for positive relations with the department; however, he didn't regret it. What the hell. Sometimes you just had to forge forward in life, and he hadn't been particularly good in that regard lately.

Although he'd overstepped bounds all over the place and if he were caught, had no backup plan, he didn't much care. Part of his "depression," no doubt, but he kinda thought his very lack of interest was the reason he'd gotten past the ME. He wasn't desperate or pushy, didn't want anything really, and so he'd raised no alarm. If he wanted to see the John Doe's body, it was fine, fine, fine. No reason to call the sheriff and check. Just go goddamn look at it already, and get out.

The dead man's image crossed the screen of his mind. The stitched Y-cut from the autopsy. The muscular build. His youth. No defensive wounds . . .

Why hadn't the guy fought back? What had stopped him? Did he know his attacker? Was he unconscious before the knife attack began?

Lang knew the man had been found by a trucker, but

unless he looked at the case file he wouldn't know the trucker's name and/or how to get hold of him. Not that he really cared to talk to the man. Not that he had any authority to get involved.

"Not my case," he said aloud.

Yet he was mildly intrigued. Mildly.

"Nobody likes interference," he added. "Curtis knows better."

Yet his partner, the bastard, had intrigued him.

Maybe it was a good thing. Time would tell.

The rain had turned his windows into a moving rain splatter and now he was insulated from view behind a gray fog of condensation, cocooned within the vehicle. Lang thought about the Jane Doe who'd been released from Laurelton General to Halo Valley Security Hospital.

Halo Valley.

He closed his eyes, breathed quietly for several moments, then opened them again. Halo Valley Security Hospital was a private institution where special funds were set aside for worthy cases. The Marsdon family being a major contributor to the hospital and the special funds made it a good bet concessions had been made for Heyward Marsdon III, yes, but the hospital served an altruistic purpose, too. Cases that might have normally been assigned to the Oregon State Hospital in Salem, the state-run facility, sometimes ended up at Halo Valley, easing costs to the state and maybe even giving the patient more intensive care.

Not that Lang would ever be a fan. Given what had happened to his sister on Halo Valley grounds, and the choices that had been made by Halo Valley staff, particularly Dr. Claire Norris, he was never going to feel all warm and fuzzy about the place. But Halo Valley was where the pregnant rest stop victim had been taken, so if he kept with this case, it might be a place he was destined to visit.

The idea brought a cold chill to his skin.

So why was he parked outside the Winslow County Sheriff's Department? Why was he listening to Trey Curtis? Why did he feel oddly committed to a case that had nothing—*nothing*—to do with him? Why this case? Why now?

Lang's hands flexed on the wheel for a moment, then he threw open the door and stepped into the rain, jamming a baseball cap on his head and watching rain slide down the shoulders of his black leather jacket. He should have worn a raincoat. He shouldn't be on this mission. He should have stayed home and watched daytime television.

It was raining the day Melody died, too. An incessant, chilling precipitation thrown around by the hand of the wind. She'd stopped by to see Lang at work, her hair wet, her face flushed from cold, raindrops sparkling under the department lights. He'd been on his way out and she'd said she wanted to talk to him. She wore a thin jacket, a summer jacket, and he could see the bare skin of her wrists and a little up her forearms. Thin, red welts showed where she'd scratched herself. Even in those few moments she couldn't stop the compulsive tearing at her own skin. He'd been worried. They agreed to meet at the house as soon as Lang was off, about three hours later. Melody had long ago moved out and been on her own. She'd been a bright star once, someone who seemed to know what she wanted. Someone in control of her own life. But things had deteriorated and Lang had tried to get her to come home to no avail. He knew about Heyward Marsdon, knew of his family and a little of his problems. Initially, he'd foolishly been relieved and happy when his drifting sister had connected with someone from a solid family. He'd felt hopeful, like she might actually pull it back together. Have a normal life. A good life. Naivete at its worst. He knew better. He'd seen enough through his years on the force to know better, but when it came to Melody he just wanted to believe in good things so badly.

She never made it to his house. He tried calling the cell phone number he had for her, but it was not hers any longer. He went to an old apartment address, but it was empty and the neighbor lady said she thought the woman who'd lived there had been evicted for nonpayment.

Kicking himself for not just leaving work with her when she stopped by, Lang tried getting in touch with the Marsdons and was coolly ignored. No, they didn't know where Heyward was. No, they had no phone number for him. No, they had no idea who his friends were. And they would appreciate not being bothered again.

And then . . . merely an hour later . . . the emergency call from Halo Valley Security Hospital was logged into 911. He'd heard the tapes enough times. A guard, Wade De-Bussy, was holding down Heyward Marsdon, and one Dr. Claire Norris was saying that a woman named Melody Stone was dead.

Paranoid schizophrenia, they told Lang. Hallucinations and delusions. Unpredictable behavior. But no one, no one, believed Heyward Marsdon would kill anyone. Certainly not Heyward Senior or Junior, who were chock full of disbelief. Why, Heyward III had just been at the governor's ball with his loving family. Yes, he'd had bouts of depression in the past, but this was entirely unprecedented. Unbelievable. There were undoubtedly mitigating factors to explain the psychological break. Drugs, maybe? He was never *that* sick.

Well, at least that was the beginning spate of excuses until Heyward Senior, who was the old man pulling the strings, saw that he'd better go for the insanity plea or his grandson would be heading straight for serious prison time. Lang suspected Heyward Marsdon Sr. was practically choking on the diagnosis for his only grandson.

Heyward III's father was like a pale shadow following the old man around and didn't seem to have any say, one way or the other. A disappointment to his old man? Maybe the reason Heyward Senior was pinning his hopes on his schizophrenic grandson, no matter the evidence to the Third's sickness?

It didn't matter. None of it.

The upshot was that Lang hadn't been there for Melody. A couple of hours on the job when he should have been with his sister. A couple of hours . . . that's all.

So he quit. Just up and quit. Couldn't do it anymore. Couldn't go to his old desk and remember how he'd turned Melody away when she'd needed him. Since then he'd had six months of idle time and one job offer from the Tillamook County Sheriff's Department, the law enforcement agency that held Halo Valley Security Hospital within its jurisdiction. Strange how the world worked. Ironic. He'd met with Tillamook County's sheriff and had hit it off sometime the spring before, and the job offer came in just about the time he quit the Portland P.D. He'd turned them down, but like Drano, the job had yet to be filled. At this point he didn't even know if he wanted to go back to law enforcement anywhere. Yet here he was, stepping forward through the rain to the Winslow County Sheriff's Department, working a case he had no business being involved with.

Now, stepping inside the department's front doors, he glanced through bulletproof glass at the receptionist whose name tag read Dot Edwards. She smiled at him and said, "That's one wet coat ya got there."

Lang glanced at his jacket. It was soaked. "It was dry when I was at the ME's."

"You came from there?"

He nodded. "Sheriff still not in? I'm Langdon Stone. Ex-homicide with Portland P.D."

"Ex," she said.

"Long, ugly story."

Dot hesitated, then gave Lang a slow, negative wag of her bleached blond head.

"Thought I'd check," Lang said, turning to leave.

"Wait a sec. Detective Tanninger might be able to help you. He's, like . . . the man everyone wants to see?" She reached for the phone.

"Is he in?" Lang asked, pausing.

She smiled and said into the receiver, "Could you check with Detective Tanninger? There's someone here to see him. Ex-detective . . . ?"

"Langdon Stone, formerly homicide Portland P.D."

She repeated the information, then hung up a moment later. "Go on through," she said, touching a buzzer.

Lang pushed through the door, feeling a little like Alice falling down the rabbit hole. He didn't know what he was doing and what he would find, and it was an adventure he maybe should have reconsidered before embarking upon.

He walked down a short hallway and then was in the squad room. Several sets of eyes turned to him, but most of the desks were empty. "Tanninger?" he asked, and was pointed toward a corner. He turned it just as a tall man in the tan uniform of the sheriff's department appeared from an office.

He stopped upon seeing Lang, and the two men sized each other up. Detective Will Tanninger—per his name tag—was one of those strong, silent types who observed more than talked. Lang thought about trying to bamboozle the man for about half a second, figured it wouldn't work, said instead, "Detective Trey Curtis, my ex-partner at Portland P.D., wanted me to jump-start my stalled investigative engine by interesting me in one of your cases. The rest stop one. So, here I am, insinuating myself into your world. Feel free to kick my ass out of here."

Tanninger half-smiled. "The truth. Interesting approach."

"I came here to talk to the sheriff, but he's not here. Dot at the desk suggested I meet with you."

"Sheriff Nunce planned to retire but no one wanted him to. He was reelected, but when he's not around I'm the next man."

"Maybe that happens a lot?" Lang suggested.

"Maybe it does."

"So, do you want some help, or am I wasting my time and yours?"

"I know Trey Curtis. Of him, anyway. And Drano."

"You know Drano?"

"We got a call from him, too. Wanted us to encourage you. Said you were a hell of an investigator. Sang your praises. Twisted our arms as hard as he could."

Lang said wryly, "I'm a charity case."

"According to them, you're the man for the job, and if this case just so happens to kick you back into gear, everybody wins."

"Well . . ." He wasn't sure what to think of that.

Tanninger said, "If you're as good as they say you are, jump in. Even if you're not. We're short-staffed right now. This damn flu has decimated us and Nunce is out sick."

Funny. Lang's lie to the ME was turning out to be the truth. "How long's he been out sick?"

"A while. Maybe a while more."

"Vacation. Sick. And still one foot in retirement?"

Tanninger shrugged and said instead, "One of our best took a bullet last year, and though she's recovered, she's about all we've got for this case. And she went home early with a cough."

"You're not bullshitting me?"

"What do you care if I am?"

"I don't know."

"There's a lot of crime out there. We don't have enough investigators on a good day for the type of attack that took place at the rest stop. No manpower. You want in, I'll meet you all the way."

"What's Drano got on you?" Lang asked.

Tanninger laughed.

"Can you give me the info on the guy who found them? The trucker?"

"I'll get you the file. We checked the license plate of the vehicle that was left on the scene. Stolen truck. It's in the file, too."

"And the murder weapon, the knife, was found at the crime scene . . . ? Anything there?"

"No prints that count. Covered in blood and wiped on the grass. Tossed into the nearby bushes."

"He or she didn't want to be caught with it."

Tanninger shrugged. "Maybe. But the doer had to be hit by the blood. There was a lot of it."

"They weren't thinking straight."

"Not that kind of crime," he agreed.

Lang nodded. "Okay."

"Tomorrow I'm heading out to interview the other victim. The woman. If you want to join on, your timing's perfect. Barb was going to head to Halo Valley Security this afternoon, but she's out sick, so I'm teed up. Jane Doe hasn't talked, hasn't even comprehended what's happened, as far as anyone can tell. It's wait and see, but we try to keep a finger on the pulse . . . so?"

Lang absorbed the news about an imminent trip to Halo Valley with mixed feelings. He could feel his pulse speed up. "Is Barb the one who got shot, or . . . ?"

Tanninger nodded. "She didn't want to go home today. She's hard to hold down, no matter what."

"No one's got in touch about Jane Doe? Or the guy in the morgue?"

"Not yet. Channel Seven's doing a follow-up."

"Pauline Kirby?" Lang managed to keep from making a face. Just.

"You don't like her?"

"Love her."

Tanninger laughed. "So, do you want to go to Halo Valley?"

Did he really want to take a trip to that hospital? See that monstrous institution and know that Heyward Marsdon was in there, albeit behind the double-locked doors to the restricted half? Have a chance to maybe interview Dr. Claire Norris?

He saw her in his mind's eye. Quiet. Serious. Slim. Brunette. Maybe a ballbuster.

Exhaling slowly, he nodded.

Tanninger stuck out his hand. "Welcome to the team."

Claire took the three concrete steps that led to her back door, balancing two bags of groceries. She'd made a quick stop at the market, buying salad fixings and boneless chicken breasts. Once upon a time she'd prided herself on her original meals. But that was when she'd been married. Happily married. Or at least believed she was happily married. A long time ago.

She dropped the bags onto her chipped Formica countertop. The rented bungalow was cute but tired. Its major selling feature was its view of the Pacific Ocean. Not a spectacular view; the homes dotting this hillside above the small hamlet of Deception Bay were built in the forties and fifties, anything but lavish, but they had charm.

Her kitchen window faced north and she could see slices of the jetty past the laurel and camellia bushes that had nearly taken over this side of the house. She could also see Dinah's cabin, smaller than hers, more of a Craftsman style, though its paint was peeling badly and the roof patches looked like acne, dotted across the whole of it.

She put the chicken breasts in a pan with a spray of olive oil, covered them, and waited for them to finish cooking. Then she tossed together the greens, added garbanzos, chopped walnuts, goat cheese, and blueberries, and pulled a favorite bottle of honey mustard dressing from the cupboard. She'd learned shortcuts since her ill-fated marriage. She'd learned she didn't have to be a perfect wife in order to matter.

Seeing a flash of color outside the window, she looked out. It was just getting dark and wisps of fog were floating by like a magician's screens—now you see it, now you don't—further obscured by fitful rain. The color splash was dullish red and came from her neighbor and friend's, Dinah's, tunic. Dinah was walking from the direction of the beach, which, though across the road and down the hill, was part of Dinah's favorite exercise venue. Walk at dawn, walk at dusk. If Claire's work schedule permitted, she would be right with her.

Quickly she unlocked and pushed up her window. "Dinah!" Claire called. "Can you join me for dinner? I've chicken breasts, salad, and wine."

Dinah hesitated, holding open her screen door. In the gathering dusk Claire couldn't see her eyes, which she knew to be light blue. "I'll be right over," she called.

Claire hurriedly uncorked the wine, put it in a chilled silver bucket, turned the chicken breasts, then headed into her bedroom to change. The bungalow was two-story: two bedrooms, one bath on the main level; a daylight basement below that faced toward the ocean, its view blocked by houses across the road.

Changing into an oversized cream cotton sweater and jeans, Claire padded back barefoot. It was chilly and getting wetter with another spate of clouds and rain. She'd just placed the chicken breasts on a platter and set out forks and knives wrapped in napkins when Dinah arrived. "Come and get it," Claire invited and they served up in the kitchen and took their plates to the covered deck, which surrounded the upper level, where Claire had placed the wine, glasses, and salt and pepper on a teak table built for two, one of the few pieces of furniture she'd taken from her marriage.

"If the rain comes again, we can head back in. Fast," Claire said.

"I like being outside," Dinah admitted.

"Me, too."

Dinah was in her midthirties, close to Claire's age, but sometimes seemed like an older sister, almost a mother, to Claire. "How was the hospital today?" she asked.

Claire peered at her. "Small talk, or do you really want to know?"

"Whichever you prefer."

Claire poured both of their glasses with the Savignon Blanc she'd recently discovered. Light. Not too astringent. Cheap enough to buy without wincing. "Do you remember that Jane Doe I told you about?"

"The pregnant one?"

"She was transported from Laurelton General to Halo Valley today. Dr. Freeson has taken her on as his patient, with the help of Dr. Avanti."

"You'd like to take care of her," Dinah guessed.

"Maybe I'd just like them not to."

Dinah cradled her glass in her hands and looked out toward the ocean, her blondish hair smooth and straight to her shoulders. Dinah had been there when the incident happened. She'd seen it on the news and was waiting for Claire to get home after all the interviews and checkups and red tape. As soon as Claire wearily stepped from her car, Dinah was there with a basket of chocolate chip muffins and a warm hug.

The warmth Dinah lavished on her foster child she brought to Claire when she needed it most. Without the thousand questions Claire expected, Dinah followed her inside that first night, dropped the basket on the table, and set about making herbal tea. Fresh herbs from her own garden. Claire, spent, sat in a chair at the table and let Dinah take over. And while the tea steeped Claire leaned forward on her elbows, head in her hands, and cried. For Melody. For Heyward. For her own inability to stop things.

Dinah pushed a cup of tea her way and said, "You need to know that this will pass. You won't be blamed forever. There are changes ahead."

"Right now, I'll be lucky to get through tomorrow."

"You are only guilty of a tender heart. It's your saving grace, but it's caused you pain. And you may be too polite. It's how they've used you as their scapegoat."

"What do you know about it?" Claire asked, surprised.

"What I saw on the news," Dinah answered, unruffled.

But Claire learned that Dinah saw a helluva lot more than was broadcast. She called it her intuition, but Claire had her own intuition about things and she knew this was something else. Just what, she couldn't say. And as they became friends, she decided she didn't care. Dinah was her therapist. A therapist's therapist. Other than her own work with her patients, the evenings she shared tea, or dinner, or wine with Dinah were the real moments where Claire felt connected to the human race.

Now she said, "I don't know how I would've gotten through the last six months without this." She motioned to Dinah and herself.

Dinah smiled. "That's what I'm here for."

"For me? Yeah, right."

"Sometimes the universe does answer."

"Mmm." Claire squinched down in her chair and gazed into the fog. "I didn't know I'd sent out a question."

"You didn't want to send it out. Others did that for you. But the message was received and now you're getting better. Stronger."

"You're a little too woo-woo for me. You know that, right?"

She smiled and leaned her head back and closed her eyes. "I shouldn't drink wine. It dulls the senses."

"All five, or do you have six?"

Dinah opened her eyes and turned to look at Claire. "You're such a believer in straight science."

"Hey, if there's something more, I'm all for it. Don't quote me on that. The hospital administration already regards me with suspicion. But I like this." She lifted her glass to toast Dinah.

Claire had told Dinah how her marriage to Ron fell apart after her two miscarriages. Dinah, in turn, had talked about Toby, about her frustration with Toby's mother, how she would love to adopt the little boy herself, but it was not to be.

Now they just enjoyed each other's company, talking about other things, the less important the better. After dinner and several glasses of wine, Dinah headed back to her house and Claire stayed where she was, her gaze on the ocean.

Later, lying in bed and watching rain drizzle down her windowpane, she wondered more about her friend. Dinah seemed to understand Claire's very soul and yet, beyond Toby, Claire knew very little about the woman next door. Some people were like that, she knew; they could give of themselves wholly without offering up a clue to their own inner workings. Claire had just never met someone so completely like that as Dinah. She felt a little guilty because it seemed sometimes like she was taking, taking,

taking and offering nothing in return except an occasional dinner or glass of wine.

She closed her eyes, thoughts of Dinah drifting away to be replaced by other more pressing issues. Tomorrow Claire was going to be bullied by the administration and the Marsdons to give a favorable account regarding Heyward Marsdon III's rehabilitation and therefore the means of his incarceration. Nobody wanted him on Side B. Not his family, and because of them, not the hospital administrators. She knew they wanted him as an inpatient on Side A.

But was it the right course to take?

The question kept her awake till nearly dawn.

Chapter 4

The hour-long eleven o'clock meeting started on time and ran an hour and a half late. Everyone Freeson had said would be there was there, along with Dr. Zellman, Dr. Prior, and Dr. Dayton from Side B—Dr. Jean Dayton being the only other woman in the room besides Claire.

The meeting was to decide the fate of Mr. Heyward Marsdon III, at least within the hospital walls. There was a lot of detailed data on his psychological state of mind, garnered over the past six months, and the first hour and a half crawled by with each of the doctors from Side B's recount. Claire was a little surprised that Dr. Jean Dayton's views coincided so closely with her own.

"Mr. Marsdon is a paranoid schizophrenic," she wrapped up in her curiously flat voice. She seemed to have next to no inflection in her tone. "He suffers delusions and hallucinations. Off his meds, he believes there are alien beings trying to kill him. That has not changed in six months, nor is it likely to in the future. I believe he should stay where he is."

"Dr. Dayton," Avanti answered smoothly, before Radke, whose face had grown tight and grim at her bald assessment, could try to pour oil on the situation himself. This was the first serious voice of dissent in their plan to move Heyward to Side A. "How often do you see Mr. Marsdon, professionally?"

"Daily," she stated.

"How often do you see other patients?"

"Daily," she repeated.

"All of them?"

"Most of them."

"But isn't Dr. Prior Mr. Marsdon's primary psychiatrist? Isn't he the one who should decide the right course of action?"

"I'm Heyward Marsdon's primary," Prior affirmed. He was a short man with a rotund stomach that he liked to rest his clasped hands upon.

Dayton said, "I'm one of Marsdon's doctors as well." Her voice took on a stubborn tone. "I think he's a danger to himself and others. Why don't you tell them what you said about him last week," she challenged Dr. Prior.

Prior sat up straight as if hit by a cattle prod."What?"

"When you and I were talking about Heyward after our weekly session together."

"I said he was doing fine," Prior declared.

"Actually, you said, 'Thank God he's on his meds. That's the only time he's fine.'"

"We all agree Heyward should stay on his meds," Avanti broke in. "But when he's on them, as he is now, he's in complete control."

Claire glanced at Heyward's family, his grandfather, Heyward Marsdon Senior, and his father, Heyward Marsdon Junior. Senior leaned forward, interested in the proceedings, but Junior looked like he was counting the tiny holes in the acoustical tiles on the ceiling.

Senior said in his gravelly voice, "I'll allow my grandson's had a few problems. He was overtaken by chemically induced visions that have altered his reality in terrible ways."

Like killing Melody Stone? Claire felt her skin tingle with shock. He was trying to negate the seriousness of Heyward's crime.

Dayton stated flatly, "If you're implying that his medications altered his reality, you are ignoring the facts."

"Dr. Dayton, we all know what happened." This time it was Radke speaking. "And we're not asking that he be released. What we are trying to discern is whether the more restrictive side of the hospital is the right place for Mr. Marsdon."

"There are some seriously psychological disturbed *criminals* on that side," Marsdon Senior pointed out.

Of which Heyward III is one, Claire thought.

"They're all treated with respect," Dr. Zellman felt compelled to put in.

"That goes for all of our patients," Avanti said. "Side A and Side B."

"All right," Radke said, closing his leather-bound notebook and leaning his arms across its smooth, black finish. His glance touched on Claire for a moment, then he looked around the room. The other doctors gazed back at him expectantly. Avanti, whose supercilious attitude was in high gear, had a faint smile on his lips, as if he knew it was already a foregone conclusion that Marsdon would be moved to Side A. He was worse than Freeson, Claire decided. A major leaguer while Freeson was still on a farm team when it came to overinflated ego, impatience, and narcissism.

The Marsdons, Senior and Junior, gave each other a look. Junior crossed his legs, twitched his knife-creased pant legs into place, then stared off into space as if he'd magically transported himself somewhere else. Maybe he had. He sure as hell hadn't been in the moment once during this meeting.

Radke said, "We've all had a chance to discuss the right

course of action for Mr. Marsdon, and though initially it seemed prudent to house him in the high-security wing of our hospital, maybe that time has passed. The focus of Mr. Marsdon's care is, by design, centered on detention in the high-security wing rather than individual treatment of his disease."

Heyward Marsdon Sr. reacted to "disease" with a jerk of tension. His white hair pulled away from his head in a wavy, Donald Sutherland style and his eyes were as blue and piercing as the actor's as well. He was heavier; his chest was wide, his cheeks fleshy, his hands meat hooks that looked as if they might have trouble handling the delicacy of a knife and fork. Claire could easily see him picking up a turkey leg in one hand and a pewter stein of ale in the other while hunching over a plate. He had that medieval look about him. She wondered if he'd been a grade school bully.

Marsdon Senior said, "My grandson needs help. Yes. But he is not the villain the media paints him. He does not belong with those vile killers in that part of your hospital."

"He did take a life," Dr. Howard Neumann reminded them quietly. He didn't want to go against the tide, but he had enough honor to want to keep the facts straight, regardless of the amount of money and influence sitting around the table.

Radke, six foot two, long-faced with salt-and-pepper hair and a lean build that made him seem taller than he was, turned his attention to Neumann, who was six inches shorter, stubbier, and tended to fidget. But this time Neumann placed one hand over the other on the table and waited. He wasn't going to let them forget what had truly happened. Claire could have kissed him.

"We haven't forgotten, Howard," Radke said. Then, to Claire, "You haven't said much, my dear."

"Everyone knows how I feel. He was remanded to

the high-security side of the hospital. Side B," Claire stated clearly.

"He was remanded to the *hospital,*" Radke corrected her.

"With the intention that he be monitored twenty-four seven. We don't do that on Side A to the extent Heyward Marsdon needs."

"I disagree," Avanti said vigorously. "Side A has more personnel. More contact with the patients."

"Side B has contact as well," Dr. Neumann started, but Marsdon Junior chose that moment to jump in with, "They're in cages on your high-security side! Only the sickest of the sick should be there."

Radke said to everyone, though his gaze was stuck on Claire, "It's up to us to decide the level of his care."

Dayton tried to get another word in. "It wouldn't do the hospital any good to have one of the patients hurt themselves or someone else."

Radke was practically willing Claire to see his side. She had no real authority. They would do what they would do. But if the press got hold of the fact that she didn't want Heyward III released from Side B, and then something happened, Claire would be on the front lines. The face of the hospital.

They wanted her on board badly.

"When Heyward was admitted to the hospital, it was with the understanding that he would be placed on Side B. That's why he's there now," she said.

"But it wasn't specifically written that he would have to stay there," Radke argued.

He was splitting hairs and they both knew it. This was for the Marsdons' benefit; it had nothing to do with what was best for Heyward III and others around him. "I know what the letter of the law is," Claire said evenly. "I also know the spirit in which it was made."

"Honey, what is that supposed to mean?" Heyward Senior frowned at her.

Claire was tired of being a dear and a honey. She met Heyward III's grandfather's eyes and said, "Everyone was stunned and horrified by Melody Stone's death at the hands of your grandson." Surprised looks abounded from other members of the staff and even Heyward Junior. Nobody, but nobody, talked back to Heyward Senior. "The public wanted him locked away forever. In a dungeon. To rot."

"Claire . . ." Radke admonished.

"He needs care. Personal care. Probably more than what he receives at Side B. But he's delusional and unpredictable and has hallucinations, like Dr. Dayton said. There's no escaping the fact that he's dangerous and needs round-the-clock supervision. If you want Heyward to receive one-on-one from Side A personnel, we can go to him on Side B. But I think he should stay there. He shouldn't be moved."

Avanti put in, "Side A can offer complete security. We can monitor his meds and the doors are coded and card-keyed. No one gets in or out without their keycard and code."

"I was overpowered by a paranoid schizophrenic," Claire reminded him. "Coded doors and keycards are only so effective."

"My grandson scared you. I understand how you feel," Marsdon Senior growled softly. His bushy white eyebrows were pulled down over his arctic eyes. "But he's not a cold-blooded killer like those men in the other rooms over there. You must agree on that, Dr. Norris."

"Not all of them are cold-blooded killers," she answered. "Some are delusional and hallucinate as much as Heyward. Some are worse. Some are better."

"So, what are you saying, Claire?" Radke asked, sounding annoyed.

Well, Emile, I'm saying you need to think in terms of

patient care and safety instead of the bottom line. "I'm saying my position hasn't changed."

"Dr. Norris, we need you to be on board with this," Avanti said in a voice that was gently threatening.

More than Dr. Dayton, it was Claire's vote on the issue that would matter. To the public. To the press.

And the press were going to be here soon to do their story on Cat.

"Only to look good politically," Claire responded to him. "You can make this decision without me."

"Dr. Norris has already said that Heyward won't receive the same level of care on Side B as Side A," Freeson suddenly popped up. "We all agree in theory."

"I can speak for myself," Claire said.

"Well, then speak," Avanti suggested, looking to the others for support. "Dr. Norris, you don't think the care on Side B is perfect for Heyward, do you?"

"Perfect? No. But—"

"Then what are we arguing about?" He turned to Radke and spread his hands. "Side B is not the best for Heyward Marsdon the Third. We all agree."

"That is where the court assigned him," Claire reminded them. "That's what they meant."

"I don't believe you're a mind reader." Avanti's dark eyes held a hint of warning.

"I don't believe you're that obtuse," she snapped back.

Silence descended on the room, and it was Howard Neumann who rescued the moment by accidentally knocking over his coffee cup and spilling the cooled brown liquid across the table. Apologizing profusely, he mopped up the mess while the rest of them gathered their notes and slid back their chairs.

Despite her strong words, Claire felt the anger that tightened her chest. She wasn't great with confrontation. She was an analyst, not a political infighter. But they'd backed her into a corner.

Freeson followed her through the door. "Claire, wait."

"Talk to me later, James. I'm busy." She kept walking rapidly away from the meeting room.

"I have some hospital business to discuss with you, and I don't feel like shouting it down the hall!"

"I'll hold the elevator," she said through lips that barely moved, then did just that as he took his sweet time joining her, just to let her know who was boss.

"You really like being a fly in the ointment, don't you?" he complained as the elevator doors closed.

"Oh. I thought I was speaking my mind and letting people know where I stood."

"Why are you fighting this so hard? It doesn't help anybody. Not even Heyward."

"I'm fighting for what I believe. You should try it sometime."

"You don't really believe Heyward should be on Side B. I know you don't."

"I don't think he should be on Side A, either. But he was remanded to Side B, no matter what spin anybody wants to put on it."

"You're overstepping your bounds," he said with a shake of his head.

"I'm always overstepping my bounds." His look of surprise was almost comical. "It's what you've always thought about me," she said. "Maybe I am a mind reader after all. Avanti was wrong."

He was staring at her as if she'd grown horns. Figuratively, she supposed she had. Good girl Claire Norris had left the building.

"What happened to your professionalism?" he demanded.

"Is it missing?"

He shook his head. "Channel Seven's going to be here

today. I don't know whether you should be available or not."

"Jane Doe's not my patient. Go ahead and take care of it."

"There's something else, too. The police want to interview her, and I've allowed it."

"Cat?"

"Jane Doe, yes."

Claire was blindsided by this turn of events. "But she's not awake."

"They don't care. Just wanted to let you know not to panic."

Not to panic. "What good is this going to do?"

He shrugged. "You don't say no to the police."

She shook her head, disbelieving. "If you think this is right for the patient, then I guess it is."

He peered at her hard. "I think there's an insult in there somewhere."

"I'd like to be there for Cat's interview, too, if it's all right."

"With the police, but not with Channel Seven . . . ?"

Claire made a sound of annoyance. "For both," she said, though she really wasn't looking forward to another round with Pauline Kirby.

The elevator doors opened onto the second floor and Freeson held them back from closing with his hand. Instead of getting out of the car, Claire punched the button for floor one again.

"You're going back down?" he asked.

"I'm going to check on Cat."

"Why?"

"Part of the personal patient care we give on Side A."

"She's my patient," he reminded her.

"I haven't forgotten."

"I'll go with you." He let go of the doors and they whispered shut once more. Claire had had about as much as she could stand of the man, but there was nothing much she could do to get rid of him.

They entered room 113 together. The blond woman stared straight ahead, not acknowledging either of them. The mound of her belly drew Claire's gaze and she walked up to her and touched her hand lightly.

"Nurse Maria will be on duty tonight. If you need anything, press this." Claire leaned across the bed, grabbed the remote call button, and laid it beside Cat's blanketed left leg.

The girl's eyes shifted. A flicker, side to side. Claire saw it and so did Freeson. He stroked his beard and said, "She's in there."

"When are the police coming?"

"Later today, I think. After Pauline Kirby."

"Make sure I'm called for both, okay?"

"Fine."

Claire turned away from him, knowing Freeson would do whatever he felt like in the end. He had no compunction in conveniently forgetting promises.

Heading for her office, Claire went back up the elevator, then passed by Glenda, the general receptionist for the medical office building, who was talking into her headset. She motioned for Claire to wait up, so Claire slowed her steps and stopped.

"A package was dropped off for you," she said, reaching behind the counter. She handed Claire a silvery box from Promise's Bakery, the size that might hold a two-layer cake.

"Who sent it?"

"Tony brought it."

Tony was an orderly who was a general errand boy for the hospital.

Claire carried the box to her office, set it on her desk, slid off the top. It was indeed a cake. Fudge frosting. She felt strangely light-headed as she pulled it from its box and stared at it. There was a card but she didn't have to read it.

She recalled the day Heyward III had asked her what her favorite cake was. She'd told him she preferred pies. Tarts. Something with fruit. They were in session and he was fixated on the idea. Wouldn't talk about issues he was facing. Didn't care that she liked pies. Was obsessed with knowing what Claire liked in a cake.

"I guess I'd say chocolate. Fudge, actually. With raspberry filling." And a glass of red wine, she'd thought, but kept that to herself.

"I'm going to get you one," he said with sudden vigor, rising from his chair.

"No, Heyward. Not now."

"Soon," he said. And then forgot the idea in the next moment.

But here it was. . . .

She didn't have a knife in her office. Carefully she ran her index finger down the edge of the cake, encountering the raspberry filling between the two layers. Heyward couldn't have done this on his own. She would bet he'd told his grandfather what she liked, and Heyward Senior sent it to her. The card read, "Wanted to get you your favorite." It was Heyward III's writing, but she could visualize his grandfather hovering over him. They wouldn't trust him with a pen.

A bribe, in its way.

She thought back on the meeting. Had she done enough to make herself heard? It was a moot point; they would do as they liked. They had before. They would again. But this time she'd really wanted to take a strong stand. No hedging. No trying to keep everybody happy. *That* hadn't worked. Spectacularly hadn't worked.

Carefully she carried the cake to the vending machine room. There was a small counter with a sink and a few haphazard chairs. Not really much of a meeting place, but then it was for the medical office staff only. She placed the cake on the counter and washed her frosting-covered finger in the sink. Gazing at the cake for a long moment, she felt her stomach growl.

Tightening her lips, she backed out of the room and headed back to her office for her purse and some change. She returned a few moments later and plunked coins into the vending machine, slamming a palm against a button for peanut M&M's. Protein. And sugar. If she had a multivitamin it would be a complete meal.

She hoped somebody would enjoy the cake. It just wasn't going to be her.

Cat was sitting in the other chair as Gibby claimed his, one eye on the lookout for Maribel, but she wasn't around. Gibby scooted his chair closer to hers and was amazed when she said, clear as a bell, "I need to get out of here."

"Out of the morning room?"

"Yes. And out the door." She leaned toward the front of the building, past the desk and the sofas where Big Jenny liked to sit, though Darlene always told her she couldn't sit there, and to the big glass windows that slid back and forth if you knew what numbers to push. Gibby didn't know the numbers. He didn't want to know the numbers. You had to have a square thing, too, or get the lady at the big desk to let you out.

"I'm scared out there," he admitted, though it was hard. He wanted the blond lady to like him. "Your name is Cat . . . like cats . . . and dogs . . . ?"

"Help me."

"Okay." She wasn't looking at him, but she was talking to him. To Gibby. Kinda made him scared, though, 'cause she was asking him to do something. He didn't know what, but he didn't think they'd like it.

Gibby glanced around the room. His hands gripped the sides of his chair. Oh! There was Maribel. She was coming his way! "Go 'way," he told her.

She strolled toward Cat, swiping at him. Gibby bared his teeth and made a face. Maribel stopped in front of Cat and stared at her. Maribel did that *all* the time.

"She has Zimer's disease," Gibby said. "Get outta here." He flapped his hand at her but Maribel just stared and stared. Cat stared back.

Donald strolled over. "Maribel, is there a problem?"

Gibby threw him a dark look. Donald always acted so smart all the time it made Gibby uncomfortable. Now he wanted to get up and go get Greg, but he wasn't around. Darlene was there, but he never wanted her. "Go 'way!" he hissed again at Maribel, stomping his foot at her.

"Fuck you," Maribel said.

"Oh, no," Donald said, sliding away.

Gibby slapped his hands over his ears. She said that *word*. She said it to *Cat*! "Noooo!" Gibby wailed. "You're mean! You're not nice!"

"Fuck you and the horse you rode in on," Cat replied.

Gibby's eyes widened. His jaw dropped. "Wha'd you . . . wha'd you . . ."

"Everything okay here?" It was Greg. Finally. And he was looking from Maribel to Gibby to Cat, but mostly at Gibby.

"She said . . . that word . . ."

Greg glanced at Maribel. "What word?"

Gibby pointed to Cat. "She said it, too. You know . . . *that word*!"

"The f-word?"

Gibby nodded furiously, his finger shaking as he kept

it directed at Cat. "She said, 'Fuck you and the horse you rode in on.'"

Greg shot a look at Cat and then demanded, "Where did you hear that, Gibby? Who said it?"

"She did!"

"I mean it. Who said it? Maribel?" Greg looked mad. He shook his head and took hold of Maribel's arm, trying to direct her away from Cat. "Was it Thomas?"

Gibby blinked a couple times and gazed at Thomas McAvoy, who was watching them with laser eyes. "No! He says that, too, but it was Cat!"

"Well, whoever said it, don't say it again." Greg was looking at Gibby as if it was all his fault!

Greg tried to move Maribel but she pulled her shoulders in and shrank down. She always did that. After a few moments Greg let go and went over to Thomas McAvoy, whose face looked just like those dead guys on TV. He was scary, too.

"You got me in trouble," Gibby moaned to Cat. He felt a little like crying.

She was still staring at Maribel, who was pulling at her hair and looking at the floor.

Gibby got up and tried to shove Maribel to one side. Maribel slugged him in the arm and jumped into his chair.

With a howl, Gibby launched himself at her and then Greg reappeared with Darlene and even Donald came back, too.

"Tsk, tsk," Donald said.

"What is with you, Gibson?" Darlene asked. "Ever since Cat got here, you're starting trouble."

"Not me!" Gibby cried.

"He repeated something Thomas said."

"Maribel said *fuck you* first!" Gibby screamed.

"Fuck you!" Maribel shrieked right back.

For the second time in two days Gibby was hauled off to

his room. He cried all the way, looking back at Cat. He watched her head turn as she examined the front door.

"She's my friend," he whimpered. "I need to help her."

But Greg and Darlene, the witch with a capital B, wouldn't listen to him.

Pauline Kirby touched at her dark hair, but every strand was held in place by one of the best hair sprays on the market. Super hold. Super expensive. But the best was the best, and Pauline liked the best. Pressing the pad of her little finger to the corner of her mouth, she looked into the hand mirror and tried on a smile. Her makeup was fresh. She looked good.

"Here." She handed the mirror to a production assistant. A gofer who hurried forward. A new one, she was pretty sure. They all looked the same. She could never remember their names and had given up trying. Long ago, she'd been the one with the eager smile and winning ways, ready to serve the talent in any way she could.

She was long over that, thank God.

Today she stood outside Halo Valley Security Hospital. Concrete and redwood in front, but the back part, the older section, was solid brick. They tried to dress up this new part: there was a portico with concrete pillars, but it still looked industrial, institutional, with maybe just a hint of architectural thought, but it sure as hell didn't transcend to anything close to beauty.

What a sorry piece of crap, she thought. Past the first roof you could actually see the razor wire that surrounded the grounds of the second brick building, the high-security hospital. No damn laurel hedge could disguise it, though that looked to be the idea. She knew of a couple real crazies who resided there. One of 'em had the gall to write to her now and again. Really filthy stuff. She showed it to her coworkers, pretending to be unaffected. She was a newswoman. A professional. But it gave her a nasty little shiver whenever she thought of that particular monster. If they ever let him out . . . ever . . . she was going to call in every favor she'd ever been owed, and there were a number of them, to make sure he was caught and hopefully killed this time.

Coming back to herself, she shook it off. She carried pepper spray. She was safe, even if she had to remember the spray every time she went through that damn security at the airport. Moron TSA agents. Acting like she was some kind of terrorist when they ripped it away and glared at her through stupid, suspicious eyes. Twice she'd been taken to a special room and had to strip down. Sickos. Full-on bull-dyke lesbians getting a thrill to see her in her Victoria's Secrets.

Fuck 'em all. She was important, and they were miserable larva.

"Hurry up," she told the production crew at large. "They're only giving us a few minutes."

"We're ready," Darrell said as he hefted the camera on his shoulder. He, at least, could get the job done.

Pauline led Darrell through the front doors; all she needed was one cameraman for the interview. She'd been granted access, but still needed to bully her way past all the hospital security. To that end, she smiled at the woman at the desk, who pressed some button and opened the doors. She looked slightly alarmed, gazing through the glass doors to the van outside, then back again to Pauline and Darrell as they entered.

"Doctor Freeson invited us," Pauline said. "He wants to get your Jane Doe's face on camera, try to find her family members."

The girl nodded, slowly, like the news was taking a

loonngg time climbing up that neuron. "I'll call him," she finally said and picked up the receiver.

"We're only here for a few minutes. We have places to be," Pauline pressed. She glanced around quickly. Entry room. Straight ahead a main room with tables, a gathering place. Several hallways branching off north and south. Stairs sweeping grandly to an upper gallery and more hallways.

"Dr. Freeson, some newspeople are here . . . ?"

"Pauline Kirby, thank you," Pauline said tautly.

"Pauline Kirby," the girl responded dutifully, but the little bitch apparently had no idea who Pauline was.

There was a brief interchange and the girl hung up, eyeing Pauline warily. "Dr. Freeson will be right here."

"Stat," Pauline said. "Good."

They moved away from the desk and Darrell said in her ear, "Play nice."

"Playing nice is for amateurs."

"And you're no amateur."

Pauline shot him a look but Darrell wisely didn't respond. They were both diverted by the arrival of Dr. Freeson bustling down the grand staircase. He was a slight man with a Vandyck beard and a fussy style that made Pauline smile internally.

He looked suitably starstruck as he came up to her and stuck out his hand. "Ms. Kirby, it's a pleasure to meet you. Do you want to do the interview here?" He gestured toward the gathering room.

"Can you take us to see the patient, please?"

"I'm sorry. That's against hospital pol—"

"Has anyone contacted you about her? Our station received a number of call-ins after our first story, but we didn't have a good picture, if you recall."

"I do. I know. That's why we wanted more exposure."

"We need a picture. Can't we just take our cameras to her? We'll be out in less than ten minutes."

"I'm sorry." He shook his head and looked like he really was very sorry. He could see his fifteen minutes of fame blowing to dust.

"Then can you bring her to us?" Pauline motioned to the general area surrounding them.

Dr. Freeson hesitated. Pauline's upper white teeth bit into her lower lip while she was smiling. A shark's look. One she'd perfected without even being aware of it. "One quick shot, and then maybe we can go into that room with the chairs and talk with you a while."

Freeson's eyes slid a look to Darrell and the television camera he balanced on his shoulder. Bingo, Pauline thought, but she kept her expression pleasantly neutral.

Everything was going swimmingly until a slim brunette in a lab coat with surprisingly good legs entered from one of the hallways. Pauline recognized her vaguely. Someone . . . oh, yes . . . the patsy for that throat-slitting by the youngest Marsdon . . . Heyward Marsdon III or IV. Poor woman. Marsdon was a real psycho if Pauline had ever seen one. Pauline automatically straightened her posture, sensing a battle about to brew.

The woman exchanged a chilly glance with Dr. Freeson. She said, "Lori called me."

Freeson glared at the receptionist, the hapless Lori, apparently. "I was going to call you," he stated stiffly. Then to Pauline, "I'll have one of the nurses see about our Jane Doe." He walked away abruptly.

Amused, Pauline watched the brunette stare at his retreating back with a grim expression. She then turned toward the news crew duo and said, "Our patient isn't speaking."

Pauline nodded. "Not responding to stimuli of any

sort. We know. It's a human interest story. There must be someone out there who's missing her."

"I'm Dr. Claire Norris. We've met before." She didn't extend her hand.

Pauline nodded. "Yes, over the murder here. How are you doing, by the way?"

"Fine. I didn't like your reporting of the so-called facts at the time. Think you can keep it less lurid this time?"

Pauline felt a tingle of surprise and Darrell made an amused sound that sounded like a half gasp. "One patient slitting another's throat in front of his doctor is kind of lurid, wouldn't you say?"

"Today's patient, the one you say you want to help, has retreated, owing to shock and fear."

"Someone tried to cut out her baby. I'm sure she is traumatized." Pauline wanted to hurry this along. She hated wasting time.

"She is." Dr. Norris was firm. "She's not talking. She's recovering slowly."

"In case you missed it, the point is, we're trying to help. We want a story and when we have it, maybe we'll find someone to identify your little mommy in the process. It's good for all of us. I'm sorry for her. I truly am. But being mad at me for doing my job isn't helping any of us. Am I coming through?"

"Loud and clear."

Her tone irked Pauline. She was so calm and cool and there was an itsy-bitsy little judgmental part of her—the stuffy doctor part whereby she had a rod up her ass—that she couldn't quite hide. "All right, let's get this little lady teed up and do our thing. We'll be out in no time. Ah!" She grinned as the blond woman in question was wheeled from the hallway by a mousy-looking aide of some kind. Freeson was hovering behind.

Pauline's focus changed to the sweet-faced victim in the

wheelchair. She was so fragile seeming. Too young to be a mommy, but then, some people just didn't see the advantage to ending an inconvenient pregnancy. Not that Pauline was pro-abortion. Not that she would admit publicly, anyway, but c'mon! This girl was a child. Barely looked old enough to breed.

She would make absolutely great television.

With an almost imperceptible motion to Darrell, who never needed cuing anyway, she leaned down toward the patient and said, "Jane Doe is no name for someone as special as you, honey. Can you look at me?" The girl's head was tilted so all you could see was her crown, her eyes downcast.

"Dr. Freeson?" Claire Norris said in a frigid tone.

"Can you just take a picture?" Freeson said anxiously. "A still."

"Sure. It'd be better if she looked up, though."

"Maybe she doesn't want the spotlight." Norris looked around, as if searching for security.

Pauline touched the girl's hand. "Hey, there," she said. "We're going to help you find your people, but we need a picture, honey. Could you lift your head?"

Freeson shifted his weight from one foot to the other. Pauline gave him her sweetest look. "Maybe you could just put your hand under her chin?"

"Dr. Freeson, if you can't get them out of here, I will," Dr. Norris snapped furiously, her feet tap-tapping toward the front desk.

The bitch was was going to ruin the whole thing. "We'll go," Pauline said.

"My interview?" Freeson said vaguely as they turned to leave.

"Your little friend kinda took that away from you, honey," Pauline told him as she turned aside. Darrell followed on her heels. They walked out the door and toward the van, climbed inside. Pauline wasn't happy as they settled into their seats. She really hated women. They got in the way at every turn.

A gray truck came up the long drive from the highway followed by a sheriff's Jeep with Winslow County Sheriff's Department written in white on its black sides. Both Pauline and Darrell examined the newcomers with interest.

"Who called the cavalry?" Pauline murmured, then motioned the driver to wait. "The guy in the black leather jacket. I know him. Who is he?"

"Last week's booty call?" The driver sniggered, but no one else in the van dared such a one-way ticket to you're-fired-ville.

Pauline sent him a scathing look, mentally reminded herself to can his sorry ass, then said, "Detective Langford Stone. Or something." She snapped her fingers a couple of times. "Lang*don*."

"The guy whose sister was killed by Marsdon," Darrell said on a long whistle.

"Kill that engine, moron," Pauline snapped to the driver. "We're sticking around."

Chapter 5

As Lang pulled into a spot in front of Halo Valley hospital, he could feel the tightening in his chest. He didn't like anything about this place. He couldn't.

Detective Tanninger was following in his department-issue Jeep. He pulled in a couple of slots over from Lang's truck. Since their first meeting, Lang had checked with Curtis about the man and had learned a few interesting facts.

"About a year ago, remember that pedophile guy with the van and ropes and stuff?" Curtis told him. "The guy that was run down by some woman?"

"Yeah. He ended up at Laurelton Hospital."

Curtis nodded. "Tanninger was on that case. Worked it hard. A lot of pieces to it that I forget the details, but the woman he's seeing now? She was someone he met during the investigation. A suspect."

Lang turned the wheels of his brain backward, trying to remember what he knew about the case. There were pieces of information before Melody's death, and pieces after. Sometimes the answers were there, but sometimes they weren't. Like he'd suffered some kind of memory leakage that he didn't care to stop. "Was she the one who ran him down?"

"Winslow County says no. Tanninger's a straight arrow. Doesn't seem like he'd be with someone who tried to kill a man, even if he deserved to die."

"Maybe that's why he's so eager to give me this case," Lang mused. "Doesn't want the drama."

"Maybe. And thanks for the beer." Lang had been the first one to see Curtis at Dooley's.

Now as he watched Tanninger stride toward him, he thought, *You never know about people.* Seeing Tanninger's attention was diverted, he followed his gaze to the Channel Seven news van parked on the far side of the hospital's front portico.

"Shit," Lang said as they met up.

Tanninger chuckled.

Claire had barely returned to her office when her intercom buzzed. "The police are here," Lori said, her voice hushed. "I already called Dr. Freeson again."

"Did he tell you to call me?"

"I did that on my own. Like with Channel Seven."

"Thanks, Lori."

"No problem." She hung up.

Annoyance. That's what Claire felt. And a little bubbling anger. Being the hospital's receptionist, Lori was attuned to the inner workings of the hospital and had landed firmly on Claire's side when the shit had hit the fan, so to speak. It was still a surprise and a pleasure to learn members of the staff felt she'd been given a raw deal and wanted to support her. And all Claire wanted now was to protect Cat, and though the authorities wouldn't learn anything from her, this apparently was part of the procedure and needed to be done. A box to check. A report to file.

Fine.

Lori saw Claire arrive and motioned outside where the

Channel Seven news van was still loitering. She realized they'd probably seen the police arrive and were curious about what was going on.

"The officers are in the private room," Lori said, her gaze, like Claire's, still focused outside.

"Thanks." Claire pulled her attention away from Pauline Kirby and company and headed to the private room around the corner, a room with low chairs and tables done in tasteful grays and tans. It was staged to resemble a den and mainly used as a meeting area for family members who wanted updates on their loved ones' conditions. Better than an office. More warm and intimate. Was it the best place to meet the police? Maybe not. Claire would have preferred the barrier of her own desk.

She pushed through the French doors, the glass currently shuttered by mahogany-stained plantation blinds. The room was dark inside, dimly lit, and Claire automatically slid the button for the dimmer up a couple of notches.

Freeson was already there, talking about the hospital as if he owned it personally, his chest pushed out, his beard quivering, his lips pulled into a smile. He glanced at Claire but didn't stop his speech. "—the finest in the region. Our care is exemplary, and funding provided by private donors has made it possible for Halo Valley Security to go toe to toe with larger institutions with our state-of-the-art equipment and top personnel."

The two men standing in the room definitely looked like The Law. One wore the tan shirt and slacks of the sheriff's department. Not Tillamook County, she realized. Winslow County. Of course. Where the attack had occurred. His hair was dark brown and he had a quiet demeanor, slightly intense, slightly careful. Claire's gaze slid from him to the other man, who, in a rain-dampened black leather jacket and jeans, looked almost rumpled compared to the first. The second man's hair was even darker, his expression grimmer. He gazed at Claire with razor intensity and her breath caught.

She *knew* him. Melody Stone's brother. Portland P.D. *What is he doing here?*

Freeson was going on: "The state hospital's beds are full, and Halo Valley takes patients from them, as well as our own, such as Jane Doe, who cannot offer financial remuneration—"

With an effort Claire quickly schooled her face, hoping the muscles weren't as tense as they felt. Too little, too late. Stone had seen her momentary shock.

"—at least not yet, since no one knows who she is. In cases like hers, Halo Valley absorbs the costs, sometimes with no expectation of reimbursement."

"I'm Langdon Stone," the rain-dampened man cut in flatly, causing Freeson to stop with his mouth open.

Claire said, "Yes, I recognize you. I'm—"

"I know who you are."

His partner turned to look at him momentarily, then, slightly bemused, reached out a hand to Claire. "Will Tanninger, detective with Winslow County Sheriff's Department. I don't know who you are."

"Dr. Claire Norris." She shook his hand. There was a spreading cold in the small of her back. *Langdon Stone?* "You're here to see our Jane Doe. I'm not sure how that can help."

"She communicating yet?" This from Stone.

"She hasn't spoken, no."

"But she's communicated," he pressed.

"She's in a catatonic state," she responded tightly. "She stares straight ahead and doesn't react to conversation or even loud noises. She's also pregnant. Seven, eight months." She turned to Freeson, who was staring at Langdon Stone in wide-eyed silence. "Dr. Freeson is her primary doctor, but anyone under the hospital's care is looked after by all members of its staff. I personally don't believe this meeting's necessary, but it wasn't my decision to make."

"As long as you're respectful of her condition," Freeson bubbled back in, "you're certainly welcome to see her. It's true, she hasn't spoken yet, but she's made great progress."

What progress is that? Claire wondered. "We're ignoring hospital policy again," she said for Freeson's benefit, wondering why she felt like the prig when she was just trying to follow orders.

"Let's see her," Stone said.

Claire resented his tone. Wanted to remind him that Cat was a person and should be treated like one, and his attitude sucked, blah, blah, blah, but decided it wouldn't change anything. She nodded curtly and swept out ahead of them, the chill in the small of her back radiating throughout her spine and down her arms and legs. What the hell was Langdon Stone doing here? All he'd done was badmouth Halo Valley and every member of the staff since Melody's death. It wasn't like she didn't have sympathy for him. He'd lost his sister at Heyward Marsdon's hands. But, even more than her colleagues, he seemed to blame her personally for what happened. She'd heard him on an unscripted television interview.

Detective Stone, do you blame Halo Valley for the death of your sister?

I blame Heyward Marsdon. Halo Valley just aided and abetted. They were the ones who ordered his release.

Anyone in particular?

Doctor Norris. The one he held at knifepoint. Glad she's not hurt, but what does it take to recognize a psycho? Especially when it's your damn job?

He'd been in jeans then, too. Dark brows slammed over intense blue eyes. He looked downright mean, and Claire had wondered straight up if he was one of those cops that could have just as easily walked the other side of the law. Probably. If she had half an hour with him alone, she thought she would be able to tell.

They caught up with her as they headed down the hall. Freeson had recovered himself a little, though he was clearly wary of Stone. He seemed to be deciding whether to say something about Melody or not. Detective Tanninger broke in before he could speak. "What do you think about Jane Doe's condition?" he asked Claire.

"Physically, she's recovering well," Freeson answered for her.

"Did you put her in front of the cameras?" Stone accused.

"They wanted a picture to broadcast in case someone recognizes her," Claire said.

"Is that a yes?"

"We need to find out who she is, and the media is a good route. Yes."

"If she's catatonic, will she even know we're here?" Stone asked.

"If?" Claire repeated.

They stared at one another, sizing each other up.

"Well, there's a question," he drawled. "Could she be faking it?"

He was baiting her. She'd been baited by the best of them. "What would be the point of it?"

"So you really don't know."

Freeson stated flatly, "She's not 'faking it.' She's suffered trauma and she's repressing reality."

"She's completely nonresponsive?" This from Tanninger.

To him, Claire said, "I honestly wish she could help you. I just don't think she can right now."

They stopped outside room 113. Claire opened the door and checked on Cat first. She was lying on the bed, on her back, her eyes closed. Langdon Stone pushed in behind her and Claire quickly moved out of the way, not wanting to even touch him. He gazed at the woman in the bed for a long moment, then lifted his head and stared through the window beyond toward Side B of the hospital. On this first level, mostly all that could be seen was the laurel hedge that blocked the view of the locked-down portion of the hospital, but the razor wire above the chain-link fence stood out. Side B was a hospital and a prison; there was no denying that. Access was only by two doors, on the north and south wings from Side A, farther down the same skyway that connected the medical office buildings to the hospital. Those doors were guarded and well locked. Claire knew Stone was thinking of Marsdon. This she understood. She thought of him a lot as well.

"She's asleep," Claire said.

Freeson squeezed around them into the room. He frowned at the patient, as if she were thwarting him directly. "We want to comply with the authorities," he said.

Claire realized that Stone hadn't introduced himself as a detective. He'd only given his name. Langdon Stone. Did that mean something, or was he off the force? And what was he doing with the Winslow County Sheriff's Department?

Freeson added, disappointed, "But as you can see, she's not really ready for an interview."

Stone was staring critically at the blond patient again, his brow furrowed. Freeson went on about her injuries and seemed about to show the detectives the marks scored across her belly, much to Claire's dismay, but Tanninger said it wouldn't be necessary. They had pictures. They knew someone had slashed at her. He, at least, seemed to respect Cat's personal privacy.

An awkward silence ensued, as if they'd all run out of things to say, which was probably the truth. Claire was about to suggest they head back toward the front of the hospital when Cat's eyes slowly opened.

They all took a collective breath.

"Well . . ." Freeson murmured.

Her head was lying on the pillow, her blue eyes staring. The emptiness of her expression was impossible to miss. Stone's grim face grew grimmer, as if he'd just realized how awful the whole thing was. Cat had a china-doll look about her. An innocence. An overall *niceness* that made the attack on her seem that much more horrific.

Freeson cleared his throat. "Hello, there," he said brightly, as if he and Cat were BFFs. "How are you feeling today?"

No response.

"These men are with the sheriff's department and they want to talk to you about what happened."

Claire had to look away, mentally biting her tongue. It almost hurt how much Freeson was trying to impress the detectives. The man was a sycophantic worm with delusions of coolness that no Vandyck and Thom McAn shoes were going to make come true.

She felt Stone's gaze upon her but studiously avoided making eye contact. She didn't like him, either. She didn't have to. The only one in the room who seemed to have something worthwhile to offer was Detective Tanninger from Winslow County.

So, what the hell was Langdon Stone doing with him?

She finally glanced back and was jolted to find Stone's blue gaze on her. "Aren't you with the Portland police?" she asked him.

"Not any longer."

"You've changed jobs."

"I quit. Right after . . ." He let it trail away, but Claire knew it wasn't to spare her feelings. He was making a point. She felt as if he'd shot a dart into the center of her heart.

"You're with the Winslow County Sheriff's Department?" She wondered where the uniform was.

"Not really," he said.

Tanninger glanced from Claire to Stone and back again.

"The department's a little shorthanded right now," he said. "Detective Stone's on a kind of furlough with the Portland P.D. He's helping us out."

Claire heard alarm bells. She didn't want him involved in Cat's story. She didn't want him hanging around, asking questions, interviewing hospital employees. She'd thought this was a one-time event, but now she wondered.

"Good enough," Freeson said. "Catch the bad guys any way you can." He enthusiastically pumped Stone's and Tanninger's hands as if his arm were hitched to an electric motor.

"That's the plan," Stone said.

"Jane Doe can't help you yet, I'm afraid," Claire said.

"No," he agreed. "And no one's tried to see her?"

"Not here."

"Not at Laurelton General, either," Will Tanninger said.

"That's why we allowed the news team in," Freeson pointed out. "To keep the public aware of her."

Stone said, "Maybe her deceased companion was her only friend."

They all silently considered that, their collective gaze on the woman in the bed staring mutely at the opposite wall. In unspoken consensual decision, they moved into the hall and back toward the front of the hospital.

Tanninger asked, "It's definite that someone tried to cut out her baby?"

"Oh, yes." Freeson's steps slowed. "She's bandaged, but I could still show you the marks."

Stone swept a hand to forestall him. "We've got pictures. Just wanted your take that medically speaking, these wounds weren't just made in the struggle."

"They were purposeful," Claire said.

"They're knife wounds," Freeson put in. "She was slashed. Someone meant business."

"The wounds weren't deep," Claire said. "They were—done a bit frantically."

"What makes you say that?" Stone asked.

They were outside their original meeting room, but no one made a move to enter. Claire drew a breath. "It wasn't surgery, Mr. Stone. It was hurried. It wasn't thought out."

"Whoever did it was clearly trying to get it done before they were caught," Freeson said frostily.

Tanninger spoke up. "The trucker who found her said the male vic was still alive when he got there. Maybe John Doe intervened and made it impossible for the baby stealer to succeed."

"Lucky for her," Stone said. "But it probably cost him his life."

Freeson started talking about the horror of violence that was such a part of everyday life these days until Stone interrupted with, "What happens when the baby's born?"

Freeson looked nonplused, like the thought had never occurred to him.

Claire said, "Hopefully, our patient will have recovered enough by then to take care of the child."

"And if she hasn't?" Stone wasn't giving up.

"Social Services will be called," she answered, the words tasting like ashes on her tongue.

"Think our homicide vic was the baby's father?" Stone looked at Tanninger, who shrugged and said, "DNA testing will tell. If he isn't, the father could still be out there."

"This is forward-tripping, and it isn't doing us any good," Claire said. "There's every indication that our Jane Doe will recover and be able to tell us what we need to know."

"That would be great," Stone said. "The question is, when."

"If there's any change, you'll let us know?" Tanninger had turned to Claire, but Freeson jumped in and assured him they would call them immediately as soon as Cat was able to communicate.

A few minutes later, they all headed for the front doors, and Claire, after saying her good-byes, hurried out ahead of the three men. Freeson, however, wasn't that easy for Claire to shake.

"Claire!" he called after her as she turned the corner for the elevator.

She pressed the button, determined to outpace him, but he got there before the car opened. They stepped inside together.

"That was Melody Stone's brother!" he declared.

"I'm aware."

"What the hell was he doing here? He's no longer a detective, is he?"

"I don't know. I don't care."

"We should talk to Tanninger only. Not Stone. Not good for the hospital. I should alert Radke about this and maybe the Marsdons. Could be trouble."

"For God's sake, stop acting so damn guilty all the time. We didn't do anything wrong. It was a tragedy. A horrible, shocking tragedy. Langdon Stone may have a vendetta against us, but—"

"A vendetta!"

"—it all comes down to the fact that Heyward had a psychotic break and thought his girlfriend and I were some deadly, evil beings. Heyward still doesn't get it, from what I've heard. Calls for me. Calls for Melody. It's . . . *awful*. Awful. And Stone may want some kind of revenge, blaming us for his sister's death. Okay. It's transference. He wants his sister back. We all get it. But don't make it worse by running scared!"

"I'm not running scared!"

"Yeah?"

"It's your name on the release form, Claire."

It felt like she'd been slapped. Again. "Oh. Thanks so much."

"I only mean, we're all in this together."

"No. You have your own cabal. I'm on my own. I always have been."

"That's the kind of talk that pisses everybody off!" Freeson declared with a shake of his head. "You're not a team player. You don't have the hospital's best interests at heart."

"I have my patients' best interests at heart," she shot back, stalking off the elevator car as soon as the doors whispered open.

"We all have to work together!" Freeson called after her.

But she'd already forgotten him. Her mind's eye was full of the sights and sounds of Langdon Stone. He hated her. Blamed her. Had undoubtedly taken Cat's case as a means to extract some sort of retribution.

Fine. Bring it on. She was tired of being everybody's whipping girl.

God, she was a frozen bitch, Lang thought, his eyes on the slim legs of the good doctor Norris as she broke away from them. Figured. This whole place was a frigid tomb. Gave him the heebie-jeebies but good. He couldn't wait to be outside and suck in some non-antiseptic-scented air. Why couldn't Jane Doe be anywhere else but here? It felt a little like Melody's ghost was hovering nearby. He definitely felt hidden eyes, and since he'd been accused by an ex-girlfriend or two of not being very imaginative, he wondered if he was changing, maybe not for the better. His subconscious was definitely trying to tell him something.

"What do you think?" Tanninger asked, his gaze on the retreating form of Dr. Freeson, who was trying to hail Claire Norris.

"I think we're going to get more out of the file than from Jane Doe herself. At least for now."

"How's that going?"

"I called the trucker, Denny Ewell. He said he'd be

happy to meet with me, but I've got a feeling I'm not going to learn much. Maybe I'll have more luck with the stolen car's owner."

The plates had been run on the vehicle left at the crime scene, the one they believed to be driven by John and Jane Doe. It was registered to a Tillamook County farmer by the name of Tim Rooney who, when called, ranted that the damn thing had been stolen and when would he get it back? Lang was going to meet with him in person and see if he could learn anything further.

"I hope Jane Doe comes back in time for the baby's birth," Stone remarked.

Tanninger nodded. "That doctor . . . Norris. She's the one who was treating Marsdon." He spoke neutrally, but he'd clearly gotten the scope of what was going on.

"She's the one."

"This case is going to throw you in with her. Still want it?"

Lang was silent, absorbing. Finally, he growled, "Yeah. I got a problem with her and this hospital, though. Doc Freeson can sing its praises to the skies, but it doesn't change anything."

"A personal problem?"

"That's about right."

"That why you took this case?"

Lang shook his head. "Coincidence. This one's just the first one my partner interested me in."

"Coincidence," Tanninger repeated, making a face as if it tasted bad. "Don't go all cowboy on me and try to do it alone. Detective Gillette will be back, and she can take over."

Lang immediately wanted to squelch that idea, but he was the outsider, so he nodded in agreement. He and Will headed out the doors to the portico together and ran directly into Pauline Kirby and her cameraman.

"Detective Stone," she said, wearing her best smile.

"Following up on the Marsdon case? Anything you can talk about?"

"There is no Marsdon case," Lang said after a moment of quiet. "He's incarcerated."

"You were against him coming to Halo Valley, as I recall. You wanted him in prison."

"I thought you reported news, Ms. Kirby. This is ancient history."

"You're making a visit here. That's news. Are you checking up on Mr. Marsdon, seeing if you can change the situation?"

Will said, "I'll talk to you later," and with a faint smile, left Lang with the barracuda. Kirby seemed like she wanted to stop Tanninger, but she was ill equipped to trap them both. Lang was ready to walk, too.

"Did you speak with Dr. Norris about him?" Pauline asked.

That did it. He was done. He turned away from her, and with a last look across the building to the bank of windows on the opposite side and a view of the locked-down section of the hospital, Lang shook off Pauline Kirby and his heebie-jeebies over Halo Valley. The heavily secured side of the hospital was blocked mostly by a laurel hedge, but you got the idea. Heyward Marsdon III was there. His sister's killer. He hoped the man was in a straightjacket in a five-by-five white, padded room, but with the Marsdon money, he probably had a pool table and cable TV at his disposal. A private masseuse. Private bathroom. Private everything.

Sick bastard.

"Detective Stone!" Pauline called to his retreating back as he headed to his truck.

He ignored her, throwing the Dodge into reverse. As he left, his eyes scanned the manicured grounds and facade of this, the benign side of the hospital. A wind was blowing the trees, exposing the yellowy underside of the birch leaves. The firs waved thick arms at him and rain dashed across the windshield. Behind the first building he could see the green and brown hills in the distance, above the roof of the locked-down side of the hospital.

"Rot in hell," he muttered, throwing the truck into gear.

He had no compassion for his sister's killer. Whatever demons Marsdon possessed had taken over and ended Melody's life. He didn't have to care. He didn't have to feel mercy. He wanted her back and it wasn't going to happen, so now all he wanted was justice.

In his rearview, he thought Pauline might be giving him the finger.

At six o'clock, Claire walked her last patient to the door, then grabbed her purse and coat, locked everything up, and left her office. She carried her raincoat over her arm as she strode across the gallery, down the front steps, and toward the hallway to 113. The morning room was mostly empty right now, but Darlene was on duty. She, too, was on Claire's side, and now she plodded up to her.

"Checking on Cat?" she asked.

"Thought I'd pop a head in on my way out."

"That was the brother, wasn't it? The cop?" Darlene threw a glance toward the front of the building, through the sliding glass doors to the portico, parking lot, and waving fir limbs beyond.

"Ex-cop," Claire said. "Melody Stone's brother, yes."

"What's he doing here?"

"Working with the Winslow County Sheriff's Department, apparently. Some kind of liaison."

"Like a deputy?" Darlene asked.

"I didn't ask specifics."

She couldn't wait to go home to her bungalow. The

coziness was calling to her. Maybe Dinah would be home. Or, even better, she wanted to wrap herself in a blanket, go out to the deck, stare toward the ocean, and simply shut her brain down.

"He was hot," Darlene added as Alison suddenly stepped into the hall ahead of them from one of the rooms. Cat's room, Claire realized, as Alison said, "Dr. Norris? Cat's trying to say something!"

Darlene and Claire picked up their pace as the aide ducked back in the room, her mop of curly hair bouncing. Claire entered and saw that Cat was lying inert on the bed, staring straight ahead, just the same as she'd left her earlier. She gave Alison a questioning look. "She was moving," the aide insisted.

"Moving how?" Claire asked.

"I don't know . . . like in distress . . . ?"

And then, as if on cue, Cat slowly lifted a hand and plucked at her hospital gown. Her blue eyes were open wide, staring ahead to some tableau only she could see. It was eerie, and Claire heard Darlene and Alison both sweep in their breath. She, too, was suspended. As they watched, Cat clawed up her hospital gown and ran her hand over her bandaged wounds. Then she curled her fingers, lifted her hand as if holding a knife, and sliced across her stretched skin.

Alison emitted a little blurp of fear, her curly mop shivering a bit. She turned to Claire with scared eyes. "She knows someone cut her! Who would do such a thing?"

Darlene stepped forward and put her hand over the patient's. The agitated motion ceased and Cat closed her eyes and sank back into the pillows as if exhausted.

A monster, Claire thought. *That's who.*

Chapter 6

Rita Feather Hawkings thought of herself as a good person.

She was good-looking, thirty-seven, voluptuous, and an LPN, licensed practical nurse. She had a good job and a boyfriend who loved her. Had loved her . . . although not now. Swallowing, Rita put that aside for the moment.

She was currently driving up the long, tree-lined drive toward Ocean Park Hospital, her place of employment, her rusted Chevy Malibu buffeted by winds off the ocean, winds that screamed up the drive and hammered at the hospital's front doors. Those trees were gnarled and stunted, their leaves hanging on by the grace of God. Ocean Park was an unassuming one-story building, but it was a general hospital that took care of the needs of the people who lived along a fifty-plus mile stretch of the Oregon coast and eastward toward the Willamette Valley.

Rita barely noticed. She pulled into an empty spot in the employee lot to the south side and snarled at the sight of her sensible shoes. She wore three-inch heels off duty. Black heels. Like her hair. Rita was over half Native American, but there was no way of telling for sure because

Rita's mother was a mixture, a mutt, the product of a whoring father whose father was a whoremonger before him.

Rita's Aunt Angela was a whore as well. But she was dead now, and Rita's mother was the only one of her family still alive. Rita's father was in jail, or so she was told, but she'd never known him anyway, so it didn't matter.

Rita's mother was a religious fanatic. A combination of Christianity mixed with Native American religious beliefs and folklore. Delores Feather Hawkings had warned Rita long and loud against the path that had led to Aunt Angela's demise.

"She whored her way to death. Men. Sex. That's how she died. That's why she burned! Don't you become like her, Rita. Don't you walk that path."

Rita ignored her mother as much as possible. She slept with lots of men, as often as possible. But she was no whore. There was no exchange of money, though there hadn't been much love, either. Except for her boyfriend, but . . . no . . . she wouldn't think of tragedy.

Sighing, she plodded toward the hospital's front doors. Thirty-seven-year-old Rita, who looked twenty-seven, had wanted a baby since she could remember how to think. When she was young, she played with dolls that looked like babies. Carried them with her everywhere. When she learned what it took to have a baby, she started sleeping around. Yes, she knew they said she was going the way of her aunt. Yes, she was playing with fire, hoping to get burned.

But it was not to be. Rita never became pregnant. All these crippling teenage pregnancies tearing families apart, and nothing for her. Nothing! Oh, the gods were against her. It just wasn't fair.

Before her slide into fanaticism, her mother had insisted that her daughter find a career. Rita had dutifully taken courses in the health care field and had thrown herself into several heated affairs with older doctors. She lied about birth control. She made certain she had sex on the most fertile days of her cycle. She ritualistically laid out corn and rice and drew her own blood, making a kind of fertility stew that she'd learned from her mother's folklore.

But nothing worked.

As she grew older, Rita became convinced her mistake was in choosing older, more financially established males. It had seemed the smart thing to do, but it had absolutely prevented her from becoming pregnant. Now she was the ultimate "cougar." She needed younger men's virility. She suspected older males were what had been the problem. It was not her. It was not.

As she entered the hospital, the receptionist threw her a look. Rita knew it was because she purposely kept the top three buttons of her blouse undone and allowed a hearty view of cleavage. She lamented the fact that she would have to change into her uniform and went into the employee bathroom with a feeling of defeat. Changing into teal scrubs, she examined her body. Round, but not fat. Soft, but not doughy. Motherly, in a womanly way, without being matronly.

Crossing her hands over her abdomen, she closed her eyes for a moment and prayed to God, to the Heavenly Spirit, to the Fertility Goddess.

Hanging up her street clothes in a locker, she dropped her purse, then turned the combination lock. She walked directly to the lunchroom as she was twenty minutes early for her shift, sat down in one of the formed-plastic chairs at a Formica-topped table, and contemplated the babies that should have been hers.

The first was beautiful Selene. She'd had her for only a matter of hours before that bitch of a so-called friend, Vonda, had snatched her away and looked at Rita as if she were some kind of monster. Vonda had left Deception Bay and never returned and Rita lost Selene before she really had a chance to be a mother.

The second was Brian. He'd been abandoned in a stroller at the Big Ten strip mall and Rita had saved him. The police had been involved that time, and though Rita explained that she was saving Brian, there had been a terrible wrangle that had only gotten straightened out when Brian's so-called mother, what was her name . . . oh, yeah, Linda, a drug and alcohol abuser, backed off and said she might have been mistaken on Rita's intent.

They were all so wrong about her!

And then . . . and then . . . a real boyfriend . . . the perfect father!

Her fingers trembled as she reached into the pocket of her uniform and felt the newspaper clipping within. She was about to pull it out when Jake Tontor strolled in. Rita removed her hand, feeling a little thrill in her center at his lean, dark good looks, skinny ponytail, and lion's prowl.

He walked past the vending machine and picked up one of the oatmeal raisin cookies from a paper plate. A gift from one of the staff do-gooders who occasionally brought doughnuts, muffins, or homemade cookies.

Rita was about to tell him that the cookie was stale, at least four days old, but didn't get a chance because Carlita Solano slipped inside the room as if she'd been following him and said, "It's a small world, y'know? A really small world. Things happen and all of a sudden you think, 'Wow, I know her!'"

Jake actively ignored Carlita, which made Rita smile. She looked him over. He was around twenty-three with long, black hair tied at his nape. His skin was dark and reddish; he could have been a member of her mother's tribe. Maybe he was. It *was* a small world.

Carlita got herself a Coke from the vending machine and said, "That girl's on the news again. The one in the coma."

"The blond good-looking one?" Jake asked, suddenly in the conversation.

"Yeah, I think I know where she's from. I mean, she looks like all the rest of them."

"Who are you talking about?"

"The cult! Those women that live at that lodge. You hardly ever see them and I've never seen this one before, but she looks like the rest of 'em. And they found her at that rest stop. Maybe she was driving from Deception Bay and heading toward Portland, trying to get away or something."

Rita's brain was rushing, fizzing, her ears buzzing. She hadn't seen the news. She hadn't seen *her*!

"She was in a wheelchair and kind of looking down."

"Well, then how do you know?" Jake was skeptical, losing interest.

"That's *why* I know. Just the side of her head, y'know?"

"Her profile."

"Yes! It reminded me of them. Especially that one that used to work at the market years ago. Did you ever see her?"

"No. I thought you said they were in a cult."

"They let that one out. Jesus, what was her name? And she was at the Drift In Market for a while. I wanted to ask her what it was like living in a cult, but I was a kid and never did."

Rita wanted to clap her hands over her ears and scream.

"But that's not this coma girl," Jake said.

"No, no. This is another one."

"You should call the police. They want to know who she is."

"Yeah, but somebody killed the guy she was with. He could still be out there."

"Call anonymously, then," Jake said, sprawling into a chair at a table far away from Carlita. She didn't take the hint and dropped into the seat across from him.

"I don't want to talk to the police. The sheriff's department arrested my brother 'cause they thought he was in a gang! That bastard Clausen is out for him."

"I heard he was dealing dope."

"You heard wrong! I'm an RN. He did something like that, I'd kill him."

"Don't let the patients hear you say that," Jake drawled.

Rita gulped long breaths and reached into her pocket for the clipping, spreading it on the table with trembling fingers. She couldn't listen to them anymore. Couldn't . . . listen . . . Her attention narrowed, tunneled, zeroed in on the well-creased newspaper clipping. She'd actually found the clipping in this very lunchroom. Wasn't one to take the paper herself.

She'd been debating what to do.

UNIDENTIFIED MAN SLAIN. PREGNANT COMPANION ATTACKED WITH KNIFE.

Rafe, she thought, her chest aching. *Rafe!*

The article was old. She'd found it in the lunchroom and ripped it out. Had spent the last week wondering and worrying, sick at heart.

Rafe. And that Tasha bitch. Pregnant. With Rafe's baby! Oh, it should have been hers. Would have been if Tasha hadn't come between them. Her baby.

Hers and Rafe's.

Rafe . . . her lover . . .

The emotions that ripped through Rita's soul made her shiver all over and she had to tuck the clipping away before she shredded it by mistake. Climbing to her feet, she scooped up and crumpled the wrapper from the vending machine crackers someone had neglected to throw in the trash. Her fingers clenched hard enough to send a pain message along her nerves, but her brain simply wasn't receiving.

Her baby.

Should have been hers.

Hers and Rafe's.

* * *

Carlita threw Rita a look as she headed out of the lunchroom. Rita Feather Hawkings was weird. A licensed practical nurse, but not a very good one. On the other hand, Carlita was a very good RN. A great RN, she believed. And a warm person, where Rita was, well, kind of sexy in a dirty way, yet cold, sort of.

But she was pretty, Carlita could grudgingly concede. In a freaky, cold, stalker kind of way. Or something. Hard to really determine.

Having worn out her story about the cult girl, Carlita sought to regain Jake's attention. "You ever notice Rita's eyes? That woman has no soul."

"Everyone's got a soul."

"Not everyone."

"Don't tell my mama that. She's very big on the soul."

"I don't think she's normal," Carlita said. "She's like a robot, but she can go all whup-ass on you so fast. One of Dr. Loman's patients complained about her and she got in some serious trouble over it. And she made one of Dr. Harris's patients cry, the other day."

"Harris is an oncologist. His patients have cancer. They probably cry all the time."

"Are you defending her?"

Jake yawned and tossed an empty Gatorade bottle that had been idling on the counter for days into the trash. "Two points," he said automatically. Then, "I think I'm related to her."

"To Rita? How?"

"Some distant cousin, or something. Her aunt, I think, was like the town whore. Disgraced everybody. Y'know, the bones they found at that house that burned a few years ago? That was her, I think."

"Wow."

He shook his head. "They're all whacked. I gotta get outta this town."

This was Jake's mantra, and it used to bother Carlita, who had no intention of leaving this section of the coast. She lived in Deception Bay, a little town just south of the hospital, and she had visions of making a home there with someone special. She wanted to settle down. Have a few kids. Live on sex, wine, and love. Jake was definitely on her radar. He was too good-looking not to be.

"Where would you go?" she asked him.

"Alaska," Jake said after a moment of thought, though Carlita suspected it was all an act. He liked saying he was leaving. Made him feel self-important. Her brother was like that, and he was still in Deception Bay working at a bar called Davey Jones's Locker, which was a lowlife hole, all dusty fishing nets and tarnished copper diving bells and beer-soaked carpet. But Jake . . . he was doing so much better than Alonzo. Jake had a career path.

Still, they both shared the need to bring the attention on themselves with macho bullshit. It was just one of those annoying things you had to put up with when you were dealing with men, and Carlita liked to think she was good at dealing with men.

"Alaska, huh," she said, sucking on the straw stuck in her Coke can. "Damn cold. Frigid. Like tundra or something."

"Yeah, well." He shoved back his chair and got up to leave.

Carlita tossed her drink in the trash and hurried after him, but Jake just strode on down the hall, his ponytail swinging in tandem with his hips. Rita Feather Hawkings was standing in the hall like she'd forgotten where she was going. She watched Jake cruise by, then turned her dead eyes on Carlita.

"Jake looks like my boyfriend," Rita said.

"You have a boyfriend?" Carlita said in surprise. "Who looks like Jake? Tell me another one!"

She laughed long and hard.

* * *

Rita didn't like Carlita Solano at all. Carlita was dark, like Rita, not like that blond bitch who'd stolen Rafe, but she was just as evil. She was just the same. Those women . . . those ones who always took the good ones. Always, always, always. "We're getting married," Rita stated flatly.

Carlita barked out a laugh and smoothed her long, sleek hair. She was athletic-club slim to Rita's curves. Rita had a sudden mental image of herself: a serious face above a good body that was maybe getting just a little heavier than it should. She would have to diet, and smile like a flirt, so that when she saw Rafe again he would notice how good she looked.

A shiver fluttered under her skin. Rafe was *dead,* she remembered with a sob of pain. And that bitch had Rita's baby inside her. She'd stolen Rafe from Rita, and Rita's baby, too.

"What's your boyfriend do?" Carlita asked. Rita didn't answer and Carlita pressed, "You got a picture of him?"

Rita walked away, the newspaper clipping burning into her skin. "Rafe . . . Rafe . . ."she murmured brokenly. What was she going to do without him? Without his baby? Her thoughts were all jumbled. She couldn't really sort through them. It was just so painful, and it was *her fault.* That blond bitch!

What hospital was she at? *What hospital?* If only she'd seen that newscast, but she couldn't bear to look at those vacant blue eyes and blond hair.

She pulled out the clipping again. What did it say?

. . . *victim was taken to a nearby hospital* . . .

Nearby hospital. She thought about it hard and knew. Laurelton General. It was closest to the rest stop. That's where the cold, evil man stealer was. That's where Rita's baby was.

That's where Rita needed to go to get her baby back.

And Rita had two days off, starting tomorrow.

Lang was driving south on 217, thinking about turning off onto Beaverton-Hillsdale Highway and a fast-food lunch, when he got the call from Curtis.

"Drano wants to see you," he said without preamble.

"When?"

"As soon as you can get here."

"I'm getting lunch."

"Come after."

"Okay."

Lang flew past his off-ramp and kept north on I-5 into downtown Portland. He didn't want to talk with Drano, to have to make plans. He wasn't ready. This investigation, regardless of its threads to Halo Valley Security Hospital, was just what the doctor ordered.

He'd met with Denny Ewell, the long-haul trucker who'd discovered the dying male victim and the unconscious female one. Ewell had been passing through Portland on one of his trips and had agreed to meet with Lang face-to-face. They'd met at a truck stop off Sunset Highway, just outside Laurelton, and the trucker had given Lang a moment-by-moment account of what had happened after he'd come out of the restroom and discovered the two injured people.

"The guy died right there, I think," Ewell finished, running a hand through his short, receding gray hair. "He said, 'The baby,' and bent over the pregnant lady. She had these marks across her belly and then the guy just keeled over. I think I touched him. He was holding his chest and there was a lot of blood."

"The pregnant lady was unconscious."

"Yeah."

"Did the male vic say anything else?"

"No."

Lang asked a few more questions, but Ewell could offer nothing further. It was about as much as Lang already knew. They shook hands and Lang thanked him for his time.

"It was bad, man," Ewell said as they walked to their respective rigs. "About as bad a thing as I've ever seen, and that's saying something."

Now Lang considered who this killer and potential baby stealer might be. Man, or woman? If it was a man, there had to be a woman involved in some way, he suspected. Cutting a baby from a woman's womb wasn't your every-day crime. It came from some twisted maternal kernel deep in the killer's brain and that said: woman. Men just didn't think the same way. The male vic had tried to stop the killer and been stabbed, murdered for his efforts. Could a woman have killed him? The height and angle of the man's chest wounds said yes.

He pulled into an underground parking structure near the Portland police station, took a ticket, and found a spot that he could back into. Old habits. He never wanted to waste time reversing in tight quarters.

Drano was in his office behind a glass wall when Lang entered the squad room. He was greeted by other officers with both welcoming handshakes and careful smiles. Lang suspected they worried he might want his job back and a number of them, like Celek, would be demoted. Celek's freckled face couldn't hide his anxiety and Lang said, "Stop worrying so much," as he cruised into Drano's office.

Drano was on the phone and he motioned Lang to a chair. Curtis, who'd also been on the phone when Lang arrived, appeared in the doorway and took another seat, shaking his ex-partner's hand. Lang said, "I owe you a beer."

"You did not see me first. I saw you in the outer hallway."

"Bullshit. The outer hallway's not visible from your desk."

"The door was cracked open. I saw you coming."

Drano slammed the receiver into its cradle. "Politicians," he muttered.

"Somebody putting pressure on you to solve a case?" Lang asked.

"Always." Lieutenant Draden clasped his hands on his desk and gazed hard at Lang. "Detective, you don't need to be here." He swiveled his head to make sure Curtis knew he was talking to him.

"This a secret meeting? I called him in for you!"

"Curtis . . ." His world-weary face looked even wearier.

Trey lifted his hands and left. "I owe *you* a beer," he stated firmly as he walked out the door.

"I thought that rule only applied when you met at bars," Drano said.

"It's everywhere, now that we're not working together."

"I got a call from Tillamook County. You want that job or not?"

Lang said, half-surprised, "I thought you were going to offer me employment."

"I would've, but I knew you wouldn't take it, so it's off the table. And now, with new budget constraints, the position's terminated."

Lang considered that information, testing his own feelings. He was surprised at the small jolt of regret. He'd had no interest in returning, yet now that the door was closed, he wondered if he'd made the right choice.

"But Tillamook County still wants you. If you want a job, you'd better take it soon. Economic climate sucks. Everybody's feeling the pinch."

Lang nodded slowly. Did he want the job? He liked what he was doing. Liked something for the first time in a long, long time. "I'll call Sheriff O'Halloran today."

"Good."

At the pause, Lang asked, "Is that it?"

Drano eyes glittered with faint humor. "You want me to ask how you're doing? See if you're mentally ready to come back to work?"

"Yeah, that'd be nice. How's that depression? You still looking for revenge? Think you're stable enough to be part of the team?"

"Get outta here." Drano waved him away. Despite his words, Lang knew the lieutenant had wanted to see his ex-detective in the flesh because he really did want to know how Lang was doing.

Lang had just passed a test he hadn't even known he was taking.

He pointed at Curtis, who, once again, was on the phone, on his way out. "Okay, I'm going to let you buy me that beer," Lang declared loudly.

He headed for his truck, a Subway sandwich, and a trip to the coast to see Sheriff O'Halloran and check with Tim Rooney, also of Tillamook, whose truck had been stolen by person or persons unknown and had apparently ended up in the hands of the victims.

Might as well kill two birds with one stone.

"Dr. Norris?"

Claire had just finished with a patient when her office phone rang. She recognized the voice of Eugenie Ledbetter, a local midwife whom they'd called on to monitor Cat's baby. Claire immediately straightened, her hands tightening on the receiver. "Eugenie. Is something wrong?"

"No . . ." But she sounded unsure.

"Are you with Jane Doe?"

"I'm in her room. She's been making motions with her hand as if she's . . . slicing her abdomen."

Claire relaxed a bit. "I know. That started yesterday."

"Have you looked at the incisions? The score marks?"

"I've seen them."

"It's just that they seem almost uncoordinated."

"Random," Claire agreed. "Made by someone who didn't know what they were doing."

"I was wondering if you thought . . ."

"What?"

"If you thought there was a chance someone *wasn't* trying to steal the baby."

Claire stared across her office room. "What are you suggesting?"

"I don't know. It's just that the marks aren't deep. They're healing well, which is great. But it's like someone just hacked at her without getting close enough to do any real damage, or they never meant to. These cuts aren't like the shoulder wounds at all."

"So what do you think?" Claire asked.

"I don't know." Eugenie sighed. "It's just an observation. Thought I'd let you know."

"Thanks."

Claire hung up, lost in thought. She'd spent the evening before lost in thought as well, half-hoping Dinah would be around, though she wasn't; half-glad that she was alone. She'd sat on her deck and let the rain-washed air dampen her face. Many of her thoughts had turned to Cat and her baby, and not necessarily from a professional point of view. Not so long ago Claire had wanted a baby very badly. She'd even managed to convince her wishy-washy husband at the time to give the parent thing a whirl. Claire suffered through two miscarriages, and that's when her husband said he really didn't want to try again; he'd never really wanted children in the first place.

After that the marriage just wasn't the same, and it fell apart. They'd been living in Salem, about two-thirds of the distance from Halo Valley to Deception Bay's one-third, in the opposite direction. So Claire left Ron and Salem and up and moved to the coastal town, making a new life for herself.

She realized that one of the reasons she felt so bonded to Cat was because of the girl's pregnancy. Didn't take a lot of professional skill to call that one. And the score marks were just so horrific; they tugged at Claire's maternal heartstrings.

But . . . Eugenie wasn't sure the score marks were an actual attempt to take the baby. That's what she was intimating, whether she'd put the thought into words or not. So what did that mean?

With sudden decisiveness, she called down to the first-floor nurse's station and asked for Darlene, who was beckoned from the morning room.

"Yes?" Darlene asked.

"I want to take another look at Cat's wounds." She explained to the nurse about Eugenie's concerns.

"Okay, I'll meet you there in ten," Darlene said. As a nurse, she would redress the wounds. Claire could do the same, but she wanted someone with her and Darlene was a good ally.

Darlene was already in the room when Claire entered and was in the process of removing the bandages that Eugenie had already disturbed. Cat's eyes were closed and she seemed unaware of the procedure.

When Darlene was finished, she and Claire gazed down at Cat's abdomen and the now scabbed-over wounds.

"They've healed well," Darlene observed.

"Very well," Claire agreed.

The wounds were like random hash marks and looked as if someone had swiped at Cat from a few feet away.

"Are you going to call Detective Stone?" Darlene asked.

"I've got Detective Tanninger's number."

Darlene nodded. "What about Dr. Freeson?"

"I'll let the police decide if this is important."

"Freeson'll have a cow."

"I'm sure he will."

Claire headed back to her office, looked up the Winslow County Sheriff's Department phone number on her computer, and placed the call from her cell phone. She gave her name to the woman who answered and asked to speak to Will Tanninger, who was unavailable. She explained that her call concerned her Jane Doe patient at Halo Valley Security Hospital. The woman at the other end assured her Detective Tanninger, or someone else, would call her back.

Claire hoped that someone else was not Langdon Stone.

Chapter 7

The Tillamook County Sheriff's Department was in a low building in the center of town, an island created by two sides of Highway 101, which broke around it like waves around a jutting boulder. The southbound lanes were on the west side; the northbound on the east. There was a parking lot on the south end of the building with a few scattered department vehicles. Lang pulled his Dodge truck into a reserved spot, as there were no visitors' spots available. Probably catch hell for it, or get his truck towed, but he didn't plan to be here long.

It wasn't the greatest start for a résumé, but it was raining like a son of a bitch and he didn't feel like walking.

Bending his head to the onslaught he hurried across the lot, up a couple of concrete steps capped by a sagging metal rail, and whooshed inside the door, making sure it was properly closed against a tearing wind, the kind the coast was known for.

He was in a short hallway that led to a reception area that wasn't much wider, at the end of which sat a heavy-set woman in a tight tan uniform.

"Can I help you?" she demanded.

"My name's Langdon Stone. I have an appointment with Sheriff O'Halloran."

"Well, if you did, you don't anymore. Sheriff's out working a case."

She had a lot of attitude in her manner. Lang pegged her around forty. Maybe divorced. Black hair with fine strands of gray pulled into a tight bun at her nape. Black eyes that warned him not to piss her off. Her name tag read Johnson.

Lang said, "I talked to him. He said he'd be here, but things change. I've got another appointment, so I'll come back."

She frowned suspiciously. "What's this concerning, Mr. Stone?"

"Employment. Specifically mine. With this department." He smiled and headed back out the way he'd come.

The rain hit him like a wall. A true Oregonian, Lang never used an umbrella. Mostly the rain, though incessant, was the thin, drizzling kind, although if he was really planning a permanent move to the coast he might have to rethink that. Here the weather was fiercer, wilder, and wetter.

He was soaked as he drove toward the farm of one Mr. Timothy Rooney, his leather jacket squeaking, possibly ruined. The farm was just south of the city of Tillamook proper, off a two-lane road that branched from 101, then branched again. He drove past the large silver mailbox nailed to a two-by-four that read ROONEY FARM before he knew it; the rain was a silvery curtain. Backing up, he turned into the gravel drive and bumped along for a quarter of a mile. On either side were sunken fields dotted with black-and-white dairy cows; the road had been built up between them. Tillamook was a lowland known for its flooding. It was also the site for premier cheese making. The Tillamook Cheese Factory produced and sold cheese nationwide, hence the dairy cows.

But in the heaviest flood season, the cows were as susceptible to flood waters as the humans; more so, given their habitat. Lang had never lived in the area, but he watched the news, and every couple of seasons farmers were scrambling to save their herds from drowning.

The Rooney farmhouse was a rambling affair that may have once been a saltbox but now had wings jutting off at odd angles, all of it decrepit with grayed wood exposed under peeling white paint, the force of nature evident everywhere, from the leaning sheds to the missing shingles on the roof. The barns beyond looked to be in the best shape. Rooney knew how to take care of his livestock.

Lang sloshed the truck through mud puddles the size of craters and parked next to a once-reddish pickup with mud-caked tires, its body being washed clean of the same by the pounding rain. Taking a readying breath, he opened the door and gingerly slid his boots onto one of the tiny isthmuses of hard ground between the puddles. He crab-walked his way to the front porch, rain running down his bent head and sliding beneath his collar. If he wasn't completely soaked to the skin before, he was now.

Knocking on the door, he shifted to one side to avoid the rivulet of water that was running through a hole in the porch roof and racing down one of the posts, dropping huge plops of water along its way.

It took several more attempts at knocking before the door was answered. A man in his seventies, back ramrod straight, opened the door and eyed him with a hard look of suspicion. His hair was gray, clipped short, and his face was weathered. He looked like he squinted a lot, and he was dressed in brown work pants and a gray shirt.

"You that detective from out of town? You sure picked a hell of a day to show up."

"They're not all like this?" Lang asked.

Rooney didn't seem to appreciate the humor. "I'm Tim

Rooney," he said, shaking Lang's wet hand. "You'd best come in, I suppose."

Lang glanced down at the wet marks his boots were making on the rough plank board floor but Rooney waved off his concern. "This is a working farm. I don't have a wife no more. Nobody cares but me."

He led the way to a kitchen with a small table crammed in the corner and motioned for Lang to take a chair. "Like a drink?" he asked. "I've got water . . . and milk."

Was that the faintest bit of humor in the older man's eyes? Lang said, "Water, thanks."

"Not enough of it outside," Rooney said.

He poured each of them a glass, then sat across from Lang at the postage stamp–sized table. "You're a time waster, son. I told you that truck was stolen long ago."

Lang nodded. They'd tried the license plates, learned they, too, were stolen, and had traced the truck's owner back to Rooney through the VIN number. It could have been through a number of thieving hands before it found its way to the rest stop victims. "How long ago?"

He shrugged. "Maybe a year."

"And you never reported it missing?"

"Nope."

"Why not?"

"'Cause I knew who took it."

Lang's brows shot up in surprise. "You knew who took it? You didn't say that before," he declared with some heat.

Rooney was unperturbed. "Nobody asked me. They asked me if it was my truck. I said yes, and that it was stolen right off my property. I asked 'em when I would get it back, and they said they were investigating a crime and would get back to me. And here you are. So, when am I gettin' my truck?"

"Who took it?" Lang could hear the frustration in his own voice.

"Well, it weren't the people you found at that rest stop, if that's what you mean. Saw that on the news," he explained. "Figured that was my truck. Cade musta sold it to 'em."

"Cade? He took your truck?"

He nodded. "Had to be Cade Worster."

"Who's he?"

"Thievin' Injun. Gave him some odd jobs around here and he thanked me by takin' my truck."

Lang wasn't sure whether he wanted to laugh or strangle the old coot. "This Cade Worster, who you say stole your truck, is Native American?"

"Part, yeah. Maybe more'n just part. Damn near all, I'd say."

Lang was having a helluva time keeping Rooney on point. "He live around here?"

Rooney made a motion toward the north. "He's a Foothiller, up by Deception Bay. You know the Foothillers?"

Lang shook his head.

"Okay, well, you got your whites, and you got your Injuns. Back in the day, this is. The Injuns were already here but then all of a sudden they had to make their way for the whites who came in and took up all the land. Pushed 'em back toward the mountains." Rooney swept an arm toward the east, in the general direction of the Coast Range. "So's then the whites take the coast land and the Injuns move east, but the two groups get a little hanky-panky goin' on and mix together and after a while, you got your Foothillers."

Lang found himself staring at the gray-haired man who spoke with such blythe, political incorrectness. "And Cade Worster's a Foothiller."

"Don't get me wrong, son. Ain't nothin' wrong with being a Foothiller. My wife was a Foothiller, bless her soul. Ain't nothin' wrong with bein' an Injun either. But a thievin' Injun is what ain't right."

"But you didn't have him arrested."

"Mister, Cade Worster is some kinda relative to me through my wife, bless her soul. Couldn't have her rollin' over in her grave just because Cade's a good-for-nothin' who's givin' 'em all a bad name. Stereotypin' them bad."

"But Cade Worster is not the man who died at the rest stop."

"Cain't be. I saw him the day after it happened, and I saw him again yesterday." He snorted. "Bad pennies always show up."

"You saw Cade Worster yesterday. The man you think stole your truck?"

"I *know* he stole my truck. Hell, son, you need to write this down? That's what I've been sayin'!"

Rooney was growing as annoyed with Lang as Lang was growing exasperated with him. "You think I could talk to this Mr. Worster?"

"You can sure as hell try, though he won't be talkin' back. He gets real quiet when the authorities come around, you know what I mean?"

"Like he has something to hide?"

"Huh." He nodded several times, as if happy Lang and he were finally on the same page. Then he skewered Lang with a look through very sharp blue eyes. "You know where Deception Bay is, right north up the coastline?"

"I know it."

"There's a—residential district, I guess you'd call it, straight east and up against the mountains, in the foothills."

"The Foothillers."

"Yessir." He wagged his head with a faint smile, as if Lang, dense as rock, was finally catching on. "It ain't a reservation. That'd be up north in Washington state."

"Got it."

"And it's not a town, really. It's a community."

"Foothillers community."

"That's it. Lot of mixin' of blood, but white folks are looked on with some suspicion."

"This community sounds like it falls under the jurisdiction of the Tillamook County Sheriff's Department."

"Have to be, I guess. You with them?" He looked over Lang's drenched civilian clothes.

"Maybe. Yeah." Lang shrugged. "I'll know in a couple of hours."

"Huh." He leaned back in his chair. "If'n you find Cade, tell him I've got some jobs for him, if'n he wants 'em."

"You'd hire him? Even though he stole your truck?"

Rooney shrugged. "The boy's got a strong back when he cares to use it. Truck wasn't worth much anyway. I am gettin' it back, though, right? It is my property, after all."

"If you own it, it'll come back to you."

"When?"

Lang spread his hands and shook his head.

"Huh," Rooney said, then after a moment, "You want some more water?"

Lang said no, thanked him, then headed out through the still pouring rain to his Dodge truck. Glancing at his watch, he saw it was four o'clock, and as he put the vehicle in gear, his cell phone rang. It was Will Tanninger; he'd plugged his cell number into his contact list and *Tanninger* popped up on the screen.

"Stone," he answered.

"Got a call from your doctor friend at Halo Valley, Dr. Norris. I called her back. Apparently there's some thought that the knife wounds on the pregnant vic's abdomen weren't meant to cut out the baby."

"What? That's bullshit!"

"A midwife pointed out that they look too unfocused,

like an afterthought. You want to go over there and check it out?"

"To Halo Valley?"

"Where are you?"

Lang opened his mouth to say, "Tillamook," but nothing came out. He was far closer to the hospital than anyone in the greater Portland area. He just wasn't sure he wanted to make another trip there.

"Stone?"

For a coward's beat, he thought about pretending his cell phone was breaking up or he'd lost the signal. Instead, he heard himself saying, "It wouldn't be till later tonight. I've got a couple appointments."

"I don't think it's urgent. You could go tomorrow. Or I could send someone else."

"What am I looking for?"

"Just check it out. Listen to the staff. See what's going on there. I don't know why they'd minimize the crime, but something's off."

"Okay." Lang said a few more words, then rang off. He liked Tanninger. He liked the work. He just didn't like the idea of heading to Halo Valley. He wasn't much for hospitals in general and certainly Halo Valley in particular.

Rita Feather Hawkings was well into her shift but her eyes were constantly turning to any clock she could find. She didn't wear a watch and she didn't own a cell phone to check the time, so she prowled by the nurse's station more often than usual just to get a fix on the hour.

"What's with you?" Carmelita asked once.

Rita ignored her and concentrated on her own plans. She would leave tonight, as soon as she got off work. It would be a bit of a problem because she shared a car with her mother, and her mother expected Rita to do all the shopping for her. If Rita were gone for a few days, Delores would wonder why.

But she'd done it before. Lots of times. That's how she'd learned that Rafe had left her bed to go behind the gates of that cult and screw the brains out of that blond whore! Tasha. One of *them*. All dressed in their printed cotton dresses, looking like they were from another century. Walking inside the property like zombies. Pale. Stupid. Lifeless.

Siren Song. That's what their place was called. Rita was pretty sure they hadn't named it themselves, 'cause she'd had to take some literature courses—as few as she could manage—when she'd first gone to school, and she knew that a Siren was a sexy, mythological female voice that called out to seamen and when they sailed toward it, their boats were smashed on the rocks. Or something like that. But it was a sexy voice, and there was nothing sexy in that compound with its blond female ghosts. They just didn't seem real. All of them girls. All of them! She'd never seen a man there, except, of course, for Rafe.

He'd been their gardener, their handyman, their deliveryman. And he'd fallen for that fucking Tasha!

He hadn't told Rita at first. *At first,* he saw them both, both Rita and Tasha. Rita had been livid when she'd accidentally learned the truth. She'd followed Rafe and seen him with *her*. Seen them groping each other under a full moon. Watched through the iron bars while hiding in the brush. *Groping*. Rafe had been all over Tasha and she'd stood there quivering, naked, her skin glowing. Rita had been sure that she herself was pregnant. She and Rafe had made love so many times. Rita was an innovative lover, not like this stick of human flesh that couldn't even move. She'd wanted to scratch the bitch's eyes out, and her hands had stretched like claws toward them before she remembered herself and pulled back.

She watched the whole act. Was somewhat embarrassed that she got a secret thrill from watching them go at it. Noticed Rafe's back muscles gleaming as he humped her hard. Tasha just stood there. Her back to the wall of the building. Her mouth open like she was going to yell. But she was silent and had to clap her hand over Rafe's mouth as he moaned, "Tasha . . . Tasha. . . . Oh, God . . . Tasha."

And then Rita saw *her* hands begin to tentatively explore Rafe's buttocks. That drove him wild and he jammed into her hard till she cried out with pleasure and Rita sank onto the ground, ran her fingers into her hair, ripping it out by the roots. She was hot herself, her center molten. Oh, how she wanted him inside her. Wanted him filling her up with babies. Her Rafe. *Hers!!!*

But that *blond bitch was fucking him!*

She decided right then she had to kill her. Had to.

She slid away from the sight of them. Moved to her mother's dark sedan, fell inside, drove home in a fury, threw herself onto her own bed, and thrashed on the bedsheets.

Nobody stole Rita's man.

Nobody.

She had visions of slicing apart the yellow-haired devil. She would find a way to get inside those wrought-iron walls that Rafe could scale so easily and stab her. Take her life.

It took a supreme effort for Rita to pull herself together that night and pretend to Rafe that she didn't know. It was so difficult. So, so difficult. Sometimes she could barely pull it off, especially when Rafe, clearly lost in thoughts of banging Tasha's brains out, could hardly get it up for Rita.

Bastard. Oh, how she loved him.

But Rita Feather Hawkings knew about game playing. She could lie. She could smile. She could seduce. She was good at all of it. That's how she'd hooked Rafe in the first place! He was the best-looking man around. Young. A little immature. But handsome as the devil. Rita had made up a potion from herbs the Fertility Goddess recommended and fed it to Rafe, telling him it was an aphrodisiac, though it was more a narcotic. Still, it slowed his virile body and mind down long enough for Rita to win him over, and once hooked, he was hers.

Until that *blond bitch* got her talons into him. From then on, Rita had to work twice as hard. She just wished she would get pregnant, then Rafe and the baby would be hers. Hers alone.

Several months passed and Rita believed things were getting better between her and Rafe. He still went to the fortress where Tasha lived, with Rita following, but Tasha didn't come out; Rita could almost believe she didn't exist.

But then, one night last April, everything changed.

Rafe, who had access to Siren Song in those days, before the cult-mother learned the truth and tossed him out, wasn't home when Rita got to his place after a long day at work. He lived in a camper on blocks, not far from Rita's mom's, and Rita paced outside the front door, knowing in her heart that something had happened. That evil witch had drawn him back.

She was about to charge to Siren Song herself when he suddenly appeared, driving the rattletrap Chevy truck with its back filled with rakes, scythes, a push mower, handsaw, and other gardener's tools. His handsome face was bright and happy, but when he saw Rita guilt raced across it.

That fucking Tasha whore . . .

"Rita," he gulped. "Sorry, babe. I can't stay. I've got . . . some work to do. Just came home to grab a few things."

"Uh-huh." Rita's blood started a slow simmer in her veins.

His black hair fell over his forehead and he couldn't stop the smile of joy that showed his white, white teeth. "But I'll be back later, okay? I'll call you."

He pushed past her, unlocking the door and disappearing inside the tiny space. The smell of leftover pizza and something sour wafted out, maybe unwashed dishes or clothes. Rita deplored his lack of housecleaning skills, but he was young. That's what she was there for. He needed her as much as she needed him.

He slammed back out and reversed onto the road. Rita waved and got behind the wheel of her mother's car, a dark Malibu that had also seen better days. When Rafe raced away, she knew where he was going: to Tasha. Rita's hopes were crushed. Rafe's and Tasha's lovemaking might have waned for a bit, but it was back on. That's where he was going. Rita was once again forgotten in his blind desire for his princess.

Rita followed a few minutes later, but she knew the routine. Rafe parked on the east side of the grounds and worked his way to one of the remotest lengths of the fence where a sumac and Scotch broom and mountain laurel all crowded together as if dying to get inside as much as Rafe was.

He climbed the bushes and the fence and threw himself over. To get back he had to go closer to the front of the lodge and climb a large rock to throw himself over. Rita knew he'd surreptitiously managed to add more rocks, creating a pile, while he worked on the grounds, thereby making his vault to freedom easier with time.

Rita parked farther away yet, nose out in the long, winding driveway of a nearby vacation home that was never used, as far as she could tell. She worked her way to the wrought-iron fence, tucked into her own viewing position, invisible in the weeds and behind a couple of scrub Douglas firs.

Sure enough, there was Rafe, just over the fence and crouched, walking fast, to the shadowed walls of the lodge. She fantasized about following him over the fence and killing Tasha with her bare hands, but she kept her cool.

And then Tasha appeared, sliding through the shadows to fall into Rafe's welcoming arms. "I got your note," he said. "Where have you been?"

"They found out," she said, her voice quavering.

"About us?"

"They wouldn't let me out of my room. But I got a key."

"I've missed you." And then he was all over her, pushing her against the wall, then pulling at her, trying to get her to the ground. "The graveyard?" he murmured, when she wouldn't comply.

The graveyard. Rita's nails cut into her own palms. It was taboo in Rita's mind. You didn't mess with the dead. But Tasha didn't care. There was no end to her badness. Rita had witnessed Rafe and her writhing away on top of a grave, had seen her enemy's breasts laid bare and Rafe's dark head suckling frantically while Tasha lay like a zombie and stared at the stars.

But tonight Tasha wouldn't leave the shadows; she kept her back against the building. Rafe was too eager to care, and he was dry-humping her in a way that made Rita seethe with fury.

Then Tasha, distraught, said in a little girl's voice, "I'm with child."

With child? Rita's brain couldn't process. *Pregnant?*

Rafe had been scrabbling with her dress, yanking the folds to her waist with one hand and jamming the other into her panties while Tasha stood stiffly.

He froze. "You're fucking kidding me!"

"Shhh." Tasha put a finger to his lips. "I can't stay here. You have to take me with you! We have to leave!"

Rafe stumbled backward, his hands raking through his hair. "Oh, Jesus. Oh, Jeez-God."

Rita's ears were rushing. With child. Tasha was with child. Rafe's child. Rita's child. *Rita's child!*

"We need to make plans," she said urgently.

"Plans," Rafe repeated.

"You and I, Rafe. For us, and our baby . . ."

Rafe lifted his head slowly and met her gaze. Rita wasn't exactly sure what happened then. One moment he was in terrible shock, the next it was like Tasha had him under her power because he suddenly bent over and kissed her stomach through her dress. Tasha held his head close and then looked over *right where Rita was hiding*! They were yards apart, there was little moonlight to see, but it felt like those blue eyes sent lasers searching under Rita's skin and finding no baby. No child. Just an empty vessel.

Rita shrank back and stared at her enemy.

It was then that she knew she had to take her baby from Tasha. She had to take Rafe back, too. Find a way to break the witch's spell on him.

But Rafe's dead. . . .

Rita came back to the present with a bang. *Rafe,* she thought brokenly. *Rafe . . .*

"Rita?" Nina Perez, one of Ocean Park's head nurses, was eyeing her harshly, enough to make Rita worry that she'd said something, given something away. Nina had caught Rita daydreaming before.

"I feel ill," she murmured.

"What's wrong?"

"Maybe the flu . . . ?"

"Well, if you're really feeling that sick, maybe you should leave."

"My shift isn't over."

"Go home. Get some rest."

"Okay."

Rita shuffled away, head down, toward the employee restroom and her locker. She rarely took time off work, was hardly ever really sick. It wasn't from a sense of duty, or even a need for money. It was camouflage. Rita, the good nurse. The exemplary employee. As dependable as the day was long.

Rita with two days off and the use of her mother's dark blue sedan.

This time Rita wouldn't make a mistake. This time Rita would slit the zombie bitch's throat and take *her* baby from its surrogate womb.

Chapter 8

Sheriff O'Halloran was back by the time Lang returned to the sheriff's department. This time he found a parking spot, though it was the only one, and he hurried in the back door with the rain letting up only slightly.

Johnson gave him the stink eye; it was like she disliked him on sight. Not an auspicious beginning, but she said, "Sheriff said if you came back to tell you to go on through."

"Thanks."

Lang was conscious of the water squishing inside his cowboy boots. He scraped as much mud as he could at the door, but he couldn't stop the wet marks that left a trail behind him. Luckily, he could still see the sheriff's prints on the scarred wood floor as well.

"Good to meet you," O'Halloran said in a booming voice that matched his large size. He was something over six feet with a wide girth that was spilling up over a belt. Lang pegged him somewhere in his fifties or sixties, with gray hair turning white and bright blue eyes. Another stereotype. The Irish cop. But there was a glint in those eyes that spoke of intelligence behind this act of bonhomie.

Lang realized this job was not just his for the taking.

O'Halloran had professed interest in him, but maybe that interest had changed?

"You got yourself pretty wet, there," O'Halloran observed.

"I was on an interview."

"Yeah? Around here?"

There was no reason to hide what he was doing, so Lang told O'Halloran about Tim Rooney and his revelation that one Cade Worster had stolen his truck, the truck that was in the possession of the unidentified deceased male and his currently catatonic pregnant companion.

"Cade Worster," the sheriff mused.

"You know him?"

"He's been in our jail a time or two. Mostly disorderly contact. Drunk in public. Possession of stolen property."

"So, you think Mr. Rooney might be right?"

"I know enough about Cade to believe there could be some truth in it."

"Rooney told me Cade lived in the Deception Bay area."

The sheriff nodded. "He's a Foothiller. Know what that is?"

"I've been educated."

O'Halloran's eyes twinkled. "This the reason you came here, or are you thinking about the job?"

"I'm thinking about the job."

"Well, good, then. One of my detectives, Deputy Marcia Kirkpatrick, up and left for a position in Phoenix. Left another detective, Fred Clausen, partnerless. We've had a few applicants. Had sort of a trial position thing going, for a time." He shrugged. "Nothing worked out. It was Clausen who knew your story, suggested I look into your employment situation, so I talked to your lieutenant, and to you, and here we are."

A detective position. With an experienced partner, by the sounds of it.

"Would it be a trial position?"

"Would only be fair."

Lang nodded. Actually, he liked that idea. A trial position worked both ways. He wouldn't have to move immediately, sell his house. He could rent something and give the job some time.

"How long?" Lang asked.

"Three months."

"When do I start?"

The blue eyes twinkled again. "We got a thing going around here. Tillamook Bay is fed by a number of rivers. Find out their names and how many, and when you're ready to start, come in here and give a report."

"Seriously?"

"You wanna finish up the case you're on, go ahead. Don't take too long. But yeah, come and give me a report and we'll put you on. You're gonna want to meet the other deputies, too."

Lang shook his hand, a little bemused, wondering if he was getting well, because for the first time in a long time he felt a lifting of darkness from his heart.

Claire checked her schedule for the next day, Friday. It was fairly light. She had an early appointment with Jamie Lou again. An extra one, as Jamie Lou was struggling to do as she'd promised and stay on her meds. Then she had a cancellation, and in the afternoon—

A light knock on her door. She turned with a racing pulse toward the door, as Glenda, her receptionist, hadn't announced anyone coming her way, and ever since the night she'd met Heyward and Melody, even though that had been a different office, a different setup, she was skittish.

But it was Dr. Avanti who ducked his dark head around the door, smiling. "Got a minute?"

She was instantly wary. Paolo Avanti was no friend of hers. "Come in."

He moved into the room with a grace and fluidity that some might have described as sexy. She just saw an adversary.

"I thought it was time we talked about the meeting." He took one of her client chairs and crossed his ankle over his knee, adjusting his lab coat like a sports jacket. He was a little too classy for the shirt open to his navel and gold chains, but the image found its way into her mind.

"Okay."

"Claire, we all know how hard this is for you. And you're one of the most dedicated doctors on staff. And everything you do is for your patients."

"Cut to the chase, Paolo." His brows shot up in surprise. "What do you want?"

He hesitated, and she could tell he was calculating what tack to take. "All right. I'll come directly to the point. We're moving Marsdon to the less restrictive environment."

"From Side B to Side A."

"We would sincerely like you to be on board with this, but it's already been decided."

Claire absorbed the information, not really surprised.

"The room will be locked. He will only go in and out with supervision. His meds are monitored."

"Did the Marsdons pull out their checkbook before or after you gave them the good news? I'm guessing before."

Avanti tried on a smile. "You really are a ballbusting bitch, Claire."

She smiled right back. "This time you get a thank-you."

"How *did* you become a psychiatrist?"

"An understanding of human nature. An ability to generally know a lie from the truth. The realization that manipulators never stop manipulating, even when—maybe especially when—they purport to be your friend."

He held Claire's gaze. "I didn't know you had it in you."

"Try having a knife held to your throat. If you get past the fear, there's a clarity that follows. Kind of like knowing your place in the world. I have less need to bend and conform."

"That can work against you."

"I could lose my job, but even so, I'm a better doctor now."

"The Marsdons are coming here this evening. They have a scheduled meeting with Heyward, who's been asking for you."

Claire regarded him warily. "What are *you* asking?"

Avanti hesitated. This hadn't gone even remotely the way he'd expected it to. "Could you make that meeting?"

"After hours, you want me to go with you and the Marsdons to Side B? To see Heyward?"

"Yes."

She shook her head. "You forget, the Marsdons specifically asked for me to be taken off Heyward's case. That request is the reason I haven't seen Heyward since his incarceration."

"Not the only reason."

Claire understood psychological warfare very well. Avanti was trying to bully her into doing as he wished. "You think I'm afraid to meet with him?"

"Yes," he admitted. "It would be a natural reaction."

"Wait. You're saying the Marsdons now *want* me to be there?"

Avanti got to his feet and straightened his lab coat, holding on to the lapels with both hands, gazing down at Claire in a superior way. She stood, too, resting the tips of her fingers on her desktop. A duel at noon in the hot sun. "They don't want you anywhere near him, but they need you. You're the fly in the ointment, Claire. You know it, and I know it."

"They're afraid I'll go to the courts. Raise a stink. Try to get Heyward's room assignment nailed down to Side B. Foil their plans."

"He attacked you. You could probably get whatever you wanted, if you decided to go that route."

"You don't think I'll do it?"

"On the contrary, I think it's very possible you will," he said. "Before that happens, you should see Heyward for yourself."

"Tonight."

"Yes."

When she didn't immediately answer, he dropped his stance and moved toward the door. "You're a good doctor, Claire," he said, a hand on the knob. "Maybe a great one. You want what's best for Heyward even though you're scared of him. You understand he's sick. You know his intent was never to hurt you or Melody Stone. You know you should help him, regardless of what you think of his family."

He hesitated, glancing back at Claire. She was regarding him soberly, struck by his words though she didn't want to be. He seemed to be waiting for her response.

"When is this transfer to take place?" she asked.

"Kind of depends on what happens tonight."

"You mean, it's predicated on how I feel about Heyward? That's why I need to be there?"

"Your opinion matters, Claire. But it won't alter the decision."

"So, basically, this transfer is imminent."

"It'll be soon," he agreed. "The Marsdons want to be here for that as well."

"Of course they do. They want to do everything for Halo Valley."

"They just want what's best for their son."

"They want what they think is best for their son," she

said. "Whether it is or not is another matter. One the hospital should really look at."

"Your feelings have been well documented."

"Yes. Theirs, too."

"So will you be there?"

Would she? Claire felt the same suffocating feeling she'd experienced when everyone at the hospital seemed to close her out. "I'll be there," she finally said. "It'll give me a chance to thank them for the chocolate cake."

The door shut behind him with a soft click and Claire sank into her chair, feeling the leaching of adrenaline throughout her whole body.

The rain would just not let up. Not. Let. Up.

Lang's wipers were working overtime, slapping water away in splashes without much success.

He had half a mind to give up for the day. It was closing on six o'clock and the light was starting to fade. If he drove up 101 and turned onto 26, it would still be an hour and a half or more home in perfect weather conditions. If he cut east toward Halo Valley he could be there in forty minutes, well, except for the blasted rain. Then it would be another hour and a half east to Salem and north to the greater Portland area on I-5.

He didn't want to see Claire Norris. Not the least because he found her attractive. Something about her control. And those legs. And a slim face with doe eyes that were filled with suspicion, at least when they were trained on him.

If he forgot Halo Valley and went north he could maybe stop at the Foothillers' residential community and learn something about Cade Worster, maybe even find him. He could potentially learn the name of their murder victim and his pregnant companion. Tanninger had said he could wait to visit Halo Valley until tomorrow. Hell, he could leave it entirely, as this was a volunteer position on his part, more or less.

Or he could go to a bar, order an Irish coffee, and wait for the storm to pass.

He was currently heading north on 101, but had barely left the Tillamook city limits. He was driving slowly, partly because of the rain, partly from indecision. Growling under his breath, he turned the Dodge around and nosed the truck toward the two-lane state road that led east to the Willamette Valley and Salem, the state's capital city, the same highway that, about a third of the way to Salem, held the turnoff for Halo Valley Security Hospital.

Might as well get the least palatable task off his list first.

He drove fifteen miles under the speed limit because the road was awash with mud-filled water with more pouring over his car as if some gleeful god had tipped a blimp-sized bucket over. By the time he reached the turnoff for Halo Valley, he was sorry he'd chosen this task today. He wanted to be home. Under the hot needle spray of his own shower. Then maybe a Scotch, maybe not. But definitely a face plant in his bed.

He drove down the long entrance lane and past the main hospital parking lot, which was surprisingly full, circled to the left of the portico, and found a spot at the far end of the medical office building, which was attached at the north end of the main building. Wishing for an umbrella, something he never did, Lang climbed once more into the soaking rain and jogged through standing water on the asphalt to the medical office building's side door, up about six concrete steps and through a door that warned it was locked from seven P.M. until six A.M.

His boots squished as he walked down a long, gray-carpeted hallway toward a central desk, a semicircular affair made from blond wood with a young man wearing a white shirt, green tie, and Dockers seated on a swivel chair behind it.

"Can I help you?" he asked, eyeing Lang's dripping jacket.

He had no identification. No credentials. "Detective Langdon Stone," he said, the lie too easy on his tongue. He sensed now that he'd never left. Not really. Not where it counted. Law enforcement was who he was; maybe all he had left. "I'm here to see Dr. Norris."

He frowned. "She may have gone home for the day."

"She called the Winslow County Sheriff's Department, and they sent me."

"Oh." He reached for the phone and punched in a number. After waiting through enough rings to convince even Lang that she wasn't in, he hung up and shook his head. "Not in her office."

"Can you page her through the hospital from here?"

"I can call the hospital front desk," he said, his fingers already on the phone again. After a brief conversation with someone at the other end, he nodded and pointed farther down the hallway, ostensibly toward the juncture with the hospital. "Go to the elevators at the end of the hall," he said to Lang. "Punch floor two, which leads to the skyway and the gallery level of the hospital. Turn right, follow the hallway, and go down the stairs to the front reception desk. They don't think Dr. Norris has left yet."

"Is that the only way to access the hospital directly from the medical offices?"

"Uh-huh."

"And what about the other hospital building? Where they house the criminally insane?"

"Ummm . . ." He was uncomfortable, but said, "Second floor is also the access to the other half of Halo Valley. It's guarded. It's really safe."

The kid acted like Lang was going to write up a safety

violation. Following his directions, Lang found the elevator, pushed two, exited onto a hallway that branched to the right, and saw a sign for the hospital. To the left there was another desk, and curiosity made him head there first. It was a duplicate of the one on the first floor, unmanned at the moment, but he could see this was the nerve center for the medical offices. Downstairs was more a security center. Here was where the appointments were booked, the insurance information taken. There was even a roped-off waiting area that patients were advised to stand back from. The HIPAA requirement to keep medical records private.

Lang then headed to the hospital. He saw the corridor branch that undoubtedly led to the locked-down half, but he ignored it for now. He didn't want to think about Heyward Marsdon III or his sister. He was here on a completely different case, and it was best if he kept it that way.

Walking across the gallery, Lang felt oddly uncomfortable, looking down on the main entry, taking the curving stairs to the lower floor, feeling a little like a debutante at her coming-out party. A few people glanced up and stared, and for a moment he wondered if he had a scarlet letter on his forehead, but then realized his soaked clothing and wet hair were the cause of interest.

"Can I help you?" the receptionist called.

"Dr. Norris, please," Lang said, approaching the desk.

A very large woman teetered from one foot to the other as she lumbered toward him. "You look like someone threw you in the river!" she declared.

"C'mon, Jenny." A woman wearing a salmon-colored uniform, one of the nurses or aides, guided her back toward the main room. Lang looked over and saw their Jane Doe, Cat, seated in a chair in front of the television.

And Dr. Claire Norris was also in the room, her attention taken by a man in a tan turtleneck, deep brown jacket, and slacks. They seemed to be conferring. Claire had removed her lab coat and a raincoat was tossed over her arm. She was definitely on her way out.

"I see her," Lang told the receptionist, who smiled and nodded. He walked to meet Claire and her male companion.

As soon as she saw him, he saw her tense. Then she stepped forward in greeting, hand outstretched. "You got my message?" she said. Her handshake was firm and she withdrew her hand immediately.

"Tanninger gave it to me." He glanced questioningly at the man.

"This is Donald Inman," she said. "Donald, this is Detective Stone."

"Not a detective at the moment," he said, shaking the other man's hand next. "But that's changing."

"Good to meet you," Donald said. "Are you here about Cat? Our Jane Doe?"

"Yes."

"Are you going back to the Portland P.D.?" she asked.

"It looks like Tillamook County Sheriff's Department."

Lang couldn't decipher the strange look that crossed her face as Inman said, "Such a horrible crime. Basically, an attempted emergency C-section to the victim when there's no emergency. A lot of complications could occur."

"I thought the question was whether that was even the intent," Lang said.

"That is the question," Claire agreed. "I didn't really expect the police to come out here again. I just wanted to pose the idea, in case it helped the case in any way."

"She's lucky to be alive." Inman gave Cat a studied look.

The television was set to a game show. Several faces were turned toward its screen, but Lang didn't think anyone was really paying attention. At that moment a woman suddenly jumped up and said, "Change the channel! Change the channel!"

The rallying cry took up and the heavyset nurse that

Lang had met before brought forth a remote only she had access to, apparently, and switched to the news.

And there was Pauline Kirby in all her glory, with a downcast Cat sitting front and center in her wheelchair, her blond crown centered in the camera's lens.

Pauline's voice-over was full of treacly sorrow. ". . . little more than a child herself. The authorities have no idea who's responsible for this horrifyingly malicious attack. If you have any information about this woman who is unable to even tell us her name, please call the station. She needs your help. Her unborn child needs your help."

The camera moved in and gave the profile of Cat's face that had been seen on an earlier broadcast as well.

"It's Cat! It's Cat!" A young man leapt from his chair and pointed at the silent girl who'd been seated beside him. "It's you! It's you!" he told her.

The nurse who'd herded the heavyset woman back now turned to the young man. "Gibby, that's enough. We all saw the broadcast." She pushed the remote and the TV screen went blank.

"But she's here! She's here! We should tell them! She's here!"

"They know she's here. They're trying to find her family."

"Excuse me," Claire said, and Donald Inman fell in beside her as they joined the group. Lang followed a couple of paces behind, watching. The blond girl in question hadn't so much as twitched.

The young man, whose face was full of earnest worry, leaned into the girl. "Cat!" he yelled loudly, as if that would wake her up. "You're right here! At the hospital with me!"

Lang flicked a look from him to the girl. Her fingers flexed ever so slightly on the chair arms.

"She moves her limbs," Claire said, anticipating the question.

Donald turned to Lang. "She's in a twilight state. Neither fully present nor fully asleep. Claire, I think we should have a consult."

"Cat!" Gibby yelled into her face.

"Not right now, Donald," Claire said tautly, moving to Gibby. "She can hear you without yelling, Gibby. We need to use our inside voice, remember?"

Lang glanced at Donald, wondering what his function at the hospital was, then turned his attention to Claire, who'd placed herself between Gibby and Cat.

"But she's here," Gibby said, sounding wounded and confused.

"Her people are out there. We hope they're watching the news, too. We want to know more about her."

"Like what?"

"Like her name."

"It's Cat."

"Gibby, you know that's just the name we call her."

"Everybody hasta have a name." Gibby glanced around anxiously. "Why don't she have a name?"

"She does. We just don't know what it is."

Gibby seemed to be working himself up to a full-fledged panic attack. "She wants to leave. She wants me to help her out the door!" He waved toward the front glass doors.

"No, Gibby." Claire was firm. "She needs to stay."

"She told me! She told me! She said, 'Help me! Help me! Help me! Help me!'"

From the back hallway came two burly-looking men. Lang recognized the muscle when he saw it and stepped out of the way. After a brief skirmish the orderlies took a protesting Gibby away from the main room, his cries diminishing slowly as he was hauled farther and farther away.

"Controlled chaos," Lang observed.

She shot him a dark look. "Gibby has made an attachment to Cat and he's become protective of her."

Donald said, "Bradford Gibson—Gibby—suffers from mental retardation. He's a permanent resident at Halo Valley."

"Yeah?" Lang looked the guy over. His hair was sandy brown, smoothly combed, and he had a sensitive mouth. He looked a little like a college professor. An aesthete of some sort. A pipe would have completed the look.

The heavyset woman had wandered over and now stood to Lang's right. He glanced at her and she smiled shyly.

"Go on, Big Jenny," Donald said curtly. To Lang, in an aside, "The mind of a two-year-old, the hormones of a horny thirteen-year-old slut."

"Donald." Claire's voice was sharp.

As Lang watched, she took Donald's arm and led him to the other side of the room, sat him at a table with a crossword puzzle. An older man stood by the window, mumbling and looking out to the razor wire–crowned wall above the locked-down side.

When Claire returned, Lang nodded toward Donald and observed dryly, "Hard to tell the inmates from the staff."

"Donald was in the mental health field. He believes he's a therapist."

"But he's a patient now."

She nodded stiffly.

Lang wasn't sure whether to be appalled or amused. "So, this is how you professionally treat him? By buying into his delusion?"

"We continually remind him of reality," Claire said with a bite in her voice.

"But it's just easier to let him wander around and act like he's a doctor."

"Even if we had the staff to tag after him and remind him every waking hour that he is not a therapist, he wouldn't be able to hear it without digressing into a state of anxiety and fear and acting out. There's a fine balance, Detective."

"Really." He could tell he was pissing her off, which was fine with him. "What happened to him?"

She seemed like she wasn't going to answer, then said, "A slow deterioration of mental faculties."

"That's pretty general."

"Yes."

"You called the station," Lang reminded her, getting to the point.

"I called Will Tanninger."

"Who called me." Lang was growing tired of their thrust and parry. "Look, neither of us has a ton of time to dance around, so let's get on with it. Tell me why you don't think someone tried to cut out Jane Doe—Cat's—baby."

They both glanced toward the blond patient in the chair. "Let's go to my office," Claire suggested, though Lang had a feeling it was the last thing she wanted.

She led the way and Lang trooped along behind her, retracing his steps to the upper level and bypassing the medical office's main reception area, down a short hallway, through a door she bent to unlock. He had a great view of her backside, the black pants that hugged her hips, the slim ankles peeking out below.

She opened the door, stepped inside, gestured for him to enter.

His heart started pounding as an imagined scenario passed in front of his eyes, one he hadn't expected to be so close to the surface: Melody . . . Heyward . . . the knife . . . a scream . . .

Claire Norris's voice, penetrating from far away. "You understand this is my new office."

"Yes." His voice sounded normal. He came back slowly, could feel blood return to his head and quell the sudden rushing.

She was looking at him hard, frowning. "Maybe I should have made that clear."

"It's not a problem." He crossed the floor and accepted a chair that sat in front of her desk, glad for the support. She moved behind the desk, smoothed the seat of her pants, and sat down. They were facing each other like doctor and patient.

She looked serious. Her skin was silken smooth and he focused on an errant tress of dark hair that curved into her chin. It was all he could do not to reach forward and brush it back.

He said, "You signed Heyward Marsdon's release when he should have been locked up."

She swallowed but her gaze didn't waver. "I can't discuss him with you."

"He killed my sister."

"Yes."

"And he damn near killed you."

"I can talk to you about Jane Doe. The rest is privileged."

Lang gritted his teeth. She was right. More than right. He'd believed he could handle this investigation without letting the past make him step outside the bounds of propriety and law. But he couldn't. He couldn't. "Privilege," he stated flatly. "That's what the whole damn thing is about. The privileged get what they want. They buy it."

"Would you like to speak to the midwife who last examined Jane Doe's wounds?"

"They bought you."

"I can't talk to you about Heyward Marsdon," she stated flatly. He could see bright spots of color in her cheeks. He was getting to her.

"Yeah, you can. You just won't."

"Heyward Marsdon the Third is a patient at this hospital."

"An inmate," Lang said.

"A patient," she repeated. "That's all I can tell you about him. If you came here to learn about his status instead of aiding the criminal investigation into Jane Doe, you've wasted a trip."

"I think you, of all people, would be interested in seeing Heyward locked up somewhere safer than that place." He inclined his head toward the other building. "Is it really safe over there? Prison safe?" Her lips parted in spite of herself. He'd hit a nerve. "It's not, is it? You're afraid he'll get out and come after you. I don't blame you. The man's a ticking bomb, waiting to go off. Slice someone else's throat."

"You need to talk to the Marsdons," she said suddenly. "Do it soon." She stood up abruptly.

"What's that mean?"

"They disagree with your feeling about imprisonment for Heyward."

Lang gazed at her. "Not exactly a news bulletin."

She seemed about to say something, then changed her mind, some overriding sense of duty or conscience keeping her from talking. He saw her eyes stray to the small clock on her desk.

"Am I keeping you from something?" he asked.

"No."

But she was lying. He could sense it. And suddenly he thought he knew what it was. "You're going to see him, aren't you? You're still his doctor."

"No." She was firm.

"Something's up with him."

As if on cue her phone buzzed. She didn't move as a male voice said over the intercom, "Dr. Norris?"

Lang's instincts went on high alert. She didn't want him to know what she was doing, but it had to do with Heyward Marsdon. He *knew* it. "They're calling for you," he said softly.

She got up and went to the door, holding it open. "I hope you and Detective Tanninger find out more about our Jane Doe."

"Dr. Norris?" the voice said with a touch of impatience. "We're waiting for you before we go through the gates."

Lang read the answer to that on Claire Norris's face. "They're here now. The Marsdons. You're all going over to the lockdown section to see Heyward the Third."

Chapter 9

Sodium vapor lights illuminated the shiny, rain-slicked parking lot of Laurelton General as Rita pulled the Chevy into a spot at the far end of the lot, a dark spot, behind a thin, swaying maple whose leaves were being flayed from its limbs by the raging wind.

The storm from the coast had made its way inland and was dumping rain in wet sheets, driven by the wind. Rita was still in her uniform, teal scrubs, and boring shoes. She pulled on her raincoat and threw the hood over her hair, then turned on the map light and glanced at herself in the rearview.

She wasn't quite sure how she was going to play this. She wanted Tasha's room number but didn't want to alert anyone to her plan.

But Rita Feather Hawkings was good at deception. She could make this work for her, just like she always did.

Head ducked, she fought her way to the front doors, slapped by a flash of rain that dampened her bangs, sticking them to her forehead. Her sensible shoes slogged through puddles. She saw herself bedraggled and forlorn. Poor Rita. Just off work and intent on seeing a sick relative.

But how to find out about the blond coma girl? They

didn't know Tasha's name, and Rita wasn't going to give it to them.

She walked through the front doors, shaking rain from her jacket on the entry carpet. Carefully, she pulled back her hood, fluffing at her bangs. What relative was she seeing? Who?

Rita couldn't risk asking questions, so she marched through like she owned the place, heading toward the elevators. She didn't know Laurelton General all that well; she'd been there exactly once, applying for a job that she didn't get. She hadn't wanted it anyway, but Ocean Park had been on a hiring freeze when she'd first tried there and Rita's mother had insisted that her daughter get a damn job.

"Make a career," Delores snapped. "Don't wait for it to happen to you. Don't fall into the trap my sister did!"

Delores was always so, so sure that Rita would become a whore. She had no idea what made Rita tick. None at all!

On the fifth floor, two up from the main level, she ran directly into a nurse. They actually smacked into each other as Rita tried to get out of the elevator and the nurse, who was in a decided hurry, was getting in.

"Excuse me," the nurse said. She was black, short and sturdy. Her name tag read Leesha.

Rita would have liked to read her the riot act. At Ocean Park, no one was allowed to racewalk like this nurse was. Instead, she said in a bewildered way, "I'm sorry. I'm kind of lost."

"Check with the front desk. Or the bathroom's that-away." She pointed down the hall. "I've got an emergency." She slammed her palm against an elevator button.

Rita took a chance and guessed, "The coma girl?"

"No. She's not here anymore."

Rita was both elated and discouraged at the same time.

Tasha had been there. She was on the right track. "Well, maybe you can help me. She looked kinda familiar."

"You know who she is?" The nurse eyed Rita up and down in a way that made her uncomfortable.

"Well, I'm not sure. Maybe. I thought if I could get a closer look . . ."

"You're not on staff here."

"No. I'm a nurse at Good Sam," she lied. "I was just in the area and thought I'd stop by."

"Talk to the front desk," the woman said, holding the doors as they started to close. "They're taking everybody's calls and routing them to the police."

"Everybody's?"

"Everybody who saw her on the news."

She lifted her finger from the button that held the doors open, so Rita said hurriedly, "She's been released?"

"Moved."

Moved? Rita stood rooted to the spot as the elevator descended. After a few moments, she pushed the call button again, waiting for the car. The second elevator opened and she stepped inside, thinking hard. She hadn't seen the news, but clearly people were calling in, thinking they knew Tasha. Maybe they did, she thought with a jolt. Maybe Rita wasn't the only one who knew who she was. That bitch Carlita had told Jake she thought Tasha was from the cult.

And what about Tasha's crazy family? Those women? They were bound to raise a hue and cry sometime, weren't they?

Either way, it was only a matter of time until the truth came out.

Moved . . .

Rita strode toward the front desk and then it came to her. A bolt of insight. Coma girl was no longer in a coma. She was physically stable and awake, at least partially. Carlita had seen Tasha's profile on the news and hadn't said her eyes were closed. So Tasha was awake, maybe faking amnesia? Some kind of head trauma?

And she'd been transferred to another facility, one more suited to her condition.

If only she'd seen that newscast! She might have been able to tell where she was, although she could almost bet . . .

She walked up to the front desk. "You're taking calls from people who think they recognize the Jane Doe that was sent to Halo Valley?"

"We're referring them to the sheriff's department," the woman responded. "Have you got some information?"

To Rita's horror the short black nurse caught sight of her and headed her way. Rita said, "I thought you had an emergency."

She nodded. "Car accident. Surgical team had to take over."

"I'm thinking about going to Halo Valley and seeing if I can recognize Jane Doe," Rita lied.

The nurse shot a look at the woman at the front desk, as if she thought she'd given the information to Rita. Rita didn't disillusion her.

"Check with Dr. Claire Norris when you're there," was all she said, her attention diverted by the breach of protocol.

Rita thanked her and headed for the front doors before any further questions could be asked. She'd gotten what she came for.

If Claire could have started the day over again, she would've. She wanted to shriek and cry and laugh hysterically. All of them: Freeson and Avanti and the Marsdons and Melody Stone's damn brother—all of them made her want to spiral into a wild primal scream.

She wanted to run from her office, run from the building.

Instead she stood in stiff disapproval as Stone ambled out
of her office, and she thrust her key in the door to lock it.
"I don't know why you're here," she told him. When he
opened his mouth, she beat him to the answer. "I know I
called the sheriff's department. I know I said Cat might not
have been attacked for her baby. But I didn't really expect
someone to rush right down and interview me. There's
nothing more to say. It's a theory. She's in a catatonic state,
and the only information we can get is through what we
observe. I wanted Detective Tanninger to know that, just
in case it mattered.

"But nowhere in there did I ask for you. Whether you
and I like it or not, we have an unpleasant history. Something neither of us wanted, something neither of us can
help. And it involves a patient here at the hospital. Someone who was once my patient. I cannot have anything to
do with you and Heyward Marsdon the Third. And I don't
want to. I don't want to explain myself to you and have you
accuse me and the hospital of negligence. And I don't want
to have you here under the guise of a different investigation just so you can vent your spleen about the Marsdon
family."

Lang had opened and shut his mouth several times. Now
he waited, his blue eyes staring hard as Claire wound
down. "Where are you meeting them?" he asked.

She swept out ahead of him, heading for the hospital.
She was blind with fury and exasperation. She heard his
footsteps behind her, a kind of squishing of water from his
boots. "Don't follow me," she threw over her shoulder.

"Why isn't Heyward your patient any longer?"

"One guess, Detective."

"You haven't seen him since . . ."

She stopped, her heart pounding, and turned, gathering
her professional skills around her once more. "Since *the
incident*?"

He flinched slightly. "Yeah."

"No, I haven't. I don't go to Side B often. There's a procedure."

"A procedure?"

"The staff is different on that side. It's more restrictive. There's a guard outside each of the two entry points on this level. If I want to go there, I ask for an appointment and the staff lets me know if and when I can come over."

"Side B." He turned in its general direction, but they were still in the hallway and all that was visible were the walls surrounding them. One of the aides walked by them, giving them a curious look as she disappeared around a corner.

Claire wondered what he would do when he learned Heyward was being transferred to Side A. "I have to go. I can't help you anymore, Mr. Stone."

"Who can?"

"Dr. Freeson. Dr. Avanti. Any of the doctors on Side B, possibly. Depends on what you want."

"Have you talked to anyone about what happened?" he asked curiously.

His question took her aback. "You mean, have I talked to a professional?"

"A shrink seeing a shrink. Yeah."

"If you think I haven't been examined from top to bottom and inside out, then you don't know the thoroughness of this hospital. I assure you, I'm fit to work."

"You seem . . . tightly wound. I wouldn't want you for my shrink."

"Assuming you have one," she said, stung. "Which seems like an impossibility, given your reckless way of achieving your goals."

"I think I make you nervous."

"Yes. You do."

Claire forced herself to hold his gaze. She was no wimp,

but he was right. He made her nervous. Very nervous. He was one of those guys who sucked up space without even being aware of it. And he was on the warpath about his sister's death. He still was. No matter how he wanted to wrap it up.

"You found your way in, I'm assuming you can find your way out." She hoped he heard her dismissal.

"But don't follow you."

"Don't follow me," she agreed and headed down the hall to the gallery stairs, both relieved and a bit wary when she didn't hear him behind her.

Jesus H. Christ. Lang watched her go, aware that his nerves were standing at attention. He wasn't even sure what that all meant. She definitely sent him vibes that reached a sexual core, but she also was trying pretty damn hard to verbally shut him down, which only managed to piss him off.

She was meeting the Marsdons. It wasn't his business. Melody was dead and gone, and whatever happened to Heyward III was someone else's problem.

Bullshit.

A few hours ago he'd almost believed he was getting better, that this was becoming a bruise, not a death blow, to his soul. Now he felt the rush of frustration, anger, and a need for revenge like lava sluicing through his veins.

He let her get out of sight, around the corner, heading toward the gallery. They would probably gather in that same meeting room; he could visualize Granddaddy Marsdon's shock of white hair and pale, blue eyes. Marsdon Junior would be bored, his gaze purposely vague and sliding away after a brief touching on others. Lang didn't know which of them was the bigger bastard. Could be a tie.

He gave himself a moment, deciding what to do. This

wasn't his barbecue. He wasn't invited. But he was here and he had questions, a right to be heard, a need to face off.

To give himself time, he walked the other way, toward the north and the gate to Side B. His long strides ate up the carpet, and after a last turn and a switch from carpet to industrial vinyl flooring in a beige color, he came to locked double doors with a button and call box. He depressed the button, which opened a two-way transmission, and said, "Detective Langdon Stone."

A male voice replied, "Could you wait a moment?" Then after ten seconds, "Your name is not on the list."

There was a small window in one of the double doors. Lang could see a guard's station situated on the north end of the ten-by-ten space with a thick window. Maybe bulletproof. Another set of double doors identical to the ones in front of him opened on the other side of the station. The guard himself, a six foot–plus black man with shoulders that said he could've been a professional lineman, was looking through the glass of the guard's station to the small square of glass Lang was peering back through. They stared at each other.

"I'm not on the list," Lang said. "How do I get on?"

"You need a Halo Valley doctor's written permission."

"Okay."

"And a medical escort."

Lang nodded at the guard and turned away. The two-way transmission clicked off, regulated by the guard inside, apparently.

Not bad security, he thought. Not a prison. But not bad. The guard was probably armed and looked like he could handle about anything thrown his way.

Feeling slightly encouraged, Lang followed in the wake of Claire Norris and strode down the curved stairway from the gallery. His feet were wet and uncomfortable; his cowboy boots looked a lot dryer than his socks. His jacket was only slightly wet, but the black leather had taken a beating. His hair was nearly dry.

The patients who'd populated the main room had been moved elsewhere and several uniformed workers, aides, maybe, were setting a series of tables with plastic plates and flatware, serving platters of bread, while the scent of string beans and macaroni and cheese swept toward him. His stomach growled. He couldn't remember when he'd last eaten.

He wondered if he should look in a mirror and thought about ducking into the public restroom near the front desk when a black Town Car pulled up in front of the building and a driver in black slacks and sports coat stepped out, came around the vehicle, and opened the passenger door. Heyward Marsdon Sr. stepped out, balancing lightly on a black cane with a silver tip and curved handle. His son kicked open the door behind him and joined his father.

Lang felt some movement beside him and half-turned as Dr. Freeson hurried toward the door followed by a more sedate man. Another doctor, Lang assumed. Dark hair, swarthy good looks, a sense of power. What name had Claire thrown at him? Dr. Avanti. He would bet this was the man.

And then Claire herself appeared from the direction of the meeting room. The look she sent him was full of mixed emotions. She was not a happy camper.

Freeson was gushing, helping Marsdon Senior inside. "Let's all sit down for a few minutes while we get ready."

Granddaddy flicked a look at Lang, didn't recognize him, said in a gravelly voice to Avanti, "I want to see my grandson."

"We're bringing him over," Avanti said smoothly.

Lang couldn't believe his ears.

Claire rushed to say, "I thought we were going to him, as per protocol."

"As Heyward's being transferred here soon, we thought it would be a good idea to get him acclimated." Avanti made it sound like a directive.

Lang must have made a sound. Maybe a growl. He certainly felt like growling. Avanti turned to him, his nose in the air, as if he were scenting an enemy or maybe just practicing being the snobbish prick he obviously was.

Claire introduced him quickly and politely. "Dr. Avanti, this is Detective Stone, formerly of the Portland Police Department, soon of the Tillamook County Sheriff's Department."

Avanti's mouth dropped open. He blinked several times. "What . . . what . . . ?"

"He's investigating our Jane Doe's attack and trying to learn who killed her companion. He's here for that," Claire said.

"I don't need a disclaimer," Lang stated flatly, his gaze on Marsdon Senior.

"Who is this man?" Marsdon Senior said imperiously. He'd picked up on the tension but Melody's last name meant nothing to him.

But Marsdon Junior had it. He was standing behind his father and now put a hand on the older man's shoulder. "We didn't know Detective Stone would be here."

Freeson's face had paled, but Avanti turned on Claire. "No, we didn't know," he said in a voice barely above a snarl.

"You're moving him to this side of the hospital. That wasn't the court's decision," Lang snarled right back.

Avanti was trying to hurry Marsdon Senior to the meeting room, but he stood stubbornly in place. Lang stared at the old man in a kind of repressed fury as the room faded back, the faces of the growing crowd of employees disappearing. "You don't give a damn that your grandson slit my sister's throat."

Marsdon's eyes widened. "Oh."

"He's a killer, and all you want to do is set him loose."

"I am sorry for your loss, but he was ill." Marsdon Senior recovered his aplomb. "Off his medications, I understand. Something Dr. Norris should have seen." He slid her a crafty look.

"He'd missed appointments." Claire defended herself, flushing nevertheless.

"He shouldn't have been released!" Lang turned on her. "He should have been locked up before this happened!"

"There was no indication of hallucinations," Freeson jumped in. "We thought he was delusional, but not hallucinatory. We didn't know he was seeing things. He was supposed to be on his meds."

"Supposed to be." Lang had heard it all before. "He's still ill. He'll always be ill."

"You have no right to talk about my grandson as if you know him!" Marsdon Senior's face was turning red.

"Mr. Marsdon," Avanti said, stepping between the old man and Lang to defuse the escalating battle. But Marsdon was a feisty bastard and shook a hand at Avanti to get him to move out of the way. Unhappily, Avanti stepped to the side and shared a look with Marsdon Junior.

"You can't control him taking his medication," Lang said to the group at large. "That's the problem. He's dangerous."

"She asked for it, you know," Marsdon Senior stated tightly. "Your sister asked him to kill her."

"You bastard." Lang was stunned. This was new territory, and he thought he'd known the script by heart by this time.

"Ask Dr. Norris. She's the one who said so." He pointed his cane at her.

Claire put her hands up in front of her, equally stunned. "That's not what I said at all."

"You told the guard that's what she said."

"That's not what happened." Claire's voice was a whisper.

Marsdon Junior spoke up, "The security guard who came

to your aid said you were coherent and that Detective Stone's sister asked my son to kill her." His supercilious tone cut like a knife through the thick atmosphere.

"They were both in a state of high anxiety," Claire said. "Heyward was clearly delusional *and* hallucinating."

"What are you saying?" Lang demanded, his voice dangerous.

"Melody wasn't really understanding what Heyward was seeing. She didn't know what to say to him," Claire answered, hearing the desperation in her own voice and hating it.

"You're blaming my sister for him killing her?" Lang's ears rang.

"Heyward was off his meds. And apparently so was she," Claire said. "You want to talk about your sister, you need to check with her doctor. I was Heyward's, not hers."

"What were her words?" Lang demanded. "You were there. What did she say to him?"

"She said, 'Do it,'" Marsdon Junior told him. "She ordered my son to kill her, and he complied. I'm sorry, but that's what happened."

Lang saw through a haze of red. He was angry. Felt murderous. Knew he was out of control. "You're all crazy, asscovering bastards." His voice was far away. "You don't give a damn about anything."

He focused slowly on Claire, who was shaking her head. She looked angry, too, and something else. Scared, maybe. Did she think he was going to hurt her?

Screw 'em.

He strode past them all. Out the front doors, beneath the portico, into the incessant rain, and to his truck, waiting at the far end of the medical building's parking lot.

Chapter 10

Claire stood on her front deck and let the rain come at her in fits, wetting her cheeks, soaking her raincoat and jeans. It was somewhere after nine P.M. Tomorrow was Friday, and she planned to just limp through it and get ready for the weekend. She expected it to be noneventful. Nothing could be as bad as today.

Dinah had been home when Claire drove up her drive; Claire had seen the welcoming glow of yellow lamplight coming through the slits of her front blinds. She'd parked her car and walked up Dinah's drive, knocked on her door, and been greeted by Dinah, who wore her caftan and whose house smelled like some kind of musky incense mixed with cinnamon.

Claire had started weeping and Dinah had led her to a cushy chair, gently taken her raincoat, then gone to get a cup of herbal tea that Claire had cradled in her hands while she apologized for her breakdown for the next forty-five minutes.

Dinah brought her a bowl of vegetable soup with an Asian flavor and two pieces of thickly sliced wheat bread. Claire tried to do justice to the food but barely made a dent.

"What happened?" Dinah asked when Claire set the food aside and lay back in the chair, spent.

And it all came out. Stuff Claire would have expected from her patients, but not of herself. The dismal marriage. The miscarriages. The turning away of her colleagues. The shock of Heyward Marsdon's release. The blame of Melody Stone's death.

Dinah didn't say anything. She'd heard some of it before, and she just listened. When Claire finally got to the last scene at the hospital with the Marsdons and Langdon Stone, she made some kind of murmuring sound that penetrated Claire's purge.

"What?" Claire asked.

"You either deserve a medal or an intervention for putting up with those *doctors*. Why have you done it?"

"It's my job."

"You could have another job."

"Could I?"

"They've made you doubt yourself." Dinah shook her head. "That's shameful."

"Melody's brother thinks I blame her for her own death."

"No, he doesn't."

"You weren't there."

"Is he a complete Neanderthal?"

Claire drew a breath and let it out. "No."

"It was a volatile situation and things were said that shouldn't have been. It doesn't change anything."

Claire disagreed. "I should call him."

"I wouldn't do that right away," Dinah said wryly. "Unless you want more abuse."

"I need to talk to him."

"To explain what?" She cocked her head. "That this whole thing was a tragic falling of dominoes that has no real explanation? What would you tell yourself, if you were your patient? Would you recommend calling Langdon Stone?"

"No."

"Then why do you want to exonerate yourself so badly, when you know in advance it won't work?"

Now, hours later, Claire thought over her conversation with Dinah and also about her meeting with Heyward Marsdon III and his family, the first since *the incident*. She hadn't told Dinah all the ins and outs of that meeting; it was privileged, and even if it weren't, Claire hadn't really wanted to discuss it.

After Detective Stone left they regrouped and headed to Side B. They took the south entrance, which did not have a twenty-four-hour guard like the north, but was monitored with security screens by the north side guard during the evenings. Their images were clear on camera, and as soon as Avanti spoke into the microphone, a soft buzzing allowed him to open the door and they all trooped through into an anteroom with more overhead cameras. The second door was buzzed open as well and then they were walking down a corridor the same width and style as those on Side A. Claire knew the general layout of Side B. She just didn't spend a lot of time there.

The outdoor area, with high chain link fencing and razor wire, was neatly landscaped with low shrubbery and a large cement slab that offered up bolted-down plastic benches. Outdoor privileges were coveted, but this evening the sodium vapor lights barely made a dent in the oppressive rain and crowding cloud cover.

Claire had been in a fog, her brain still processing the scene with Stone. She'd thought it was bad when she'd been thrown to the wolves by the likes of Freeson and Avanti; seeing Langdon Stone's face full of revulsion in believing she was blaming Melody for goading Heyward . . . it was enough to make her stomach revolt. There was no explaining what had really happened. No way to put it in perspective without making it seem like she was making excuses for herself.

There were varying levels of incarceration and care on Side B, from the very restrictive and intense, to nearly as open and relaxed as Side A. Nearly, as anyone who ended up at Side B came there for one of two reasons: they were a danger to themselves or a danger to others, or both.

How strictly they were monitored depended a lot on the patient. Most of the inmates on Side B had committed egregious crimes. All were considered mentally unable to stand trial. Some were believed to be candidates for reentering society; others were disaffected lifers, unable to understand the most basic human emotion, intent upon destruction.

Heyward leaned to the less restrictive side. On his meds, he was a model patient. Claire knew she'd built up an aversion to him based on her own experience but had been unwilling to go see him. Now was the time, and at some level, she sensed it was a good thing she was so preoccupied with her anguish over what Langdon Stone thought of her; it kept her from making too much of this first meeting.

They walked past Heyward's room on their way to Side B's central meeting area, a much smaller area than Side A's, as fewer patients and staff were allowed that kind of freedom. Heyward wasn't in his room, which looked sparse but comfortable. His door was generally locked but, being under less restrictive care, he was allowed out for meals, therapy, and even some closely monitored interaction with other patients. Claire got a quick look inside as part of the tour that Avanti, and Side B's Dr. Jean Dayton, had coordinated as they continued to the central patient meeting area, a mirror-image location to Side A's morning room.

Heyward III was seated on a chair at a table, his attention directed through the window to the rain that was snaking in drizzles down the windowpanes and the drenched outdoor area beyond. He didn't turn as their group moved into the room.

"Heyward," his father said, trying to put a smile in his voice, though it sounded stiff.

He slowly turned around. He was twenty-eight but with a drawn expression and unfocused eyes that made him look closer to forty. Claire found herself holding her breath and expelled it quietly. Her heart was drumming in her chest. Her reactions were all from expectation, she realized, because seeing him was like opening a dam, letting her built-up resistance wash out in a rush. He was not a scary monster. He was sick. And lost.

His gaze traveled over the group and fell on Claire. "Dr. Norris?" he said with a note of hope.

"How are you doing, Heyward?" Her voice was steady. She told people on a regular basis to face their fears. She hadn't known hers were so intense, but they were insubstantial. She could almost see them floating away like cottonwood fluff.

"Where's Melody? She's okay. Tell me she's okay." He half-rose from the chair and Dr. Dayton crossed to him and soothingly reminded him of reality. His eyes beseeching Claire, he sank back down, defeated. Claire went to him on stiff legs and managed to say a few words of comfort about Melody, but clearly all he wanted was to hear she was alive, and Claire couldn't let him believe that delusion.

Marsdon Senior and Junior took turns saying hello to him, both of them clearly uncomfortable with the surroundings and Heyward himself. Ironically, Claire found herself keeping the conversation going as an intermediary, and eventually they all headed back to Side A.

"He shouldn't be there," Marsdon Senior declared, his bushy white eyebrows a drawn line about his fierce blue eyes.

"Their treatment isn't helping," Junior said.

"He responded to Dr. Norris," Avanti pointed out.

Neither Marsdon wanted to hear Claire had any influence on him whatsoever. She was a loose cannon, prone to her own independent thinking. To negate her, Marsdon Senior said, "He became more confused when Dr. Norris arrived."

"He's not processing Melody's death and his part in it," Claire responded. "Even on his meds. He's a long way from recovery."

They didn't want to hear *that*.

"When are you moving him?" Senior asked Avanti.

By this time they were facing the cameras on the south entrance of Side B, waiting for the doors to open. Avanti heard the buzzer and led them inside and to the opposite door before answering. "By the end of the month."

"Not good enough!" Senior declared.

"Can you give us a specific day?" Junior asked. It was clear he didn't care as much when the deed was done. If his father, Heyward's grandfather, weren't so adamant, Junior might let Heyward stay on Side B indefinitely.

The family dynamics were a study in power and selfishness. Claire wanted no part of them, but seeing Heyward had gotten to her. She was still convinced he should stay on Side B; his hallucinations weren't over and they were dangerous to everyone. But she found herself wanting to help him.

"I'll let you know when it will be as soon as I know," Avanti said as the door closed to the anteroom behind him and they were safely on Side A. Dr. Radke, the hospital's administrator, was there to meet them, and Marsdon Senior forgot about them at once and bent Radke's ear with Junior following along.

Avanti said to Claire, "Having Stone meet the Marsdons was irresponsible."

"Yes, I planned that to embarrass the hospital."

She stalked away from him, gathered her personal items, slopped through the rain to her Passat, and drove home, her head swirling equally with thoughts of Heyward III and Detective Langdon Stone.

Now Dinah's question floated across her mind. *Then why do you want to exonerate yourself so badly, when you know in advance it won't work?*

She couldn't answer that. In the overall scheme of things, Langdon Stone's opinion shouldn't matter. He wasn't unbiased. He wanted to blame someone for Melody's death. He thought she was using the ultimate cop-out, believing, in so many words, that Claire was saying Melody had asked for it. It was damn frustrating, not being able to explain the truth, but what good would it do her anyway? Closing her eyes, she gritted her teeth and sighed. Why did Stone's opinion matter so much when she didn't give a damn what her colleagues felt about her? What was it about him that got to her?

Lang stood under the shower for the second time that night. He'd driven home on automatic, thrown off his clothes, headed straight for the shower. The only reason he stopped was because he'd run out of hot water.

After dressing, he'd gotten back in his truck and headed to the nearest fast-food burger joint. He'd gone inside and eaten without tasting, then he'd returned to the house, watched ESPN until his eyes ached, then returned to the shower.

Now it was late and he was spent. He'd dozed and Melody had been with him. Half awake at times, he tried to imagine her goading Heyward Marsdon into slitting her throat, but the image was impossible to grasp.

But the influence of drugs . . . and Heyward's mental illness . . . it was a powerful and deadly combination.

His thoughts drifted to Claire Norris. She was taut and reserved and a psychiatrist. Anathema. She also had flawless skin, large dark eyes with thick lashes, nice ass and legs and breasts.

She tried too hard. Seemed locked in some kind of need to preserve order at all costs. Even when chaos was all there was. Something from her childhood? Job? The result of witnessing a death and having a knife's blade pressed into her neck enough to draw blood?

That last one would do anyone in.

But who the hell was she to blame Melody for her own murder?

Feeling exhausted, he headed to bed early, expecting to lie awake for hours but falling into his own comalike sleep, flat on his back.

Rita Feather Hawkings arrived at Halo Valley Security Hospital around ten P.M. and determined that the place was situated in a hellhole. In the middle of nowhere, about forty minutes from the coast, and sixty to Salem. There was nothing on this stretch of highway. Nothing. Until you were almost to Salem, and then there was a steakhouse that had exchanged its cowboy-chic decor for something clubbier. Dark, red leather circular booths. Even darker atmosphere only a blind man could travel without knocking a shin. Ice-cold martinis in sweating silver shakers.

Rita rarely drank liquor. Aunt Angela knew how to swill rotgut whiskey, gin, and what have you, then go prowling for a customer. She'd had herself a couple of kids. A little bit younger than Rita. Rita's cousins, but they were both gone now. Rita's mom believed it was payback for Aunt Angela's sins. All Rita knew was that their branch of the tree was withering without new life. New life that needed to be seeded in Rita's womb.

Tasha had stolen that from her.

Now Rita drove slowly up the long access road to the hospital. More sodium vapor lights. They tried to make the front of the place look like a resort with its tall portico and square columns. But Rita knew about the razor wire around the perimeter of the other side. The place for the real crazies. Killers, too.

Her eyes narrowed and she reached a hand in the side pocket of her driver's door. Her knife was there. The one she always carried. The one she'd taken to the rest stop. Oh, how she'd wanted to stab that bitch dead. She managed to get her in the shoulders but she'd come back fighting and then they were rolling on the ground. Rita wanted to stab her in the throat. Stab her dead. But she was worried about the baby. How long would it last after Tasha was dead? Rita had hesitated and then, and then . . .

Oh, Rafe!

A tear trickled down her face from each eye. *Rafe, oh, Rafe, oh, Rafe . . .*

It was Tasha's fault he was dead. Tasha's fault.

Rita parked away from the portico and adjusted her rearview mirror to see the front doors. There was a woman at the front desk with a small desk light switched on; the only illumination. The glass doors would undoubtedly be locked. She would have to get the woman's attention for access and she couldn't think of any kind of plausible reason why she would be there.

There were lights on in some of the rooms; some of the residents were still awake. Rita's eyes wandered across those rooms, wondering where the blond whore was being kept. She knew she would have to come back. Tomorrow. Her first of two days off.

Rita thought about that for a while, studied on it. A break from her job. A job she plodded through at her mother's insistence that she have a career. A job close to her home, a home she shared with her mother.

It wasn't a life she lived. It was a prison sentence. Rafe was all she'd had. Rafe. It should have been Rita running away with him, not that man-stealing bitch!

She whimpered and held her palms to her abdomen. Why wasn't Rafe's child inside her? Why was Tasha carrying it?

She had to have the baby. The baby inside Tasha was Rita's. Rita Feather Hawkings's.

She could almost cry over the unfairness of it all. Rita needed *that* baby! Rafe's baby. Rafe and Rita's baby, not that pale little whore who—

A man appeared inside the hospital, heading toward the glass front doors, saying something to the woman at the desk as he reached them. He hesitated and she must have pushed a button that electronically unlocked the doors because he strode outside and the receptionist pushed the button again, the doors sliding shut behind him, shivering a little when they reached their endpoint. Some kind of locking mechanism. Huh.

The man was dark, somewhere in his forties, too old for Rita. He kept on striding to a black Lexus whose surface must've been waxed to a high gloss 'cause the rain just ran off it in sheets.

He was a doctor, she realized, though she had no real way of knowing. Just a feeling. And he sure as hell thought he was hot shit. Somebody important? In the overhead light while he fired the engine she examined the back of his head. She liked his neck. Strong.

Maybe he wasn't too old . . . maybe . . .

Switching on her ignition, Rita backed out of her spot slowly, waiting till the man in the Lexus was just a set of red taillights down the entry lane. She nosed along behind him, catching him turning east onto the county highway toward Salem and I-5. Probably lived in the valley. She hesitated. She should really turn right to the coast and her own bed. But he'd looked . . . important.

Licking her lips, she turned east and followed after him through the drowned night, wipers slapping angrily at the rain, her agile mind working on scenarios. He was *some-one* at Halo Valley. The girl at the desk had practically fallen all over herself trying to get that door open.

She wasn't surprised when he pulled into the club-type steakhouse, which was still about ten miles away from the interstate. A man like him wanted something good before he went home. A drink. A succulent piece of red meat. Maybe some company.

Rita felt all her hormonal juices slip through her system. Didn't happen that often with old guys, but once in a while one of 'em could warm her up to a simmer. Once in a great while she could even boil.

The place was called Vandy's and it let you know in scripted red neon along top its low-peaked shake roof. There was an assortment of pickups and trucks, some Ford and Chevy sedans, and a few expensive foreign cars, her guy's Lexus, a couple of Mercedes, and a white convertible BMW getting pounded by rain that Rita bet was leaking in under its canvas roof.

Rita parked her rusted bucket of bolts along one side, away from the front, away from the only light in the parking lot. Didn't want her quarry to see her climbing out of such a sadly cared-for vehicle. She would have liked to have been driving in his polished black Lexus. Looked like a car for a money man. A doctor.

She pulled a tube of frosted pink lipstick out of her purse and ran it over lips that felt fatter than normal, hotter.

She was getting herself all pumpy. Could feel a wetness inside her. The Fertility Goddess sending her a message.

Popping the trunk, Rita climbed outside, into the

damned precipitation, and hurried to haul out a suitcase. Quickly, she threw it in the backseat, climbed in after it. Yanking out a black, clingy dress, she shook it free of wrinkles, then ripped off her teal scrubs and changed clothes. The shoes inside the case had four-inch heels. Hooker shoes, Delores would have railed had she seen them, but Rita took care not to have her mother, whose knees were bad and who didn't move as well as she once had, find her outfits.

She paused for a faint moment, thinking of Rafe, broken inside. For him, she'd given up her trolling. He'd been *the one*. She'd known they were meant for each other, meant to have babies together.

But Rafe had died. His betrayal, his fascination with— Rita would not think of it as love—Tasha had killed him.

Rita had not stabbed him. That wasn't her. She would never do that. No, his evil whore had killed him. Or maybe Fate had stepped in. It had not been Rita Feather Hawkings. She loved him too much.

Except her body was all loose and hot and willing now and she hurried through the rain, sidestepping puddles, balanced on her heels. She pushed through the doors and smelled the scent of broiled steaks and garlic and heard the sound of country western music, kept low except for some pulse-thumping bass.

Stepping past the maitre d's stand, she stood at the edge of the main dining area for a moment, taking in the red leather booths, most of them empty. Then she turned toward the bar, which was blocked by a wall of rough-hewn boards, and up two oak steps into a room with more booths tucked into the edges, a grouping of bistro tables on dark carpet ringing an oak dance floor where no one was currently dancing, and a long bar with glittering bottles under soft lights.

Her quarry was seated in the center of the bar. A couple

sat on one end, a group of three women on the other. Rita assessed the situation with a predator's eye. She walked up to the seat next to him and brushed rain from her dress, catching the bartender's eye. "Rum and Coke," she told him, then adjusted the line of her dress, making sure her cleavage was at its soft, billowy best, before seating herself beside the dark-haired man.

He was studiously ignoring her, his eyes trained on the bottles in front of him, his and her reflection glowing in the mirror opposite them. She slid a glance across to him, wondering if she could meet his gaze, but he was determined to pretend to ignore her. Because he was pretending. She could feel his attention even though he tried to disguise it.

"Wet night," she said to the bartender as he brought her drink. Rita smiled and drank lustily. Though she wasn't fond of alcohol, men at bars were leery of women who completely abstained.

"Really wet," the bartender agreed, his gaze lingering on her cleavage.

"Like a monsoon."

The man on the seat beside her was slowly turning his drink around and around on the bar with his right hand. Every so often he would lift it and take a gulp. Though he'd gotten inside the place about ten minutes before her, she suspected it was his second drink. He didn't want to go home just yet.

Perfect.

Rita closed her eyes and started softly humming to the current song coming through the speakers, something by Garth Brooks, she thought. She slowly opened her eyes and caught him just turning aside. He'd been looking at her.

"You're a doctor, aren't you?" she said.

Now he gave her a full-on stare. "Do I know you?"

"I'm a nurse at Ocean Park. But I've been to Halo Valley Security Hospital. That's where you work, right?"

"You've been to Halo Valley?"

"Very nice facility."

"And you're a nurse."

Rita Feather Hawkings was both slow and smart. Slow when it came to working in complex social situations— like dealing with women. Smart when it came to sex and men. "Yes," she said. "I'm Rita."

"I'm Paolo." He was reluctant to say it. Reluctant to give away his name. It took an effort. But it was like the first crack in the dike; it would grow faster and easier with time. Very little time by the way his eyes goggled over her boobs.

Rita was feeling very, very wet. "What's your specialty, Paolo?"

"That's a leading question, if I've ever heard one." He smiled, showing even, white teeth.

"Are you someone important at Halo Valley? You look important."

He glanced around. "Want to move to a booth?"

For an answer she slid her drink from the bar and swung ahead of him from her seat.

It was only a matter of time now before she had him inside her.

Bam!

Tasha's eyes flew open. She was lying in a bed in a strange room, and rain and wind were slamming against her window. The limbs of a hedge were waving madly, as if trying to get her attention.

Bam! Bam! Bam! They slammed against her window.

Where am I? she thought fearfully, her hands clutching the bedsheets.

Her gaze shot to her wrists. No shackles. Her heartbeat was so hard she could see her chest rise and fall.

She'd been dreaming, she realized, recalling fragments. Something bad had happened and she'd been blamed. Again. And instead of listening to her, they'd bound her to the bed with leather straps. They were horrible to her. Jealous. Mean. Her sisters. Catherine. Horrible.

She turned on her side, squeezing her eyes shut, and felt something move inside her. One hand curved over her hospital gown and under her protruding abdomen. A baby?

How?

How long had she been asleep?

What did she last remember?

She closed her eyes, tried to recall, felt a familiar, age-old blockage to her own thoughts and forced herself to relax. It was better to just let herself go to that twilight place, somewhere between the here and now and the world of dreams. She'd had to escape there ever since she was a little girl. Ever since she was old enough to realize she was in a prison of women.

There was Catherine, of course. She pretended to be your friend, to have your best interests at heart, but she really only wanted control. She'd gotten rid of someone, an evil being, whom she blamed for everything that had gone wrong in their world. Tasha believed it was her real mother, but no one wanted her to know the truth. She was deliberately kept in the dark, deliberately kept away from their secret meetings. Oh, but she'd seen them. Before she was old enough to make them worry, she'd pressed her eyes to a crack in the door and watched them carry candles to the upper attic, wearing their long dresses, their hair swinging to their hips. An army of angels, but they weren't angels.

Before the evil being was banished, there were different rules. Dangerous behavior that worried Catherine and the disciples. Tasha, too, was a disciple and she went along with them, believed in them, until she saw past the wrought-iron gates to another world. It came as a shock to learn that they were the oddity. Outsiders called them a cult. Some had even named them: The Colony. And the name of their home, their lodge, was Siren Song, though where that came from had never been completely explained.

There were rules everywhere. Rules for waking. Rules for washing. Rules for eating. Talking. Working. Praying.

By the time Tasha was seven she started doubting the rules. Too wise and old to meekly abide, she'd stood against them. Too naive and young to understand there was no other side but theirs, she'd been contained to her room. Shackled. Prayed at. Even by the Indian man considered a shaman by his people and maybe by Catherine and the disciples as well.

He'd scared Tasha. Lying on her bed. Helpless. He'd swept in like a fog and leaned over her, his face lined by age, maybe by a hard life. He mumbled something, maybe in a native tongue, maybe just gibberish. Terrified, she felt him touch her forehead with a cool, dry palm.

Whatever he was supposed to accomplish didn't happen. Tasha felt the same. Always felt the same. But the one thing she learned was to lie, to pretend. She couldn't fake an epiphany; she'd never had one. But she could pretend to slowly come about to their way of thinking.

They believed in God. They believed in Indian spirits, later changed to Native American, as Catherine, one of the only ones allowed outside the gates and who was friendly with the Foothillers, became enlightened to a new political correctness. The disciples all followed, but Tasha sensed they were all playing at belief and rightness. They didn't *feel* it.

And then there was the other doctor, whose hands had strayed some. She hadn't told about him. She'd kept her own counsel. And, by being patient and keeping her mouth shut, she gleaned information. She learned by chance that the gates had not always been closed to the disciples. One or two had been given away as babies. One or two had run away. One or two had been allowed to come and go, work in the neighboring town of Deception Bay.

Then the gates had closed. Catherine had disallowed anyone to leave. Tasha did not know why, and none of the disciples seemed to really know, either.

Except dull, wheelchair-bound Lillibeth, who believed they were imprisoned because of their mother, Mary. "Catherine's worried she'll put a curse on us," Lillibeth whispered one night in a squeak of fright. "Another one! Worse than the last one!"

"Catherine's our mother," Tasha blurted out without thinking. Her rule was get information, don't give it out.

But Lillibeth was too alarmed to hold back. "Mary is our mother. Catherine is her sister, our aunt. Mary was cursed with a sickness that made her crazy. She never knew right from wrong. She slept with many men. Catherine is trying to keep us safe. We all are cursed, but Catherine can help us." Upon which she began ululating like she suffered from the craziness she claimed they all possessed.

Her revelations made Tasha ask questions. Careful questions. She didn't want to seem too eager to learn. But Catherine saw more than she should. She turned her sharp blue eyes on Tasha, and it felt like a beam of intense heat that burned through the small white lies and down to Tasha's core truth.

"What are you planning?" Catherine accused.

"I just want to know about my mother," Tasha answered right back.

"Your mother made a pact with the devil, who filled her with lust. She dropped you children like a she-cat drops kittens. She slept with every tom. She made only one good decision: she asked me to take care of you all."

"Where is she?"

"She's dead."

"She's not dead." Tasha knew it like she knew many things she didn't understand. "Why are you lying?"

"She has to stay away from you for your own salvation."

Catherine would say no more and Lillibeth suffered a minor ostracism for confiding in Tasha and would speak of Mary no more. Tasha was the outsider. Always the outsider. She lived her days in a kind of ritualistic haze. A woman, part Native American, came in and taught with Catherine overseeing. Tasha learned to read and write, and she had a grasp of mathematics that seemed to alert Catherine to some new problem.

"Manipulation," Catherine said one night when Tasha awoke screaming from a dream. "You learn very quickly."

The dream still hanging on raggedly, Tasha said without thinking, "Like my mother."

"Just like your mother."

Catherine left and Tasha recalled the dream. Her body was tingling. Alive. She wanted to touch herself all over.

So this was the curse. Sex, she learned later. Desire.

Now Tasha lay breathing hard on the bed, staring out the window, hearing the whistle of the wind. Sex . . . desire . . . she must have experienced both, because how else was she pregnant? She knew about pregnancy. The teacher lady had waddled in right before she had her baby, and all the disciples were wide-eyed and excited. Therein followed a lesson on childbirth that had made Tasha feel slightly ill on the one hand, and worry desperately that she would never experience it on the other. How could she? Locked inside those cold walls.

She had to get out. She had to find a life to live.

Had to, had to, had to . . .

She saw now that she'd found a way out. This place, wherever she was, was not Siren Song. She had a life inside her. With exploring fingers, she slipped under her nightgown and felt the taut-skinned mound.

And there were scabs. Something . . . what?

Drawing up the gown, she gazed through the dim, nearly nonexistent light from the window, at her belly. Lines. Scratched across her.

Death lines.

She began shivering like she was about to explode. Scrabbling for the covers, she pulled them to her chin and lay beneath them, quaking furiously.

Help me, she thought. *Help me.*

I have to get out of here.

Help me!

Rita sat astride Paolo as if she were riding a bucking bronco. He lay beneath her and grabbed her breasts and humped upward and sweated and made a lot of *huh, huh, huh* sounds and then started screaming, "Baby, baby, oh, baby . . ." And that made Rita think about needing a baby and all her wetness started drying up and she worried that Paolo was too old. His chest hair was thick and graying, far more than the hair on his head, but maybe he used one of those products.

Still . . .

"C'mon," she whispered against his ear. It was kind of off-putting, the little hairs that sprouted out like wires against her lips. *"C'mon."*

"Baby . . ." He was breathing like he was going to have a heart attack. "Baby . . ."

Maybe she should be on the bottom, not the top. She needed to hang on to his sperm, if, and when, he finally gave her some.

"C'mon!"

"Huh, huh, huh."

"Come . . . on."

"Baby. Oh, baby! Ahhhh!"

And finally, there it came. Rita squeezed down hard, then slipped off him. She hoped she hadn't made a mistake by getting on top.

"Hey," he said, after a couple of minutes of getting his breathing under control. He slid his fingers lightly up and down her arm. "When I woke up this morning, I sure didn't know this was going to happen."

"Let's make sure it happens again," she said.

"Want to make another date?"

Rita wondered if it was the right time to ask for a job, decided it wasn't, and leaned into him, reaching a hand down to start stroking his shaft. She didn't have a lot of time. Tasha could be out of Halo Valley before she knew it. "How about tomorrow?"

"Same time, same place?"

"Can you get off earlier?"

He stared into her eyes. He was halfway to being her complete slave. Rita had seen the signs before. "Yes."

"See you at six?"

"Yes . . ." He closed his eyes and she examined the skin along his jawline. A little tough-looking. A little old.

If she couldn't get a baby out of this old fart, she was pretty sure she could get a job. But maybe she could get both.

Chapter 11

Lang drove west on Highway 26 and south on 101 into Deception Bay. The town was built on both sides of the highway and was like so many small, coastal Oregon beach towns, dotted with a few quaint restaurants and a couple of tired ones that looked as if they only survived on the good grace of a few dedicated locals. There was one gas station and one grocery store, the Drift In Market, if you didn't count the snack wall behind the gas station cash register. Just off the rocky coastline was an abandoned lighthouse, the squatter's home to a nutcase who'd killed a number of women and who was also incarcerated at Halo Valley Security Hospital. Beyond the lighthouse was a small island, as rocky and inhospitable as the cliffs along most of the shoreline. Lang felt like he knew some history about the island but it escaped him at the moment. He thought he should do a little Internet research, or maybe he could learn more from the locals.

But today he was looking for Cade Worster.

About a half mile farther he turned onto the two-lane blacktop road that led east toward the Coast Range foothills and, he hoped, some answers. He'd called Tanninger and had a talk with him about what he was doing, and also brought up his soon-to-be job with the Tillamook County Sheriff's Department. Of everything Lang said, it was Deception Bay Tanninger had focused on.

"Deception Bay," he repeated, sounding surprised.

"What?"

"Nothing. My girlfriend has ties to Deception Bay. Never heard of that town till a year ago."

Lang had sensed a lot of unspoken information in the man's voice and had probed around, not letting Tanninger off the hook, though he seemed to be instantly sorry he'd said anything.

Finally, he admitted, "Gemma's been looking into her own history. She was adopted, but her birth mother's from that area of the coast, apparently. She's been looking for her."

"Did she find her?"

"No. Could be a woman in a care facility around there whose mind's not tracking and hasn't been for a while."

"So she's not a Foothiller?"

"I hadn't heard that term till you said it."

His tone was so careful, as if he were vigilant about every word. Like there were dangers, minefields, that he had to step around. "For Pete's sake. What is it you're not telling me?" Lang demanded.

"Nothing. Nothing that's related to your investigation, anyway."

Lang recalled Curtis telling him that there was still some mystery surrounding Tanninger's girlfriend, so maybe this was it, but he agreed that it was merely a sidebar to his own interest in the area. "You want me to ask around about your girlfriend? Gemma?"

"God, no. Gemma's on that all on her own. Just let me know how it turns out with Worster."

"If I find him."

So now Lang was heading east toward the mountains,

driving down a corridor with tall Douglas firs on either side, waving limbs dashing rain at his window in fits. It was less stormy than yesterday, but that wasn't saying a hell of a lot. Eleven o'clock in the morning, and threatening clouds made it feel like night was approaching.

Tim Rooney was right, Lang realized as the road opened up to the Foothillers' community's sloping fields and gravel streets, which formed squares, the residences built like 1950s ramblers on block after block, some of them having been updated and remodeled, improved and/or bastardized depending on your way of thinking.

Lang first drove by the address Rooney had given him and saw that the place looked abandoned. Weeds had grown up in the drive, which was two ruts dug through gravel. No one answered his knock on the front door, and when he walked around the back, it was more of the same. He glanced around the area, but there was an overall feeling of desertion along the whole block. Maybe they were at work. Maybe there was simply no one around.

He drove around some more and came to what could be considered the main drag. There was a pharmacy, of sorts, that doubled as a liquor store. In Oregon, hard liquor was regulated by the Oregon Liquor Control Commission, the OLCC, and was only available at businesses with a proper license. But beer and wine were available at any grocery store, and down the street could be purchased at a general store that sported an honest-to-goodness hitching post in front. It was more for show than anything else as trucks, smaller pickups, and a few older-model American cars vied for space every which way in front of the place. He could hear music coming from the back, some shitkicker country song that he couldn't make out the words, only the mournful tone of loss in the man's warbling voice. Though he wore cowboy boots as a habitual part of his dress code since he'd left the department, country music wasn't

Lang's thing. He knew a few crossover artists who'd managed to find their way to pop music, but even there he was iffy. So, though he half-looked the part as he strode through the general store that occupied the front of the building, then past the café in between, and finally into the tavern at the rear, he was definitely a fish out of water.

Especially when about a dozen Native American faces turned his way, regarding him with serious suspicion. And he didn't think that was wine or beer being served up in old-fashioned glasses, though the bartender did an admirable job of sleight of hand, switching out beers for whiskey and bourbon.

"What can I do you for?" the bartender asked him. He wore a black shirt and faded blue jeans and cowboy boots.

Lang didn't waste time trying to win their allegiance. They looked at him like he was the enemy, so no amount of bullshitting was going to lower their defenses. "I'm looking for someone who may be able to help solve a homicide."

"Homicide." One of the men, whose hair was short, a thick, steel gray, and whose face was as weathered and red-hued as pine bark, straightened in his chair. He sat at a small table near the back door with a younger man.

"A man was knifed to death at a rest stop off Highway 26."

"Who you lookin' for, boy?" This from a man who couldn't have been much older than Lang himself. He wore a lumberjack's plaid flannel shirt and jeans that looked like they'd been outside working since the day they were sewn. His boots were mud-caked and came up nearly to his knees.

"Cade Worster."

"Cade!" The first man shook his gray head. "Well, you won't find him, that's for sure. He don't stay in one place long enough to leave tracks. But he ain't your man, if that's what you're thinkin'. He's a thief, for sure. But he ain't no killer."

"He coulda killed somebody by mistake, Gordon," the

second man said to the first. "If he got caught stealin' from 'em, and they caught him at it."

"It doesn't appear to be that," Lang said. "Looks like Cade stole a truck from a farmer in Tillamook."

"Rooney?" Gordon asked.

Lang was surprised they knew so much. "Rooney says Cade took his truck about a year ago. Cade might not be the killer, but could he be the victim?"

"Cade? No." The second man shook his head. "He was walkin' around yesterday."

"Walkin', 'cause he sold that pile of shit to his cousin." The younger man sitting with Gordon spoke up for the first time.

"Cade sold Rooney's truck?" Lang asked.

Gordon said, "Well, it ain't really a sale. He loaned it to him."

The second man said, "Well, it ain't really a loan 'cause it wasn't his truck in the first place."

"Who's this cousin?" Lang asked.

"You with the sheriff's department?" the younger man asked. "You don't dress like you are."

"I've taken a job with them," Lang said. "Haven't got the dress code down yet. Who's Cade's cousin?"

"Rafe." Gordon shook his head. "Rafe Black Bear."

"Rafe's father was a fuckin' asshole, rest his soul." The second man looked back at Gordon, who nodded soberly.

"Killed hisself by mistake," Gordon said. "Got drunk, got a little too friendly with Tommy-John's widow, got shot in the heart with a twenty-two."

"Suicide by stupidity," the younger man said. "You can check with the sheriff. Happened a coupla years ago."

"I'm more interested in Rafe," Lang said. "Has anyone seen him around lately?"

They all looked at each other, but no one answered. Lang could see the realization dawn on them.

"Not Rafe." The younger man stood up sharply, knocking the table with his knee.

"I have a picture of the victim in my truck," Lang said. "Could one of you look at it and see if it's Rafe?"

"Cade's his next of kin," Gordon said. "Let him do it."

"I don't know where Cade is," Lang responded.

"He's at home. We just didn't know you, so we didn't want to give him up," the second man said. "You need the address?"

"I was just there," Lang protested. "There's nobody home."

"He's there. Go talk to him." Gordon motioned for Lang to go back out the way he'd come in. "And remind Sheriff O'Halloran, when you see him, that Cade's a good man. Don't wanna keep him locked up too long."

Lang walked back through the café and the general store and into watery sunshine filtering through fast-drifting clouds. For the first time in days there was a break in the rain. Maybe that meant something.

Friday morning. Appointments till noon, then nothing. Claire's attention was shot and it was harder than normal to listen to her outpatient clientele regale her with their fears, concerns, and general discontent. Mostly she was in the moment. Today she felt like she was on another planet.

Jamie Lou Breene was her last appointment, and she looked far worse for wear than she had at their last meeting. There was a bruise on her cheek that was turning green and yellow, and her hair was unwashed and lank.

"What happened?" Claire asked straight out.

"I got arrested!"

"Oh, Jamie Lou, why didn't you call me?"

"I called Barry, okay? He came and got me." She closed her eyes and looked like she was going to cry.

Then she proceeded to tell Claire a story of how John, her current lover, had left her for someone younger with fake boobs, and how she'd kicked the little whore in her big butt, and how she'd then stolen John's car and ended up being chased down by the police, landing in the Clackamas County jail. Barry was Jamie Lou's ex, and she was lucky he'd come to her rescue, which Claire told her in no uncertain terms.

"Barry only cares about himself," Jamie Lou said. "I was at the jail for hours before he showed. Look at me. He kicked me out of the house!"

Claire said, "He's your ex-husband. You don't live with him. You're lucky to have him in your life at all, tenuous as the bond is."

"You always take his side. Always!"

"Someday you are going to have to take responsibility for your own actions, Jamie Lou."

"What was I supposed to do? John was banging this stupid whore the whole time we were together. I just wanted to kill her." She started weeping violently.

"Jamie Lou, we've talked about this. It's a pattern, one you don't want to break, or even recognize. You like being a victim. And you like being the center of attention to the point of self-destruction. That's what you're looking for. It's what you're always looking for. John is only your latest means to star yourself in the Jamie Lou show."

Although Claire's diagnosis was really nothing new, it was the first time she'd been so final. To date, she'd led Jamie Lou down paths of self-recognition, trying to elicit her own words of ownership to her misdeeds. To date, that hadn't worked worth a damn, and Claire's patience, usually so long, was gone.

"I love John," she said stubbornly.

"You physically fought with a woman he was seeing, stole his car, and ended up in jail."

"I'm saying I love him!"

Claire inclined her head. "Do you think we're making progress together? Are these sessions helping you?"

"No! You're just like the rest of them."

"I'd like to help you, Jamie Lou. I really would. But you enjoy making me part of the problem as well."

"Well, then, let's quit this. How about that?"

"The object of these sessions is to help you change your self-destructive behavior, but you make your therapist part of the process. There's you, there's the current lover who eventually leaves you for someone else, and there's me."

"We can quit right now."

Claire gazed at her for long moments, assessing her sincerity. With Jamie Lou, it was hard to tell. Finally she said, "We'll make another appointment. Stay away from John and men like him. Don't rely on your ex-husband. How's your job?"

She worked at a grocery store in the Salem area and had managed to hang on to it throughout her trials, mainly because the manager was a recovering alcoholic who had taken her on as a personal mission.

"I'm still working."

"Good. Stay on your meds. Next time we'll see."

"You're a hard-hearted bitch," she declared.

"So I've been told," Claire said dryly. "Go do something positive, Jamie Lou. Start putting one foot in front of the other."

There was no one at Cade Worster's abode; it was just as abandoned as it had been earlier. Lang climbed back in his Dodge and fiddled with the truck's radio, finally finding a station that came in with bang-up clarity, though it was country-western.

He wondered if he'd been shined on by the men in the

bar. He'd got the sense they were playing with him a little, but that was okay. Part of the game. But he didn't think they'd completely led him wrong. If Rafe Black Bear was the dead man, and he was Cade's cousin, then Lang needed more than an identification anyway. He needed background on Rafe, maybe a clue to who blond Cat was.

Still . . . an hour went by. Lang watched a hawk glide by overhead and land on a post at the far end of the block. Beyond was a field with a house on the far side, maybe several. He suspected there were more houses buried inside the massive tangles of Scotch broom that rimmed the west end of the field, running parallel to the coastline, but it was hard to tell as the hardy plant was greedily taking over the farmland as fast as it could. If somebody didn't root it out, and soon, there would be little land for planting left, if that's what the Foothillers used it for.

The hawk rose up and up, then suddenly dived down, coming away with some small creature in its talons that made Lang grimace. Goddamn nature. He might dress somewhat country but he was a city boy at heart. He'd much prefer chasing a perp down a smelly, rat-habituated alley than across a piece of grassland filled with any manner of cute little critters whose intentions might be a whole lot more deadly than any garbage-seeking rat. And this hawk thing . . . danger from the sky? No thanks.

Lang was about to give up when he saw in his rearview a guy walking up in a green army jacket, jeans, and work boots and carrying a pizza box. He'd bought it at the general store, Lang guessed, as it was the only game in town. If so, it was one of those cheapo pizzas with a crust as hard as asphalt and barely enough pepperoni to call it nonvegetarian; he'd seen a couple of those under heat lights on his way to the café.

If this was Cade, he'd shown up at the general store after Lang's meeting with the men in the bar, though he didn't appear to know anyone was looking for him. He was just shuffling along, sorta tired-like.

Lang let him get to his house, watched him fumble for a key, slide it into the lock. Shoving a shoulder against his stubborn driver's door, Lang stepped out of the truck as Cade passed inside. He loped across the street, reaching the porch about fifteen seconds after Cade closed the door behind him.

Lang rapped lightly, then took a step back.

"Yeah?" he heard from inside. A suspicious voice.

"Cade Worster?" he called back.

Silence.

Damn it. He should have stopped him before he went inside. He'd just been afraid that Worster might run. Why, he couldn't say. It had just seemed that way, and now—

Slam!

The back door crashed against the house. Lang jumped off the porch, ran around the side of the house, and got to the rear just in time to see Cade Worster beating feet down the gravel road behind the house and heading for the open field.

Well. God. Damn.

Lang took off after him, hoping to high heaven he didn't break an ankle on the uneven ground ahead.

Halo Valley looked different during the daylight, Rita determined. More hospital-like, less inviting, and if you got a view of that razor wire, well . . . the place was a damn prison.

She hoped to hell it was easier to get someone out than it looked.

She was wearing black slacks and a peach-colored blouse that hugged her maybe a tad too closely around the breasts, so she'd opted for a black cardigan. It was her Take

Me Seriously outfit and she pretty much hated it, but whatcha gonna do?

Looking around the parking lot, she didn't immediately see Paolo's car. Paolo Avanti, that was his name. Dr. Paolo Avanti. Not that much in the mattress department, really, though he sure thought he was. She wondered idly if he was married. He hadn't said so, but there was something rusty about him, like his dick might not get much of a workout. *She'd* certainly given him that last night. Woke him up but good.

A quick tour around the lot convinced her the Lexus wasn't there, and as she was thinking that over, the car itself pulled into the lot and slammed to a halt in one of the reserved spots. She stepped behind an SUV, screening herself, and watched Paolo hurry inside. He looked sort of stern. Maybe he was late. It was damn near two o'clock in the afternoon, but she didn't really think he had working-stiff hours. Still, it was kind of hard when you were trying to make an impression on other employees, something she'd sensed from some of his conversation the night before.

Not that he'd told her much. But something had gone down because his cell phone had rung and though he hadn't wanted to take the call, he'd glanced at the number, thought about it for a moment, then answered tersely, "Avanti." A pause and Rita had whispered, "I'll be in the bathroom," but then had been able to close the bathroom door and reopen it a crack without him noticing as he was standing by the door of the Salem hotel room. His back was to her anyway, like that would close her out. Hah.

"She's coming around. She was affected by Heyward," he said. "She knows the change'll be good for him." Another pause, longer. "Stone's a dick, in more ways than one. I don't know how he got there, but there's no reason for him to come back. I'll call the sheriff's department myself. No. I'll make her do it. Finish this damn thing. I'm sorry we ever got Jane Doe, but that was her fault, too!" Another pause while he listened, then, "I'll take care of it tomorrow. We may have to do something. I don't feel like having Pauline Kirby around anymore, either. She's done all she can for us, whether she knows it or not. Yeah. . . ." And then he snapped the cell phone closed.

Now, as she walked to the front desk, Rita had a blinding moment of realization that caused her head to hurt. She'd understood that Jane Doe was Tasha, but she now also understood that "have to do something" might mean moving Tasha out of Halo Valley. She needed this job. She needed it today. There was no time to waste with the whole human resources department. She had to leapfrog in.

"I have an appointment with Dr. Avanti," she said.

"He just arrived," the girl said, eyeing Rita with some surprise. "I'll page his office, but I'm not sure he's there yet."

"I'll wait."

She found a seat on a chair across from a love seat, a grouping intended to make the front lobby more intimate and inviting. Glancing over, she saw a number of patients meandering around another room that looked suspiciously open to this room. How did they keep those crazies in check?

And then she saw the blond hair. In a chair, facing the TV. Some kid who looked kind of retarded was talking to her but Rita didn't think she was responding. Of course not. She'd been in a coma, or something. Maybe still sort of was. She'd seen that kind of thing before. They were there, but they weren't. Eyes open but the rest was shut down.

It was her! The blond bitch! *Tasha!*

Her heart started pounding. What if Tasha saw her? What then?

She had to leave. Had to get out now.

Had to!

She stood up, intending to tell the girl at the desk that

she had another appointment and couldn't wait, but the retard suddenly turned Tasha's chair around, gesturing right at Rita.

"Go!" he said. *"Go on!"*

Tasha stared at Rita and Rita stared at Tasha. Both frozen. Each waiting for the other to make a move. In despair, Rita realized she'd left her knife in the car.

Tasha gazed toward the front doors. Gibby flailed his arms and did his bestest to get her to take this chance. "You can *go!*" he cried. "You need help!"

Darlene was suddenly there. And Donald.

Donald said, "You must calm down, Gibson."

"Donald, let me handle this," Darlene said with an edge.

"You're a bitch with a capital—" Gibby sputtered.

"Gibby, you have to leave Cat alone," Darlene said. "Every time you do this, you know what happens."

"Nooooo!!!!"

He held his arms out to Cat. "She needs help! She said so!"

"We'll get the wheelchair and take her back to her—"

"She can walk!" Gibby eased away from Darlene and Donald, beseeching the girl in the chair. "Show them, Cat. Show them what you can do!"

Donald looked concerned. "Should we contact Dr. Norris? Perhaps some Thorazine is needed?"

"We don't need to medicate him," Darlene said shortly. "Gibby, stop speaking for Cat."

"She wants me to!"

"Haldol?"

"Donald . . ."

Darlene looked like she was going to pop a blood vessel. That's what Thomas said. Pop a blood vessel. Gibby glanced over at McAvoy, who stood with his arms folded, watching them. "You know!" Gibby screamed at him. "You've seen her move!"

"She walks with help. We all know," Darlene snapped. "Try to refocus."

"What's going on?" a male voice snapped.

Gibby gazed around and saw that the dark-haired doctor with the scowl had approached. He didn't come around much. He just shook hands with men in suits, mostly.

"We're redirecting, Dr. Avanti," Darlene said. She pretended to be nice, but Gibby was pretty sure she wanted to pop a blood vessel, too.

Dr. Avanti glanced toward the outside doors and his whole body seemed to jerk. He was looking at a dark-haired lady who was staring down Cat. Gibby realized Cat was staring back.

"Who is she?" he asked, rushing to Cat's side. "Who is she!"

Chapter 12

Oh, holy mother . . .

Rita felt like she was in slow motion. She saw that bitch's eyes and she wanted to claw them out. But Tasha could finger her, and she couldn't have that.

There was a commotion. The retard was yelling; the staff was trying to hush him. Rita tried to turn away just as Paolo Avanti, alerted by the front desk, came into the room, scowling, looking slightly alarmed.

"What's going on?" he demanded.

"We're redirecting, Dr. Avanti," the heavyset nurse answered.

And then Paolo's gaze met Rita's and she saw the flash of remembrance of their lovemaking cross his brain. It was powerful, and if she hadn't been so freaked by Tasha, she might have experienced a little thrill as well.

But all she felt was urgency.

Paolo had inadvertently blocked her from Tasha. Rita was torn between running away and still meeting with Paolo. He made the choice for her, pretending to just meet her with a pumping of her hand, then another hand in the small of her back as she was escorted toward a room just around the corner of the south corridor. The heavyset nurse was helping Tasha from the chair and guiding her toward Rita and Paolo. Rita quickly ducked in the room, which was semidark and private, her attention on the hallway. Tasha never moved her gaze from straight ahead. She lumbered, her belly protruding. Rita's baby . . .

Tasha hadn't seen Rita at all. Still in a coma? Catatonic state?

Rita was shaking, she realized. And Paolo Avanti was furious with her.

"What are you doing here?" he hissed.

"I told you I wanted a job."

"I don't do the hiring!"

"You could put in a good word for me."

"No! It would be an anomaly. I don't do that kind of thing." He was fit to be tied, but his eyes were all over her, hugging her curves.

"I want to get on my hands and knees and have you do me right here," she whispered.

"God, Rita."

"You can lock the door. We'll be quick."

"I can't put in a good word for you," he pleaded, his eyes goggling as she turned the lock herself, then was as good as her word, unzipping her pants and stepping out of them, hooking her scrap of lacy underwear with one finger, dragging it down her legs. She then positioned herself on the floor, her hair over one shoulder, her gaze intense as it met his eyes. His mouth was on "O."

Rita wriggled her ass. "Come over here. . . ."

Lang's lungs were on fire. Damn, but the Worster kid could run, work boots and all. Of course Lang was in cowboy boots, so it was probably a draw. But he had ten years on the kid, too, and that's what he was currently feeling in every aging muscle.

He slowed down, his breath coming in gulps. Cade had zigzagged across the open field and then slid into the Scotch broom. Lang had veered toward the Scotch broom, which was damn near as tall as he was, and now he was kicking himself for getting drawn into this insanity. He should go back to Worster's house and simply wait. Eventually, the kid would come back.

With that in mind he took stock of where he was. There was no sound from within the thick shrubbery apart from his own ragged breathing. Why had Cade run? Because he knew something about the attack on his cousin and Jane Doe? Or because he was a thief and recognized instinctively that Lang was part of the law?

Either way it was a pisser. Lang just wanted some answers.

Annoyed with himself, he brushed Scotch broom needles off the arms of his jacket and slopped back across the field to Worster's place.

A large dog started *boo-woo-wooing* somewhere ahead of Lang and to his right. He glanced over. Damned if that speedy little shit Worster wasn't already halfway back to his house! He'd circled around toward the west and was hugging the houses there, trying to stay under Lang's radar.

Lang let himself drift back to the protection of the Scotch broom and hesitated a moment, watching as Worster scurried across the road and to the back of his own house. He returned to the worn-down rambler home like a homing pigeon.

"Must be really jonesin' for that pizza," Lang muttered, annoyed.

It was humiliating to be so outrun by the little bastard. Time to get back to the gym before he started with the TCSD.

* * *

Paolo was on Rita in an instant. Fumbling with his belt, dropping his trousers, grabbing at her butt and pushing hard. It wasn't the most romantic of meetings, but she'd had worse. Then he was slamming into her and trying to balance himself and grab her breasts with one hand under her blouse.

"Baby, baby . . ."

She wished very definitely that he would stop saying that. It made her head feel like it would explode. Blocking out his crooning voice, she tried to concentrate on the moment. The moment. If she could think about Rafe. His hard body, his deep penetration, his—

"Jesus!"

The harsh whisper accompanied a last thrust and Paolo collapsed against her like he'd run a marathon. Rita had to balance his unexpected extra weight and it really torked her that she could feel his life-giving sperm spilling out as he pulled away with a groan. She did a mental count. She knew enough about her cycle to think she could get pregnant. *Be fertile. Please, please . . .*

"God," he said, stumbling away, reaching for his belt and trousers.

Rita found her panties and slipped them on, squeezing as hard as she knew how to keep him inside her. The whole thing was over in less than five minutes. It wasn't the greatest sex and he wasn't the perfect lover by a long shot, but he was perfect for her plans.

"I'd like to help you, but I can't," he apologized.

Oh, sure. Now that he'd been satisfied, he sounded less frantic about the whole thing. Detached, even. Rita gave the thought of blackmail a whirl. His colleagues wouldn't think kindly on what had just transpired on their well-respected hospital's gray carpet. But that was a card she was not quite ready to play.

Instead, she pushed aside her misgivings and sashayed

toward him. He looked kind of concerned, which torked her off some more. Rita Feather Hawkings wasn't used to rejection of any kind. But then, she also knew how to turn a man's head around, and in this case, that meant ignoring all his crap and pretending they were longtime lovers and she had full access to him.

He tried to draw back, but she wouldn't have it. She moved in close, grabbed his face between her palms, and kissed him hard on the mouth, sticking her tongue inside his and running it around his teeth. He made a soft, protesting sound but didn't pull away. He was starved for sex, she thought with an inward smile. Married, unmarried—whatever his situation was, he wasn't getting any. "We could meet like this every day," she said, breathing into his mouth. "Or somewhere more private, if that's what you want."

"This can never happen again!" he sputtered wildly.

"Why not?"

"Not at the hospital!"

"Somewhere more private, then. Like last night . . . ?"

He ran his hands through his hair and looked around, blinking, as if he couldn't believe this was happening. He probably couldn't. His life was filled with work and maybe not much else. That's where his power came from: work.

But she was showing him another way.

"Rita Feather Hawkings is a good nurse," she said.

He shook his head, but she could tell he was weakening.

"We're good together," she said, slipping her hand inside his pants and giving him a squeeze. Then she strolled out the door, throwing a look down the hall where they'd taken the blond whore, but she was now nowhere to be seen.

She forgot Paola Avanti as soon as she was outside of the room. He was a means to an end. A fairly pleasurable one, but he was no Rafe.

Soon, she thought, as she approached the girl at the front desk and asked to be directed to human resources and an employment form. Soon, she would be back at this hospital as an employee. Very soon. Time was of the essence. She needed to slit the bitch's throat and take her baby out of that black womb. Save the child and destroy its evil mother before that whore's body decided to give birth.

Lang had chased thieves, murderers, and criminals of all sorts in his years with the Portland PD. He'd never thought about it much, just gone ahead and done it. But then, that was the case with his whole career. He'd just gone ahead and done it. Until Melody's death. Until his faith in humanity and overall fairness was destroyed.

Still, it came as a small shock to realize he was out of shape, that he couldn't just fire up the engines and expect to run at breakneck pace, full-on, for as long as it took. Not only did he see long hours in the gym ahead of him, he saw a possible fine-tuning of his diet. Fewer burgers, fries, and greasy fast-food chicken. More salads, fruits, and vegetables lightly sauteed in olive oil. That was fine by him, but he was no gourmet cook. If it didn't come out of a drive-thru window, it was kind of off the menu.

The fact that Cade Worster had brought him to this realization put him in a foul mood, and that foul mood made it impossible for him to feel kindly toward the fleet-footed thief.

He walked right around the back of the house and didn't have to knock, holler, or attempt a break-in because Cade was coming out of the back with a hastily thrown-together black duffel bag in one hand and his precious pizza box balanced in the other. He was holding a slice of pizza in his teeth, the cheese and pepperoni sliding with gravity.

"Don't move," Lang said in his cop voice. He didn't have his gun. It was locked in the glove box. Didn't have anything but his anger, but by the wide-eyed fear in the younger man's eyes, he thought it might be enough.

A piece of pepperoni hit the ground. Lang didn't drop eye contact with the kid.

Cade's shoulders slumped. He slipped the pizza box under his chin, opened his jaw, and dropped the piece of pizza atop the cardboard. "Ah, man . . ." The duffel bag hit the top step and bounced down to Lang's level.

"I just wanna talk about your cousin, Rafe. That's all."

It took a while for that to register. He was either slow or scared. Maybe both. "What?"

"You sold a Chevy truck to him."

"Sold it? Shit, no. He borrowed the fuckin' thing for forever! He owes me!"

"This is the same truck you *borrowed* from Tim Rooney, about a year ago?"

"Don't know what'cher talkin' about."

"Let's go in and sit down and I'll make myself clear."

He didn't want to. He didn't really get who Lang was and what it was all about, but that suited Lang just fine. He hated the waste of time it took to play by the rules, and anyway, Lang didn't give a rat's ass about what Cade stole from whom and why.

Cade picked up his pizza box and shuffled back in the house and Lang took the two steps in one stride and followed him in. Cade stood in front of the refrigerator and Lang positioned himself to face him with his back to the counter. If the kid decided to escape again, Lang could leap either way and make a great stab at stopping him.

"Who are you?" Cade decided it was time to ask.

Lang ignored him. "I think your cousin Rafe is dead. I think he took your truck, with or without your permission, and left with his pregnant girlfriend. But something happened at a rest stop on Highway 26 and he was stabbed and killed. The pregnant girlfriend was attacked, too."

Cade had set the pizza box on the counter and it was a

good thing, too, because his arms went slack to his sides and his jaw dropped. "Bullshit," he said.

"You haven't seen the news?"

"I saw about the pregnant girl—don't know her—but Rafe? Nah, man. You gotta be wrong."

"I've got a picture I could show you."

"A dead picture?" Cade's brows lifted in dismay. "Like of a dead person?"

"Yeah."

"I don't want to see it."

"I kinda need an identification," Lang said.

"Who are you, man?"

Cade was getting upset, so Lang told him about working with the Winslow County Sheriff's Department and his pending job appointment with Tillamook. Cade's attention faded away early on but Lang realized it was because he believed him, didn't much care, and was processing the information about Rafe.

"Rafe Black Bear's your cousin," Lang finished, trying to nail down the facts.

"Yeah, man, but his name's not Black Bear. People just call him that 'cause it was his dad's name, but his mom and dad never married. His dad was an Injun. But Rafe's a Worster, like me. His mom and my dad are brother and sister."

"So you're saying that Rafe took your truck without your knowledge?"

"That's about it."

"You know when?"

"Uh . . . a couple weeks ago?"

"Are you asking me?" Lang almost smiled. It was the classic attitude of a kid who was searching for the right answer to keep himself out of trouble.

"I don't know, man. Why don't you just leave me alone." He wrapped his arms even closer around his chest.

"If it's Rafe, and somebody killed him . . ." Lang tried.

"It's not Rafe. He's too real to die."

"Too real?"

"Look, he's a pain in the ass, okay? But he's all right."

"Maybe I'm not making myself clear. I've got a picture of a homicide victim. I'm pretty sure he's your cousin. I just need some identification. And then I need to find who stabbed him, and you might be able to help catch his killer."

"You got it wrong. It's not Rafe."

"Denial isn't going to change the truth," Lang said. "Let me go get the picture."

As he turned to the door, hoping to high heaven that the kid wouldn't start running again, he saw Cade's gaze drop to the floor. He seemed to shrink in upon himself. "Ah, man . . ." he said with a catch in his voice, sliding down the front of the refrigerator to sit on the floor, his forehead touching his knees, his hands clasped on his head.

He was finally getting the picture.

Feeling like a heel, Lang hurried to his truck for the manila folder that held Rafe Worster's photograph.

Claire's intercom buzzed. "Yes?"

"There's a call for you from Leesha at Laurelton General," the receptionist said.

"Put it through."

A moment later, Leesha was on the line. "How're you doing? How's our Jane Doe?"

"Getting better. Still unaware. Still pregnant," Claire said with a smile in her voice. "How are things going with you?"

"The emergency room's run over by people who think they've got the flu. I was just wondering . . . did that nurse ever get hold of you? The one who thought she could identify Jane Doe? Dark hair. Medium tall. From Good Sam?"

"No one's contacted me. Maybe she talked to Freeson, though I think he would've said something."

"I gave her your name specifically."

"It didn't happen."

"Huh." Leesha sounded perplexed. "Maybe she changed her mind. I was kinda pissed, 'cause I thought the girl at the front desk gave out Jane Doe's whereabouts, but she said no. This nurse must've figured it out on her own. She sure acted like she was going to come your way."

"I thought the authorities were sifting through would-be identifiers."

"They are. It just seemed like she might know something . . . hmm . . ."

They chatted for a few more minutes before Claire's next appointment knocked on the door, a stunning athlete whose dream of playing college football had been dashed when he'd been diagnosed with an enlarged heart. He was having serious trouble redirecting himself and was so low that Claire had prescribed antidepressants and made sure he was never alone.

She hung up as he slouched himself into a chair. "How are you doing, Jeremiah?" she asked and spent the next hour pulling out monosyllabic replies that didn't bode well for his overall mental health.

Cade was still in the same position when Lang got back. He lifted his head a little, peeking from beneath dark brown bangs, as the back door squeaked open and Lang reentered the kitchen. His gaze zeroed in on the manila envelope in Lang's hands and he swallowed hard. Lang pulled out the photograph, the one of the victim on the ME's stainless steel gurney, most of his body covered by a sheet, though a stab wound near his collarbone was plain to see, and held it up for him.

Cade swallowed. "Shit," he whispered.

"It's Rafe?"

"Fuck . . . oh, God . . . holy shit . . ."

"Put your head between your knees," Lang ordered, seeing the color drain from his face. When Cade didn't seem to hear, Lang dropped the picture on the floor and pushed Cade's head down for him, using more speed than finesse. Cade was gulping air.

"Can you tell me about him?" Lang asked after a couple of moments. "He was your cousin and a friend. You both grew up around here."

He lifted his face and his eyes were red. He wasn't exactly crying; Cade was a tough guy. But he sniffed and wiped his nose on his arm. "Rafe's dad was never a real dad, y'know. He was gone early. I don't know. Maybe somebody knows where he is, but Rafe didn't. And he didn't care. His mom died a coupla years ago. Some kinda cancer. Rafe was rentin' with me for a while but he moved."

"To where?"

Cade shook his head, either not knowing or maybe just not eager to tell.

"You haven't been aware that he's been missing," Lang said.

"He goes off sometimes. He just works in people's yards and doin' stuff like hauling crap away and fixes fences and stuff."

"A handyman."

"Yeah, a handyman, I guess. And a lover." He shot Lang a weak smile. "Really got the girls. Just, they were all over him."

"A good-looking guy," Lang said. In this kind of interview, it was all about keeping them talking.

"Yeah, but, more'n that, too. He was kinda stupid-good? Never really knew what was going on with women, what they were thinking. He just sorta ignored all their shit and was okay with it? You know what I mean?"

"I think so." Lang's own experience with women was limited to a couple of half-assed relationships that he sensed might be his own fault. He sorta ignored them, too, but he wasn't really okay with any of it. He just thought they should stop acting hysterical or emotional or ridiculous, and they had a tendency to object to that opinion.

"Women are all over that shit," Cade said.

"Was he dating a blond woman? Someone around twenty, maybe?"

"Nah."

"No? He was with a young blond woman who was pregnant."

"Hell, no!" Cade blinked a couple of times. "Maybe you got the wrong guy! Rafe was with Rita. She just, like, took him over!"

"That couldn't be this girl?"

"Nah, she's part Injun. Dark hair. Kinda fierce-lookin' in that cool way, like she's gonna eat you alive, y'know? He was really hot for her . . . although . . ." He thought a long moment, staring off into space.

"Although?" Lang prompted.

"Although, I don't know. He didn't talk about her much lately. I haven't seen him a lot, really. He was busy at that job with the cult."

"The cult?" Lang was half-amused, half-exasperated. Cade's rambling view on women and relationships, and now the mention of a cult, made him wonder how much of this recount was truth and how much was Cade's own weird take on life as he knew it.

"You know them? The ones that live at the lodge with the big fence around it? Been there forever, like some of them are really ancient. I've seen some younger ones, though. Once in a while. They all wear those long dresses and their hair's up." He motioned upward in a spiral that Lang took to represent a bun. "Rafe's been doin' work for them for a while. They really don't let anybody in but him."

"Could this girl have been from there?"

"Was she wearin' a long dress?"

"Uh . . ." Lang wasn't sure. "A smock, or something. She's pretty pregnant."

"Too bad you can't just ask her," Cade said.

"No one's come forward to identify her, even with all the press."

"Bet she's from that place, then." Cade nodded. "They don't have TV. They don't do nothin', like, modern. It's like *Little House on the Prairie*. You ever seen that old show?"

"I know of it."

"That's what they dress like."

"Are they blond?"

Cade rolled that over. "Maybe. I've seen the old lady. She's gray. And she's the one who lets you through the gate, or not. Mostly not. The younger one I saw mighta had a hat on. Coulda been blond."

"Maybe I should go talk to them. See if one of them's run away."

"Good luck with that." Cade snorted. "I bet you don't get past the gate."

"Where is this place?"

Cade described it as being closer to the highway, near Deception Bay, with a view across the road to the ocean but back down a long, rutted lane. "You know where the lighthouse is?" he asked.

"Yeah."

"And then there's an island out there? Rocky and kinda in like a hospital?"

"Inhospitable?" Lang guessed.

"Yeah, that's it. Their lodge looks right out over that. If you're on the water, lookin' back, you can see their place. All fucked up, spookylike. Candles and shit. Looks like it's lookin' back at ya? You know what I mean? Like its windows are eyes and it sees you."

"Uh-huh . . ."

"But don't go out on the bay if you don't know what you're doin'. That's why it's called Deception Bay, y'know. My dad told me. Because boats get smashed against the island, or the lighthouse, or the jetty. Lots of accidents with stupid boaters who don't know what they're doin'."

Lang realized Cade had a lot more imagination than most thieves he'd run across. Most of them were in the clutches of meth or heroin or some other addictive drug that forced them to steal to make money to buy more drugs. Maybe Cade had an addiction problem, maybe he didn't. But he sure as hell wasn't the usual lost soul Lang ran across.

"I'm going to give your name to a friend of mine at the Winslow County Sheriff's Department."

"I told you everything I know! What do you mean? Thanks a lot, you bastard. I don't have the truck no more. You guys have it! It's not my fault it's stolen!"

"Actually, yeah, it is. You stole it first," Lang corrected him. "But that's not what I meant. We need someone from Rafe's family to make arrangements for the body."

"Oh, shit, no."

"Looks like it's you, unless he has some other closer relative?"

"No . . . no . . ." He was on his feet, absorbing, starting to pace.

"Can you name me another relative? What about your dad and mom?"

"Mom's remarried. She's not around. Dad lives in Seaside. You can call him." Cade looked relieved. "That'd be about it."

"Okay. Thanks." Lang picked up the picture and slid it back into the folder.

"Dad doesn't like Rafe. He thinks he's a bad influence."

Since Rafe had a job and it looked like Cade's source of income was from criminal activity, Lang wondered who was the bad influence on whom.

"I know you're tellin' me the truth," Cade said, "but I still think Rafe could walk in here any minute. I don't really believe he's gone, though I know he is, y'know?"

"Yeah."

Lang left, thinking about Melody all the way back to his house.

Chapter 13

Lang had a laptop as old as Methuselah. Its wireless capabilities, though it purported to have them, were cagey. Sometimes they acted like they were there, but then, mysteriously, they were gone. He couldn't remember the last time his laptop had connected to the Internet unless it was actually plugged directly into the modem. Maybe never.

"Gotta stop paying for that service," he said to the empty family room. The television was on, flickering with an action movie he thought he'd seen before but couldn't quite place. Not that he was paying much attention. His thoughts were elsewhere, on his case that wasn't really his case, and on his upcoming employment with the TCSD, and on Claire Norris, though he sought to deny it.

It had been an interesting week and a half.

He'd been to Seaside to talk to Cade Worster's father, Silas Worster. Silas was a developer whose business had died in the housing slump and now he worked as an electrician, his original trade. More accurately, he was currently an electrician's assistant, as the amount of work had dwindled from a rushing river to a trickle that sometimes was a mere drip.

Lang met Worster outside Palmer Electric, which Worster

suggested after Lang called the office and left a message on the man's cell phone voice mail. Worster was picking up some supplies before his next job the following morning, and when Lang connected with him, it was while he was checking off a list he had on a clipboard of various and sundry wires, tools, and equipment.

"You're the guy who called?" he questioned, giving Lang the once-over.

Worster himself was about five-ten, going to gray though he still had most of his hair, lean enough except for the beginnings of a middle-aged belly. He wore gray work pants, a long-sleeved black T-shirt and a Columbia Sportswear jacket with a hood and a lot of pockets, most of them weighted down with tools of the trade.

Lang introduced himself as working with the Tillamook County Sheriff's Department and explained about the body at the Winslow County ME's office, waiting for identification and dispersal. He showed him the picture of Rafe's body on the gurney.

Worster turned back to his checklist. "Cade gave you my name."

"Yes."

"Well, that's just about what you'd expect. Pass the buck. Make dear old dad clean up every mess."

"This isn't about Cade," Lang said slowly, feeling his way.

"My son and I don't talk. We don't really like each other. The only time he contacts me is when he needs something from me."

"He said that Rafe Worster was the man in the picture and that Rafe is his cousin. He also said there's no one else in the family except him and you."

"Well, he was telling the truth there, for once." He tossed the clipboard into the back of his truck and slammed the doors shut. "So, how'd Rafe get himself killed?"

Lang explained about the rest stop and the knifing, and Silas Worster suddenly woke up.

"Shit, man. The murder. Holy Christ. That was Rafe?"

He hadn't looked at the picture closely enough to even notice the knife wound, Lang realized. No love lost in this family. He'd seen it before, but it never got any easier to understand, especially when he himself missed his sister every day. A part of him wanted to shake Worster and tell him to make up with his son, no matter what it took, but he also knew some things that were broken simply couldn't be fixed.

"You may have seen on the news about the girl he was with. She's not been responsive since the attack."

"Yeah, yeah, yeah. The pregnant one. I saw her on that channel with the Kirby woman."

"Channel Seven."

"Jesus . . ." It seemed to finally penetrate once he realized Rafe's murder was a top news story. It took Lang another twenty minutes to get him to agree to make arrangements for Rafe's body, muttering all the way about the expense.

Lang had already called Will Tanninger after his meeting with Cade, and they agreed that Lang should stop by the sheriff's department after seeing Cade's father. He waved at Dot on the way in and she buzzed him through. When he entered Will's offices he met the other detective, Barbara Gillette, slim, with short dark hair, whose caseload was enough that they'd allowed Lang to come on board. She'd been on medical leave for a while, Lang recalled, but she seemed fit and determined and slightly suspicious at their first meeting. Lang didn't blame her. If the situation were reversed, he'd wonder what the hell was going on.

After Lang brought them both up to date on what he'd learned about Rafe Worster, Tanninger said he would co-ordinate with O'Halloran and the TCSD to do further follow-up on the man's history—where he lived, his job, if there were any other living relatives, what events had taken place directly before his death—anything at all that would help with the investigation. He concluded by thanking Lang for his help.

Lang responded with, "I've got a lead on Jane Doe." Both Tanninger and Gillette looked up with interest, so he then explained the intricacies of Rafe's active dating life, per Cade, and brought up the lodge in Deception Bay.

"Cade called it a cult," Lang finished with a shrug. "I don't know about that. I banged on the gates for quite a while but no one heard me. Either that, or they just didn't pay me any attention."

Tanninger looked surprised. "I know of that place," he said, to which both Gillette and Lang turned to him with upraised eyebrows. "My girlfriend, Gemma, was from Deception Bay originally. She went there to see what she could find out about her past."

"She learned something about the cult?" Lang asked.

"The name of the lodge where they live is called Siren Song, and the townspeople refer to the women who live there as the Colony."

"They're all women?" Lang asked.

"Seem to be. When you get to TCSD, check with Detective Clausen. Gemma talked to him about her mother, and both he and O'Halloran told her more about Siren Song."

"I'll do that," Lang said.

"Looks like this investigation is moving your way geographically, so do you want to continue?" Tanninger asked. "Or do you want Barb and me to take over?"

"I can keep going." Lang wanted to, actually, but he didn't want to step on any toes.

"Fine by me," Barb said.

"Think O'Halloran or Clausen will know of a way to get beyond the cult's gates?" Lang asked.

"O'Halloran's the man to ask. Siren Song's in his jurisdiction, and everybody in Deception Bay seems to have an opinion about the place." He made a face. "That whole town's a magnet for the strange and weird. O'Halloran's words, not mine."

Lang shook Will's hand and promised to keep in touch. He'd then had another meeting with Sheriff O'Halloran; Detective Clausen wasn't around when Lang arrived because he was following up on Rafe Worster.

"You won't get Catherine to give you the time of day," O'Halloran predicted when Lang said he wanted to find a way inside Siren Song. "She knows me and we leave each other alone."

"Catherine is the older woman who runs the place?"

The sheriff nodded. "There's a whole history to them. It's common knowledge, or lore, I guess. You can hear any number of stories about them and other crazies by just sitting at the Sands of Thyme bakery, or on a bench at the beach, or just walking through the town."

"Other crazies?" he asked, thinking of Will's girlfriend's mother.

"You know last year when that serial killer was attacking women along 101 and 26? The one at Halo Valley Security Hospital? He squatted in that lighthouse that's in Deception Bay."

"Turnbull," Lang said with a small shock. He'd been so focused on Heyward III that he'd forgotten who else was incarcerated on Side B.

"That's the one." O'Halloran nodded. "Talk to Clausen. He and his old partner were involved in corralling him."

"You'd think this Catherine would want to know where one of her missing flock was," Lang said.

"If she's even one of 'em." He frowned. "You say this girl is pregnant?"

"Seven or eight months."

"Then I doubt she's one of the Colony."

"Why?"

"'Cause they don't leave that place. And there aren't any men there. No way to get pregnant."

"Rafe Worster worked there, according to his cousin, Cade."

O'Halloran sniffed, disbelieving. "Okay, sure, that's a possibility, I suppose. But if a man was anywhere around her girls, you can be sure Catherine had them all in chastity belts."

"She rules with an iron fist."

"She rules. Her way. The only way. That's all." He shook his head, then asked, "So, when are you coming on board?"

"Next week? I've got some moving to do. And I told Tanninger I'd still work on the rest stop murder."

"Good."

Lang made a face. "I can't demand those women let me through the gates, seeing as I have no real authority right now. Any way we can get a warrant and storm that place?"

"Find me some probable cause. I think you'd do better with your charm."

"I've driven to the gates twice and stood there like an idiot. I can't get anybody inside to even look at me."

"Oh, they're looking," O'Halloran said.

"If they don't respond soon, I'd like to take more serious action."

O'Halloran sighed. "Before it becomes a battle, make sure that this Jane Doe is really one of their own or we'll be crucified by the press for forcing the law upon a private home that houses a group of passive, peaceful, law-abiding citizens, all of whom happen to be women."

Lang did see the problem. Still, from all accounts, this Catherine of the Gates seemed more like a dragon lady than a serene keeper of the faith.

Lang had then said his good-byes and asked O'Halloran

to have Clausen give him a call. As he was heading out the door, O'Halloran hollered after him, "Got those five rivers for me?"

"Still working on it," Lang yelled back.

Which brought him full circle to the problem of his grinding laptop and its lack of connection capability. One more thing to do before he left the greater Portland area: buy a new computer.

Glancing at the clock, he grabbed up some boxes that were hurriedly packed and ready to go, carried them outside, and stowed them in his truck. Since meeting with the sheriff he'd started packing up his house, and he'd already half-filled his vehicle with his belongings. He'd done some halfhearted apartment hunting, reluctantly putting down a deposit on a unit in downtown Tillamook, close to the department. He already knew he wouldn't be there long, but it was at least someplace for now. Eventually he planned to rent a house. Even more eventually, if the job worked out, maybe even buy a place. Time would tell.

Also since the meeting with O'Halloran, he'd made another fruitless attempt to engage Catherine of the Gates, but the lodge seemed almost abandoned. If they were watching him, they were damn stealthy about it. It was frustrating. He decided to shove a note through the bars in the hopes that someone would come and pick it up.

"Candlelight," he muttered aloud.

Talk about the dark ages.

He'd wondered over the past couple of weeks if Catherine and the other women could be behind Rafe Worster's murder. It wasn't impossible. If Cat was from the Colony, maybe her pregnancy could cause a violent reaction? Was he being overly melodramatic? Stranger motivations had definitely surfaced throughout his years in law enforcement, and O'Halloran had mentioned the chastity belt thing. Catherine clearly didn't want her chicks defiled.

But if they were involved in the murder, how could he find out?

Maybe from Cat herself . . . ?

He realized the idea had been rolling around in his brain ever since he'd learned of Siren Song, and now as the thought crystallized into action, he decided to make one more trip to that hellhole known as Halo Valley Security Hospital and speak to Cat herself. This meant, of course, getting past the hospital staff, which was almost as difficult as Catherine of the Gates. It also meant he expected Cat to be able to communicate.

He thought about his last trip there and made a face. Not his most shining moment of restraint. He'd wanted to punch out both Marsdons and had pretty much thrown Dr. Norris to the wolves.

But she'd lied about Melody and what she'd said . . . hadn't she?

Lang shook off a faint pang of remorse. To hell with all of them. They deserved whatever they got. They were bound and determined to move Heyward III to Side A, and he owed them nothing.

Grabbing the strapping tape, he pulled a strip across the top of a box of office supplies. Stacking it with a smaller box, one that had been sealed for some time that contained family mementos—Melody's meager belongings—he toted them to the Dodge.

The transfer of Heyward Marsdon III from Side B to Side A was done quietly and without a lot of folderol. Claire felt suppressed anger toward Avanti and Freeson and even Radke, the head administrator, the way they'd professed to need and value her consent and then had gone ahead and done what they wanted anyway.

She was no longer Heyward's doctor, but he didn't seem

to understand why not. Freeson was in charge of him and he took over the job with relish. In his way, Heyward III was a celebrity, and Freeson loved that kind of spotlight.

By default, Claire had been given care of Cat. A kind of consolation prize. An appeasement. Claire had accepted the assignment with a nod of her head while inside she'd been more than happy with the exchange. She'd always wanted to be in charge of Cat's care, but Freeson had superseded her. And she knew she couldn't have been fair toward Heyward, given the circumstances, even if the Marsdons and the rest of the staff had believed in her.

But that didn't mean she was comfortable with having Heyward on her side of the hospital. Logically, she could tell herself that he was no threat when he was on his meds. She knew that to be true. But fear was irrational at the best of times. It was gut deep. Lodged in her cells. She was superstitious enough to walk a little faster past Heyward's door than anyone else's, which was ridiculous, and she would never admit it to anyone.

Now Claire consulted her watch. Eleven o'clock. She'd already met with several patients earlier today in her office and she was en route to Cat's room to check on her. Then lunch, followed by a one-thirty appointment and a surprisingly light afternoon, as her three o'clock had canceled.

As she passed by the morning room she saw Cat sitting quietly in a chair, so she turned toward her, making a mental note to get Cat some maternity clothes as she was still in a hospital gown, though she was at least wearing her own shoes.

"I was just coming to see you," Claire said. "I think maybe we need to get you some more clothes."

The girl's eyes shot to Claire's, filled with what looked like panic.

It was a surprise, but a heartening one. She really was

coming out of it. "Not the clothes you were wearing," Claire assured. "Some new ones. It'll be all right."

Cat went back to staring vacantly straight ahead. Claire tried to engage her some more but she'd lost contact, and after about ten minutes of a running monologue that Cat didn't seem to hear, she told her she'd see her again later and headed out for lunch.

Tasha surreptitiously watched the doctor leave, sliding a look from the corner of her eyes.

I think maybe we need to get you some more clothes.

Fear had stabbed an icy dagger in her heart.

Not because of the clothes. She wanted clothes. Needed clothes. What she couldn't bear was thinking it was something for her distant future! They believed she was going to be there forever! They thought she was sick. Here she was, in this place with all these lunatics. Trapped. She'd spent her entire life trapped inside her aunt's austere prison, and now this. She had to get out. Had to live.

And she couldn't wait for someone to bestow a wardrobe upon her. She had to leave *now*. Like she'd tried to leave with Rafe.

Rafe . . . she thought despairingly, closing her eyes, remembering.

She heard Gibby drop into the chair next to hers, shifting around. He couldn't sit still. If Catherine were there, she would lash him down, tie his feet and hands, castigate his behavior.

She reopened her eyes and Gibby was leaning toward her, his face right in front of her, like a bobbing clown. "Hey!" he said loudly. "There you are!"

Across the room that weird Thomas was staring at her as if he wanted to do something to her. Tasha pretended to stare back blankly, like she'd been doing for days, keeping her awakening to herself, as all the staff members remarked whenever she even fluttered her lashes. She didn't want to talk to them. Didn't want them to know who she was until she figured out how to escape, find some transportation away from here and to freedom!

She looked down at her hospital gown. It was a smock that tied in the front and touched just below her knees. A kind of dress, but it wasn't good enough. She needed more clothes, and she couldn't wait for the good doctor to get her some. Her shoes were fine, but the clothes she'd been wearing were gone. Covered in blood, no doubt. Shivering, she covered the mound of her abdomen protectively with both hands and thought hard.

Beyond clothes, she needed help. Some way to get past the guarded door. The girl at the desk opened the doors by a remote mechanism, and the staff members had plastic cards that they slid into slots and then punched numbered buttons. She'd watched it all. Taken notes. She didn't have much experience with their world, but she sure wanted to join it.

She'd picked up some interesting language while she'd been here. That Maribel used words that made everyone react with displeasure. And Thomas McAvoy. Borderline personality, whatever that meant. He wanted something. *Wanted* it. They gave him a lot of pills but he tried not to take them. He surreptitiously stuffed them in his pants pockets, then later he took them out and put them inside a small brass pitcher that was used as a bookend on one of the built-in shelves at the end of the room. He was pretty good at being sly, but Tasha knew his game.

She didn't know what those pills did, but they were always handed out when McAvoy started getting tense. He would fight them, pretend to swallow the tablets, stealthily transfer them to his pocket, then later, maybe hours later, maybe a full day, he would wander over to the pitcher and plunk them in. Once he'd caught her staring at him and she pretended to be blank. He'd glared and glared, and then, right before dinner, he came by her chair and whispered in her ear, "You fucking fake," then cruised away.

The two older women inmates who were never more than four feet from each other gazed across the room at Tasha as if she'd done something wrong. Mrs. Merle and Mrs. Tanaway. No one ever called them by their first names. And there was Lester, mumbling and looking outside. And that Donald with his incessant diagnosing.

It was all too much for Tasha. She would never belong there. She needed a plan to get away.

Her gaze swung to the other side of the room. The kitchen was through a swinging door that was locked when they weren't bringing out the swill they fed to the inmates. Twice Tasha had planted herself in a chair near the door and stared out the window to the laurel hedge and razor wire beyond like Lester, her senses attuned to the room around her, and, when no one was looking, had peeked into the kitchen. Kitchens had knives. As careful as Catherine was, they all worked to put meals on the table, even Tasha, when she wasn't in trouble, and that's how Tasha had found a way to steal her knife, the one she'd had in her pocket when she and Rafe made their escape.

The baby kicked and Tasha inhaled sharply. She didn't know much about pregnancy; it was a taboo subject, though all the girls wanted to know every last detail. They'd learned it took sex with a male to get the job done, but this changing of her body was kind of frightening. How much further? How much bigger?

She'd learned that there was a time after dinner that she could sneak into the kitchen if she needed to. It might not be a bad thing to have another knife. Especially the way McAvoy looked at her.

"Hey, hey," Gibby said now, waving his hand in front of her face.

"I need help," she told him.

"I know. I wants to help you!"

She and Gibby shared conversations; she'd spoken aloud to him on more than one occasion. Gibby wasn't lying about that. But she needed this deception to keep her safe, to fashion an escape, and she was always fighting the dark curtain that was both a blessing and a curse. Her gift, such as it was. A double-edged one. Not nearly as useful as Cassandra's powers of seeing into the future. Or even dim Lillibeth's crystal clarity that popped out at the oddest times.

Tasha would have liked something better. Her sisters were blessed with deeper gifts. The ability to see someone's intentions. Future calamity. The darkness of the human heart. A man's devotion.

But instead, she had this darkness that crept around her consciousness. She didn't really understand it, didn't want it half the time, but there it was.

She was still silently lamenting her lack of special gifts when the air pressure changed, someone coming up behind her.

"Hello, Cat," a female voice purred in her ear.

With an effort Tasha stayed staring straight ahead. She wanted to twist around and see who'd spoken.

And then the dark-haired nurse walked into her line of vision, and Tasha's pulse rocketed. She'd seen her upon occasion the last couple of weeks, had thought she recognized her, had hoped, prayed, that it was her imagination.

But it wasn't.

Rita!

Now the witch gazed down at her hard. It was all Tasha could do to keep up her act. Rita the nurse. Rafe's Rita. Rita, who'd chased them down to the rest stop. Tasha had thought that's who it was, but she hadn't believed her bad luck. It couldn't be. Just couldn't be! But it was. Rita had been hovering around for days, but this was the first time she'd actually spoken to Tasha directly.

"She doan talk 'cept to me," Gibby said, smiling widely at Tasha.

Rita gazed at him hard. "What does she say?"

"Oh, she needs help. Lots of help."

"What kind of help?"

"She needs to get away."

Tasha wanted to kick Gibby but remained frozen, staying put in her distant twilight.

Then Rita's gaze dropped to Tasha's protruding belly and Tasha felt an inner horror and a need to squirm away as the woman placed her hand atop the mound and said, "My baby."

She was ready to throw off her deception and attack her, but then Rita let her hand slide possessively along Tasha's rounded belly before walking away. Tasha automatically touched the stab wounds at her shoulders. Rita had stabbed her hard. Deep.

She needed clothes now!

"I doan like her," Gibby said.

"She wants to hurt me," Tasha said.

His eyes rounded. "She does?"

"I don't have any clothes. Can you get me some of yours? Pants. And a shirt?" They wouldn't fit well. Gibby was shorter and rounder than Tasha, but it was better than these gowns the hospital supplied. Tasha had never worn a pair of pants. She hoped she could anchor the waistline somehow beneath her baby.

"You has no clothes?"

"No. And you have to bring them to me in secret. I have to make sure she doesn't find out." Tasha's voice was a harsh whisper.

"That bad nurse woman?"

"That bad nurse woman."

"Okay. . . ."

"Tonight. After dinner."

"Okay!" He was growing excited, bouncing in his chair.

"Shhh," she warned. "Settle down. Don't let them know or they could take you back to your room."

He glanced around, his head swiveling hard from side to side. "No!"

"Let's watch TV," she said to distract him.

"They gots the controller." But he was already signaling one of the apelike orderlies. It was Greg who came to see what he wanted. He threw a glance at Tasha, who blinked slowly and dully, and soon the television was softly squawking away and Gibby settled into his chair. She would have to remind him again, just before dinner, but if all went well she could be out by tonight.

She just needed a distraction to get past the woman manning the front door. A distraction and a keycard. Maybe she could steal one, somehow. She needed to escape. Today.

Rita had quickly grown accustomed to her job at Halo Valley. She'd been there for over a week and had seamlessly fit herself in with the staff, though it was with an effort, as Rita wasn't one to warm up to people. Normally careful and spare in her words around women, she'd gone out of her way to be friendly to the staff, especially Lori at the front desk and Darlene, one of the floor nurses. She was working on Maria, one of the night nurses, though she wasn't sure she'd had as much success with her yet.

It was all an acting job for Rita. Her emotions were only engaged around babies and certain men. Paolo Avanti definitely engaged her, though not in the same way as Rafe.

But now she was here. She'd managed it, with the help of Dr. Avanti's good word—reluctantly given as it had been, the bastard. He'd been nervous about having his lover on staff, but she'd managed to convince him it would be to the benefit of both of them.

And then there had been a bit of stickiness when she'd put in her resignation at Ocean Park. Nurse Perez, superior busybody that she was, had been appalled that she'd given such short notice.

"What is it, Rita?" she asked. "Has something happened?"

Rita hadn't told them she was moving to Halo Valley when she quit. She hadn't been officially hired at the time she tendered her resignation, and she wouldn't have cared to let them know anyway. None of them were her friends, though when Jake strolled by she felt a pang of loneliness for Rafe that left her momentarily choked up. That's what Nina Perez saw and misunderstood.

"Does this have to do with Dr. Loman?" she'd asked quietly, a hand on Rita's arm, gently steering her away from listening ears in the hallway, guiding her to the employee room. The nosy bitch then looked around, and seeing they were alone, gazed at Rita with fake concern and added, "He was pretty negative about your care for Teresa Warnock."

Teresa Warnock. The snotty lawyer's wife who lived in that fancy house where she'd slipped on her marble floors and broken her wrist in two places, coming under Rita's care at Ocean Park. Teresa Warnock was a friend of Dr. Loman's, the hospital's osteopath, who was old, old, old— too old to perform surgery anymore. Teresa had taken offense to the way Rita simply tuned the withered hag out when she blabbered on and on and on about her wrist. The bitch had then complained to Loman, who was basically retired and out of it, but who'd had the nerve to dress Rita down anyway! Rita really hadn't taken him seriously. He was too ancient. Tall and lean, with a neatly clipped ring of white hair, he'd scowled down at her with what she suspected was his mean look and told her her attitude was unacceptable. Rita had simply listened and thought that he'd probably been handsome as the devil in his youth, though those days were long behind him. And his mind wasn't what it once was, though nobody at Ocean Park was saying it. She figured he would never remember later whom he'd dressed down anyway, and though she'd seethed about the injustice at the time, Loman really wasn't worth the energy.

Still, when Perez suggested this was the reason she was leaving, Rita seized on it like a lifeline. "He hurt my feelings, Nina. Mrs. Warnock lied to him about me, but Dr. Loman was good friends with her and he wasn't about to listen to someone as low as Rita Feather Hawkings."

"Rita, you know that's not true."

"I don't know. I don't think I can work here anymore."

"Dr. Loman is retiring soon. Don't let this dictate how you feel about Ocean Park Hospital. It's a good place to work. We need nurses like you."

Rita was almost swayed. Almost. Even though Nina Perez was a liar and was just trying to get what she wanted. But Rita had a different life for herself in mind, an alternate future.

Carlita had chosen that moment to push into the employee room. She stared hard at Rita and Nurse Perez. "You guys got some kind of powwow going on here?"

"Carlita!" Perez took instant offense to what she believed was Carlita taking a swipe at Rita through her Native American heritage. Rita knew that was just how Carlita talked; she didn't mean anything by it. But Rita pretended affront as well, glaring hard at her.

"What?" Carlita demanded.

"I gotta go," Rita said, and walked out. It was a good way to leave things. Clean. Over. No unanswered questions.

And then she'd started at Halo Valley. Of course they'd

asked her all kinds of questions to test her psychological health; Rita had been through that a number of times. She knew the answers, though sometimes she got called out for not having the correct expression and tone for the words. She just couldn't muster the big bright smile they seemed to want. They worried she was too serious, a code phrase meaning she might be too emotionally remote. She parried that with a good line about keeping a balance between herself and her patients: she worked hard to keep from caring too much.

One moment it seemed like they were actually going to turn her away, then, after another grab-and-stroke session with Avanti, which set up his recommendation, she was given the job. She actually kind of liked working here. Everyone tried so damn hard with the crazies that they seemed to spend less time trying to tell Rita what to do. If she was there helping, well, that was good enough. No one cared whether she was smiling or not, whether she was emotionally engaged.

Rita wondered if there was a way to keep her job even after she found a way to remove Tasha from the hospital's guarded walls. She thought she might be able to swing it. She knew a lot of ground along the foothills of the Coast Range where no one ever went.

How hard would it be to hide a body, once the baby was taken?

No one ever had to know.

Chapter 14

As Lang pulled into the parking lot of Halo Valley Security Hospital, his cell phone went off. He didn't recognize the number, so he answered, "Langdon Stone."

"It's Fred Clausen. O'Halloran said you wanted to talk to me."

Detective Fred Clausen. Lang's soon-to-be partner with the Tillamook County Sheriff's Department, most probably. "Hey, thanks. Have you learned anything more about Rafe Worster?"

"Pretty much what you found out. Turns out he lived in an RV camper that's on blocks down the street from his cousin. Not a lot of belongings. Worked as a gardener and handyman around Deception Bay and the Foothillers' community. The last year or so, he's been doing work at Siren Song."

"Think that had anything to do with his homicide?"

"I don't know. Maybe. More likely it's something he got caught up in outside of the cult. His cousin's a thief. From what I've learned, Rafe didn't have any problem with that. He pretty much took Tim Rooney's truck from Cade for himself. People liked him. But nobody's acted like he was

Mr. Responsibility. Kinda lived day-to-day. Had a lot of different girlfriends. Pretty much what Cade told you."

"You heard we think the girl might have come from Siren Song?" Lang asked.

"Yeah." Clausen sounded skeptical.

"You don't think so?"

"Sheriff said she's pregnant. That would be unusual from what I know of the place, which isn't much."

"What can you tell me?" Lang asked.

"Well, I worked a case, almost two years ago now. Caught the tail end of it with Kirkpatrick, but the detective in charge was Sam McNally, out of Laurelton P.D. Case started there and wound its way to the coast."

"Kinda like this one has," Lang observed.

"Yeah, kinda like it." Clausen snorted. "Anyway, we caught this guy and he was squirrel nutty. He's at Halo Valley and he ain't coming out anytime soon. This nutcase thought the Siren Song women were the devil's daughters or something. He was targeting anyone he thought was connected with them. After he was caught, O'Halloran met with Catherine, the girls' leader, about it. She allowed him inside the gate but not into the lodge. She said she didn't know anything about the crimes, but the sheriff thought she was holding back."

"The sheriff acted like he and Catherine stay out of each other's way."

"Yeah, well . . . she's not a woman with a lot of warmth."

"You've met her?"

"I've seen her around Deception Bay a time or two. She reminds me of one of those really mean nuns who rap you on your knuckles or get out the cane and whup your ass. But she's more than that, too. She's . . ." He searched around for a bit, then said, "Otherworldly."

Otherworldly. It sounded strange in Clausen's gravelly voice.

"Catherine and Siren Song are just part of the landscape around here," Clausen went on. "Everybody's got a story about them."

"So, what do I have to do to reach them? Catherine? I want to talk to her about Cat, the Jane Doe who was attacked at the rest stop, and see if she knows her. That's all."

"Did I hear you left her a note?"

"Yeah. Threw it through the bars."

"What did it say?"

"Just told her to call me. I said I was a detective with the TCSD, which is only a lie for the time being, and I left my cell number."

"Well, don't expect miracles." Clausen was dry.

"Why?"

"You didn't give her any information. She's not going to bother with you."

"I didn't really want to go into the whole thing in a note."

"I hear you. I'm just saying."

"Are the women always locked away inside there? Don't they ever come out?" Lang couldn't believe how he was stymied.

"They used to. A couple of 'em left or were adopted out, early on. One of 'em worked at the Drift In Market for a while. They're not prisoners, though sometimes it seems that way."

"What happened to the one who worked at the market?"

"You'd have to ask them. I don't know."

Clausen didn't have much more to go on, so he and Lang ended the call. As soon as he was off the phone, Lang looked through his rearview at the front of Halo Valley. The rain was threatening, but there was a slight break. The wind was blowing the maple trees around, waving orange and brown leaves on the end of spindly leaves, daring him to enter.

Early October.

He was in jeans and his black leather jacket, which had
survived its drenching. Just. His cowboy boots had been
cleaned; no trace of the muck he'd covered them in after
chasing Cade across the field.

He strode forward and hit the buzzer at the hospital's
glass doors. The woman at the desk asked his name through
the speaker. He gave it and was admitted. Once inside, he
wished he could just join the inmates in the morning room.
He could see Cat's blond head, but the front guardian was
gazing at him suspiciously.

"Dr. Norris," he said.

She hesitated, giving him a long look. Lori, her name
tag read. He realized she'd witnessed the brouhaha that had
ensued the last time he'd been there. She probably also
knew something about his feelings for the doctors at Halo
Valley, especially Dr. Claire Norris.

He didn't offer up any further information and Lori
touched the intercom button and spoke softly to the person
on the other end.

Come on down, Dr. Norris . . . he thought, girding himself a little for the battle that was sure to follow.

Claire replaced the receiver and paused, wondering if
she should call Freeson and tell him Langdon Stone was
back in the building. What he would do when he learned
Heyward III had been moved was anybody's guess. He
would undoubtedly go to the press and make the decision
public, and then there would be hell to pay. Claire knew
she could pick up the phone herself at any time and be that
teller of tales. Pauline Kirby would be all over the Marsdon story.

But Claire was facing a moral dilemma where Heyward
was concerned. She was starting to wonder if he really did

belong on Side B. She'd been so sure before, but was that because of her own fear? He wasn't a psychopath. He was a paranoid schizophrenic who suffered hallucinations and delusions. A sick man who needed professional help. And it wasn't as if he were allowed to just roam around Side A; so far, he'd been confined to his room. Locked in. Able to page the staff but kept separate from the rest of the patients. Radke, the hospital administrator, might bend to the Marsdons' wishes, but he wasn't taking any chances.

Besides, she really thought if anyone should go to the press about Heyward's transfer, Langdon Stone was the man.

Claire made a face. She wasn't going to call Freeson. She would never call him. He was worse than useless, in her mind. Let them figure out what to do when Stone exploded. Maybe it wouldn't happen just yet as Heyward was being kept in his room, unable to enjoy the full privileges of Side A until such time as it was proven he was, in fact, a true Side A candidate.

Glancing at the clock, she mentally logged the time. One thirty. How convenient for him that her three o'clock had canceled and she was free for the day. The man was lucky—if a meeting with her could be considered luck, she supposed.

She headed out, using her keycard and punching in her code to take her from the medical office building to the hospital. Since Heyward's transfer, they'd increased building security to include all hours of the day.

As she was walking across the gallery she passed the new nurse, Rita, who read her name tag but seemed to turn away rather than engage Claire. She realized this had happened almost every time they'd run across each other and wondered if she intimidated her in some way.

Or maybe she'd already heard that Claire was being

blamed for the incident with Melody Stone and had chosen the other side.

"Or maybe you're being paranoid," Claire murmured aloud as she descended the steps to the first-floor lobby where Melody Stone's brother stood, legs apart, eyes serious, waiting for her arrival. She forced herself not to glance down the hall toward Heyward's room.

"Did you decide our Jane Doe's abdominal wounds were worth a second trip?" she asked, stopping about two feet away, giving herself ample personal space.

"No . . ." She nonplused him a little. "I have some information about Jane Doe."

She nodded. "Okay."

"It's not verified, but I'm a little stuck, so I decided to bring it to you now." He thought a moment while Claire waited, then said, "I think she belongs to this group of women who live together in a lodge at the coast."

Claire frowned, bringing her thoughts back to the moment with an effort. "You mean Siren Song?"

"You know it?" He was surprised.

"I live in Deception Bay. I've only been there a couple of years, but yeah, I know the lodge. You think Cat's part of the Colony?"

"Pretty sure."

"I don't know . . ." She glanced away. Where was Freeson? If he were to suddenly decide to bring Heyward down the hall at that moment, while Stone was there . . .

"She's pregnant. I know," Stone said, sounding like he'd covered this ground a thousand times. "And nobody from there can get pregnant."

Claire gave him her full attention again. "Pregnancy just . . . it's not their way."

"So I keep hearing. But even preachers' kids get pregnant," Lang pointed out dryly.

"In some cultures it's more taboo than others, and in the

case of the Colony . . . in their particular culture, I'd think
it's still pretty taboo."

"You know a lot about them?"

She shrugged. "They're old-fashioned. In dress as well
as thought. Maybe they have a totally progressive stand on
sex, but I wouldn't bet on it."

A door squeaked open at the end of the hall and Claire
nearly jumped out of her skin. Stone made silent note of
her discomfort, then turned to look in the same direction.

"What makes you think Cat's from Siren Song?" she
asked quickly, seeking to regain his attention.

"A number of things." He quickly gave her a rundown
of his interview with Cade Worster, finishing with, "Rafe
Worster's the homicide victim. Stands to reason Jane Doe
could be from this Colony, or whatever."

"Have you told them? The Colony members?"

"Oh, sure. I walked right in and sat down with Catherine and the girls. We just talked and talked and talked."

Claire forced herself not to look directly down the hall,
but in her peripheral vision she got a quick look at Heyward and Greg.

Aware she was distracted, Lang asked, "What's going on?"

"Nothing."

He stared into her eyes for long moments until Claire
had to look away. Then he turned slowly and saw for himself. "Jesus," he muttered. "He's here."

"You can't go there." Her hands shot out to stop him,
arms straight.

"I haven't moved a muscle, Doctor. I don't plan to see him."

His voice was like a razor. She nodded, feeling idiotic.
"I'm sorry."

"You're sorry." His voice dripped sarcasm. "And you
keep saying my sister asked for it."

"I'm not your enemy," she said a bit helplessly.

He looked like he was going to argue. The scowl on his

face reflected his anger. But with an almost physical effort, he clamped his lips shut and pulled himself together.

"To hell with it," he muttered, thinking of turning away.

"If you really want to talk to the Colony, why can't you?" she burst out. "I mean, essentially, aren't you the law?"

He didn't want to be here anymore. He was done. She was the enemy, even if she didn't know it. She and Halo Valley Security Hospital.

But he'd come here for a different reason. Arguing with her about Marsdon wasn't it. "Even the law isn't going to hit their gates with a battering ram or yell at them through a bullhorn without some kind of proof of a crime. I can't really force them to talk to me. They don't have phones. Electricity is iffy, maybe a generator for the first floor. They wear long dresses and their hair up in buns. I've called to 'em. I shoved a note with my cell number through the bars, just in case they find a phone somewhere. I told 'em I'm with the sheriff's department. They know I'm trying to reach them, and they now know how to reach me, but so far, nada."

She nodded, clearly surprised that he'd been able to put Heyward Marsdon aside.

He shook his head, wondering what the hell he was doing.

"Cat can walk by herself now, though we don't let her without staff nearby," she said diffidently.

"She talking?"

"No."

"I'd like to ask her about the Colony anyway."

"I don't know . . ."

Heyward and Greg came their way, Heyward looking hopefully toward Claire, who nodded but stayed where she was. Lang watched them slowly move on by, his body tense.

With an effort, he dragged his attention back to their conversation. "Maybe she's listening. If she's a member, maybe she'll snap out of it."

"It doesn't usually work that way," she said carefully.

"How the hell does it work, then, Doctor?" he demanded.

"She's just not responding that well."

"Why don't we go try it on her? You and I. Right now."

He turned toward the hallway, and short of physically blocking his way, Claire could do nothing but fall in step beside him. At Cat's door they turned to face each other. Squared off.

"Let me talk to her first," Claire said.

"I want to be there. See her reaction."

"If there is any."

"If there is any," he agreed flatly.

"I think I should go in alone first."

"Bullshit protocol," he said. "What's the worst thing that'll happen?"

"She'll relapse."

"Into what? Catatonia?"

"You don't know anything about it," she said stiffly.

"I know a lot about it," he snarled. "I had a sister who suffered from schizophrenia. Don't tell me I know nothing about it."

"Cat's going to have a baby very soon," Claire said, losing the battle, stinging from his arrows. "I'd like to know who her people are in case she cannot care for this child immediately."

"So would I. Lead the way," he challenged.

She pulled out her cell phone. "We have a midwife who's associated with Ocean Park Hospital who's been looking in on Cat, monitoring her pregnancy. I need to check with her."

"More bullshit," Lang concluded, but he waved a hand, telling her to get on with it.

Claire turned away, ostensibly to hear the call, more because she needed a semiprivate moment. Lang wasn't completely wrong. There had been nothing in Eugenie Ledbetter's reports on Cat's condition that would suggest the pregnancy was anything but textbook. Claire just wanted to keep the power play between herself and Stone under control. Eugenie answered directly and when Claire posed the idea of having Cat interviewed, Eugenie didn't see it as any kind of problem. "Has she come to?" was all Eugenie asked, to which Claire answered, "Not really."

"She wondered why you called her," Lang observed with a small smile as Claire hung up.

Annoyed, she turned to Cat's door. She would have liked to thwart him in some way. He really, really got to her in ways that probably needed to be assessed, but right now she didn't have the energy or inclination to go there. Cat came first. As her hand reached for the knob, she asked, "Does arrogance always work for you?"

"A lot of the time," he answered without missing a beat.

"Part of your police procedural?"

"More like a natural gift."

"Let me broach Siren Song to her," she ordered, slipping into the room.

"You're the professional," he said, and she was pretty sure she heard a gibe in there somewhere.

He didn't want to like her. Or be attracted to her. Or even notice any little thing about her. But Dr. Claire Norris was a stunner. Not traditionally beautiful, maybe. Her face was narrow, her profile sharp. But she had sleek, dark, winged brows and warm, liquid brown eyes and a mouth that was a bit too generous, the lips, even without lipstick, like now, soft and pliable and welcoming even while her words were taut and hostile. As they walked in he had to drag his gaze from her slim waistline, a blue satiny blouse tucked into a black skirt beneath the open lab coat.

Cat looked much like he had the first time he'd seen her. Unresponsive. Staring straight ahead. She was blond and blue-eyed and projected an almost eerie innocence, too perfect to believe in.

Otherworldly, Clausen had said of Catherine. It was true, too, of Cat.

"Detective Stone of the Tillamook County Sheriff's Department has come back to visit us again," Claire Norris said, leaning a bit toward the patient. Lang was conscious of the swell of her hips beneath the lab coat. His gaze traveled to her calves, trim and tight, with neat ankles and a pair of black flats.

What would that leg and foot look like in a three-inch heel? he wondered.

"He thinks you may have come from the town of Deception Bay. There's a lodge there called Siren Song."

Black patent leather, shining, tap-tapping against a wood floor as she walked away from him and—

"Detective?" The woman in question turned toward him, her brown eyes assessing.

"What?"

"She's responding."

His gaze flew to Cat's face. Those blue eyes were now staring straight at him now, unwaveringly. Waiting.

It was enough to send a cold little shiver under his skin. "We think you may be from Siren Song."

Was he imagining it, or did her eyes dilate?

"We've been trying to learn something about you. Your name. Where you come from. Your family members. We're in contact with someone from the lodge. Catherine," he added, pushing the truth.

She turned her head away. Slowly. To stare at the wall again. But before that Lang had noticed her skin quiver a bit. From fear? Cold? It was like an oven in this damn room, as far as he could tell, so that didn't make sense.

"Does any of that sound familiar?" Claire asked her.

Cat didn't respond, but Lang could tell her breathing was faster and shallower. Something was going on there.

"We've identified your traveling companion, Rafe Worster," he added. "He was a homicide victim the same night you were attacked."

No response to that. Lang brought up finding her and Worster's body at the rest stop, but she was gone to whatever world she'd escaped to. There were no more responses.

After a few more moments, Claire motioned for him to head out of the room. Reluctantly he let himself be banished to the hall as Norris assured Cat that she was safe at Halo Valley, that she needed to take her time in remembering, that everything was A-OK.

When Claire came out they walked together back down the hall. Lang asked, "Does that work? All that pacifying?"

"Everyone needs to feel safe."

"Is that the driving force of her catatonia? How do you know that?"

"I don't know the driving force," she said. "But given the circumstances that brought her here, I think a need to feel safe would be right at the top of her list."

"I'll buy that. She's scared. Someone tried to take her baby, or at least tried to cut her there. Wound her. Maybe kill her. And that same person killed her boyfriend."

"If he was her boyfriend."

"It's an assumption I'm going with until I hear differently," Lang said. "Makes the most sense, and it goes with what Cade said. Rafe, the sometime womanizer, worked at Siren Song around all those young women under Catherine's charge. He got to one of them: Cat. They started an affair and then . . . *bam*! She's pregnant. Bad news for everyone. So then . . ."

They were back in the lobby, but Claire had drifted toward the empty morning room. Lang followed her and they moved in unspoken decision toward the bookcase along one wall.

"So then?" she prompted.

Her face was close to his. For a moment he lost his train of thought. There was a strange intimacy about being in this corner, their voices low, their dialogue concerning a sexual affair. "So then they have to get out. Away from Catherine and all that repression. They run away together."

"Hmm . . ." She sounded unsure.

"What are you thinking?"

"By the time they run, she's seven or eight months pregnant. Her pregnancy has to be obvious to everyone. It's not like they could hide it."

"Lots of times women hide pregnancies. Teenagers hide them from their parents all the time. Some women don't even know they're pregnant until they deliver."

"That's the rarity," she said, but her tone was thoughtful. "They wear dresses that are almost smocks."

"So maybe Catherine didn't know?"

"You think Cat hid her pregnancy, and then ran away with this Rafe, who was her lover, before anyone could find out?"

"Maybe."

Claire's brow furrowed. "I'm not saying Cat's from Siren Song, but if she were, she might have felt it was imperative to leave when she did."

"To keep the news from Catherine. To save the baby. But then Catherine found out and went after them, found them at the rest stop, took out a knife—"

"No." Claire shook her head. "Not in her character. She's raised all those girls, apparently. She wouldn't do that."

"Anybody can kill," Lang argued. "And Catherine seems to be a woman of rigid rules. This could have been a

Nancy Bush

complete betrayal. What if she tracked them down, planning on—I don't know—forcing an abortion."

"What a sick mind you have," she sputtered.

"Coming from you, that's saying quite a lot. You being the expert on sick minds."

"I don't think that's Catherine's M.O., either. If Cat is really a member of the Colony, and she took a lover and became pregnant, that might certainly stir up some strong emotions in Catherine, but I don't think it would set her on a path of murder. Either the baby, Cat, or even this Rafe."

"Then why won't she even talk to me?" Lang demanded.

"You haven't given her a clue what it's about."

"She knows Cat left. She has to be worried about it. But for some reason she doesn't want to face it, and why would that be? Because she's at fault in there somewhere. Maybe criminally at fault."

"You're trying to force facts to fit your own theory."

"Well, why are you so dead set on defending a woman you don't even know?" Lang demanded.

"Why are you so dead set on making her out to be a monster?"

"Because she's holding those girls hostage. Not letting them out of that place!"

"You don't know that."

He snorted. "You say you live in Deception Bay? Well, how'd you miss the four-one-one on Catherine of the Gates? From what I've learned, she makes Nurse Ratched look good."

"So she follows Cat and her boyfriend and attacks them with a knife? Killing him and stabbing away at Cat's belly, with no real direction, then leaves her and the baby to die, too? If she's as concerned with rules as you say, she wouldn't break so many of them."

"You just want to defend her because she's a woman," he said.

Claire's eyes flashed. "You're going to make this about gender?"

Her eyes weren't totally brown. They had gold specks inside them. Gold specks that glowed hot. "It is about gender. You don't think a woman could be diabolical enough to chase them down and knife them to death?"

"Oh, yes, I do. Women can surprise you with their strength, fury, and commitment. I just think you're totally off base with Catherine. You're objecting to the circumstances in which the Colony women live. You think it's a kind of forced slavery. So Catherine is the head evildoer. You're focused on her, and it's taking you away from the real killer."

"I'm just letting this go where it goes," he countered. "Investigations are like that. You just follow them. They lead you where they're gonna lead you. To Catherine, or maybe to someone else. But she's my impasse."

She thought that over for a moment, turning slightly as if listening to something.

"What?" he demanded.

"It is about gender," she said, reversing her earlier stance.

"Wait. Really. My head's spinning," he said wryly. "Now you think I'm right?"

"You can't reach Catherine because you're not a woman," she said, ignoring his sarcasm.

But he saw where her thoughts were heading. Wasn't sure he agreed.

"Her world is all about women. Men are—"

"The enemy?" he guessed.

"I was going to say, men are a foreign culture. She doesn't understand them and doesn't want to deal with them."

"So I should go with a woman next time? Or send one?"

"You can go with me."

* * *

The words flew out of Claire's mouth before she really knew what she was saying. The discussion with Lang had been low and intense, and Claire, though she didn't really want to be so near him, felt strangely certain that she was on the right track where Catherine of Siren Song was concerned. And she wanted to help Cat. She wanted to be a part of this. With or without Langdon Stone, though she knew she couldn't just charge out on her own without him.

"No," he said.

"I can help you with her." Claire was calm and certain.

"You're out of bounds."

"Really?"

"Yes."

"How?"

He was on the defensive and it pissed him off. "I don't know," he admitted, "but you and I—face it, lady. We've got problems enough already, and I don't want to have you under my care."

"Under *your* care."

"Let's not . . ." He stepped away from her, hands up, as if she were some armed villain.

"You don't have to like me," she said determinedly. "But no matter what you think, I'm good at what I do. I'm going to try to talk to her. On my way home. You can join me if you want, but you can't stop me."

She didn't wait for his response. Didn't wait for anything. She swept past him and up the stairs and took out her keycard and let herself out of the hospital and into the medical office building.

Chapter 15

Claire took her own car, but she was completely attuned to the gray truck following her Passat as they drove west toward the coast. Detective Langdon Stone was following close behind her. She was pretty sure she'd taken complete leave of her senses.

"Is that a professional opinion?" she asked herself grimly. The answer was yes.

She shouldn't be doing this. Sure, she was trying to learn more about her patient, but rashly telling Langdon Stone that she was heading to Siren Song wasn't exactly part of the job description.

Why? Why had she jumped at this opportunity?

Claire took a corner too fast and forced herself to slow down, easing her foot off the accelerator. The rain was in abeyance but that didn't mean she should be driving at the mercy of her emotions. She was normally pretty good at self-assessment. Years of practice, she thought with a faint inner smile. When her marriage had broken up, she'd examined all the reasons, picking them apart, spreading them out, examining each one. Her ex, for all his faults, of which there were many, wasn't a bad guy. They just hadn't been on the same page.

Not all his fault. Not all hers.

Claire had done what so many had done before her upon the disintegration of their marriage: she'd thrown herself into her work. Her job was the one place she felt truly competent. She was good at it. She understood her patients. She made serious headway and glowed under the compliments of a particular one who'd overcome a crippling shyness, got promoted at her job, and gave all the credit to Claire.

Then came Melody Stone's death . . . at Heyward Marsdon III's hands.

Claire's professional foundation had crumbled and she'd been working to restore it ever since, sometimes with success, sometimes not.

And then Langdon Stone had entered her world and, well, here she was, making rash and strange decisions, acting anything but like her normally rational self.

"Do you have something to prove?" she asked herself as she turned north onto 101 and toward Deception Bay. "What are you doing?"

Glancing into her rearview, she could see Stone's wide shoulders above the dash and steering wheel.

"You want his approval? You can't get it this way. You know that."

With an effort Claire shut her brain down on the subject. She was committed to this task, come hell or high water, so she might as well just follow it through. Time for postmortems and recriminations later.

She drove past the cutoff to her rented cottage on the way, giving it a quick glance as she passed by. It was getting dark and she could see lights on at Dinah's place. As soon as she'd completed this harebrained attempt to solve the mystery of where Cat came from, she would have a drink with Dinah. Maybe two. Wine, not tea.

The turnoff to Siren Song was along the road that led to

the Foothillers' community, but it was a long, twisting turn and a rutted lane to the front gates. Claire pulled into a spot, bumping over gnarled roots and flattening waist-high grass. There was no parking area, as such; the Colony members didn't need one.

Lang's truck bumped along slowly toward her as Claire climbed from the Passat. She could see him swaying back and forth inside the cab as the wheels hit potholes. He turned in next to Claire, a small pine limb brushing his truck's side, and he had to push hard on the driver's door to extricate himself, some kind of catch there, Claire surmised. When he got out he surveyed the damage from the limb. His vehicle had seen a lot of hard use, and it amused her that he frowned at an apparent scrape.

"Maybe you can claim it on your insurance," she said. "Or, since you're working for the police, maybe they'll step up." She shrugged.

"It's not that bad."

He walked past her to the gates. He'd either missed her sarcasm or was too single-minded to care. Beyond was the lodge, and so far there were no lights shining from its windows at all in the gathering gloom.

Claire was leaning against her car and he gave her a hard look. "So, okay, you're the woman. See if you can get a response."

She walked over to the gates and peered through. The twin ruts continued on the other side and circled around to the back of the house. Huge laurels and Scotch broom and a row of twisted pines, tortured by the winter winds, crowded toward the lodge, whose boards had silvered over time. It was a pretty place, by all standards, but it had a tired, can't keep up feel to it. Claire bet if they could ever draw nearer, they would find signs of both dry and wet rot. The roof shingles looked okay; there were patches where new light tan ones had been nailed over broken gray ones.

Lang had come up beside her. She could feel heat radiating from his body to hers. The October air felt dense with moisture and night was falling, dropping the temperature. Still, she felt hot and prickly.

"What's your plan?" she asked him.

He gave her a long look. "You're the one who stormed over here because Catherine needs to see a woman."

"It might be better if I were here by myself."

"You want me to go hide in the bushes?"

"I'm just pointing out that your presence might be the problem."

"I think I'll stick around, all the same."

Minutes passed by. Claire felt a little foolish, but at least she and Lang weren't in open hostility at the moment, a miracle, given that he now knew that Heyward III had been moved out of criminal lockdown. Inwardly, she winced, knowing this was transitory. He'd granted a cease-fire, but the war wasn't over; she suspected it never would be.

Rain clouds scudded overhead, gathering ominously, darkening the already deepening shadows. Claire had thrown on her raincoat, but it offered little protection against the cold. She tried not to shiver, didn't want to show too much vulnerability, but after forty-five minutes of waiting she was fighting full-blown shakes.

"You're freezing," he observed. "You should go."

"What about you?"

"I don't know. I'll write another note." With that he pulled a pen and small pad of sticky notes from his jacket pocket and scribbled something down. "My cell number," he explained. "Like last time."

"Maybe you should offer something more?"

"I am." He was still writing, ripping off one sticky note, continuing onto another, and another, and then sticking them together by their glued edges. Carefully, he slipped them through the wrought-iron bars. He then searched around for something and Claire watched him pick up a rock, which he placed over the note. "It's gonna rain," he explained, and almost as if his words turned on the spigot, a deluge poured from the sky, sending Claire scurrying to her car.

"You're soaked!" she called to him over the roar of the downpour.

He nodded, but his gaze was on the lodge.

"Follow me!" she called.

"Where?" he yelled back.

"My place."

Claire slammed the door behind her and twisted her key in the ignition. The Passat fired right up and she backed around until she was facing out, driving carefully down the now rain-filled ruts.

Definitely, she'd taken leave of her senses. Definitely.

Two women stood inside the three-story foyer with its rough-hewn beamed ceiling and plank board floor, peering through peepholes strategically placed to offer a view of the front gate and unwanted visitors. Behind them, the wide stairway rose to a landing, turned, then led to the second floor. The lodge had been built by laborers from an architect's design, to the specifications of Catherine's ancestors. She'd lived here all her life; planned to remain here for the rest of it.

The woman beside her was half her age and confined to a wheelchair. She was slow by normal standards, but her insight was deep. Shockingly so. Like instinct.

"Are they here about Natasha?" she asked.

Catherine watched the strangers climb into their respective vehicles and drive away, then she pulled out the note that she'd carefully folded and tucked into a hidden pocket in her dress. It only listed the man's name and telephone number. Langdon Stone.

The girl leaned over to look at the note. "What does cell mean?"

"I believe it's his telephone number."

"What does he want?"

"I think you're right. They're here because of Natasha."

"They know where she is?"

"Come along, Lillibeth." Catherine grabbed the wheelchair's handgrips and pushed her through the Great Hall toward the kitchen area and the anteroom beyond, an adjunct storeroom that had been converted into a room that the outside world would have called a den. There were two settees against opposite walls and a wide, square, low table covered with hardbound books. Another young woman was already seated on one of the settees and folded her hands in her lap as they entered.

"What are we going to do?" she asked.

Catherine didn't immediately answer. She'd ignored the first note, but she'd seen him place another and mark it with a stone. Though her face and demeanor gave nothing away, she was in inner turmoil over Natasha and her child's impending birth.

"He was with a woman," she said aloud.

"Are you going to meet with her, then?" Lillibeth's eyes were wide.

"He left another note. When the rain abates, I'll collect it. Then we'll see."

She was talking to herself more than either Lillibeth or Isadora.

"Can I tell the others?" Lillibeth asked.

Catherine nodded. "Tell them to meet me in the Great Hall in an hour. It's time for decision making."

* * *

Rita felt a smile hovering on her lips as she stared at the ceiling while Paolo pressed her against the wall, grunting and fondling and slamming into her. He probably thought it was the height of sexual wildness, being there in the sole empty room on Side A, meeting with his secret lover. They'd been there exactly nine minutes, about all the time he needed. He'd grabbed her in the hall and pulled her into the room, and she'd let it happen. It was dinnertime for the residents and there was little chance of anyone surprising them. Rita was allowing the indiscretion because she was about to break up with him.

Her period was four days late.

Four days late.

She was pregnant. Had to be. Her only regret was the baby wasn't Rafe's.

His breath was hot against her neck. She glanced at the clock on the wall. Ten minutes.

"I've gotta get back on the floor," Rita whispered.

Paolo increased his rhythm and reached an instant climax. He fell against her, groaning. She'd learned more about him the past couple of weeks. He was divorced twice. No children. That had worried her at first, but he'd admitted that his first wife hadn't wanted kids and his second had suffered a miscarriage. Why the marriages had broken up didn't interest her.

"I don't know what I'm doing," he muttered, one of his favorite lines, as if this made it all okay.

It really pissed her off, the way it was always about *him*. That wasn't the way it was in Rita's world.

Quickly she grabbed her underwear and teal scrubs and slipped herself back inside them. She left while he was still buckling his belt. Bastard, she thought without heat. Fucker. She was through with him.

But when she entered the hall she nearly ran straight into Dr. Freeson, who slid her a look as she passed, his goatee quivering a bit. Weasel. He was always lurking about. Well, that was Paolo's problem. She would deny everything.

She walked on past him, her lips twitching. Pregnant. A baby . . .

Her happiness took a hit as she cruised by the morning room and checked out the diners. Tasha was there, big as a house. Rafe's baby would be here soon.

Rafe's baby.

She closed her eyes and found her way to the staff room, leaning against the wall for a moment. Then she headed into the adjoining bathroom and stall for a cleanup. She didn't want Paolo leaking out of her and—

No. No! Oh, no!

Rita's buoyancy disappeared in a whoosh. Her period had started.

No. Her heart beat hard, hurting. Maybe it was a mistake. Nothing to worry about. Maybe it would be okay!

But no . . . she recognized it for what it was.

No baby.

It took her twenty minutes to pull herself together. Twenty minutes before she could look at her face in the mirror as she washed her hands. She was dizzy with disappointment. Could hardly keep her balance. The old joyless Rita stared back at her. The one that could take over like another personality and do what was necessary to achieve her goals.

She cruised back by the morning room. Most of the residents were gone, but Tasha still sat there, as if she were waiting for something to happen. Gibby hovered nearby and Rita wanted to suddenly smack him silly. She was furious. She wanted to fucking kill him!

But no . . . this was not the time for rashness. She needed a plan. A plan.

Tasha. Rafe's baby. That's what she'd come to Halo

Valley for. Paolo Avanti had been a means to an end: to get a job. She'd made him her lover to get hired and had almost lost sight of her goal because she'd wanted so much to be pregnant herself!

Now she let out a little mew of hopelessness, then immediately clamped down on her emotions, her mouth hard, her expression stony.

Rita Feather Hawkings never gave up. Never.

"Tasha . . ." she said aloud, softly.

Lang yanked on the emergency brake of his truck and cut his headlights after seeing Claire Norris motion to him to join her as she scurried up the back steps of her home, her head covered by her raincoat hood.

He glanced down a sloping split in the driveway to another house, where he could see candles and blue, red, and gold refracted light, as if fed through a prism or crystal of some sort. A woman walked by, stopping for a moment and looking out as if she might be able to see him, which was impossible.

With a sigh, he climbed from the truck and walked steadily through the pounding rain and up the steps to the back door, which Claire was holding open. This was insanity, but he felt powerless to stop.

"Hurry up before we both drown," Claire said, and he stepped inside, rain puddling at his feet. She'd hung her raincoat on a hook and he took off his jacket and watched water drip rapidly onto the vinyl flooring beside the puddle from her own garment.

What am I doing here? he asked himself.

As if she'd heard his unspoken thought, she said, "You looked so wet, and I felt like it was my idea to go to Siren Song today."

"I would have probably been out in the rain with or

without you." He inhaled carefully; he didn't want to relax too much around her.

"You want to come in the rest of the way?"

She'd taken off her shoes, and after a moment's hesitation he yanked off his cowboy boots. His socks were damp but at least they wouldn't leave a wet and muddy trail. Running a hand through his hair, he followed her through a small galley kitchen to a sitting room with windows that looked out through the storm toward the ocean.

"I don't have food," she said, reaching into a cupboard. "But I've got wine." She pulled out a bottle of red.

"Thanks, but I've got to go soon."

"All right. I'm going to have a glass," she said, peeling off the foil, then opening a drawer and finding a corkscrew.

Lang felt completely out of his element. This wasn't how this day was supposed to go. He should be talking to her about Heyward Marsdon, berating her for going against the intention of the courts, arguing with her over what really happened in her office, what Melody might or might not have said. But he didn't doubt that she wanted to help their Jane Doe/Colony girl, and that's what he was there for now.

"What did you put in the note?" she asked, pouring the red wine into a stemmed glass.

"I gave them your name and profession. Thought that might stir things up. Not just a woman. A woman doctor."

His gaze fell on the glass of wine and, seeing that, she held it out to him. Feeling like he was falling into a trap, he reluctantly accepted the drink. There was something sensual about the rain and the wine and the storm outside, and it made Lang feel like a traitor.

"My sister didn't ask to be killed," he said again, taking a quick gulp of the wine.

She didn't respond, just poured her own glass with a concentration that spoke volumes.

"Nobody asks to be killed," he said hoarsely.

"I'm not going to argue with you."

"Why did you tell the guard she said that?"

"Because she did," Claire stated flatly. "I'm sorry. I should have kept that information from Wade, but I was in shock. I spoke the truth without censoring myself."

He thought that over. Finally said, "My sister was screwed up, but she wasn't suicidal."

Claire started to say that it wasn't about suicide, that Melody's plea to "do it" stemmed from her delusion, but stopped herself. Instead, she said, "If I engage in this argument, we'll fight, but it won't alter the facts."

"Great deflection. They teach you that in shrink school?" he demanded.

She took a heavy swallow. "In shrink school, we learned that sometimes we're the object of transference."

"You think I'm transferring my anger over my sister's death to you?" he asked with an edge of danger.

"Yes."

"So what I'm feeling is simply misdirected anger. Great. I feel so much better. Thanks for the cure, Doc."

"You *should* be angry," she said tautly. "We should all be angry. We failed. The system failed, and nobody wants to admit that Heyward Marsdon the Third is a ticking time bomb. A man—a very sick man—who will likely go off his meds again, and then anything's possible. Yes, I know, Detective. I'm not hiding my head in the sand. I don't think he should be on Side A, but does he belong on Side B?"

"Yes." He was adamant.

"Maybe. Maybe not."

"Then where does he belong?" Lang demanded.

"I don't know."

"Oh, finally. An honest answer."

"They've all been honest."

He wanted to come back at her. He really wanted to yell at her. The cooler she seemed, the hotter he got. But he could tell that she was bothered that Heyward had been moved. Bothered and unsure. Well, hell, why not? The bastard had held a knife to her throat, too, hadn't he?

A knock sounded on the back door and Claire whirled around, sloshing a bit of wine, her free hand to her throat. Tense, Lang thought, again, understanding how fragile her own state of mind was; no matter how logically she spoke.

"Dinah!" she said a moment later as she headed to the back door.

A moment later a blondish woman walked in, having deposited her own coat and boots in the mudroom. She wore a dark blue caftan and her hair was long and braided. He realized she was the neighbor even before she introduced herself.

"I'm Dinah, from next door."

"Langdon Stone."

They shook hands, assessing each other. Claire poured the newcomer a glass of wine and handed it to her. "Detective Stone was with the Portland police and is starting with the Tillamook Sheriff's Department soon."

"Detective," Dinah repeated, frowning. "You're not . . . ?"

"Yes. He's that Detective Stone." Claire didn't look at him.

"What are you doing here?" she asked, turning to encompass both him and Claire, clearly knowing that he was Melody's brother.

He opened his mouth to explain but Claire stepped in, telling her about Cat and the circumstances that had pulled him into the investigation and how it had led to Deception Bay and Siren Song.

Dinah listened intently, jerking a bit at the mention of the cult's lodge. Lang narrowed his gaze on her and said, "You're familiar with Siren Song?"

"Anyone who lives here knows about them," she side-stepped. "I still can't get over that Claire let you into her space. All that compressed negative energy. It's unhealthy."

He slid a look out the rain-washed window in the direction of her home. "You some kind of New Age quack?"

"That's one definition, I suppose." Her mouth quirked.

"A quack's quack?" He looked from her to Claire. "Beautiful."

Claire held her tongue with a comeback, but with an effort, he could see. She said tightly, "You're very quick to name call."

"I'm a two-year-old inside. I've been told that before. In all my relationships."

"You don't seem like you've had many relationships," Dinah said. "Not ones that count, anyway."

"Oh. You're a seer, too," he said. "This gets better and better. Do your colleagues at Halo Valley know about her?" he asked Claire.

"Do you want to start a fight with me?" Claire asked.

"I've been trying all night, lady."

Dinah said with amusement, "I think I walked into a lover's quarrel. The 'seer' missed that one." She started to head out.

"Don't go. I'm on my way out." Lang set his empty glass on the counter. "Thanks for the help, Dr. Norris. If Catherine of the Gates ever gets back to me, I'll be sure and let you know."

"You want to know about the Colony?" Dinah asked.

Both Claire and Lang turned to look at her, hearing something in her tone that arrested them both. She motioned for Lang to return and walked into the living room, curling herself into a chair, much like a cat, tucking her feet under her legs.

"What do you know?" he asked.

"Quite a lot, actually. My father wrote the book on them. Literally. He amassed a history of the Colony complete with old letters and newspaper articles. The works. And he knows Catherine personally."

Catherine looked over the sea of blond female heads and felt every one of her fifty-seven years. Her own hair was going gray, still threaded with blond, but those strands were diminishing day by day. She'd done her best to keep them all safe. She would continue to do so. But the breach of Natasha's disappearance was bringing the outside world too close. She hated the outsiders. Hated them all. They were too inquisitive and their sole aim seemed to be to strip Catherine and her charges bare of all their secrets. The outsiders called them the Colony and had latched on to the whimsical name of Siren Song for the lodge itself—Mary's name for it. Both tags had been adopted by the women inside as well. They were the current generation of the Colony and they lived at Siren Song. So be it.

But Catherine wanted no further influence from them, and tonight's meeting was called to ensure all of their agreement.

"Natasha has been found," she announced.

There was a murmur through the crowd. Anxious faces turned her way. Catherine spread both notes on the table; she'd braved the rain to collect the second one.

"I am going to meet with the sheriff's department," she went on. "I should only be gone several hours. As ever, Isadora is in charge."

"Lillibeth said there were two of them at the gate this time. The man, and a woman?" Ophelia said, her eyes bright. She was the youngest and the most interested in the outside world, an interest Catherine was desperately trying to quell.

"That's right," Lillibeth piped up.

"Let Catherine speak," Isadora intoned. She was the oldest and the most like Catherine . . . the least like Mary.

Catherine glanced down at the second note. "The woman's a doctor. Dr. Claire Norris. A psychiatrist." That announcement met with silence and Catherine almost smiled. "She will not be treating any of us."

"Is she Natasha's doctor?" This was said fearfully from Cassandra, who worried almost as much as Catherine about the outsiders and their influence.

"I will find out."

The girls—women, really, though Catherine had trouble thinking of them that way—asked more questions that she had no answers for. After a while the discussion dwindled and the girls trooped into the kitchen to finish the preparations for dinner. Lillibeth hung by Catherine, as she was always wont to do, but eventually Catherine turned her over to Augustine, who was the most nurturing of the group.

Catherine then mounted the back stairs to her room, an austere single room at the northwest corner of the upper hall with a view of both the front gate and the Pacific Ocean. The abandoned lighthouse was a deeper black shape in an already black sky. The island was an ugly hump of rock, also a faintly darker outline against the curtain of night. She could see a flicker of light from the island. Mary's island, she thought grimly, though it was known on maps as Echo Island because of the way sound refracted off its sharply planed rock walls.

She stepped away from the windows long enough to scrape a long wooden match across the stone tabletop of her nightstand and light an oil lamp, waving out the match and replacing the glass surround. She then carried the lamp to a small wooden desk on the opposite wall from the bed and sat down in the matching chair. Picking up a modern ink pen and a cloth-covered notebook, she began making a list of items to buy while she was on her errand. Groceries. Paper supplies. New bedding, as some of the duvets were too worn to last out the winter. Catherine could appreciate ready-made items; she wasn't as backward as the outsiders would believe. They even had electricity on the first floor and indoor plumbing.

But she had a wall to keep fortified. Lives to protect. If the outsiders should ever understand the extent of her girls' gifts . . .

Disasters had already struck. Tragedies heaped one upon another. Lifetimes of troubles that had spilled over into these modern times despite Catherine's best efforts.

There was an account of the Colony's history, written down by a man who still set Catherine's teeth on edge. One of Mary's many lovers. A self-proclaimed historian who'd been old enough to be Mary's father! A profligate who'd roamed the coastline and taken more women than any man had a right to, dropping children in his wake without a care. He'd wanted to be in the pages of the history he detailed. He'd known of the Colony womens' powers and Mary's inability to turn from Satan's grasp, and he'd wormed his way into Mary's bed, seduced her with grand gestures and his damn evil book that was filled with half truths and outright fiction. Oh, but Mary had wanted to believe! And what she'd done to be with him. The lies. The evil tricks.

The fornication.

Catherine squeezed her hands painfully together as she recalled her sister's cries of ecstasy from wild sex acts with him . . . and so many others. It was only when Catherine wrested control of Siren Song away from Mary that the lives of Catherine and Mary's string of children had settled into a righteous path.

But now Mary was gone and the historian was in a care facility, his brain riddled with as many holes as a block of

Swiss cheese. She was glad he couldn't remember. Glad he was no longer a threat to them. If she could have gotten her hands on his account, she would have destroyed the manuscript immediately, but by a series of events it had found its way to the local historical society, a group of well-meaning but fairly stupid do-gooders who had no idea what the Colony, and Catherine herself, were about.

She'd actually gone to the old church that was now the Deception Bay Historical Society and examined the book herself. They'd known who she was and had stared at her, so it had been impossible to steal the leather-bound scrapbook of notes and letters and fiction. She'd wanted to tell those wide-eyed women a thing or two. She'd wanted to negate everything about her family as lies. But she'd kept her thoughts to herself, glad, at least, that the account ended with Catherine Rutledge and Mary Rutledge Beeman. No more names listed. None of Mary's many female children.

The problem was, there could be more pages out there. Somewhere. Written down by either the historian himself or the doctor who had been entrusted with the book until his own death, whereupon it had somehow become property of the historical society. In that regard, Catherine would have preferred it was still in the hands of the historian himself; she could have found a way to get it back. Now it was public record. Compiled and collected and written down all in one place. Easy to access, if you knew what you were looking for, and it had already surfaced a year and a half ago and been pored over and examined, and people had come to her gates asking questions.

Catherine closed her eyes and sighed. She didn't want to think about it anymore, but now there was this latest problem of Natasha. Natasha, who'd never been happy with Catherine's precautions, who'd longed to join the outsiders though Catherine's own visions, and Lillibeth's instincts, had foretold of death and madness should Natasha be allowed to leave as others had in the past.

And then there was Natasha's baby.

Lang sat on the edge of Claire's couch, processing the history that Dinah had shared with them about herself and her relationship to the women at Siren Song. Dinah's father, Herman Smythe—Herm, to his friends—had written an account of the Colony, and it was now at the local historical society. Herm, who was in his eighties, was currently living at a care facility outside Deception Bay, but he'd spent some time within Siren Song's walls when he was younger.

Which basically added up to jack shit, when you thought about it.

"You want me to put that information on a note and throw it through the gate to them?" Lang suggested. "That'll get me inside?"

Claire, however, was more encouraged. "Could we visit your father?" she asked Dinah.

"I don't know how lucid he might be, but sure."

"How old is he again?" Lang asked.

"Old enough to be my grandfather," Dinah admitted. "He was a man of excess, in love and life. I know more about him from afar than as a true father. My mother raised me. Alone. He popped in now and again, was thrilled to see me for a good ten minutes or so at a time, but then he'd go."

"Where's your mother now?"

"Remarried. Moved to California last year. My mother is twenty years younger than my father."

"And your father knew—knows—Catherine?"

"He knew Mary a lot better," she said with pointed meaning. "It's quite possible some of the women who live there are my half sisters."

Chapter 16

"Your half sisters," Lang repeated. He looked over the slim woman with her blond/light brown braid. "You're one of them?"

"No."

"Who are you?" he asked, feeling like there was more going on in this room than he'd been led to believe. "How do you know Dr. Norris?"

Claire intervened. "We're neighbors. Friends." She turned to Dinah. "You seriously think they're your sisters?"

"I think my father had sexual relations with Mary," she answered. "He's as much as said so. He could be one of them's father. Or several of them . . . it's not clear."

"Start at the beginning," Lang said in his investigator's voice, then, as a thought occurred to him, "Did you work at the local grocery store?"

She gave him a funny look. "The Drift In Market? No. Why?"

He shrugged.

"I'm not one of the girls from Siren Song," she stressed again. "My mother was a local townie from Deception Bay who got swept up in romance by my father, but twenty years is a pretty big gap in age. The romance didn't last. They split up not long after my birth. I was raised by a single mother. My dad has always just been around the area. I was never close to him emotionally, although we're more like a father and daughter now that he's in the care facility."

"What happened to Mary?" Lang asked.

"I don't know."

"Your father's book . . ." Claire said thoughtfully. "Do you think there's anything in it that would help us in connecting with Catherine and the girls?"

Dinah shook her head. "Let me explain something. The girls you speak of are *women*. The oldest ones are in their thirties and they go down to, I don't know, early twenties, maybe?"

"Cat's in her early twenties," Claire said.

"But I don't really know them," Dinah went on. "Nobody knows them. They stay in the lodge. There was a time when the state tried to go after them for lacking education requirements, and after a wrangle, Catherine allowed them to be supervised and take their GEDs. No problem there. They were well educated and passed easily. They keep to themselves by choice."

Lang said, "All we want to do is talk to them."

"Are they all Mary's daughters?" Claire asked.

"Probably. Or Catherine's, I suppose."

"How many of them are there?" Lang asked her.

She shook her head.

"Would your father know?" he pressed.

"Maybe. You can ask him. Does it matter?"

"If Jane Doe's one of their own, why aren't they moving heaven and earth to get her back?" he demanded, half angry. "Catherine doesn't let them leave, as a rule, apparently, so why hasn't she come looking for her?"

Claire said, "Maybe they let her leave."

"Why?" he demanded.

"Her pregnancy?"

"From what she's saying," Lang said, pointing to Dinah, "that's not much of an issue after all. This Mary had affairs and a lot of children. Kinda flies in the face of this old-fashioned, morally strict life they supposedly live."

"Mary's affairs were long ago. And Catherine's, too, if she had any," Dinah said. "They do live an old-fashioned, morally strict life now."

"The person who knows is Jane Doe," Lang said. "If Catherine won't talk to us, maybe she will. Soon." He glanced at Claire. "She's walking already."

"There's no guarantee," Claire began, but Lang made a sound of frustration.

"A man is dead," he stated flatly. "There's a killer out there. I'm not going to wait around for Catherine to talk to me, or Cat to wake up and point the finger at her attacker."

"What are you going to do?" Claire asked.

"I don't know yet. Something." He suddenly strode toward the mudroom, yanked on his boots, and threw on his jacket. "Thanks for the wine," he said, then banged out the door into the wet and windy night.

Claire felt strangely bereft. She didn't want him to go. Didn't want to give up his *maleness,* for lack of a better word.

"He's something," Dinah said, pointedly looking at Claire.

"Don't go there," Claire warned and Dinah smiled.

"Would you like to talk to my father?" she asked.

Claire turned back to her. "Yes, I would," she said without hesitation.

"Tonight? We could be there by seven thirty."

"Well . . ." Claire set down her wineglass. "Why not? Let's stop for sandwiches on the way. I'll buy."

Tasha allowed herself to be wheeled back to her room by Maria, careful to hide the clothes Gibby had brought to her beneath the wheelchair's cushion. Gibby had wanted to shout to the whole world about how he'd helped her, but Tasha had shushed him into silence. She just hoped he would stay that way until she got away.

It seemed to take the night nurse forever to settle Tasha in and leave. Twice Tasha glanced fearfully toward the wheelchair because the cushion was tilted and lumpy and a tiny bit of fabric stuck out like a tongue. Tasha was nearly weak with worry that Maria would notice, but the nurse was completely oblivious as she talked both to Tasha and herself, finally dimming the overhead light on her way out.

In darkness, Tasha slid out of the bed, feeling cumbersome and off balance. Sometimes she couldn't believe she was going to have a baby. Rafe's gift. The one Rita wanted so badly.

She had to leave tonight!

Fumbling around, she yanked the cushion off the chair and tossed it on the ground. Her fingers closed over the pants. She found the zipper and arranged the pants so that it was in front, then stepped first one leg, then the other, into the canvaslike material. Pulling them up, she smiled into the darkness. Pants. She was leaving one world behind, joining a new one.

She couldn't get them zipped all the way unless she kept the waist under her protruding belly. Good enough, she thought, though the hemlines dragged on the ground. Gibby might be short, but there was still too much pant leg and she couldn't bend over to roll them up. Feeling precious time slipping away, she sat down in the wheelchair and tried to perform the task, frustration and fear nearly boiling over. In the end she lowered herself to the ground and bent her feet inward to reach the hem. Quickly rolling the legs up, she then found her shoes and slid her feet into them.

Gibby's shirt was next. She tossed off the hospital gown with disdain and buttoned up the plaid long-sleeved shirt.

It nearly burst the buttons across her abdomen. Then tiptoeing to the door, she glanced both ways in the hall. No one around.

But how, how was she going to get through the locked exits? She couldn't push her way out and if she even tried, alarms would sound. Distantly. In one or several of the staff rooms. She'd heard it before when Maribel had banged against one of the bars, crying that she was going to miss the bus.

Only the keycard and code would let her out noiselessly.

Could she risk turning on the light? she wondered. Just for a moment? Just to look at herself?

She debated, then finally flipped the switch, the room flooding with light. Quickly she examined herself in the mirror and smiled a bit in awe. She looked *modern*. Sure, the clothes were masculine, but it was so much better than either the hospital gown or the gingham or printed ankle-length cotton dresses she'd worn her entire life.

She was sick of being part of the Colony. Sick of being different. Penned up. Told what to do, what to think.

The new Tasha was through trying to conform. There was no Natasha from Siren Song any longer.

She was reborn.

Her finger was touching the light switch when the door swung inward. The moment before she plunged the room into darkness, she saw Rita's face.

And the knife in Rita's hand.

The care facility where Dinah's father resided was called Seagull Pointe and it was composed of white-painted cinder blocks and sprawled around a parking lot with a center island where a wind-whipped pine waved its branches at approaching vehicles. Its utilitarian design seemed born in the fifties, and what it lacked in architectural interest it made up in maintenance. The place looked freshly washed and painted, and when Claire and Dinah walked inside, a faint citrusy scent overlaid the sharp odor of ammonia and chlorine from cleansing products.

The woman manning the front desk knew Dinah and said that Herman was sitting by the nurse's station, one of his usual haunts, apparently. They found him in a wheelchair, idly chatting with a younger woman and holding her hand.

Dinah threw Claire a look. "Some things never change," she said.

One of the attendants greeted them with a big smile and said loudly, "Look who's here, Herm. Dinah and a friend. They've come to see you."

Herm had a full head of silvery white hair, light gray eyes that seemed slightly unfocused, and a lean body dressed in jeans, sneakers, and a gray V-necked sweater vest over a white shirt. Seeing Dinah, he patted his companion's hand, then got to his feet, leaving her for his daughter. He bowed low over her hand.

"You want to walk to your room?" she asked, grabbing the handles of his empty wheelchair and pushing it forward.

"Sure thing. Exercise is good for you." He gave Claire a long, glittering look from eyes that seemed to suddenly come alive.

"I'm Claire," she said.

"Are you a doctor?" he asked, surprising her. Before she could respond, he said, "Dinah always wants me to see another doctor." In an aside, he said, "She thinks there's something wrong with me."

"Claire's actually interested in the Colony," Dinah said as they headed down the hallway, three abreast.

"Ah . . . the Colony. I wrote a history about them, did you know?" he said. "Where is that book?"

"It's with the historical society," Dinah reminded him. "But Claire was wondering about the women, the girls, when you knew them, who are under Catherine's care. You remember them?"

"Sure, I remember them. So many girls, and it was too bad about Nathaniel."

"Nathaniel?" Claire asked.

"Terrible accident. Died very young. He's in the grave-yard, but the book . . . it's with Parnell," he stated with sudden certainty. "I didn't give it to him. He took it. I think he meant to give it back to them. Did he ever do that?" He turned to Dinah for verification. "It wasn't his to give!"

"Parnell is dead," Dinah said carefully. "He's been dead for years."

"Killed himself," Herm remembered. "Where's the book?"

"At the historical society, Dad, but it only follows the Colony through Mary and Catherine's generation. Nothing about the women who live there now."

"Hmm." He thought that over. "I'm sure there's more. Much, much more." He turned to Claire. "Parnell threw himself off the jetty. Did you know that?"

"I've never heard of Parnell," she admitted.

"Well, he was their doctor. The cult's. Dr. Parnell Loman. He attended them and he had a daughter of his own. I always wondered if he took her from them. She never had a mother that anyone knew of."

Dinah said for Claire's benefit, "There were two doctors. Brothers. Both in my dad's generation: Dr. Parnell Loman and Dr. Dolph Loman."

"Dolph!" Herm sneered. "Pompous ass!"

Dinah went on, "Parnell's dead but Dolph is still on staff at Ocean Park. Semiretired, I think. Dad was kind of in competition with both of them for the ladies' affections around here."

"I was quite a swordsman in my day," he said, leaning toward Claire with a wink. "Still am."

"I see." Claire was amused.

He made a face. "But Parnell, though. He liked 'em young."

"Takes one to know one, Dad," Dinah said with a laugh.

They'd reached his room and Dinah wheeled the chair inside as Herm and Claire followed. Herm seated himself back in the wheelchair with a sigh. He wasn't as strong as he would like them to believe. The room held a twin bed and there were two orange molded plastic chairs, which Claire and Dinah each took. A wheelchair-accessible bathroom was attached.

"What do you want to know, girl?" Herm asked, folding his hands in his lap.

Claire thought about it a moment, hardly knowing where to start and what to ask. She finally told him of the general belief that Cat had come from Siren Song, and after glossing over the attack at the rest stop, explained about Cat having an accident and that she was unresponsive.

"She in a coma?" he demanded.

"In a manner of speaking," Claire said. "A catatonic state."

"She blond? They all are, you know. Blondish, anyway. All of 'em."

"Yes," Claire said.

He nodded. "There's a bunch of 'em there. And there are some that have left. They used to give 'em away, you know. She had so many of 'em, and Catherine got sick and couldn't take care of 'em and Mary was—well, I guess you'd call her a loose woman. Hah! Damn near pornographic, she was. Sexy. I was trying to interview her and she dragged me into her bed so fast I never got my shoes off! My pants were down at my ankles!"

Dinah stared off into space, long suffering, clearly having heard her father's embellished stories too many times to count.

"She dropped babies faster'n you could count," Herm went on. "Screwed everything in pants. Mind you, I left that out of the history. Kept those lurid parts to myself."

"So, the women who live at Siren Song now are Mary's children, not Catherine's?" Claire asked.

"Catherine's legs have been clamped shut since the Ice Age, dear girl. She had to clean up Mary's messes, didn't she. I always kind of liked her, but she hated me. She hated every man who Mary took to bed."

"How many children did Mary have?" Dinah asked curiously.

He shrugged. "I wasn't a regular guest after the first couple of times. Mary told me some history, and from what I already knew, I compiled the book. Showed it to Mary. I was going to include the babies, but Catherine came at me with a fire poker once, and I quit being invited. Never got their names down, but Isadora's the oldest. Then there was Jezebel, but she was adopted out, I think. And then another one was adopted out. Or two or three. Don't rightly know. Go ask Parnell. He's their doctor."

"Parnell's dead," Dinah reminded.

"Ask that cold bastard Dolph, then. He would know." He nodded his head and stifled a yawn. "Catherine . . . She and I have run into each other a few times over the years. She's never forgiven me for the book, though it's just facts. I didn't put their weirdness in it."

"Weirdness?" Claire asked.

"A lot of interbreeding in that family, through the years. Strange things develop. And there was this shaman that Sarah slept with."

"That's lore, Dad. Not fact."

He waved a hand at Dinah. "Unverified facts are still facts."

Claire was beginning to see that Herm Smythe's

supposed book about the Colony might be more fiction than truth.

A nurse entered the room and looked apologetic. "I'm sorry. I didn't know Herm still had visitors."

Herm yawned again and Claire said, "We were just leaving."

"Don't go!" he implored.

"I'll be back later, Dad," Dinah said, and then she and Claire were in the hall. "Did any of that help?"

"I don't know," Claire said honestly. "I'll talk about it to Cat, see if she reacts to anything. Maybe a little history of the Colony might jar something loose."

"You might want to leave out the part about my father being a swordsman in his day," Dinah said, her lips quirking.

"There will undoubtedly be a few remarks that I'll edit," Claire assured her.

In the moment after Tasha recognized Rita and her intention to kidnap her from the hospital, there was a chance she could get away. That she could win. Turn the tables on her. A single moment were she tensed, ready to leap away.

But Rita Feather Hawkings, Rafe's ex-girlfriend, was strong, determined, and mean. She grabbed for Tasha, who stumbled backward, would have fallen if Rita's arms hadn't caught her and dragged her to her feet.

The knife was against her neck. Tasha still had the wounds on her shoulder and back from Rita's first attack.

And in her moment's hesitation, Tasha lost.

"I won't let you take my baby," Tasha said, eyes closed, body tense.

"You want to get out of here. I'm taking you out of here." She pushed her into the wheelchair. "If you fight me, I'll have to stop you."

Kill you. That's what she meant.

"You have my baby," she stated flatly.

Tasha understood fully the complexity of Rita's problems. Rafe had mentioned her. Tasha had seen her standing outside the bars of Siren Song, eyes burning, hands bent into claws, breathing fury at both her and Rafe.

She had to fight Rita but knew she would lose.

But if Rita could get her outside these walls . . . ?

"I won't fight you," she said.

And with that Rita led her to the side door, using her keycard and punching in a code, and then they were into the raging, wind-tossed night where rain and wet leaves flew around her and Tasha greeted them with growing excitement.

And felt a gut-twisting contraction, as hard as anything she'd ever experienced.

Lang drove all the way back to his house outside Portland through a black night full of flying leaves, small limbs, and slamming rain. He made a quick stop at a fast-food restaurant for three crunchy tacos and a cola, and when he entered the house, he set down the cola, threw off his jacket, then headed straight to the refrigerator for a beer. Lost in thought, he munched down the tacos and drank the beer, not remembering much of either.

A lot of information had been gleaned and discussed in one day. A lot of miles traveled. A lot of surprising moments, not the least being his own attitude around, and interest in, Dr. Claire Norris.

He'd been a jerk in some ways. Reminded himself of how he'd been with women in his youth. *His youth.* Weren't those embarrassing high school and college days behind him? Good God, he'd said some dumb things.

He should be furious with her over the hospital's

arrogance in moving Heyward Marsdon from the lock-down side of their facility. He was furious.

But it wasn't really her fault.

Melody's death wasn't her fault.

Nothing was her fault.

"God. Damn. It."

Annoyed with himself, he fell back onto the couch and raked his hands through his hair. Was he doing the right thing? Moving to Tillamook? Leaving the Portland area and all the bad and sad memories? Leaving his friends, too?

Was he wandering around in this investigation that really wasn't his own because he was paralyzed by indecision? Afraid of commitment?

But no. He'd committed to O'Halloran and the TCSD. He just hadn't pulled the trigger about coming on board. Why? he asked himself now. Why, why, why?

There was no answer. He was in a self-imposed limbo. The same limbo he'd wallowed in since Melody's death, and maybe even before . . .

Grimacing, he thought about his last year with the Portland P.D. He'd done his job. Had even had moments of brilliance. He'd enjoyed being partnered with Curtis, whom he considered one of his closest friends.

But . . .

He'd been itching for something, some kind of change. In his personal life. Something meaningful. A direction. A plan.

A woman.

And then Melody died and his focus shifted. Sharply and completely. All he could think about was revenge and justice, not necessarily in that order. He'd wanted Heyward Marsdon to hurt. He wouldn't have cared if the man died. A part of him wanted him scrubbed from the planet.

And he wanted the damn supercilious Marsdon family to hurt like he hurt. He wanted to be the one to *make them hurt*.

And the lovely Dr. Claire Norris with her shining dark hair, serious eyes, careful words, and deep trauma was someone else he could focus his anger and frustration on. Even though she was a victim, too. Of both Heyward III and the damn, miserable hospital bureaucrats who worshipped funding over all else.

This case, which Trey had asked him to take, had undoubtedly conspired with Drano for him to take, along with the willing cooperation of Sheriff Nunce and Detective Will Tanninger of Winslow County . . . this case had thrown him right back into direct contact with Halo Valley Security Hospital and the woman who'd treated the man who'd killed his sister.

Was that karma? Bad luck? An opportunity to finally deal with his own unresolved emotions?

He jumped off the couch and headed to the refrigerator for another beer, except the refrigerator was empty. Hanging on the door, he stared into the empty shelving under the bright bulb. No food. No clothes, really, either. He was packed up and gone. This was just a side trip, a zigzag, a lateral move away from the path he'd chosen. A respite. A retreat.

A run away . . . from Claire Norris.

He closed the refrigerator door.

"I like her," he said aloud to the empty room, then shuddered. Jesus, he was an idiot.

Before he could descend further into self-flagellation, he headed for the bathroom and a hot, or maybe a more deserved cold, shower.

Tasha was in Rita's car, and Rita was driving fast down black highways with dim light from the lamps on the front of the car. Headlights. With barely enough illumination to make out the broken white lines in the middle of the road.

Tasha didn't know how to drive. Her trip with Rafe had been one of two other car rides she'd even experienced in her life. That night she'd buried her head against him, almost afraid to look out to the road. It made her feel kind of queasy.

But tonight she was focused. Watching. Every nerve fiber on alert. Like the funny feel after an electric storm. The lifting of the hairs on her arms.

She felt the wave of another contraction begin. She wished she could time them. She knew she had to time them. But they were no more than five minutes apart. Was that close? Was birth imminent? She didn't know.

She closed her eyes, retreating into a distant world. But she had to stay alert. Had to stay in front of the blackness that wanted to come for her.

Her body was making up its own timetable about when this girl child would come into the world. She knew it was a girl. It was always a girl with them, wasn't it? Except for Nathaniel. And he'd been sick. Worse than Lillibeth, by far, even before her accident. He wasn't meant to survive. Tasha had known that early on.

"What's wrong?" Rita asked sharply.

She couldn't tell her about the contractions. Couldn't let her know. Had to hide it if she could. "Keep your eyes on the road, bitch," she said through gritted teeth.

She felt rather than saw Rita's surprise. It was always that way. No one expected a girl with angelic looks to be so harsh. Oh, she knew what she looked like. She knew the effect she had on strangers, though Catherine had done her best to keep Tasha hidden away, locked up, imprisoned.

"You fooled Rafe, but you don't fool me," Rita said.

"They'll look in on me. They'll know I'm gone."

"You were leaving anyway. Or trying to. It's no different."

"They'll come find me."

"They're going to realize that you killed Rafe," Rita said as if it were complete fact. "They're going to figure it out."

"You killed Rafe," Tasha said.

"I loved Rafe. And you took him from me. Forever." Her voice was toneless, emotionless.

The edges of the dark curtain were coming closer. *No . . . not yet . . .*

Tasha fought the blackness, nearly paralyzed with fear. Sinking into her seat, she squinched her eyes closed, gripping her hands together as another wave of pain squeezed her from the inside out.

Chapter 17

The phone call woke Lang from a light sleep. He'd gone to bed early from the simple fact that he had no TV at his house any longer and there had been nothing to do. He was mildly surprised that he'd actually fallen into slumber. Groping around, he found his cell on the floor beside his bed, the only piece of furniture still in his bedroom. Had to move the damn thing soon and finish the move. Needed a little better weather before he strapped it onto his pickup, and he didn't feel like paying some moving guy a minor fortune for the honor of the duty.

"Stone," he rasped.

"It's Claire Norris." She sounded slightly panicked. "I'm sorry to bother you. Cat's gone. Jane Doe!"

Her voice washed over him, strong and full of emotion. It took a moment for him to hear her words. "Gone. How?"

"Maria, one of the night nurses from Side A, just called me. She went to check on Cat and her room was empty. Cat left her hospital gown but took her shoes. I was going to get her clothes but I haven't yet. I don't know what she's wearing, where she could be. There's been an all-out search of the hospital, but no one can find her."

Lang blinked several times, trying to get his brain in

gear. "Okay, slow down. Could she get past the doors to the medical offices?"

"I don't see how," she said, then, "I called Dr. Freeson, who already knew about Cat's disappearance because Maria phoned him first. And Avanti was on call, so I'm playing catch-up. Freeson said they'd apparently looked everywhere. Even checked Side B, but she would have been seen on the monitors, and anyway, I don't see how she could get past any door. She doesn't have a keycard. She doesn't know the code."

"Did anyone come in to see her?" He was out of bed, searching for his clothes in the dark. "If she's really gone, someone had to help her."

"No one's been to see her. She doesn't have visitors."

"Claire, consider this. Could she have been faking all this time?"

"No." She was positive. Then, "At least not in the beginning. She was out of it."

"What about now?" he pressed.

"She's been reactive. You saw. And able to walk. She just hasn't spoken to anyone yet." She inhaled sharply suddenly.

"What?" he demanded.

"Well, Gibby—Bradford Gibson, one of the patients—says she talks to him. But Gibby thinks everyone talks to him and that's not necessarily true."

"You're on your way to the hospital?" He looked around for a clock but the room was pitch black. His watch was on the bathroom counter, so he stumbled into the bathroom and flicked on the light. 10:30 P.M.

"I should be there in thirty minutes."

He should have stayed at the coast. "It'll take me two hours to get there," he said, pissed all over again that he hadn't completely moved to Tillamook, where he would be forty-five minutes from the hospital on the outside.

"I called you just to let you know. Because of the investigation. But there's no need for you to come to the hospital tonight."

"I'm coming. If she's up and moving around, maybe she's able to talk more than we've thought."

"She's got to be on the premises. I just . . . wanted you to know."

"I'll be there as soon as I can."

"Thank you," she said humbly.

He snapped the cell phone shut, stubbed his toe on the edge of the bathroom door in his hurry, swore violently, and hopped back into the bedroom to find the rest of his clothes and boots.

Rita parked the car in her mother's driveway. Delores would be asleep, and if she wasn't, Rita had sedatives that would take care of that matter. She couldn't bear the thought of her mother's nagging. She had important matters to deal with.

Tasha's eyes were closed, her whole body clenched. She was breathing shakily and moaning. At first Rita thought it was an act, which infuriated her, but now that they were stopped and she could look at her, she thought maybe Tasha was really in labor.

The baby was coming!

She couldn't leave her in the car while she dealt with Delores. She didn't trust that Tasha wouldn't run away, although how far she would get in her condition, Rita couldn't say. Not far.

Rita hurried around the back of the car to the passenger door, her hair wet and straggling in the rain. She yanked open the door and pulled Tasha out by sheer willpower and strength. The girl dropped to her knees in a mud puddle but Rita prevailed, arms under hers, dragging her toward the short flight of wooden steps that led to the back door. She banged inside, smacking her elbow. Tasha groaned and jerked, but she was only half-conscious. Good.

"Rita? What are you doing?" her mother called from the bedroom.

Rita manhandled Tasha to the couch, a sagging affair with worn cushions and arms. Tasha was soaked to the skin and pale in the faint light thrown from the windows of the nearest house, the only light available as the community didn't have streetlights.

A sorry place to live. A sorry place to be. Rita Feather Hawkings and her child were going to run far away from here. They had to.

She felt a pang for the job she'd briefly enjoyed, but it was nothing. Nothing!

She was going to have a baby. Hers and Rafe's!

"Rita!"

Tasha's eyes moved behind closed lids. She was trying to wake up.

Rita hesitated briefly, then scurried to the kitchen. Quickly, she poured a glass of water and shook out a tumble of pills from the bottle she kept inside a high cupboard. One sedative normally did the trick, but two would guarantee Delores would remain under longer. Deeper.

She took three. A gamble. But worth it. Hurriedly, she crushed the tablet on a small plate with the back of the spoon. Then she slid the powdery dust into the glass, stirring it quickly with the spoon.

"Rita! Stop ignoring me at once!"

A quick look in on Tasha. She was writhing on the couch.

"Rita!"

"Coming, Mother," she called, racewalking down the hallway, balancing the glass.

"What are you doing? Why are you banging around,

making so much noise? Who's here? Did you bring someone home with you? You're late!"

Delores was in bed. She was ambulatory, though she walked very slowly and precisely, but she chose to stay in bed and let Rita wait on her if she could. Now she glared at her daughter as Rita handed her the glass. Delores took the drink and threw it onto the floor. "What are you trying to do?" she yelled.

Rita stared at the dripping liquid spreading on the threadbare carpet. "Mother!"

"I don't want a drink. Do you know how late it is? I haven't had dinner yet!"

Rita couldn't think. Could not think. Her brain whirled and whirled, but no thoughts evolved. "What about Sharon?" she finally asked, referring to the woman who lived down the end of the block and helped out when Rita's hours prevented her from getting her mother's meals ready. This dependency of Delores's was new and growing bigger, a yawning, sucking hole of quicksand that Rita was determined to escape.

"Sharon has a family. Like you do. She can't be here every minute. Where have you been?"

"The hospital. My new job." Rita stumbled back toward the kitchen and the pills. She would force them down her mother's throat if she had to.

Her hands shook. She poured out three more tablets. Shook out a fourth. For a long moment she looked at all the tablets in the bottle. Her mother wanted dinner. There was nothing in the house except canned goods.

"I'm making you soup," she called loudly.

"I don't want soup!"

Cold fury ran through Rita's veins as she turned on the only working electric burner, grabbed a can of chicken noodle soup from the cupboard they used to store their meager supplies and a saucepan from its place on the dish rack where Sharon had left it. Then she yanked out a handheld can opener from the drawer, furiously turned the handle until it was open, and dumped the contents into the pan.

Soup was what her mother was going to get.

She crushed four tablets and added them into the mix. Maybe she should make it five?

As if coming out of a trance, Rita suddenly realized she hadn't heard Tasha moaning.

She stumbled into the living room and to her disbelief realized the blond bitch was gone! *Gone!*

How? She'd been unconscious. In labor.

Hadn't she?

Rita raced outside and glanced around, shielding her eyes to the rain. There was blackness all around. And wind and flying leaves and small sticks.

"You can't hide!" she screamed into the night, lurching around the corner of the house.

Tasha bent over, hidden behind a stack of fir chunks three houses away, her hand clamped over her mouth. The contractions were still coming, but they weren't as intense as she'd led Rita to believe. What she'd thought were labor pains had lessened. She was beginning to think that maybe this wasn't the baby coming immediately. Maybe it was false labor. Or her body's reaction to extreme fear.

Whatever it was, she was capable of movement. Escape. She could find help.

She knew where she was. She'd listened hard to Rafe's loose accounts of his life and how he knew Rita Feather Hawkings. They lived in the same community. A small town in the foothills of the mountains, not all that far from the lodge. She also knew, probably far more than he did, that his community had been founded by Native Americans. The people in the foothills served Tasha's ancestors at the lodge and the town of Deception Bay. Rafe was half Native American, and Tasha thought she might be distantly, distantly related to him. She'd stumbled upon the fact that a member of her family had once had a torrid affair with an Indian shaman. Catherine denied that fact as fable, but Tasha knew Catherine would do anything to keep Tasha and her sisters from knowing anything about their past, and Tasha hoped it wasn't the shaman who'd scared her as a child.

But Rafe was no longer here. Rafe. Innocent, trusting father of her child.

Rain ran down Tasha's face and she brushed water from her eyes and off her nose.

And then she saw Rita rush into the road, whose shallow ruts were rapidly filling with water, the scattered gravel nearly flooded. She was staggering in the downpour, her head whipping from side to side. Fearing detection, Tasha folded herself even farther behind the woodpile and pressed herself to the concrete basement wall of the adjoining house.

She wished she'd had time to get a knife from the hospital.

She had to get away from Rita.

Had to save herself and her baby.

But how?

And who? Who could help?

Rita threw herself forward, half-running into the rain, and Tasha, peering from behind the woodpile, soaked to the skin, suddenly knew where she could hide.

All she had to do now was find the place.

Why did you call him? Claire asked herself. *Why? What do you want from him?*

She wheeled the Passat into the nearest spot to the hospital portico, wheels sliding in the standing water. At the corner of the building one of the drainpipes was dumping a torrent of water onto the saturated ground.

She wanted to thunk her palm to her own forehead. She was losing it. She found him attractive, too attractive. Hadn't wanted to see him leave earlier.

But it was professional suicide to bring him to Halo Valley, right into the snake pit with Freeson and Avanti.

"Damn," she muttered fervently, jumping out of the car. She flipped up the hood of her raincoat, holding the two sides close with one hand, not bothering with the zipper. Hurriedly, she ran through the rain to the portico, pulling out her keycard and punching in the code. Lori was long gone from her desk but there were floor lights illuminating the rug and dimmed overhead can lights keeping the place from total darkness.

Avanti, Freeson, Maria, and Greg were standing in a tight circle in the foyer. They waited for her to enter, then waved her toward the meeting room, heading that way themselves before she'd actually crossed the hospital threshold. She hurried across the carpet and caught up to them as Avanti pressed the button and flooded the meeting room with light.

"She has to be here," Claire said, before anyone could speak.

"She can't be gone," Avanti agreed. He looked bedraggled and kind of rumpled, far from his usual sleek, in control self, but then the weather was horrendous.

Freeson said, "Well, she's nowhere. Explain that." He seemed to expect an answer from Claire.

"You've checked all the rooms?" She turned to Maria, who looked half-panicked.

"She wasn't in her room," the nurse said, shaking her head. "She left her hospital gown."

"She's naked?" Freeson looked scandalized.

"Tell me what happened," Claire said, ignoring him.

"I was making sure everyone was in their room before I turned on the alarm," Maria said. "It was about nine. But when I got to Cat's room, it was empty."

"What about Marsdon?" Claire asked.

Avanti said flatly, "His door was, and is, locked. He's inside. This has nothing to do with him."

"His room was checked?"

"Yes." Avanti was positive.

"About half of the rooms were checked before it was lights out," Freeson said. "Marsdon's was one, even though it's always locked."

Claire nodded. Although most of the patients could come and go as they pleased during the day, the rooms were equipped with alarm locks at night, which kept patients from wandering the halls but also alerted the staff that they were trying to get out, which could mean they needed help. Maribel, for instance, could never remember to press the lighted button on the call buttons that were located in both her bedroom and bathroom. If she needed something, she banged against the door until someone came to her aid.

"She was definitely gone by nine P.M.," Freeson said.

"Naked," Avanti reminded.

"Someone would have noticed if she didn't have clothes," Claire said. "She had to have been dressed."

She then asked which rooms still needed to be checked and Freeson swept a hand toward the north hall.

"So you haven't checked Gibby's room yet?" Claire asked.

Maria shook her head. "Maybe we should wake him and ask him about her."

"What's he going to say?" Freeson turned to Avanti as if he couldn't believe Claire's questions. "You're in charge of Jane Doe's care now, Claire. Has anything happened recently? Has she said something? Did you notice anything different?"

"She's become more responsive, but you already know that. Gibby might be able to help."

"Well, it's too late tonight," Freeson said.

Claire's cell phone rang at that moment. She paused before looking at the caller ID, dreading what she knew she would see: Lang's number. She said, "I have to take this."

"At this time of night?" Avanti asked. "Who is it?"

"Langdon Stone," she admitted, punching the answer button.

"Langdon Stone?" Avanti sputtered and Freeson made a strangled sound.

Claire turned her back to them and took the call.

"I'm making good time," Lang said. "I'll be there in an about an hour."

"I'll let you in." Claire hung up.

"He's coming here?" Avanti's nostrils flared.

"No!" Freeson was appalled. "You told him? Called him? I don't believe you."

"I didn't expect him to come."

"For God sake, Claire. You'll get yourself fired and all of us brought before the board. Unbelievable." Freeson was furious.

Claire didn't relate her own worries about inviting Lang, not the least being she was attracted to the man. She knew she would have to do a self-examination of her motivations later, and she already suspected she wouldn't like what she learned. Claire Norris didn't fall for men. Even her ex had been the one to do the chasing, and she'd let him. She hadn't fallen for him, either, really. Had just chosen the path of least resistance, and it hadn't worked out in the end.

And she especially stayed away from controlling, demanding, unattainable men who were clearly bad for her. Langdon Stone fell into that category completely.

"I think we should wake up Gibby and talk to him," she said, which met with a chorus of disapproval.

"You know Gibby. He won't be able to tell us anything," Freeson said. "Certainly nothing that matters."

"He's lucky you're not his doctor," Claire said.

His jaw dropped open. He was infuriated, but Claire had suffered all she could stomach.

Avanti ordered, "You need to call off Detective Stone. It's ridiculous, his involvement. I don't want to hear he's let the world know we temporarily lost a patient!"

Claire pointed out, "He could let the world know far worse if he puts a call into Pauline Kirby about Heyward being moved to Side A."

Both Freeson and Avanti stared at Claire in horror. "What?" Freeson whispered.

"I can't call him off," she said. "He's investigating the attack on Cat. We need to talk to him." *Deal with it,* she thought fiercely.

They argued about whether they should enter any of the patients' rooms that hadn't been searched yet, this late at night. Avanti wanted to go home and Freeson seconded that opinion, but neither of them would budge until they were assured Claire wasn't going to let Lang inside the hospital. Claire used the time of their indecision to check down the halls herself and ended up herding Donald Inman, who refused to go to bed, sure he could be of help, back to his room.

Finally, her phone rang again. She answered to learn Lang was about to turn into the hospital's long drive and she clicked off to inform the others. When she got to the hospital foyer, she saw Avanti and Freeson standing with arms crossed over their chests, waiting like sentinels.

"He's almost here," she said, taking out her keycard and waiting by the front entrance.

And then she saw him, ducking his head to the rain as

he strode toward the glass doors. Claire punched in her code and used her key, and the doors slid open as he stepped inside. For just a moment he and Claire were very close to each other, long enough for her to inhale a lungful of his scent, a dampness mixed with something male and spicy and surprisingly sensual. Her head whirled a bit. Too long a day. Too much wine. Too many events and revelations.

"Lavender," he said to her, and Claire felt the blush sweep upward. He'd smelled her scent as well.

"Most of Side A has been searched except for some of the patients' rooms," she told him, trying to get back on an even keel. "Maria and I were going to check Gibby's room. Bradford Gibson. He's kind of a friend of Cat's." She looked around for Maria, who was waiting for her while Greg had gone back to his duties.

"I didn't know she had friends," Lang said.

"We don't need your involvement," Avanti told him as Lang, Claire, and Maria moved to where he and Freeson were standing.

Maria said to Lang, "Gibby sits by her. In the morning room. They watch TV and he treats her like a friend."

"Okay," Lang said.

"There is no need to wake the patients," Avanti said in a voice edged with ice. "We can wait till morning."

It was a battle of wills, Claire saw, which pissed her off. "We need to find Cat."

"This is a hospital, and we have to consider all our patients' needs," he stated.

"I don't think waiting till morning is the answer, if one of your patients is missing," Lang pointed out, which caused Avanti's lips to compress. "How would someone exit the hospital on their own?"

"We've already discussed that," Freeson said witheringly. "You cannot get egress without a keycard and code."

"Egress," Lang repeated, lifting an eyebrow in Claire's direction.

Her heart twisted uncomfortably in her chest. She liked it that he included her in this odd little war with Avanti and Freeson. He was undeniably attractive, undeniably male, and it just killed her that she noticed.

"So someone had to help her get egress," Lang said. "Who would that be?"

"We don't know that she's left. It would be practically impossible. I don't think we really need you here, Detective," Avanti said, trying to wrap the words in a smile and failing. "This is an internal problem, not really a job for the police."

Lang ignored him and turned to Claire. "Did she have a friend on staff? Someone who could help her? Or, maybe this Gibby person?"

"We need to do a more thorough search of the hospital before we assume she's outside the building." Avanti couldn't bear someone usurping her authority.

"But you don't want us to wake any of the patients," Claire pointed out.

"Gibby couldn't help her get past the doors," Maria said. "Only a staff member could."

"But he could hide her in his room? If he thought she wanted that?" Lang suggested.

"This is ridiculous!" Freeson's goatee quivered. "Bradford Gibson can't hold one idea in his head longer than two seconds! He can't know anything."

"He likes Cat," Maria said softly. "A lot."

"You're turning this into a circus, Claire," Avanti accused.

"I don't think talking to Gibby qualifies as a circus," Claire responded.

"If we don't wake him up, I'll just hang around till morning so I can talk to him then," Lang said.

"You have no authority!" Freeson could hardly get the words out.

"It just seems like you're trying hard to be obstructive rather than helpful. But then . . ." Lang almost smiled. "I already knew that about this place."

Avanti ran a hand through his hair and muttered something under his breath. Annoying as he was, he didn't appear to be his usual self. Claire wondered why he seemed less in control. Where was his big personality? His overbearing surety in all things Avanti?

Then she caught a whiff of alcohol. Scotch, maybe. He'd been drinking, she realized, though it was a no-no when you were on call. He wasn't drunk per se, but he didn't want anyone to know.

But Lang was really pissing him off. "Fine. You want to talk to Bradford Gibson? Go right ahead," Avanti snapped. "I'll make sure Dr. Radke knows just whose idea it was," he added, glaring at Claire.

Lang drawled, "I'm sure you always do."

Claire felt as if she were standing in a play where everyone knew their lines but her. She moved toward the hall that led to Gibby's room and Maria and Lang followed after her.

"Is it always like this?" he asked quietly. "The cold war between you and them?"

Claire didn't answer, and after a moment, as if she couldn't help herself, Maria squeaked out, "Yes!"

"They don't trust me," Claire said, her eyes straight ahead. "Seems to be the effect I have on people."

Lang didn't rise to the bait, which was just as well because Claire was feeling a little out of control about everything. The whole evening had a surreal quality to it, starting with standing outside the gates of Siren Song, to drinking wine with Lang and Dinah, to meeting with Dinah's father, to learning about Cat's disappearance, and now this.

Maria entered Gibby's room first, and there was a faint beeping sound from an electronic receiver in her pocket. She pulled it out and punched in a code and the sound stopped. There might be no locks on the doors, but when the alarm was tripped, only a staff member with the proper equipment could nullify it.

There were night-lights in the room and Gibby's prone form could be made out in his twin bed. He was sleeping soundly, his breathing deep, not quite a snore. Maria turned on a bedside wall lamp and said softly, "Gibby? It's Maria. Gibby?"

He blinked several times but was still in the land of dreams.

She gave him a little shake. "Gibby!"

He snorted to wakefulness, his eyes flying open in fear. "Ohhh! Ohhh!" he cried.

"Gibby, it's Maria. I'm here. I'm here."

"And Dr. Norris," Claire said in a calm voice. "We're sorry to wake you, Gibby."

"Wha . . . ?" He sat up, wearing a flannel pajama top that buttoned down the front, and looked around in a daze. "It's still night-night time."

"Gibby, Cat's missing," Claire said. "We were wondering if she came to see you?"

"Noooo. She wants to leave. She doan like it here, even though the food's good."

"Did she say she was going to leave?" Claire asked.

"She was waiting for the dinnertime. I got her the clothes."

"Clothes?"

Gibby blinked at Lang. "You want to take her away?" he asked, growing upset.

"No." Lang shook his head. "We want to make sure she's all right, and that she's still here."

"She was leaving." Gibby was positive.

"You got her what clothes?" Claire asked.

"Pants and shirt. She had some shoes."

"She dressed in your pants and shirt?"

"She took them. Under the wheelchair."

"Under the wheelchair?" Claire repeated and Gibby nodded at her solemnly. "What does that mean, Gibby?"

"Under the wheelchair!"

Maria said, "The seat cushion wasn't on the chair in Cat's room. It was on the floor."

Claire thought a moment. "Gibby, do you mean she put the clothes you gave her under the seat cushion of the wheelchair?"

"Yes!"

"Okay," Claire said. "It's okay. We just want to help Cat."

"Stop calling her that!"

Lang put in, "Your friend. She was leaving the hospital. By herself?"

Gibby turned to look at him, his brows knit. "She needed helped. I helped." He lifted his chin with pride.

"She told you to get her the clothes," Lang repeated, to which Gibby nodded vigorously. "And that she was leaving the hospital."

"She said, 'I needs help. Please, please help me. Bring me some clothes, Gibby. After dinner. When no one's around.' She said doan tell." His gaze flew from Lang's face to Claire's, stricken.

"We won't tell. It's all right. We want to help her, too," Claire said.

Maria had walked through the adjoining bathroom and come back, shaking her head. Cat was not anywhere in Gibby's small room.

"She need to leave here," he said seriously. "She was afraid of them."

"Who was Cat afraid of?" Claire asked.

"Her name is Tasha. She tole me."

"She's afraid of someone called Tasha?"

"*No!* She has a name! Tasha! Not Cat!"

Claire exchanged a glance with Lang, then concentrated on Gibby once more. "She told you her name was Tasha?"

"Uh-huh. Can I have apple juice?"

"Sure." Claire turned to Maria who headed out to fulfill the request. "Who was Tasha afraid of?"

"She was afraid of them."

"Do they have a name?"

"Baby." Gibby looked down at his body and patted his stomach.

Watching Claire interview the boy, Lang was impressed in spite of himself at her patience and kindness.

"She—Tasha—said she was afraid of *them*," Claire repeated, trying to keep Gibby on track. "Who do you think they are?"

"They hurt her. She had to leave." He looked up at the ceiling and the shadows that were created from his bedside wall lamp. "They will hurt her some more. My baby." Gibby wrapped his arms around his own neck covering his mouth and nose with his elbows. "She is scared," he said, his voice muffled. "She doesn't have Zimer's disease. That's Maribel."

Maria returned with a small glass of apple juice and Gibby brightened, taking the glass and gulping half of it down. "Mmmm," he said.

"She talked to you, Gibby? Tasha spoke to you. Aloud?" Lang asked.

Gibby put his finger to his lips. "Shhh. It's secret." He drank down the rest of his juice and handed the glass to Maria. "Thank you," he said soberly.

"It's a secret that she can talk," Claire said.

"You can't know!" he said, suddenly alarmed.

"I'm not going to tell anyone. It's still a secret," Claire assured him. "But I'm worried about the bad people."

"The bad woman. Like Darlene." He nodded sagely.

"Who's Darlene?" Lang asked.

"A nurse who works here during the day," Claire informed him.

"She's too mean." Gibby shuddered and sank down into his pillow. "Night night," he said firmly.

"You think Darlene's mean?" Claire tried.

"Really, really mean." He turned his head away and closed his eyes, and no amount of talking to him could get him to say anything further.

"What do you think?" Lang asked when they were walking back down the hall to the foyer. Avanti and Freeson were still there, clearly waiting to leave only after they were convinced Lang was on his way out, too.

"I don't know," Claire admitted. "We'll search the other patients' rooms, but . . ."

"You think she's already gone."

"I think Gibby was telling the truth about talking to her. He wouldn't just make up Tasha as her name. That's not like him."

"And this Darlene?" Lang asked.

"Gibby might not like her, but Darlene's entirely trustworthy. Been on staff here for years. I suppose Darlene could have scared Cat . . . er, Tasha."

"Are you finished?" Avanti asked loudly as they crossed toward him.

Lang and Claire exchanged a look and he nodded to both Avanti and Freeson.

"I told you you wouldn't learn anything from Gibby," Freeson said with a hint of triumph.

"I'll call you tomorrow," Lang said to Claire, and she smiled faintly.

She let him out of the front doors and only realized after he was out of earshot that she had forgotten to tell him about her trip to meet Dinah's father.

* * *

The rain pounded down and the wind blew it into Tasha's face as she stumbled around the back of the houses, shivering, frozen to the bone. She ran in the opposite direction of Rita and crouched in the carport near an open field. There were blocks of look-alike houses on gravel streets. Too many. She'd thought it would be so easy.

And then suddenly, there it was: the camper on blocks. Rafe's home. He'd described it to her. Told her where it was. Now she yanked on the handle and wanted to cry when it wouldn't open. Locked.

"Hey!" a voice called. A male voice.

Tasha crushed herself against the side of the camper, willing herself invisible.

It didn't work.

"Hey, you!" He ran toward her through the rain, visible only in the faint light from the nearest house.

Tasha turned quickly, slipped, went down on one knee. A knife! If only she had a knife!

She was on her feet again but he caught her by the arm and spun her around.

"What are you doing?" he demanded. "Trying to break in?"

"It's my boyfriend's place!" she cried.

That startled him. "Who's your boyfriend?"

Tasha gave him a long look. "His name's Rafe."

He dropped her arm and staggered back a step, staring at her, rain pouring down his dark hair and forehead, into his hooded eyes.

"Rafe's my cousin," he said.

She couldn't believe her good fortune. "Are you Cade? You're the person I've been looking for! Rafe told me to come to you if I ever needed help. I'm Tasha. Rafe's girlfriend. He and I were running away to get married!"

Chapter 18

It felt wrong to go home after searching all the rooms. Wrong to drive away in the wee hours of the morning. Wrong to leave Cat/Jane Doe/Tasha missing with no explanation to where she'd gone.

Claire tumbled into her bed sometime after three A.M., slept until eight, then raced through a shower and threw on her clothes, her hair still slightly damp as she drove back again to the hospital.

Darlene was already on duty when she arrived, and as Claire had a nine o'clock appointment with Jamie Lou, she didn't have time to do more than ask if anything more had been learned of Tasha's disappearance.

"Who's Tasha?" Darlene had asked, and when Claire explained about Cat, Darlene looked thoughtful.

"I think I heard Gibby call her that once," she said.

Claire hurried to her office, her head full of unanswered questions. Jamie Lou came through the door with resentment stamped across her features, but at least the bruises had disappeared and she looked put together. She started right in complaining about how Claire had intimated she couldn't be her doctor any longer.

"I've been working and working and working," Jamie

Lou said tightly. "That's all I've been doing, and you don't care."

"That's not true."

"John left that bitch and we're back together," Jamie Lou shot back. "He loves me. We want to get married, maybe have more children."

"Jamie Lou." Her name came out in a rush of disappointment. Claire was too distracted, too focused on other things to hide her feelings.

"See?" she declared. "You're judging me! All you do is look all serious and *pretend* to listen. You don't care what happens to me. Not really. You don't want me to call you with my problems. You want to brush me off like dog hair!"

"I just don't want your self-destructive behavior to get the best of you."

"I'm going to go see John," she said, ignoring everything Claire was trying to do and say. "He loves me. None of the rest of you care what happens to me. You'd be happy if I was dead!"

"That's not true." Claire denied it again, but Jamie was already running out of the office to her next uncontrollable calamity.

Lang clicked off his cell phone, having rented a U-Haul van to move his bed. He would load up the rest of his items and finalize his move. That, at least, would be done, and then he could concentrate on finalizing this case as well.

He'd dreamed of Dr. Norris. Visions of her shapely legs, serious manner, wide eyes, and generous lips ran across his mind in a loop that left him a little worried for his own sanity.

He drove his truck to the rental station, collected the moving van, and was nearly finished putting his belongings inside when his cell phone rang. Claire, he thought, quickly pulling the phone from his pocket.

But caller ID said it was the Tillamook County Sheriff's Department.

"Stone," he answered.

"Clausen," the deputy responded back. "I'm calling for O'Halloran, who's in a meeting with Catherine from Siren Song. She just walked in. Apparently, she got your notes."

"My God, I'm in Portland!" Lang said, frustrated. "Is there any way I can see her later?"

"The sheriff tried that, but she doesn't seem receptive. He'll call you as soon as they're done."

"Ask if I can come to Siren Song later."

"Okay." He sounded dubious about the success of that.

"Jane Doe is missing from Halo Valley," he added before Clausen could hang up.

"What?"

Lang gave him a quick rundown of what had transpired the night before. "Nobody knows where she is. How she left, if she did. I'm going to call Dr. Norris and see if they've learned anything else, and if she's a missing person. I'll let you know. But tell the sheriff to bring it up to Catherine. See how it plays with her. She may know something about it."

"I'll tell him," Clausen assured.

Lang hung up and was consumed with frustration. Damn! What the hell? Catherine's timing was diabolical.

Quickly he finished packing the van, then burned out of the driveway on his last moving trip to the coast. There was no way—no way—he could get there in time to talk to her. It just wouldn't happen no matter what kind of vehicle he was driving.

As soon as he was under way he punched in Claire's cell phone number, but it went straight to voice mail. He left a message asking her to call, explaining that Catherine had shown up at the department unannounced.

"Maybe taking Claire to the lodge was a good idea," he realized after he'd ended the message.

Maybe that's what had brought Catherine out from behind her gates.

Seated in an interrogation room, Catherine was disappointed to realize that the man who'd left her the notes and the woman doctor were not available. The sheriff, O'Halloran, was explaining that the doctor was affiliated with some psychiatric hospital between here and Salem, and that the man with the notes had been hired by the department but wasn't actually on the roster just yet.

"He asked me to call him on his telephone," Catherine stated.

"He has a cell phone. A mobile phone," O'Halloran said with a nod. "But since you're here, I can go over what he wanted to talk about with you."

Catherine waited, her hands in her lap. She didn't like being there. Didn't like sitting in a chair like a schoolgirl in front of a disciplinarian.

"The detective's name is Langdon Stone, and he's working on a homicide case."

"Homicide," Catherine repeated, startled.

"The victim's name is Rafe Worster. He was traveling with a young woman who is in her third trimester of pregnancy. This woman was also attacked, but her injuries weren't life threatening. However, she has not spoken since the attack. From what I understand, she's been in and out of a catatonic state."

Catherine, under control again, said, "I know the young man."

"You do?" O'Halloran looked surprised by her admission.

"He worked for us as a gardener and handyman. We haven't seen him in a number of weeks."

"And the girl?"

Without hesitating, Catherine said, "No. I don't know her."

There was a knock on the door and one of the other officers took O'Halloran into the hallway for a brief consultation. The sheriff returned shortly and picked up where he'd left off.

"Detective Stone thought she might be from your . . . family," he said.

"I'm sorry. No."

O'Halloran looked at her hard. Catherine could tell he didn't believe her, but she had no intention of admitting that Natasha was one of their number. She felt a twinge of conscience about the baby Natasha was carrying, but there were good reasons to keep denying Natasha's existence. The need to keep everyone safe superseded everything else.

"Could you give me a little background on your group?" he asked. "I'm not sure I've ever heard your last name."

"I'm surprised," Catherine said dryly. "As your local historical society has a document purported to be an authentic history of my family."

"You're saying it's not authentic?"

"It's not accurate."

"What is your last name?"

"Rutledge. It's not a secret." Catherine got to her feet.

"The pregnant Jane Doe has gone missing from the hospital," he said, trying to forestall her.

Catherine felt a chill slide down her spine, but she kept a stone face for the sheriff. "Was there anything else the detective wanted to know?"

"He would like to talk to you personally."

She lifted her chin and met O'Halloran's curious gaze.

They'd known of each other for years but had never really gone head-to-head on any issue; there had been no need. "I will see the woman doctor," she said. "You can tell him that."

She then strode determinedly out of the room and out of the department, her bun of gray hair, stiff back, and long dress drawing a number of looks from other personnel. Catherine was used to it. They didn't understand. How could they?

None of them knew of the evil that constantly tried to envelop them all. None of them knew of all the devices she used to keep it at bay.

Claire left her office for the hospital after Jamie Lou flounced away. Darlene and Alison, the aide, were busy in the morning room with Thomas McAvoy, who'd taken exception to something Big Jenny had done. Jenny just stood and blinked at him, which brought up a spew of invective from McAvoy.

"Where's Gibby?" she asked Greg.

"Wanted to stay in his room. Guess he's upset that Cat's missing."

"He calls her Tasha. Says that's her name," Claire said.

"Well, whoever she is, she's not here. We've gone through every room."

"How did she get out?" Claire shook her head, not accepting.

"Like the detective said. She musta had help."

Finally Darlene and Alison broke up the altercation between Thomas and Jenny. Maribel took over Gibby's chair, but since he wasn't around, she lost interest and started wandering, touching all the books in the bookcase.

"Darlene . . ." Claire called her to one side. The heavy-set nurse looked at her askance. "Gibby said Tasha was scared of *them,* and that they were mean, and that she told Gibby that she had to leave."

"He thinks everybody's mean because we don't give him his way all the time," Darlene said.

"Anyone in particular at the hospital? Someone Tasha might think was mean, too?"

She thought about it. "Gibby doesn't like Thomas."

Claire looked over at McAvoy, who was seated at a table, hunched over, waiting for lunch though it was several hours away still. "What about someone on staff?"

"We're all mean. He doesn't like Greg, either. Or any of the other orderlies, physical therapists. None of the men."

Claire knew it to be true. "I thought maybe there was someone or something specifically. Hmm."

She left Darlene, wondering what to do next. Call the police and report Tasha as missing? Was she? Did she leave under her own power? *How?*

She was debating on whether to call Lang again when her cell buzzed. She checked caller ID to find the man in question on the phone. "Hey," she answered. "I was just going to call you."

"Learn anything new?"

"Not really." She related her conversation with Darlene and told him Gibby wasn't up yet.

"Well, I've got something for you," he said, and in turn told Claire about Catherine's unexpected appearance at the department and how she knew Rafe, but negated knowing anything about his companion.

"You're kidding!" Claire said.

"It's a lie," he stated, sounding like he was holding on to his temper with an effort. "Jane Doe is part of their cult; I'm sure of it. I don't know what the hell Catherine's deal is."

"Do you think that's where Tasha is now? Back at Siren Song?" Claire heard the hope in her voice.

"No. I don't think Catherine went out of her way to get her back, if that's what you mean. Since she's denying even knowing her."

"I'm really worried about Tasha."

He grunted in agreement. "So here's the kicker: Catherine's willing to meet with you."

"What?"

"She must feel more comfortable with women. You were right. So, I was wondering if sometime today you could go to Siren Song? I'm sure Catherine's lying and I want to know why. Keep this thing going. Keep the pressure on. Something's strange about it all."

"Very strange," she agreed. "Are you planning to come with me?"

"Yeah, but I have a feeling I won't get inside the gates." He then added that he was at the tail end of a relocation to Tillamook, but would be available in the afternoon. "What's your schedule look like?"

"I can rearrange a few things," Claire said, after a moment of thought, "and be out of here by three. Should we meet at my place?"

"See you then," he said, and hung up.

Claire studiously ignored the anticipatory thrill that ran through her like hot liquid.

Tasha lay snug in Cade Worster's bed while he slept on the living room couch. She'd stripped off Gibby's clothes and wrapped herself in a tattered quilt in a log cabin style—Tasha had hand-sewn clothes and quilts and pillowcases all her life—and fallen into tortured slumber.

In her dreams Catherine was chasing her. Catherine, the mother, though she was really her aunt. But Nathaniel had been Catherine's son, Tasha was pretty sure, though Catherine denied it mightily. Now Nathaniel was gone except in her nightmares. In them he rose from the grave and stared at her out of eyes that were black holes of death.

In her dreams he was an apparition now, appearing before her, silently accusing. Tasha turned and ran and nearly tripped over silly Lillibeth in her wheelchair.

She felt Nathaniel's cold breath on the back of her neck and screamed herself awake.

Blinking, frightened, unsure of where she was, she felt another contraction. The real thing or false labor? Whatever it was, it *hurt.*

Where am I? she thought wildly. Then, *Cade's house.*

She relaxed a moment. Just. Because there was danger here, too. She could feel it. Rita would find her. Rita would come to Rafe's cousin's home. It was logical, and Rita might be crazy but her obsession made her smart.

Tasha had to keep away from her.

Carefully she slid off the bed, the quilt around her naked skin, and tiptoed to the back window. It was daylight outside. Dark and dreary but getting on toward noon, she thought.

Where was Rita? This community wasn't that large. Rita would find her.

She had to convince Cade to save her. Take her away. Like Rafe had tried to do.

She had to *escape.*

Before Rita found her.

Rita glared out the kitchen window at the dark day.

Late for work.

Because of that blond whore who'd run off with her baby. *Again!*

Beside herself with fury, Rita phoned Halo Valley, pinching her nostrils together and wheezing to Lori about how she'd come down with a virus. This god-awful weather. Should she talk to one of the doctors? Possibly Dr. Avanti?

She was told that Avanti wasn't in yet, either. Lori then spilled about the missing patient, whom they were now calling Tasha.

Rita's blood ran like ice. "Why Tasha?" she asked, worrying that Lori might hear the little quiver in her voice.

"Gibby says he talks to her and that's what she calls herself. We're taking our cue from Dr. Norris."

Dr. Norris . . .

Rita hung up and stood staring into space for a full minute.

"Rita!" Delores yelled from the bedroom.

Rita didn't hear her, didn't even process. She'd spent hours the night before looking for that wretched little bitch. She'd been mud-soaked, drenched with rain, cold to the bone, and it had taken half the night to get warm and clean and her mind was a muddle of fury.

Tasha had tricked her into believing she was in labor. She had tricked her.

Tricked her . . .

Rita could scarcely see. Her vision was red. Filmed. Blurry. She wanted to kill her. Needed to.

Rita was going to kill her and take Rafe's baby.

"Rita!"

Tasha took Rafe away from her.

Rafe. Her one true love.

Rita Feather Hawkings's one true love.

"Rita, for God's sake. If you're not going to work, make some lunch! You're starving me!"

Rafe had a few close friends. No family, really, lucky him. She shot a dark look full of menace down the hall.

Except for Cade. Cousin Cade.

"Rita!" Delores banged the television remote against the wall.

But the house was empty.

Rita was gone.

"Let's take two cars," Lang said as they stood beside their respective vehicles in Claire's driveway. The rain had abated earlier in the morning but the steel clouds hung low in the sky, threatening to open up at any moment. It was three thirty, as both of them were running a little late. "If Catherine lets me in, great. A bonus. If not, I've got a couple of things I could do."

"Okay."

"Any further ideas on how Jane Doe got out, if she did?"

"She's not hiding in any closets or cupboards. She must have had help."

"Who would help her?"

Claire had a funny tickling of her memory, but couldn't place it. She shook her head, then said, "I went with Dinah to meet her father last night. I've been meaning to tell you, but with everything else it just didn't seem important."

"How was it?" Lang asked, so Claire gave him a quick rundown on what Herman Smythe had said about Siren Song. Lang listened intently and when Claire finished, said simply, "Interesting history."

"Seemed a lot more relevant before Tasha disappeared. I was going to bring up some of it to her, see if she reacted. I don't know."

"We're definitely calling her Tasha now?" Lang asked.

Claire nodded.

"Okay."

He then went to his truck and led the way back to the lodge, driving the nose of the gray Dodge past the scrub pine and mountain laurel and making room for Claire to park beside him. Climbing from their respective vehicles, they came to stand by the gate, both Claire's shoes and Lang's boots squishing into the mud.

"A strange way for us to keep meeting," Claire observed.

"A strange cult of people," Lang observed.

"Why won't she admit to knowing Tasha? Is there any chance we could be wrong? That Tasha's not from here?"

"Sure." He shrugged. "But she was with Rafe, and she fits the description of a Colony member, and no one else has come forward to claim her."

"She's close to having that baby."

"We're going to find her. Someone had to help her."

"Who?" Claire asked.

"Someone who knew she was at Halo Valley."

Another flash of quicksilver memory that Claire almost grasped. "She came from Laurelton General."

At that moment a figure stepped through the front doorway and into the rain. Not Catherine. A younger woman, her blondish hair scraped into a bun at the back of her neck, her slim figure encased in an ankle-length waisted dress with a gathered skirt. Her shoes were practical. Black soft-soled leather slip-ons.

Claire realized, "Tasha had similar shoes. Those are Easy Spirit, maybe Eccos, or something like them."

"Guess they don't make their own shoes," Lang observed.

"Tasha's from the Colony." Claire was positive.

"Got no argument from me."

The woman walked up to the gate and Claire realized she was much older than she'd first assumed, closer to Claire's age. She had pale blue eyes and a generous mouth, and the resemblance to Tasha was unmistakable.

"Catherine would like the doctor to come inside," she told them, then pulled out a large ring of keys and threaded a long one into the lock, giving Lang a warning look as she did so. He stepped back as a matter of course, reading the unspoken command. She then swung the heavy gate open and Claire stepped through.

"I'm Isadora," she said, then with a hard clank she shut and locked the gate again, inviting Claire to walk ahead of her across the flagstones to the front door.

As she started out, Claire sent Lang one silent glance before turning her attention to her feet and heading to the lodge.

Chapter 19

As soon as she was out of sight Lang wanted to call her back. He felt unnaturally apprehensive. What if the damn cult swallowed her up and never let her out?

Irrational. Crazy. Dr. Claire Norris was going to be fine.

But he couldn't deny the tightness of his chest. The anxiety that had him in its steel grip.

He had to do something. He'd told her he had things to do. But damn if he could remember even one!

"Hellfire," he muttered, turning to his truck. He didn't want to leave. Didn't want to stay. He sat in the cab, immobile, and swore violently and pungently, finally switching on the ignition. She had her own car. He'd arranged it that way. There was no reason for him to feel this way.

They were only women. She was safe.

But every one of his nerve endings was alive. His emotion concerning her was so intense he felt almost physically ill. He wanted to hold her, kiss her, feel his body moving with hers in that age-old dance. His head was full of thoughts of having her in his bed, being inside her, feeling her skin, her mouth, her tongue.

It was fear that sent these messages down his nerves, changing to pent-up desire.

If she came out safely—*when* she came out safely—he was going to his damnedest to make her his. Dr. Claire Norris. His onetime enemy.

It was staggering, but he wanted her more than anything.

Cade Worster was both enamored with and dumbfounded by the pregnant girl. "It's Rafe's baby?" he asked, just to be absolutely certain. He'd found her some of his clothes and she'd dressed in them, her other pants and shirt being caked with mud and soaked with rain.

"Yes," she said. "It's Rafe's."

Her admission left him shaking his head and trying not to stare. Cade's clothes were bigger than Gibby's and she had to roll up the legs of the pants even farther and cinch the waist with a belt. The arms, too, needed to be folded back at the cuffs several times. He gave her a pullover cotton sweater that had seen better days.

The effect was she looked younger than her years, too young to be having a baby.

Tasha sized up Cade quickly. "Rafe's ex-girlfriend is trying to take my baby," she said.

"Rita?"

So he knew. It worried Tasha greatly. "Yes."

"She the one who attacked you at the rest stop?" Then, "Holy shit," when Tasha nodded. "You're not saying *she* killed Rafe!"

"Yes, she did!"

"No . . . she was nuts about him."

"She's completely mad," Tasha assured him. "She would do anything to get what she wants. She wants to kill me, too." She went on to tell him how Rita had sprung her from the mental hospital. "I was planning to leave, to get away from her. But she just kidnaped me before I could!"

"You need to call the police," Cade said.

"No!" Tasha was horrified. "They'll send me back to the lodge and Catherine. I can't go back there. I can't!"

"Well, where were you and Rafe going?"

"Anywhere. Portland, maybe. We just wanted to get away! To be together and raise our baby . . ."

"Where's Rita now?" he asked.

"Looking for me," she said gravely.

"There was a policeman who came by, asking about Rafe. He wants to help. You need real help."

"I need *your* help," Tasha implored.

"I can't. Rafe took the truck!" he declared. "He always took my truck, and now it's gone for good."

"Can you get another one?" she asked anxiously.

"Steal one, you mean? I don't know. No . . . but I know a guy . . . maybe . . . who has cars."

She placed her hand on his arm. He was wearing a black hooded shirt and dirt-crusted denim pants. He looked like he could sorely use a bath. Rafe had told her his cousin was a ne'er-do-well of sorts. She could feel time tick, tick, ticking away.

"Cade, please . . ."

"All right." He swallowed. "You stay here and hide. Rita's mom's house is only a couple of blocks away. She could be there."

She is there, Tasha thought. *Or was.* And now, in the light of day, it was going to be damn near impossible to move around without being seen and wondered about. Rita had to suspect where she was. The fact that she hadn't stormed Cade's house suggested to Tasha that she was planning an ambush.

Thinking about it, Tasha realized that Rita would wait until nightfall. Wait till the screen of darkness.

Closing her eyes, Tasha remembered all the times she'd tried to escape herself, and all the punishments she'd endured for her attempts. Oh, how she hated Catherine. How she hated all of them!

Cade left and was gone for several hours and finally, in the late afternoon, she heard the rumble of a vehicle that proved to be a black Jeep Wrangler with flaps for windows and doors.

"Come on," Cade said hurriedly. "We gotta get outta here before somebody notices."

"Whose is this?"

"A guy I know." He tried to toss it off.

"You stole it?"

"Get in."

The vehicle was old and had been hard used, and the seat Tasha sat on was split down the center. She suffered another several contractions; every time she moved too sharply or felt too much anxiety, her whole body clenched. This baby was going to come. She had to get somewhere safe, and soon.

Rita cruised through the Foothillers' community in Delores's rusted Chevy, keeping a sharp eye on Cade's place. There wasn't much happening there, but then Cade was a night owl. A thief with thieves' hours. He was handsome enough, though. If she'd been in the mood she might have tried to seduce him. He wasn't as sexually attractive as Rafe, but then who was? Not Paolo Avanti, for certain, but he, at least, was a doctor. Somebody smart, which really couldn't be said about Cade.

She waited outside his house but a couple of blocks north, near the field, hoping he didn't recognize her parked car if he came out the door. She'd pulled in behind the Blackburns' RV, angled slightly so she had a line of sight to Cade's place without being too conspicuous. If he looked her way he wouldn't see more than a front fender of her car.

So he surprised her when he suddenly drove up in a dilapidated Wrangler. Roberto's car, by the look of it, she realized. She hadn't seen Cade sneak out the back, which he must have done, because there he was, big as life.

And then the bastard was bringing Tasha out the front door!

Her hand clung to his arm like the piece-of-shit damsel in distress she pretended to be. Out of the corner of her eye, Rita caught the twitch of curtain from the Blackburns' front window. Damn the old busybody, Portia. She and her husband Cliff were nosy-nosy. They'd stared through a telescope across the field from their big house to her aunt's smaller place, spying on Angela and her two sons, gleefully making up stories about what they saw. They'd even gone as far as labeling her a witch and a whore, convincing the dumb-ass Foothillers that Angela was somehow involved with Tasha's people! That she possessed special, evil powers because of it!

All lies, but it didn't matter. The lies had been believed by many.

Rita hated the Blackburns almost as much as she hated Tasha. Their nasty, flapping tongues had sealed Angela's fate and she'd been killed as a result, the field torched behind her place.

Now Rita sank down in the seat and willed herself to be invisible.

Cade and Tasha climbed into the Wrangler and Cade tried to back it out and it just stopped, the engine whining and whining. Rita watched curiously as Cade got out and opened the hood. He pretended to look under it but instead just waited a minute or two. Then he returned to Tasha's side of the vehicle, shaking his head.

What's he doing? Rita wondered.

He opened the passenger door and helped Tasha back out, though she clearly didn't want to come. She wanted to stay in the car, wanted to leave. There was something of an argument. Then hurrying, surreptitiously looking around, Cade urged her back up the front steps and into the house.

Shenanigans, Rita thought, trying to make sense of it. She knew Roberto, knew how he valued and loved his cars. Cade had either borrowed or stolen Roberto's Wrangler, and Rita would bet there was nothing wrong with it.

Cade's reasons escaped her but she didn't care. As long as he kept Tasha at his home, that's all that mattered.

She checked once again to make certain her knife was in the side pocket of the car, an obsessive search of her fingers that she performed without thinking.

Tonight, she would need to have it near.

She glanced back up at the Blackburns' house, but the curtain was still.

Claire felt as if she'd stepped back in time to another century. The lodge was all wood, rough-hewn and hand-carved, she suspected. The furniture was the same and the oak table was a slab of wood, the breadth of which made her lips part.

But it wasn't the lodge that amazed her the most. It was the women. All of them with blond or light brown hair, blue or green or hazel eyes, printed floor-length dresses, black walking shoes like Tasha's, serious expressions, silence as their universal greeting. One was in a wheelchair, but she looked exactly the same as the rest.

Everyone looked like Tasha.

Only Isadora spoke. "My sisters," she said.

Catherine stood to one side and up close Claire could see she, too, was older than she'd first thought. Somewhere in her midsixties, she thought, though her face was remarkably unlined. She wondered if any of them ever went out in the sun.

The resemblance among them was deep. Once Claire had gone with a friend to a dog breeder's home where the breeder had raised pugs. When Claire walked by their pens, she was slightly unnerved by all those look-alike black faces silently following her every move, the way their heads turned in unison as she passed. These women were like that, their eyes watching her every move. She had the same eerie feeling now.

Catherine said, "We didn't know that Rafe was dead."

The one in the wheelchair asked, "Did Natasha kill him?"

Claire stared at her and she seemed to realize she'd said something wrong, for she pushed herself to Catherine's side for protection. Claire sensed that her mental development might not be as advanced as expected for someone her age.

"Lillibeth," Catherine said, by way of introduction.

"Is Natasha sometimes called Tasha?" Claire asked.

One of the youngest ones piped up. "That's what she calls herself."

"Ophelia," Catherine snapped, and Ophelia's lips tightened for a moment but she dropped her gaze.

"Why don't you come in and sit down," Catherine said to Claire, motioning for the other women to move aside. They scattered from the room by some prearranged command, Claire guessed.

Claire took a seat at the long end of the table and Catherine sat at the head. "I went to see the sheriff this morning," she said. "He told me about Rafe. We didn't know."

Claire nodded, waiting. She knew, from long practice as a therapist, that Catherine was trying to decide just how much to tell. Sometimes it was best to just stay quiet.

"I had no intention of discussing Natasha with him," she

said, her lips tight. "But like Ophelia said, she likes to call herself Tasha."

"She is from here. Why have you been so reluctant to claim her?" Claire asked when Catherine didn't continue.

"She doesn't want to be a part of us."

"You know she's pregnant."

"She didn't try to hide it," Catherine stated flatly.

"You knew Rafe was the father?"

"There really could be no one else. We don't allow many men inside the gates, as a rule."

"Any longer," Claire said. When Catherine stared at her questioningly, she said, "The women—the sisters—each have a father or fathers. I'm assuming that at some point he or they had access to your lodge."

"Whom have you been talking to?" she demanded.

Claire had a feeling she was about to be thrown out. "I don't mean to pry and make you uncomfortable. The reason I'm here is that I'm interested in Tasha's welfare, and her baby's. She's missing from the hospital."

"The sheriff mentioned that," she said carefully. "She walked out?"

"She couldn't have." Claire explained the locked doors. "Someone may have helped her. Someone she knew?"

"If you're thinking it's one of us, you're wrong. I'm the only one in the house who drives our car, and that's very rarely. From what you've said, it's someone who works there. Someone with a key. Unless Natasha stole it."

She said it so matter-of-factly that Claire sensed something similar might have happened before. "You think that's possible? That she would steal it?"

"You don't know Natasha, Doctor."

"Then tell me about her. Let me help her. We need to find her."

Catherine seemed to struggle with herself, finally saying, "I'm worried about the coming child."

"We all are. That's why we need to find Tasha."

"She won't be able to take care of it. She has . . . an affliction she cannot control."

"What do you mean?"

Catherine hesitated, then said, "She has spells. She retreats to another world and is uninvolved in this one."

"Catatonic states," Claire said. "She's had them before?"

"Put any name you like to them."

"Has she seen a doctor about them?"

"When she was young, we asked the shaman to drive the evil spirits away. He was unable to help. And then we had the doctor who tended to Lillibeth. He gave Natasha medicine, but it made no difference. She is what she is."

"What doctor?"

"He passed away some time ago."

Claire flashed on Herm Smythe's recital. "Dr. Loman?"

Catherine met Claire's gaze with cool suspicion, but admitted, "Yes."

"Who took his place?"

"No one."

"None of them have had any medical attention since Dr. Loman's death?" Horrified, Claire looked around the room, taking in its rustic appointments. "Catherine, that's not safe."

"The only way we stay safe is to live the way we do."

Claire wasn't sure she agreed with that, but there was no way she was going to convince Catherine otherwise. "What happened to Lillibeth? What was the accident?"

Catherine got up abruptly from her chair. "You came here about Natasha, not Lillibeth. Not any of the rest of us. I will help you as much as I can concerning Natasha and her baby."

Claire heard the ringing finality in her voice and saw that she was being asked to leave. Reluctantly, she, too, got to her feet. "Do you think she will come back here?" Claire asked.

Catherine's smile was ironic. "If you find her, please contact me. I would like to know the baby is well. But as for Natasha . . . we would be the last place she would return."

Lang drove into Deception Bay and, as if by magnetic force, ended up at the historical society, a freshly painted white building that had once been a church and still had the steeple to prove it.

Inside it was one big reception room, but instead of pews there were glass cases with artifacts and curiosities from the last several centuries. A middle-aged woman with narrow glasses perched on the end of her nose smiled in welcome. "May I help you?" she asked.

Lang was still feeling like a stranger in his own skin. He could hardly reckon the man he'd become—the one who felt anxious, protective and possessive of Claire Norris—to the man he'd been a scant six months earlier.

"I'm looking for a book on the Colony," he said. "The women who live at the lodge called Siren Song. I understand you have something here. A history?"

"An undocumented history," she said, eyeing him curiously. "Left by the estate of a local doctor who attended to the women at the lodge before his death."

Lang nodded. "But written by someone else."

"Yes . . ."

She seemed reluctant to show him the book and Lang was about to ask her why when she mentally shrugged and took him to a bookcase where it was tucked between two thicker, hardcover volumes. The account itself looked like an unfinished manuscript with a laminated cardboard cover that had clearly been added later to keep the pages from shredding.

"Do you have a particular interest?" she asked.

"Mostly I'm just passing time."

"There's a general interest in the women who live at the lodge. A lot of people describe them as a cult. You don't seem to fit the image."

She drifted away and Lang thumbed through the account of the Colony, skimming. Mostly it concerned the relationships of the ancestors of Catherine Rutledge and her sister, Mary Rutledge Beeman, and the suspected intermingling with the local Indians regardless of whom they were married to, especially one very talented shaman. There was mention of dark gifts present in the female offspring.

Dark gifts, huh. Lang wondered what the hell that meant. After about twenty minutes he put the account back in the bookcase, thanked the woman for her help, then left the building. Shocking though it might be to Catherine, Lang thought it a fairly tame account. Mary Rutledge had married a man named Richard Beeman and given birth to several children, unnamed, their sex undocumented. That was where the account ended.

It wasn't of as much interest as he'd hoped. He'd learned more immediate information from Dinah.

He was heading back to Siren Song, watching the clock, when he caught sight of the sign for the Drift In Market. Turning the wheel sharply, he found a parking spot right in front, then strode up a wooden ramp to a sliding door on rails.

The Drift In Market was cramped, with tall shelves and narrow aisles set on a beat-up wood floor. The one checkout line was attended by a very large woman who wasn't going to win a record for speed. Several people were waiting patiently to be helped.

Lang walked past them and through the store. A man in his thirties wearing a dark blue apron with the store's name and logo in white—a piece of driftwood underscoring the market's name—was cleaning up some spilled grain from one of the plastic bins where you could scoop it yourself, if you were so inclined.

"You work here long?" Lang asked.

"A while."

"Do you know the woman from the lodge, Siren Song, who used to work here?"

"Uh. No. Heard about her."

"Did she work here long?"

"You could ask Julie, at the register. She's been here a long time."

He believed it. "Thanks."

He picked up two bottles of wine, one red, one white, thought about adding some beer to the mix and then changed his mind. Then he got in line behind the others at the checkout, waiting somewhat impatiently for his turn.

Finally Julie picked up his first bottle of wine and Lang casually asked her about the woman from Siren Song who had worked there. "She was here for a while," she said. "Nothing remarkable. She wasn't weird or anything."

"I didn't think they ever left the lodge," Lang said.

"I asked her about it once. The owner had to tell her to get some different clothes 'cause she looked pretty old-time, y'know? She said she wasn't forced to stay. It was up to her."

"Are we talking about the same group? I didn't get that impression."

"I know, right? But that's what she said. Is that all?" she asked, as she'd rung up the wine.

"Yeah." Lang reached in his wallet for payment. "Do you remember her name?"

"Laura. You a cop, or something?"

"Or something." He smiled and left.

Back in the truck, he checked his watch and headed back to the lodge in a hurry.

Dark gifts.

"The Wrangler's beyond broken. Can't get 'er going," Cade said regretfully, tossing the keys on the kitchen counter. "You gotta stay here."

"I have to leave." Tasha was serious.

"No, now, you gotta take care of yourself. Rafe would want me to keep you and his baby safe. You look like you're gonna pop."

Tasha gazed at him squarely. Where was the man who'd been so eager earlier to help her? The one who had warned her about Rita being near? "Are you lying to me about the car?"

"No! Hell, no." He ran a hand through his hair, then said, "But I've been thinking. You're gonna have that baby, and you can't be in a car when you do it."

"Let me decide what I need to do," she told him, angry and scared. "She'll find me if I stay here."

"I'll keep you safe."

As she watched, he pulled a handgun out of a drawer. She'd never seen one before. Knew what they were from books. "Is it loaded?" she asked.

"Well, yeah. I don't wanna kill Rita if I don't have to. But I will. You bet I will. She killed my cousin and she attacked you. We'll stay right here and wait for her. That's what we'll do."

Tasha wondered. Her instinct was to flee, run away, get as far from everything as she could. Freedom. She ached for it.

But Rita would come and find her wherever she went. Rita wanted Rafe's baby and she would do anything to have it. Confronting Rita, finishing this between them, maybe that was a better plan.

Cade was now looking at her that same way Rafe had, with starry-eyed love and adoration. He wanted to protect her. Thought he could. And was risking her window of escape with his own needs and overprotectiveness.

Tonight Rita would come. And Cade would shoot her dead.

Then Tasha would leave. Away from the sisterhood. Away from the hospital.

Away . . .

Chapter 20

Claire was escorted to the gate by Isadora, feeling like she knew almost less about the Colony than she had before. Lang's truck was slotted next to her car and she suddenly felt weak in the knees from emotion. She wanted to throw herself into his arms and damn the consequences.

Pulling herself back to the present, she said to Isadora, "I'm worried about Natasha. She could have her baby at any time, and someone did attack her and kill her companion, Rafe Worster."

"Catherine doesn't want us to talk about her," was her response, but Claire saw some unidentified emotion flit across the other woman's face.

"Don't you want her and the baby safe?"

"We're all extremely worried, too," she said with feeling.

"Why wouldn't she come back here to her home? Catherine said she wouldn't."

"Natasha has free will. Just like all of us."

"You choose to be here? You could leave at any time?"

They were at the gate and Isadora was twisting the key in the lock. She threw a cautious eye at Lang, who had climbed from his cab and was waiting in the dying light for

Claire to join him. He looked tense, Claire saw, glancing his way, but her attention was on Isadora.

"This is not a prison." She pulled the gate open and Claire walked through. The scrape of the key in the lock signaled that their interview was over.

"Claire?" Lang said.

Something in his tone, some element of concern, reached inside her. There was no reason for it, she told herself staunchly. Nothing had happened to her. It was just reaction to the series of events that had brought her to this place.

"Tasha is one of the Colony," Claire said as Lang took her arm, helping her through the slippery mud. "Catherine admitted it."

"I could tell by the resemblance." He gazed past her to Isadora's retreating form. "Why was it such a secret?"

"I don't know."

"Do they know where she is?"

Claire shook her head and turned toward her car. "Her full first name's Natasha. She did talk to Gibby. He knew."

"Maybe she's on her way back here."

"Catherine claims it's the last place she would come." Lang held open her door a moment while Claire climbed into the driver's seat. "Come back to my place and I'll give the complete report," she said lightly.

"Let me take you to dinner," he said.

"Thanks, but I'd rather eat in. If you're up for a tuna fish sandwich, I can make us some."

He inclined his head and closed her door.

Ten minutes later he was hauling his bottles of wine from his truck and following Claire inside her bungalow. It was starting to feel familiar, and though he knew he should proceed with caution, he didn't want to, and knew he wasn't going to.

"I'm on call," Claire said when she saw the bottle of

wine. "But the corkscrew's in the drawer," she said, pointing. "Please help yourself."

He did as she directed and poured himself a glass of white as she made the sandwiches. She seemed dead on her feet and he sensed it was more emotional than physical. He felt a lot the same way. Weary. Soul deep.

They ate in companionable silence, and when Claire tried to clear their plates, Lang took the task from her. "Sit down," he ordered. "You want tea or something?"

"Thanks, I'm fine with this." She lifted a glass of water, then said, "I was so sure Tasha's disappearance was related to the Colony. She was scared and needed help, and I thought they'd come for her, I guess. Save her. Take her back. I thought maybe Catherine was hiding the fact that she was back inside Siren Song already."

"But Catherine said differently and you believed her."

"I did. I do."

Lang nodded, not as convinced as Claire, but willing to explore the possibility. "Go back to Gibby. What did he say about Tasha?"

"He knew her name. She talked to him. She said she needed help. He got her a set of clothes and then she was gone."

"Catherine and company didn't help spring her," he mused aloud. "They don't have spies everywhere. They're pretty much insulated in their lodge."

Claire shook her head. "She's either hiding in the hospital somewhere we can't find her—"

"—or someone's hiding her."

"Or someone's hiding her . . ." she repeated slowly, thinking that over. "Or she left, either on her own power or with someone's help."

"With someone's help makes the most sense," Lang pointed out. "It just wasn't anyone associated with Siren Song."

"Who, then?"

"Whoever killed Rafe," he said seriously. "Look, I know you thought the knife wounds on her abdomen seemed like someone just hacking away. Maybe that's what they were, but maybe it was just someone who didn't really know what they were doing."

"Then it's someone who knew Tasha was pregnant, and that means they knew her *before,* and how can that be? She was behind the gates of Siren Song. She never left."

"That Catherine knows of," Lang proposed.

"I don't think there's any way she snuck out of there without Catherine knowing."

"She got out of the hospital," he pointed out. "We're assuming Rafe's killer and the person who tried to take Tasha's baby are one and the same. Agreed?"

Claire nodded. "Agreed."

"Would you say that's a man or a woman?"

"A woman," Claire answered readily, and then her conscience twigged her again. She stopped, hesitated, then said, "A friend of mine from Laurelton General said there was a woman—a nurse—who said she thought she knew Jane Doe. Leesha, my friend, gave the woman my name. Leesha called later and asked me if the woman ever contacted me, but I told her she never had."

"A nurse?" Lang repeated.

Claire nodded, then thought of the recently hired nurse at the hospital who never quite met her eyes. She'd put it down to something else. Newness. Shyness. Whatever. But suddenly it seemed more sinister.

"What?" Lang asked, sharp-eyed as ever.

"We have a recent hire at Halo Valley. A nurse. Talking about this reminded me of her."

"How recent?"

"Last couple weeks. Since Tasha arrived at Halo Valley."

"You think she's after Tasha?"

"I don't know. There's just something."

"Go with your instincts," he said. "Might be a good idea to check with Gibby, too."

"Oh, I'm on that. First thing tomorrow." She tried to stifle a yawn and failed.

Lang took his cue to leave. He set his empty wineglass down on the kitchen counter. Realizing she'd sent him an unconscious message, Claire got up abruptly and said, "Thanks. I'm sorry. I feel like I've been concentrating on all the wrong things. Dinah's father. History of the Colony. Other things."

"Catherine wouldn't talk to us, so it was research. No harm done. I checked the book old man Smythe wrote about them while you were inside the gates. Pretty much genealogy with a few side notes. Nothing really since Catherine and Mary."

"I wonder what happened to Mary," Claire mused.

"And all her men," Lang said with a slight smile.

Claire looked at Lang's empty glass and the hand he had wrapped around the edge of her counter. His hips were balanced against the counter's edge. There was something completely male about him that she hadn't noticed in a man in a long, long time. "If Mary was as promiscuous as Herman Smythe would lead us to believe, it might explain Catherine's austerity now. A kind of knee-jerk reaction."

"Unbridled sex in the nineteen seventies and eighties. Repression in the nineteen nineties and two thousands."

"It would make sense. I wonder when all that long-dress wearing began. Could have always been there and Mary just spat in the eye of convention."

"You think she's dead?" Lang asked.

"I guess so." They thought about that a moment, then Claire said, "I hate thinking of Tasha, so pregnant, out God knows where. She needs to be found. I keep hoping that if someone helped her escape, that it's because they care about her."

"Not because they want to steal her baby."

"Yeah." Claire reached for the empty glass, intending to put it in the dishwasher, but her hand swept against it, sending it crashing into the sink, glass splintering. A piece shot up and grazed Lang's cheek, though he ducked down instantly.

"Oh, my God! I'm so sorry." Claire was mortified, coming close to examine the cut.

"No big deal." He shifted away.

"No, please. Let me look. I can't believe I did that."

"You're distracted. Tired. Really, it's okay."

"Stop shifting." She spread her fingers around his jaw and twisted his face to the right so she could see the jagged slit. It was bleeding like a son of a gun. "I'm sorry," she said, heartfelt. "No, don't move. Just wait."

"I'll just tell people I cut myself shaving," he called after her as she disappeared into the hallway and the bathroom. "Really, I'm fine."

"No, you're not." Her voice was muffled.

She returned a few moments later with a first aid kit and a box of tissues. Blood was running from the cut on his upper cheek down the side of his head and sending small drips down to the collar of his shirt. "Head wounds," she murmured.

"Bleed like they'll never stop."

"The head is so vascular."

She dabbed at the cut and then put some rubbing alcohol on a piece of tissue, dabbing some more. Lang squinted against the sting and Claire apologized again. "I am going to live," he assured her wryly.

She lifted the tissue and her fingers gently probed the skin surrounding the injury. "You could use a couple of stitches," she said, though the bleeding had stopped.

"No, thanks."

"I have some butterfly bandages. I can close it, but seriously, I think stitches would ensure it doesn't reopen."

"You're making more of this than I need."

In truth, he didn't need any of it. She was too damn close. An attractive, verboten woman who nevertheless was the only one he could think of in his bed. Jesus. And if she didn't stop tenderly exploring with those fingers, he was going to simply lose it!

His hand shot out to stop her just as she was saying, "I'll go get the bandages and—"

Her breath swept in at the way he held her wrist, tight and tense.

"Don't," he said.

"Don't," she said simultaneously, resisting his grip, her hand clenched.

They stood frozen for a moment in that position, staring at each other.

For Lang, it was a watershed moment. A release of every brick of resentment and blame that he'd built in a wall against her since Melody's death. It wasn't her fault. It had never been her fault, and he'd known it all along. He'd just been too arrogant and blind to admit it.

Now he let go of her wrist to lift his hand to her face, laying it gently against her cheek. Claire's eyes were wide, her expression faintly anxious, but she didn't move. Her breathing was short and erratic.

"What are you doing?" she asked in a stranger's voice.

He didn't answer. Instead he bent his head to hers, capturing her mouth in a hard, pent-up kiss. She shivered. She was quaking all over, but . . . she was kissing him back.

"What are *you* doing?" he asked, his lips curving against hers.

"I don't know. Nothing I should."

"You sure?"

"No."

And then he was kissing her harder and her hands, clenched and frozen, unfurled and slid up his chest and to his shoulders, clinging. Lang pulled her to him until her breasts were pressed against his chest and he could feel the edge of the counter digging into his hips and lower back. Claire made a protesting sound in her throat that only urged him on. He yanked her blouse from her slacks and slid his hands beneath the fabric, her skin quivering at his touch.

Claire, for her part, had not engaged in anything remotely resembling sex since early in her marriage, and her ex had lost interest in any kind of foreplay, even kissing, shortly after he and Claire had entered into wedded "bliss." She'd forgotten what it was like to want to die for the feel of a man's lips, forgotten the unbearable pleasure of having her skin caressed and loved, forgotten the thrill of hearing a man's moan of desire.

It came flooding back with every moment of this fevered embrace. Her head rushed. She felt like she was back to her teenaged years and the blazing excitement of discovery. The hint of fear at being caught was there, too. The knowing that this was destined to be wrong. A mistake.

But she didn't care. She'd led too careful a life.

She pressed her hips to his and felt the evidence of his arousal. A delicious power slid through her veins, utterly intoxicating. She spent her days advising against dangerous behavior, just this kind of thing! She allowed herself this moment because she believed she was insulated against it. She knew it wouldn't be good for her. She also knew it wouldn't ruin her life. She wouldn't let it.

But he was doing things with his hands that were playing havoc with rational thought. He'd unbuckled her thin silver belt, unbuttoned the top button of her pants, thrust his hands inside.

"God," he murmured.

She should protest, she thought. She should make some attempt to stop this madness.

She knew she wouldn't.

And she wanted him to hurry. *Hurry, hurry, hurry.* Because if either of them had time to think, it would be over as quickly as it had begun, and she couldn't bear the thought.

They were crazy. Squirming against each other. Half-slipping to the floor. Losing their strength along with their common sense. Laughing softly.

"Come on," she whispered, grabbing one of his marauding hands and leading him toward the bedroom.

And then there were no more intelligible words, just mews and whispers and groans of pleasure. He divested her of her blouse, pants, and undergarments and she lay still and let him. And then he yanked off his own clothes and she had a glimpse of hard muscles and taut skin and an overwhelming sense of maleness before his body covered hers on the comforter of her bed.

"Touch me," he groaned and her hands slid down and grabbed his shaft, stroking him, loving the feel of his hardness. She could feel her own body respond and when his fingers invaded her insides, her wetness caused him to moan with pleasure.

She wanted him. Hard inside her. Pushing. Thrusting. She wanted it *now*!

Her hands eagerly guided him toward her, her hips undulating against the continued stroking of his fingers.

And then he swept her hands away and his shaft was teasing against her wetness. Claire heard the little mewling sounds and realized they were from her own lips. She felt weak, liquid, melting. Her consciousness slipped into a place where there was no thought, just feeling. Her hands found his buttocks, grabbed the hard muscles. She pulled gently at first, then urgently, desperately wanting him fully inside her.

He moaned something, maybe her name, and then thrust hard against her. She lifted her hips in glorious response and cried out, her whole body tense, writhing, eager.

And then they were in rhythmic unison. He pulled back to look at her and she met his gaze, loving the familiar features that had once been her enemy, the man who blamed her above all else. Her fingers lightly touched the cut on his face.

Then those thoughts splintered. Spiraled away. Were dust.

All she wanted was to love him. Keep loving him.

"Lang," she whispered urgently.

He drove into her harder. The right answer to the question. Faster and faster. Until Claire exploded in desire, her body arching, her cry loud enough to cause her embarrassment later.

"God . . . Claire!" he burst out and then followed her into a shuddering climax that left them both gasping for breath. When he collapsed against her she couldn't find her voice. Couldn't *think*.

And when he finally lifted his head and swept back her sweat-dampened bangs and smiled at her, she felt awe and wonderment that they'd found each other.

"Wow," he said.

"Wow," she said back.

And they both burst into laughter.

Chapter 21

Claire's cell phone buzzed, lighting up on the dresser and bringing her out of a languid state of bliss. The real world was something she didn't want to rejoin just yet, and Lang's groan of protest echoed her own feelings.

"I'm on call," she reminded him when he reached a hand out to stop her.

He made a garbled sound of rejection, which brought a smile to her lips.

"Claire," she answered.

"Dr. Norris, it's Alison." The aide's voice quavered. "Thomas hasn't been taking his meds for a while, apparently, and he's angry and threatening. He threw a book at Gibby."

Claire was already searching for her clothes. God, where were they? Her underwear was tossed by the door. Almost in the hall. Her bra the same. "Is Greg there?"

"Alphonse is on. He's getting him under control. But that's not all. It's the patient from Side B. Heyward Marsdon? He won't go back in his room. He was on a supervised walk, but he refuses to leave the morning room. He keeps asking for you."

Claire's chest felt like there was a weight on it, forcing

out her breath. She struggled for air. "I'll be right there. Any other doctors still around on Side A?"

"I think Avanti's here."

"Have him talk to . . . the patient," she said, unwilling to say Heyward's name aloud with Lang in the room.

"Okay, but he's asking for you."

"I'll be there as soon as I can." She clicked off.

"What's wrong?" Lang asked, leaning up on one elbow. He'd thrown the comforter over them and now, as she gathered up her undergarments and pants and blouse, she could see his chest and upper arms and the line of his hips in the dim light sneaking around the door from the hall.

"One of the patients is off his meds, apparently. He's combative."

Lang checked the time on his watch. Just after six thirty and black as pitch already. "I don't want you to go," he admitted.

Claire smiled, tucking in her blouse. "I don't want to go."

"When will you be back?" he asked suggestively.

"As soon as I can?" She left it as a question, and for an answer he came off the bed like a lion and backed her against the wall. Claire was laughing madly and Lang's growls of amusement matched hers.

Finally, breathless, she pushed him away from her, but kept him at arm's length, admiring his naked form in the half light. She touched his chin and turned his head, examining the cut. "I could still get the butterfly bandage."

"I'm fine."

"Okay. What are you going to do while I'm gone?"

"Stay in bed. Wait for you."

She would have laughed if thoughts of Heyward Marsdon hadn't been crowding her mind.

"Actually, I've been thinking," he admitted. "Unless Tasha was kidnapped, she would have no idea where to go but Siren Song except maybe the Foothillers' community, since that was Rafe's hometown and it's close to the lodge. Maybe she'd go there? Cade didn't know her, but maybe Rafe confided in someone else."

His cell phone rang before Claire could answer, sounding muffled because it was inside the pocket of his pants. Lang casually went over and picked it up. His naturalness was a powerful aphrodisiac and Claire had a bit of difficulty heading into the hall in search of her purse and coat.

She heard him say a few words and then hang up. A few moments later he appeared, shirtless, but snapping the top of his jeans. "That was Clausen, from the department. They had a complaint from a couple who live on the edge of the Foothillers' community. Someone sitting outside of their house in a car."

Claire gave him a strange look, waiting for the punch line.

"They live on the same street as Cade Worster."

"That's . . . coincidental."

"Yeah. This couple apparently makes a habit out of calling the police and reporting on the neighbors. But Clausen knew I'd be interested because of Cade."

"Call me and tell me if you learn anything," Claire said.

They looked at each other for a long moment. Slightly flustered, she turned toward the door. "You can push the button in to lock the door behind you."

"What? No kiss good-bye?" he asked.

She glanced back, a smile hovering on her lips. Then she shook her head and disappeared into the dark night.

Rita had moved her vehicle to the block that lay on the back side of Cade's place. The houses on this street backed up to the ones on Cade's, and an alley ran between them, giving access to both the rear of Cade's house and the rear of the homes on his street. Rita didn't dare drive up the alley, as it was seldom used by cars.

She couldn't trust the Blackburns. They'd seen her sitting in her car. Even if they didn't recognize her, they were alerted to her presence, so she drove away after Cade helped Tasha back inside his house.

Now she didn't have the same line of sight, and she'd spent some fretful hours until nightfall. But there were lights on in Cade's house and the Wrangler wasn't moving, so it looked like maybe he and Tasha were in for the night in spite of themselves.

Knife in hand, Rita moved like a wraith between the houses that faced the street where she was parked, coming into the alley on the north side of Cade's house. What a piece of shit it was. Worse than her mother's. Someday she, Rita, would have a loving family. A baby. And a father. And all these fuckers who looked down at her could go fuck themselves.

Rafe had been her ticket out of here. Rafe.

A tear slipped from the corner of her eye. *For you, Rafe,* she thought, moving up the back stairs. *For you.*

Dr. Paolo Avanti paced the hospital's empty morning room, worried he'd made a huge mistake with Rita.

She was just the kind of woman he knew better than to involve himself with. He'd learned the hard way that the power of sex could be his ruination. Rita was a nightmare girlfriend. She'd already pressured him for a job and he'd allowed it. His dick was constantly hard, thinking about their next liaison in one of the bedrooms, or a closet, or a staff room. Anywhere. All he wanted to do was thrust himself inside her and slam away.

And she knew it. She understood. She'd awakened the slumbering beast inside him that he thought he'd slain once and for all after his last loveless marriage. He'd taken the position at Halo Valley to concentrate on his career.

Halo Valley was in the middle of nowhere, for all its prestige, and he'd thought that would be good for him, but it wasn't. He longed for something more sophisticated than Vandy's cowboy bar, or that dive of a place in Deception Bay, Davey Jones's Locker. He'd been there once and found a woman, and she'd blown him in the backseat of his car and then passed out. It was all he could do to wake her up and stand her outside so he could drive away.

And then a long dry period. And then . . . Rita.

God. He was glad she was sick and been out today. In his mind, he was trying to come up with some reason to have her fired. He needed her out of Halo Valley before he was completely under her power and discovered. Freeson was already looking at him sideways, as if he had an inkling.

But he wanted to screw the hell out of Rita once more. Wanted to buck himself against her raised ass. In the meeting room. Or in the supply room off the kitchen.

"Avanti?"

The questioning female voice brought him back with a thump. Claire Norris was looking at him strangely. She'd just come in and he hadn't even heard her, he'd been so lost in his fantasy.

He had to turn away, waiting for his hard-on to dissipate. Had she noticed? It wasn't the kind of thing the doctors at this place missed. "What?" he demanded, surly.

"Where's Heyward? I heard he wouldn't go back in his room."

"Who told you that? He's in his room. Go look." He waved her away, his back still turned.

"What about Thomas McAvoy?"

"Alphonse wrestled him into restraints."

"Restraints." He could hear her wince. "Is Gibby in his room as well?"

"I don't keep track of every patient here, Dr. Norris."

He heard her departing footsteps as she headed in the direction of Marsdon's room. He was sorry, now, that he'd been instrumental in moving Marsdon. The kid wasn't much of a threat, but he was fixated on Claire, and that in itself caused friction with the Marsdon family.

Paolo closed his eyes and breathed in noisily. Oh, he didn't want to leave this place, even if it was provincial, but if things kept going with Rita, he might have to. Rita. He imagined his hand capturing a swelling breast and his dick jumped to attention again. If Rita had a cell phone he'd call her up and demand she come and suck him off. The idea made his head swim a little. But she didn't have a phone. She was a fucking dinosaur when it came to technology.

"Rita," he muttered through his teeth.

Lang drove by Cade's house on his way to the Blackburns', turning at the end of the block, which was also the edge of the field where he'd chased after Cade. Cade's house was completely dark. He wondered briefly if the kid was out doing some nefarious deed. He wasn't a bad sort, but he wasn't a straight arrow, either.

The wind had kicked up, throwing shivery torrents of rain around from every direction. Lang bent his head into a gust as he climbed from his truck. He was fairly certain he was running a fool's errand, but he nevertheless trudged up a set of brick steps to an upper porch and more wooden stairs. The Blackburns' house, unlike most of the one-story ramblers, was a three-story Victorian whose front porch looked northward across the field. Their home was on the edge of the Foothillers' community and Lang guessed the sprawling, mostly Native American residential area had grown from the base of the Coast Range toward the sea, the Blackburns' land being the most northern point and nearly the most western as well. The plots of land grew larger from here toward the sea; the community less central.

He pressed his finger to the button beside the door and heard deep within the house a resounding bass ding-*dong*. Very funereal.

A porch light went on overhead, and an older man's voice asked, "Who's there?"

"Langdon Stone. The Tillamook County Sheriff's Department sent me." The Blackburns phoned so often, apparently, that the department limited the number of times they actually got in their vehicles and made a house call. Most of their complaints were appeased by simply having someone listen to them.

The door cracked open, spilling dim, yellow light onto the porch. An old gent peered out at him, then opened the door. Both he and his wife were backlit, and they shuffled aside as the man said, "Come in, then. I'm Clifford. This is Portia."

"We're so glad to see you!" Portia said enthusiastically. "Come in, come in."

Lang stepped across the threshold and they ushered him into a front room filled with antique furniture. The lights flickered ominously as the wind rattled around the outside eaves.

"Oh, I hope we don't lose power. Sit down, please," Portia invited him, eyeing the overhead lamp anxiously.

Lang really preferred to stand, but they were so overly excited to see him that he perched on a maroon velvet settee. Portia was small, round, and white-haired with bright eyes and Clifford was tall, lean, slightly stooped, and had a tendency to squint.

"You called about someone waiting in a car. A woman," Lang said.

"Yes, sir. I think it was Rita." Portia folded her hands primly and lifted her chin.

Lang's interest dwindled. He'd known it was a long shot, but he'd hoped it was Tasha. "You know her, then."

"Oh, yes. She's one of the Indians. I shouldn't speak badly of her. I don't even know her. I just know the family," Portia said meaningfully.

"Uh-huh," Lang said.

"Aren't you going to write this down?" she asked.

Clifford said, "I could get you a notepad, if you don't have one."

"Why don't you tell me about Rita, and we'll go from there," Lang suggested. He wondered what time it was, what Claire was doing, if she'd learned anything more from Gibby, if she was thinking about spending the night together in bed, making love until dawn.

"She was sitting out in that car. I believe it might belong to the family. I don't know what she was doing. She was pointed in the other direction from her aunt's house."

"Her aunt's house?"

"Across the field." Portia gave him a stern look. "They just discovered her bones last year, you know. But she was killed here a long time ago."

"Years," Clifford said with a nod. "And he burned the field to hide it. Nobody knew."

"Angela was a prostitute," Portia said through tight lips.

"And a witch," Clifford said in a hushed tone.

As if hearing him, the wind howled outside and the lights flickered again. But as they all glanced around, distant bells rang in Lang's mind. He recalled a little about a woman's bones that had been dug up behind her home about a year earlier. The news had reached statewide and he and Curtis had talked about it even though it was in Tillamook County, because the locals had called her a witch.

Now he realized those locals were probably Portia and Clifford Blackburn. "TCSD dug up the bones," he said.

"That's right!" Clifford was pleased he remembered.

"Rita is the dead woman's niece, and she was outside your house today, sitting in her car," Lang said. He thought he could end the interview by promising to look into it.

"She was watching down the street," Portia said. "Waiting for someone."

"She was friends with the boy that was murdered. I saw her with him at the camper," Clifford said. "But she was waiting for someone else."

"She glared at me," Portia said, sniffing. "I just looked out and she glared at me!"

Lang's attention snapped back hard. "This Rita was friends with Rafe Worster?"

"Rafe Black Bear," Portia corrected. "Poor soul. Have you found out what happened to him?"

"We're working on it. What's Rita's full name?" Lang asked.

"Rita Feather Hawkings," Cliff told him. "She lives with her mother, Delores, over there." He waved a hand in the general direction of the Foothillers' community. "Delores's sister, Angela, was Angela Feather Haines."

"The prostitute," Portia reminded. "Across the field."

Cliff said, "I don't think I ever heard that Delores took her married name. She still goes by Feather. But she was married to Hawkings once, I believe."

"Rita could be a bastard child," Portia responded quickly, sounding both elated and scandalized. "I want to know why she was out there. Just waiting."

"Which house is Delores Feather's?"

"If you're going to talk to Rita, don't tell her we talked to you!" Portia looked worried suddenly.

"Rita coud be at the hospital," Cliff said, also looking concerned. "Keep our names out of it."

"She's at a hospital?" Lang asked.

"She's a nurse at Ocean Park," Portia said.

The hairs on the back of his arms lifted. Claire's friend said a nurse, or someone wearing nurse's garb, had claimed to recognize the pregnant and catatonic victim of the rest stop attack.

"Her aunt's a witch," Portia said with a quiver to her voice. "Angela was crazy, you know. Sexually crazy. She had two sons from two different fathers and they were both not right, either. We were afraid of them, but they're both gone."

"Rita could be just the same." Clifford echoed his wife's fears.

"We don't know why she was parked outside!"

They were working themselves up and Lang did his best to calm the waters. "I'm sure it was nothing, but I'll talk to Rita. You said her car was facing away from the field? Toward Cade Worster's house?"

"In that direction," Clifford answered. "Cade's a thief, you know."

"So I've heard," he said. "His cousin Rafe was with a companion when he was killed," he tried out. "A pregnant woman who we think may have been his girlfriend."

"What did she look like?" Portia asked.

"Blond. Blue-eyed. Do you know who she could be?" he asked, not wanting to give them more information than they already had.

He stumped them with that news. They both shook their heads, regretfully on Portia's part. She looked crestfallen that she hadn't been on the forefront of new gossip.

"You don't mean she's from that cult, do you?" Clifford asked slowly.

"Oh, my stars! They're all mixed in together." Portia placed a hand to her mouth. "They're witches, too."

"I'll talk to Rita," Lang said. "Do you know her mother's address?"

Clifford gave it to him, then warned again, "Leave our names out of it."

"Make us an unknown source," Portia suggested.

Lang promised to be discreet.

"Dr. Norris, you came!" Heyward said when she entered his room. "Thank you!"

He was sitting in his bed, wide awake but glad to see her, and Claire, who'd steeled herself for this moment, felt her own tension slide away. "How are you doing, Heyward?" she asked.

"I didn't mean to kill her. You know I didn't mean to kill her. I love Melody. I want her back. I want her back!"

"We all want her back, but you know it can't happen," Claire said.

"It wasn't Melody in that room. I wouldn't hurt her."

"I know, Heyward."

"It wasn't you, either." He looked stricken, eyes stretched wide. "It wasn't."

"Dr. Prior is your doctor," Claire reminded him, naming the psychiatrist from Side B who still was in charge of Heyward's care.

"It wasn't you!"

"I'm going to call him now," she said, though she knew he had undoubtedly already left hospital grounds. After-hours rotations were for interns and residents, and Zellman was one of Halo Valley's more prominent and celebrated psychiatrists, who tended to treat the most dangerous and/or infamous patients on Side B, of which Heyward could conceivably be both.

"You don't have to call him." Heyward stuck out a palm to stop her. "I know what happened. I'm on my meds now.

I know it was a hallucination. I just wanted you to know that it was real to me. I never wanted to hurt anybody." His eyes watered with the remembrance. "I'm so . . . sorry. Did you . . . get the cake?"

"Oh, yes, Heyward. Thank you," Claire said, meaning it.

She heard someone come in behind her and jumped, but it was only Avanti.

"What are you doing?" he demanded, seeing Heyward's unshed tears.

Claire looked at the man in the bed. All she saw was a lost, confused, and mentally ill patient who was not the monster of her nightmares. "Heyward was apologizing," Claire said to Avanti. To Heyward, she added, "Apology accepted."

"Thank you. Thank you," he choked out.

She left the room, affected by his misery. She still wasn't convinced he was on the correct side of the hospital. Off his meds, he was a real danger to himself and others. But on his meds there was no question that he was horror-struck at what he'd done, nearly unable to comprehend that he was truly responsible.

She really didn't know where he belonged.

When Lang knocked on Delores Feather's front door there was no answer. The place was completely dark, not a light on, even though it was only a few minutes past eight. Were they out? Asleep early? He walked around the building, looking for answers.

Why hadn't Claire called him? He thought about phoning her, but she'd been the one called to duty, so to speak, and it would be better if she contacted him.

When he'd circled the whole house and received no sense that it was inhabited, he gave up and decided to head instead to Ocean Park Hospital. Maybe Rita was working tonight. Maybe that's why the house seemed deserted.

As he walked back to his truck the wind slammed hard, plunging the whole area into complete darkness. Power outage. Yanking on his driver's door, he climbed into the cab and drove down the debris-battered street, watching leaves slap onto his windshield. He swung by Cade's place again on his way out. Black as sin. No sign of life. The only vehicle on the street was a Jeep Wrangler that had seen better days.

His mind was on Rita Feather Hawkings. A nurse. A friend of Rafe's. Who'd been seen on the street by the Blackburns, waiting in a car. Watching Cade's house, maybe?

Waiting for . . . Tasha? Maybe Tasha's *baby*?

He shook his head. He knew nothing, really. It was no good jumping to conclusions. He needed to talk to Rita herself and find out how much of the Blackburns' rambling account of mental illness and hypersexuality was real and how much was fabrication. Rita could well be the victim of a smear campaign; Portia had admitted right off the bat that she didn't even really know Rita.

A faint, uncertain light suddenly emanated from the front window of Cade's house. As if it were coming from the back of the house, near the kitchen.

Lang got a cold feeling. He suddenly wondered if he should take his Glock out of the glove box. After a moment of suspended animation, he did just that, slipping it into his right hand. Then he shouldered open his door and eased it back shut just enough to turn off the interior light, not enough to make much noise. Cade had probably seen him already, but he didn't need to announce his arrival to the whole neighborhood. He moved up to the front door.

The light was gone.

"Cade?" Lang called softly, twisting the handle. The door was locked.

No answer.

He circled around to the back porch, knocked again. Again, no answer.

. "Cade, it's Langdon Stone," he called, louder this time. "We talked before?" He rattled the back knob and was surprised when it turned in his hand. Carefully, he eased the door open. "Cade?"

The door suddenly stopped short, hung up on something.

Lang pushed harder and whatever was in the way gave, making a scraping sound against the floor. "Cade?" he called again.

And then he saw what had impeded the door. A pair of jean-clad legs.

He jumped inside and slammed his left hand against the wall, automatically searching for a light switch. Encountered it. Flipped it up. No power.

Cursing himself for forgetting, he bent over the figure on the floor. The windows offered a lighter darkness than the interior of the house and illuminated Cade's wide-open eyes. Lang leaned toward him. Listened. Faint breathing.

"Cade!"

Lang set down his gun and put his hand on Cade's chest. Felt wetness. Noticed the spreading black stain across Cade's shirt.

Blood.

He yanked his hand back, dug in his pocket for his cell phone. Fumbled it. Dropped it to the floor with a clatter. Reached for it. Felt the cold outline of a handgun—not the Glock.

Fear crawled up his spine. He scrabbled for the Glock, shoved it in the back waistband of his pants. Found his phone and punched in 911. Asked for an ambulance. Gave them Cade's address. Explained it was a gunshot wound and gave them his name.

"Mister . . ." Cade whispered.

"Don't talk. Save your strength," Lang ordered. He was leaking blood. Lang applied pressure to the wound, praying it would help.

Cade swallowed. "She . . . she . . ."

His mouth went slack and his head slipped sideways, his eyes closing.

"Stay with me," Lang ordered. "Stay with me."

And then the same uncertain light glowed from down the hall, penetrating the kitchen's gloom. A candle?

He looked around, felt the muscles on the back of his neck tighten. He jumped up, on the balls of his feet, reaching for his gun, heart thundering, as the candle carrier moved into view.

"Rita?" he rasped, leveling the Glock to the approaching light.

But it wasn't Rita.

It was a blond angel carrying a candle. Heavy with child. Breathing hard. Crying silently.

"Tasha?" he said in disbelief.

Her knees wobbled and Lang leapt forward to catch her. A thin trickle of dark blood ran down her hand and onto the floor.

"She stabbed me," Tasha said in a whisper. "She . . . stabbed me . . . again."

Chapter 22

Come on, come on, come on!

Lang gently positioned the nearly unconscious woman in the passenger seat of his truck beneath the kaleidoscope of the ambulance lights. She moaned softly, as if in pain, and tensed up as he worked the seat belt. A contraction? God, he hoped not.

The EMTs were moving Cade. There'd been nothing more for Lang to do, so he'd opted to take Tasha himself. After speaking she'd lapsed into her same nonresponsive state, eyes open, unaware.

Except she was in labor.

Closing her door, he half-ran, half-slid in the now pouring rain, grabbing on to the hood of his truck for support. His door was stuck and he gritted his teeth in impotent fury, yanking it free, cursing the fact that he hadn't gotten the damn thing fixed. Inside the cab he snatched up his cell phone, called the sheriff's department, and tersely told them about the dead man and gave them Cade's address. He told them he was on the way to Ocean Park Hospital with a victim of the attack, who was possibly in labor.

He drove with deep intensity, wanting to race, keeping

himself in check, aware he could endanger them both by hurrying too much.

Carefully, his eyes glued to the road in front of him, wipers slapping madly against the rain, he phoned Claire.

Gibby had been awake and sitting up in bed, much like Heyward, when Claire entered his room. "Are you all right?" she asked him.

"Thomas threw a book at me!" Gibby declared. "He hit me!"

"I know. I'm sorry. Did he hurt you?"

"Nah . . . I'm okay." He gazed at Claire with innocent eyes. "But he doesn't like her. He said she was lying!"

"Is that what started the fight between you?"

"He said Tasha was a fucking liar! He said Tasha was a fucking liar!"

He started throwing himself around in the bed and Claire quickly stepped forward, putting her arms around his shoulders, trying to calm him. "Gibby. Shhh. Gibby, it's okay. You can't listen to Thomas."

"He's *mean*."

"I know. Shhh."

"She's a'scared of him, too," Gibby declared.

"Like she's scared of the mean nurse," Claire said.

"Yeah . . . she scares me, too. 'Hello, Tasha,'" he suddenly said in a low, threatening tone. Then, "My baby . . ."

Claire felt her skin shiver at Gibby's sudden change of voice and attitude. "Did you hear somebody say that?" He nodded jerkily. "Who?"

"The mean lady who Tasha's a'scared of." He wrapped his arms around his neck again, his elbows in front of his mouth and nose, like he had the night before. Now Claire saw his fingers sliding around his back shoulders. "She hurt her here," he said, tapping his back.

He meant the stab wounds to Tasha's shoulders, Claire realized. "Who is this person? Is she a nurse?"

"A bad, bad nurse."

"Not Darlene," Claire confirmed.

"No!"

In her pocket, Claire's cell phone rang softly. She ignored it. "Gibby. Think hard. Please. For me. This bad nurse . . . is she the new one at the hospital? With the dark hair?"

His elbows were still in front of his mouth and nose, but his eyes rolled fearfully. "Bad, bad nurse." He gulped and cried again, "Thomas said she was a fucking liar!"

Claire's phone buzzed insistently. Frustrated, she snatched it from her pocket, her annoyance dissipating when she saw it was Lang. "I'm kind of in the middle of something. Can I call you back?"

"I found Tasha," he clipped out. "She's in the truck with me now, unconscious. We're on our way to Ocean Park. Cade Worster was shot."

"What?"

"I don't know details yet. Tasha's in shock. Maybe in labor. I've already alerted the hospital that we're coming and I've called TCSD. The ambulance is bringing Cade."

"Is Tasha okay? She isn't responsible, is she?"

"Doesn't look like it. There's some blood from a cut on her arm. Looks superficial." Gibby started crying in earnest at something he saw in Claire's face. She pulled herself together with an effort as he added, "Claire . . . I think I might know who did this."

"Who?"

"Meet me at the hospital. I'll tell you there."

"I'm on my way." She clicked off and flew out the door.

"My baby," Gibby repeated in his strangely threatening voice, the sound following her like a curse.

* * *

Tasha's hands were clasped across her abdomen, her eyes closed, as the policeman drove through the evening's rain and wind to the hospital. She didn't know if she'd been saved, didn't trust this man's, or anyone's, motives. The last person she'd trusted completely was Rafe, and Rafe was gone.

She heard him on the phone making terse commands and comments, though he thought she was unaware. She had drifted off for a bit to that place of nightmares. It was something she couldn't help, though she'd suffered a lot of blame for it over the years.

She understood that this man was worried, that he'd been stunned by Cade's bloody corpse. Rita's fault. Always Rita's fault.

She could have told the man that she was okay, but she felt silence might aid her better. She'd seen him before; he'd come to the hospital and tried to engage her in talking, but she'd kept mum then, too.

They drove several miles before they found an area with power again, lighted windows suddenly popping up from houses along the highway. Tasha could feel another contraction coming on and took a deep breath in preparation.

He suddenly turned the truck off the highway, and she squinted her eyes open to see a long black-topped road flanked by gnarled trees. At the end of this drive the lane opened up to a hospital's central parking lot, more open than Halo Valley's. The building was low and light spilled from every window. It was welcoming in its way, but Tasha knew it was merely another trap. Another prison. She had to be careful.

They were met by a team of nurses and doctors. Blurred faces. Rushing her inside. She closed her eyes and pretended to be unaware as they seated her in a wheelchair and pushed her through the whooshing sliding glass doors.

"She's in labor?" one of the nurses asked.

"Something's going on," the man who'd brought her answered.

"Can you hear me?" another nurse queried, close to Tasha's ear.

"Are you a relative?" a new, authoritative female voice apparently asked Tasha's driver.

"No," he answered. "Langdon Stone. Tillamook County Sheriff's Department."

"Nina Perez," she said brusquely. "What's the patient's name?"

"Tasha," he said.

Tasha's heart flipped over. They knew? They *knew*? Gibby, she thought darkly. He'd probably told them about the clothes as well.

"Last name?"

"Not sure. She's from the Colony."

Now she could *feel* them all turn and look at her. Tasha inwardly shrank from the sea of curious faces. She felt faintly ill. Catherine and the sisters had stared and stared at her, accusing her, enprisoning her. They wanted to dislike her, blame her, make her their scapegoat.

They blamed her for Nathaniel . . .

An ambulance came screeching in, sirens blaring. Tasha slowly opened her eyes and stared straight ahead as a team ran outside to greet it. She saw them pull a collapsible bed from the back and was mildly shocked to see Cade Worster's body.

He was dead. Cade was dead. She wondered why they bothered bringing him to the hospital. Someone muttered, "DOA," and she wasn't sure what that meant.

"She's awake," one of the nurses said. Her name tag read Carlita Solano.

"She's having a contraction," the authoritative one, Nina Perez, said grimly. "Jake," she said to a dark-haired man in deep blue cotton top and pants. Scrubs. That's what they were called. He reminded her a little of Rafe, and her heart clutched as he grabbed the handles of her wheelchair and took her behind a curtain that was suspended from a track in the ceiling. A makeshift examining room. Carlita and Perez left and a doctor bustled in. Young. Male. Lots of dark hair. He put his hands on her belly and felt around. "Where's Gallippo?" he demanded.

"On call," Jake said. "The midwife's here."

"Bring her in."

"What about her arm?"

The doctor lifted Tasha's arm and examined the bloody sleeve. "Give me the scissors." But Jake was gone, so he reached over and grabbed them himself, cutting straight through the sleeve. He made a *hmm* sound at the long slice and said, "I'm going to stitch this up."

Tasha could scarcely feel the cut or the needle as the doctor went to work. Rita had wielded a knife and she'd slashed wildly. Cade had jumped for the pistol and Tasha had pushed Rita with all her might.

And then . . . and then . . .

Another blurry nightmare threatened to overtake her. Fighting against it, Tasha stared overhead at the bright lights, breathing deeply, concentrating on the contraction that was overtaking her. They'd been on and off, some strong, some weak. Her little girl was getting ready to arrive.

The midwife was familiar. The same gray-haired woman who'd examined her at Halo Valley. Tasha hadn't liked her then and didn't like her now.

Then she heard a familiar voice outside the curtained room. The crystal diction sent shivers along her arms and legs. He'd scared her when she was younger, as much or more as the shaman had. Dr. Loman. The other one. The brother of the one who'd attended them before his death. The ultra-critical man who even seemed to cow Catherine upon occasion. Catherine didn't like him and neither did any of the sisters, herself included.

But he'd been "a necessary evil," as described by Catherine.

To Tasha's utter shock she heard the man, Langdon Stone, ask if a Rita Feather Hawkings was employed at the hospital. Carlita responded that Rita used to work there, but that she'd quit a few weeks ago. Dr. Loman demanded to know if Rita was the rude nurse. Nina Perez said shortly that Carlita was correct. Rita was no longer with Ocean Park.

Dr. Loman knew Rita? Tasha looked around the examination room wildly.

"Well, there you are," the midwife said, catching sight of Tasha's moving eyes. "Your baby's fine. You're having some contractions, I'm sure you can feel them. They haven't settled into a rhythm yet, but I think we should admit you."

Tasha stopped gazing around and stared up at the lights.

Langdon Stone's voice reached her. "Did Rita ask for a reference when she left?"

"Human Resources could tell you," Perez answered.

Tasha's pulse ran light and fast. They didn't know Rita was at Halo Valley Security Hospital. Yet.

She heard the emergency doors whoosh open and shut several more times. New voices joined the group outside. More officers, apparently. Their tone was low but Tasha knew they were discussing Cade's death. She heard "gun" and "blood" mentioned and "fingerprints."

Rita's face swam into Tasha's memory. She'd come through the back door looking murderous, charging Tasha. She hadn't immediately seen Cade but then he'd lunged for the gun and Rita's knife scraped down Tasha's arm and then *blam, blam, blam*! Cade jerked like a marionette and went down hard.

And Rita turned to Tasha and said, "You killed him," which was a lie!

Now Tasha quivered and shrank away, for once wanting desperately to go to that world inside her own head, away from all of this. She could still see Rita's mouth, screaming and shrieking and babbling, and she could see the glint of the knife blade, the arc of her swinging arm.

Like at the rest stop.

"What?" the midwife asked and Tasha realized she'd made a gurgling noise.

With an effort, she closed her eyes and willed herself away to that netherworld of demons and nightmares, where she could hide.

Claire arrived in a blast of driving rain. She'd grabbed her coat but hadn't put it on and she didn't bother now as she slammed the car door and scurried through Ocean Park's Emergency Room doors.

The first person she saw was Lang, in deep conversation with a silver-haired man of fiftysomething wearing a TCSD uniform. They both looked up at Claire's arrival and Lang introduced Detective Fred Clausen before stepping forward, clasping her forearms as if to steady her, his eyes saying something far more intimate. She could scarcely believe how short a time had passed since they'd made love. She wanted to touch the cut on his face, but caught herself.

"You all right?" he asked.

She nodded jerkily. "How's Tasha?"

"Wound on her arm's been stitched. The midwife says her contractions are getting stronger."

"What happened?"

"I don't know. Tasha hasn't been able to tell us. Cade was shot in the chest multiple times. A bullet pierced his heart. He bled out."

Claire shook her head in dismay and looked toward the emergency room examining cubicles.

"She is talking," Lang said, pulling her to one side, away from the others. "She said, 'She stabbed me. She stabbed me again.' I think she meant a nurse who used to work here at Ocean Park, Rita Feather Hawkings." Quickly, he gave her a rundown of the crux of what he'd learned from the Blackburns and about the nurse, Rita, who'd recently quit Ocean Park.

"Rita! She's the recent hire at Halo Valley!" Claire quickly brought him up to date on what Gibby had said. "I've seen her around and she would never meet my eyes. Like she was hiding something. Oh, God. I think she's been terrorizing Tasha."

"Well, she's safe now, whatever happened."

"It must have been Rita's keycard that Tasha used to get away." Claire suddenly shivered. "Where is Rita now?"

"Good question. She wasn't at the site. We've got a team doing an ongoing search at her mother's house, where Rita lives. Clausen's waiting for a call."

"Leesha told me it was a nurse who said she knew her," Claire murmured. "I should have checked."

"You're not blaming yourself," Lang told her sternly. "We don't know anything for sure yet."

"I wish Tasha could say something."

"She said 'she stabbed me,'" he reminded. "Probably meant Rita."

"Where could she have gone?"

He shook his head. "Detectives practically beat down her mother's front door, were about to break it in rather than wait for a warrant, when the mom, Delores Feather, finally answered. She was using a walker and a bit confused, but she's allowing the search."

"No Rita so far."

"No Rita so far," he agreed. "If she's our would-be baby stealer, she killed Rafe and now Cade, too."

"Why?"

"Because they got in her way?"

"Lang." It was Clausen, calling him over.

Claire listened from afar and heard that they'd found nothing at Delores Feather's house, but that Rita's mother's car was discovered on the block behind Cade's house.

"She has to be close by," Lang said.

"We'll keep looking," Clausen answered.

One of the nurses wheeled Tasha from behind the cubicle curtain and into the main emergency room area. A young doctor followed them, his expression serious.

Claire stepped forward. "I'm Dr. Claire Norris of Halo Valley Security Hospital. Tasha's been a patient there."

"She seems fine, physically. Baby's fine, too, according to Eugenie."

At that moment the midwife stepped out and, seeing Claire, came their way. "I think she should be kept overnight, just to be safe."

"Is she about to have this baby?" Claire asked.

"Sometime in the next several days. She came to a little bit while I was examining her, but now she's faded back."

"You want to put her in a room?" the young doctor asked and Eugenie nodded.

Claire said, "I think I'll stay with her." She thought about getting a message to Catherine, but how? It was dark and wet and stormy and she didn't feel like standing outside the gates and shouting. Tomorrow. When it was light.

"This Rita still has a keycard to Halo Valley," Lang said, thinking aloud.

"We'll change her code," Claire answered. "She can't get in without both. And if by some chance this is all a big mistake, we can figure it out when she shows up for work."

"I'm going back over to the mother's place. I want to talk to Delores myself."

"And maybe check the house for yourself?" Claire guessed.

"Something like that." His hand touched hers surreptitiously. "You're staying here all night?"

"I plan to."

He nodded. "Okay."

They looked at each other, the moment suspended. "I don't know where this is going," Claire said. "But it's good, isn't it?"

"It's good," he agreed.

Delores Feather was tired of the policemen stomping through her home. Tired and scared. One had posted himself in the living room in case Rita showed up, and it was a nuisance that made Delores want to scream.

What had Rita done?

She'd hobbled back to her bedroom but she couldn't stand the not knowing. They'd come in when she was barely dressed! Didn't they know how to treat a woman? Brutes, all of them!

Looking at herself in the mirror, she tucked an untidy strand of steel gray hair behind her ear and then examined her nightgown. Embarrassing to be caught like this. Carefully, not trusting her damn, fragile, arthritic legs, she moved to the closet, pulling out a decent enough looking robe. If she was going to entertain male visitors, she was going to do it properly. She wasn't that old. Her hair wasn't all gray and her face was relatively unlined. She'd just been unlucky health-wise, but she was still a looker, in her way. Rita was a handsome woman herself, and she was not like Angela! She had not taken that path.

But what had happened? Why were the police here?

Where *was* Rita?

Delores shuffled with her walker into the bathroom, opened a drawer, and eyed her makeup collection critically. She needed something to make her eyes pop; they were sunken into their sockets.

She worked carefully, making sure she neatly outlined the orbs. She'd just finished when she heard someone else arrive. Her heart clutched in fear. *Not Rita. Don't let it be Rita.*

But it wasn't.

Delores stumped her way into the living room to encounter a tall, handsome man in a beat-up black leather jacket and mud-spattered jeans and cowboy boots. The latest spate of rain had found him, and drops of water were coalescing in his dark hair.

My, my, my, Delores thought.

"I'm Langdon Stone," he said. "Has anyone told you why we're looking for your daughter, Rita?"

"No one's told me anything other than they think I'm hiding her!" She glared at the other sheriff's deputy, who pretended not to hear.

"There's been a homicide," he said, to which Delores's mouth dropped open.

"My Rita couldn't possibly be involved in that!" she declared, to which he told her the events that had brought him to her door.

What Delores heard was baby. Pregnant. Knife. Her eyes strayed of their own volition to one of the pictures on the little corner hutch. Langdon Stone followed her gaze with his own eyes and moved toward the collection of photographs. He picked up the one she'd been looking at and said, "Is one of these women Rita?"

The picture was of Delores, Rita, and Rita's good friend Vonda.

Delores unconsciously licked her lips. "Rita's the taller

one." He nodded, staring at her in a way that made color creep up her neck in spite of herself. *Don't ask,* she thought. *Don't ask.*

"Who's the other woman?"

"Vonda. She doesn't live here anymore." Delores clamped her lips together.

"She a friend of Rita's?"

"No."

"A relative?"

Why was he persisting? Delores didn't want to look at him anymore. He was attractive, but he was digging, digging, digging. "Just some people we know. Not very well." She flapped a hand at him.

"They live in the community?"

"Not Vonda. She left."

"But her family's still here."

"Rita isn't like Angela!" Delores burst out. "Angela was a whore! But Rita's nothing like her. Rita's a good, decent woman with a job. A career! You can't listen to what people say. They're jealous!"

Lang suggested softly, "Would Rita turn to Vonda's family if she needed help?"

"No. Oh, no." She shook her head.

"I'd like to talk to them anyway. Could you give me their address?"

Delores didn't want to. She wanted to help Rita. But she needed Rita home, too, so she gave the handsome detective the address and wondered if she'd done the right thing.

Claire sat in a chair in Tasha's hospital room, her mind full of the images from the last few days: Herm Smythe and his odd recital about the women of Siren Song and his written history; Catherine and her reluctance to talk about Tasha and the Colony; Gibby and the way he wanted to abet Tasha's escape and rose to protect her honor against Thomas's slander; Rita, the nurse who they thought was tracking Tasha, trying to steal her baby; Cade Worster's murder.

She wanted Lang to call and update her on his search for Rita.

She wished she could just ask Tasha the right questions and finally get some answers.

As if reading her thoughts, Tasha stirred in the bed, opened her eyes, blinked twice, then focused on Claire.

"I saw Catherine today," Claire told her quietly. "She let me inside the gates of Siren Song. She confirmed that you're from their family."

Tasha stared. Claire stared right back.

"And I spoke with a man named Herman Smythe who wrote an account of the Colony, some of it more lore than truth, I suspect," Claire went on. "You've led a sheltered life. I think maybe Rafe was handsome and attentive and you wanted to leave with him. He offered you . . . a way out."

Now Tasha was fully listening; Claire could tell.

"Langdon Stone found you at Cade Worster's house. Do you remember what happened there?"

Her lips quivered and fear settled in her eyes.

"He said you spoke to him," Claire urged gently.

Tasha suddenly drew in a sharp breath and her eyes fluttered closed. Claire realized she was having a contraction and came and took her hand. "You're in labor," she said.

Tasha, after holding her breath for as long as she could stand, let out a long, low moan.

"I'll get the nurse," Claire said, nearly cannoning into one in the doorway.

"We'll get her hooked up to an IV and fetal monitor," the middle-aged woman said crisply.

"Thank you," Claire answered gratefully.

"Are you family?"

"No."

"Then please step out of the room."

She was all brisk efficiency, and rather than argue, Claire did as she was told, watching from the hallway as more hospital staff entered and the requisite equipment for the impending birth was wheeled into the room.

Tasha was screaming inside. The low moan that issued from her mouth was nothing compared to the raging shrieks ricocheting through her brain. *IV? Fetal monitor?* What did they mean?

And then they all came in with that rattling machinery! She wanted to fight them. Yanked her arm back when they pulled out a needle and tubing and a hanging bag that swayed menacingly.

"Ma'am!" one of the nurses admonished, surprised.

She wasn't going to let them do it. She wouldn't allow it. She'd been strapped to a bed before and she would never be again!

"What's your name?" the first nurse asked, then swiveled to look out the door to where the doctor from Halo Valley had gone.

"Tasha," Claire said from beyond the door.

The nurse's lips were tight. Her manner was too much like Catherine's for Tasha to want to comply. "Well, Tasha, stop flailing around," she ordered. "The baby will be fine, but dramatics will only get in the way. Understand?"

She was starting to feel a familiar panic. The same one that crept in and smothered her. For an answer she threw herself out of the bed, knocking the head nurse aside.

"For God's sake," the nurse sputtered, stepping back as Tasha stumbled into the hallway.

"Tasha!" Claire called, scared, and Tasha, unable to stop

the creeping shadows coming up through the corners of her eyes, overtaking her, simply said, "Help me," throwing a hand against the wall to break her fall as she crumpled downward.

Vonda Youngley's family lived outside of the Foothillers' community and on the southern side of Deception Bay. Lang found it without too much difficulty and was glad to see that their power was restored, if it had gone out earlier.

He pulled into their driveway, wondering what they would think about having a stranger knock on their door so late in this stormy evening. But Cade Worster was dead and Rita Feather Hawkings, their most likely suspect, was at large, and these people's daughter had once been Rita's friend.

The Glock was once again in his waistband at his back, tucked beneath his jacket. He didn't want to freak them out, but he also didn't want to meet up with Rita unarmed.

He rang the bell and heard it make a buzzing sound inside the sixties ranch with the sagging carport. Fingers spread the living room window blinds and a face scowled between them at him.

The porch light flashed on. One of those curly fluorescents.

The door cracked open an inch. "Can I help you?" a man's voice asked in a tone that said clearly that he wasn't planning to no matter what Lang said.

"Mr. Youngley, I'm with the Tillamook County Sheriff's Department," Lang said, "and I would like to ask you a few questions."

"Show me your I.D.," he demanded before Lang could further explain.

"I don't have it with me, but you can call the department for verification. My name's Langdon Stone. I would like to know if you've seen Rita Feather Hawkings this evening, or anytime recently."

The door shut with a slam. Lang waited patiently, and when finally it opened again, Lang found himself looking at a woman in her late twenties or early thirties. She had short brown hair and wore a sweatshirt and jeans, and she swung the door open and motioned him inside.

"Vonda!" the older man yelled.

"Dad, he wants to know about Rita. I'm only too happy to tell." She eyed him critically as he crossed the threshold. "You don't look like a crazed sexual predator or anything. What do you want to know?"

"You're Vonda, Rita's friend?" Lang asked.

"Was," she stressed. "Was her friend. Not anymore." She closed the door and crossed her arms, looking Lang up and down. "What's the deal?"

"Vonda," her father said again.

"I'm visiting my parents," Vonda said, by way of explanation to Lang. "I don't live here anymore, and you know why? Because of Rita. That's right. Rita Feather Hawkings."

"Vonda . . ." her father murmured a third time, long-suffering.

"I don't come here much," Vonda said tautly. "And it's a shame, because it would be nice for Selene to know her grandparents. But that woman—my *friend*—took Selene from me when she was an infant!"

"She was just babysitting," her father said weakly.

"The hell she was! She took my baby and didn't tell me where she was for hours! She stole Selene and she meant to keep her."

"She stole your child?" Lang asked.

"Rita's obsessed with having a baby. She would go to any lengths—any lengths!—to have one." Reaching down,

Vonda swept up a well-loved, tattered pink blanket from where it lay over the back of a chair. "Just thinking about it makes me crazy. Rita would never be allowed past our front door. I don't trust her. She's sick." She paused, giving Lang a long look. "So, tell me why you're here. Why you would even think my family would be seeing Rita again. And then after that, I'm going to go take my daughter her blanket, kiss her, hug her, and just make sure as hell that she's still in bed where I put her!"

Chapter 23

"She's out," the nurse said as Tasha crumpled to the floor. "Get Jake! We need to get her back to bed."

One of the younger nurses squeezed past the group that had accumulated in the hall while the older nurse, whose name tag read Brenda Baransky, and Claire leaned down in tandem over Tasha's inert form.

"Tasha's a patient at Halo Valley Security Hospital," Claire said tersely to the nurse, then went on to explain that she was a doctor and what her relationship to Tasha was. She'd just finished her quick recap when Jake, apparently, appeared, followed by several more staff members, one pushing a wheelchair, and an older man wearing a white coat. Claire's gaze swept his name tag: Dr. Dolph Loman. Momentarily distracted, she was pulled back to the moment when Tasha moaned again.

"She's going to have this baby on the floor if we don't move her now," Nurse Baransky declared, motioning for Jake and another orderly. They picked up Tasha with practiced efficiency, slipped her into the wheelchair, took her into the room, and transferred her to the bed. Immediately they began hooking her up to the fetal monitor and drew the needle to slip into her wrist for the IV.

"Is she going to start throwing herself around again when she wakes up?" Baransky asked Claire.

"I hope not."

She snorted. "I don't want to have to strap her down."

"I'll watch her," Claire said.

When they were finished and Tasha was resting quietly, everyone moved out of the room except Claire and Nurse Baransky. "Our OB-GYN's on call," Brenda said.

"I saw Eugenie Ledbetter earlier," Claire said. "She's been monitoring the pregnancy. She suggested Tasha spend the night even before the contractions increased."

"If she's still here, I won't call Dr. Gallippo."

"Thanks."

She stepped out, but then a long shadow fell over Claire, spooking her to where she jumped.

"I didn't mean to startle you," Dr. Dolph Loman said in a brittle voice. "Is this pregnant girl truly from the group known locally as the Colony?"

Claire gave him a long look, taking in his carefully clipped horseshoe of white hair, his stiff back and manner, and his piercing blue eyes under a ridge of thick, white brows. She hadn't forgotten Herm Smythe's comments about Dolph Loman, which had been peppered with phrases like "pompous ass" and "cold bastard." In fact, Herm's words to Dinah when she'd wanted to know more about the Colony and Catherine's sister, Mary, had been, "Ask that cold bastard Dolph, then. He'd know."

Now Dolph gave Claire a harsh look at her hesitation in answering. "Well?" he demanded.

"According to what Catherine said, we believe this is Natasha."

Now Dolph really looked at her. "Who spoke to Catherine?"

"I did."

"How did you manage that? They don't throw out the welcome mat to just anyone."

Claire was beginning to see what Herm's objections had been. "Tasha's been my patient for a while at Halo Valley."

That really wrinkled Dolph Loman's brow. "Those women are all my patients," he told her flatly. "They have been for years."

Claire had no intention of getting in a turf war over the rights of the Siren Song women. "How many are there? I saw some of them when I was invited in, maybe six or seven?"

"Why do you want to know?" he asked suspiciously.

"Family history. They're Natasha's sisters."

"Sounds to me like rife curiosity," he bit out.

"One of them, Lillibeth, was in a wheelchair. Is she your patient?"

He didn't deign to answer, just looked down on Tasha in the bed, bending over her in an imposing way.

"Well, unless you plan to birth this baby yourself," Claire said, "you might have to hand over this patient to a professional."

He shot her a dark look and swept out.

"Pompous ass," Claire murmured, then made sure she was out of the way as Eugenie Ledbetter and a team of nurses came into the room and took over Tasha's care as the young woman's contractions increased in frequency and strength.

Like an unwelcome memory, Claire remembered why Tasha had come to be here at all. "Where's Rita?" she wondered aloud.

The light from all the windows of Ocean Park Hospital beamed out cold, white and harsh. Rita had worked at the institution for a number of years but she'd never noticed before what a truly awful place it was.

But . . . there were no locks on the doors. She could walk right in and take her baby away.

Unless they knew about her, knew who she was and what she planned. Just thinking about it gave Rita a host of heebie-jeebies, sliding up and down her arms, burrowing into the base of her spine and leaving a frigid knot behind.

She sat in Roberto's Wrangler. Nothing wrong with it at all. That stupid Cade had wanted the blond whore for himself. Figured. And he'd conveniently left the keys for her on the kitchen counter. She'd seen them as soon as she walked in.

What had happened there? Rita felt like her head was full of muck. Dull. Overrun with goo. She couldn't think past the image of Cade waving a handgun at her and Tasha standing by smugly, her huge belly about to burst with Rita's baby!

Vaguely she remembered lunging at Tasha, connecting, maybe. And then Cade was on her, slamming her against the counter, screaming to leave her alone!

And then *blam* and Cade was spinning away from her. And *blam blam blam* and he was clutching his chest, his mouth an "O," and he was toppling.

And Tasha had the gun, and Rita was screaming and screaming and she had Tasha by the hair and she was banging her head into the wall and Tasha was *biting* her!

Now Rita lifted her right arm and pulled back the sleeve. The bitch's teeth had broken through her forearm. Left a perfect dental match on her skin.

And it hurt!

A frustrated cry issued from her throat. She'd stumbled out of Cade's house in shock, bleeding, wondering why Tasha had let her live when she'd shot Cade in cold blood.

Now she knew. Tasha planned to blame her.

But I didn't kill him! I didn't!

She pressed her hands to her mouth. Tasha had taken
Rafe from her, taken Rita's chance to have her own baby!
And now she planned to frame her for Cade's death. Oh,
Rita saw it now. Everyone already believed she had killed
Rafe. But it was Tasha. She was the killer. She was the evil
one, not Rita!

And she has my baby . . .

With sudden decision she switched on the Wrangler's
ignition and drove out of the hospital and north toward
Seaside. She needed a disguise. A wig, at the very least.

Tomorrow. Tomorrow she would go into the hospital
and take Tasha out of there, one way or another. And then
she was going to get her baby. Kill Tasha if she had to.

And then she was going to drive away. Far, far away.

While Tasha was in labor Claire spent some of the time
in the room with her, but most of it in the general waiting
area. At one point she thought about going home to meet
Lang but he appeared around eleven o'clock while she was
still debating and took her away to one of the area's bars,
Davey Jones's Locker, a dive, really, but the only game in
town at this time of night where they could order food—
bar food—chicken fingers and jo jo potatoes.

He told her about meeting Vonda Youngley, and Claire
in turn brought up her conversation with Dolph Loman.

Then they were both quiet. Claire saw lines on his
face that hadn't been there earlier. "I'm sorry about Cade,"
she said.

"What happened there tonight?" He shook his head.
They'd worked through most of the chicken fingers
and were eyeing the jo jo's with less interest. "What
happened?"

"I don't know."

Lang picked up his glass of water and took a long

draught, trying to shake it off. "She killed him. Rita shot him? Why?"

"She's a woman with a dangerous obsession that has taken her over. Rational thought is missing. She wants Tasha's baby."

"Cade was merely in the way," Lang said, reiterating. "He was collateral damage. Rafe, too, apparently. The Blackburns said Rita was a friend of Rafe's. Cade didn't know about anyone from Siren Song, but he said Rafe's had a girlfriend or two. Maybe Rita was one of them."

"She's targeted Tasha's baby for some reason," Claire agreed. "If Rafe dumped Rita for Tasha, that would qualify."

"And she killed Rafe, too."

"I think she must be the nurse who talked to my friend Leesha at Laurelton General. She was looking for Tasha. Something went wrong at the rest stop and Rita was on Tasha's trail."

Lang nodded. "And after she found out Tasha was at Halo Valley, she quit her job at Ocean Park and took a position at your hospital."

"Happened pretty fast," Claire mused. "I'm going to look into that tomorrow. Check with Human Resources."

"But where is she now?" Lang asked. "Deputy Burghsmith is standing guard at Rita's mother's house. The car's been impounded. So where is she?" he asked.

"Somewhere around the area."

"She's either on foot or found some new transportation," he agreed, frowning. "She doesn't own her own car, as far as we know."

Claire shook her head. She had no answer for him.

"And what exactly happened at Cade's house?" Lang circled back to the issue that was under his skin. "Rita stabbed Tasha, so where did the gun come in? Musta been Cade's. And if so, he had it out for a reason."

"Tasha knew Rita was coming for her," Claire suggested. "She told Cade."

"She remembers everything," Lang said. "That's what you're saying."

"Well, I don't know if she remembers *everything*. She . . ." Claire inclined her head, thinking hard. "Catherine said she had an affliction. She didn't specify. But Tasha seems to go in and out of consciousness. In and out of reality."

"She's in labor now. That baby's coming, right?"

"Yeah. Let's go back. I want to be there when it happens."

"Okay."

Lang drove them back to the hospital and then, though Claire assured him he didn't have to stay, they both kept vigil. She marveled at how far they'd come in their "relationship" in such a short period of time. She already felt connected to him, dependent on his company. An unexpected pleasure.

By the time the gray light of morning was reaching through the windows, Claire was already awake from a brief sleep. She got up from her chair and stretched. Lang was standing by the window and, seeing she was awake, said he'd go look for coffee for them both. "I'll check on Tasha's progress," Claire said.

She'd barely taken ten steps when Nurse Nina Perez pushed through the doors and nodded at Claire. "Nurse Baransky sent me to find you. She's pushing."

"Tasha's awake?" Claire hurried after Perez.

"In and out. Eugenie's delivering."

They entered the room and heard Eugenie counting and saying, "Relax, relax, baby's here," and Tasha seemed somewhat alert and the little girl slipped out, purple as babies are, and Eugenie was cutting the cord and placing the child in Tasha's arms. Claire was in awe, overcome, but when she turned to Tasha she saw that she'd slipped away again. Nurse Baransky scooped up the baby girl and handed it to another nurse to take care of.

"She keeps going out," Baransky said. "Dr. Gallippo is on his way, but I'm wondering if she needs a neurologist."

"Her aunt told me she's had this all her life." Claire looked with concern from Tasha to the little girl, who was suddenly crying at the top of her lungs.

"The baby looks great," the younger nurse said with a smile for Claire.

"Good."

Eugenie and Baransky examined Tasha's vital signs. "She would come to when the contraction got hard enough," Eugenie said. "I never knew whether she understood what was going on. But she seems stable."

"Good news all around." Claire said it as a statement, but Baransky heard the unspoken question.

"Looks that way," she said. "Ah, Dr. Gallippo . . ."

The serious-faced, middle-aged obstetrician came in briskly, took in the scene in a glance. Claire, whose overall feeling was relief, left them to go in search of Lang. He was waiting in the main seating area, holding two Styrofoam cups of coffee.

"Tasha's slipped back into unconsciousness, but her vital signs are good. New baby is terrific."

He smiled, his first since he'd heard of Cade's death. "Let me take you home," he said, and Claire agreed.

Catherine stared out the lookout slots by the front door to a gray morning where tiny tree limbs lay in a jumble of debris across the walkway to the gate. It would be difficult to get the car out, if she wanted to leave. She would have to wait until tomorrow when their weekly gardener/cleaner/handyman, Earl, who'd advised her to hire Rafe Black Bear in the first place, returned.

Isadora came up beside her and said, "Cassandra had a nightmare about Natasha last night."

"Remind her that Natasha is not here. She's on the outside."

"She said there was a baby in the dream."

Catherine stood stiff and silent for long moments, then said, "Dr. Norris will call on us after Natasha has her baby."

"You think it's happened?"

"What do you think?" Catherine asked the younger woman.

Isadora nodded. They all possessed the ability of second sight sometimes, and Cassandra was particularly gifted. "I hope Dr. Norris calls on us soon."

Claire and Lang returned to her house and Claire put in a call to Halo Valley, saying she would not be in until the afternoon and to cancel her morning appointments. It was rare that she gave so little notice, but then the events of the last couple of days had thrown her world into a tailspin.

She slept till noon in her lover's arms, though she had the sense that Lang got up several times. Finally, when she snapped into full consciousness, it was because she heard him on the cell phone, his voice urgent and tense, and she was awake and out of bed, recognizing a crisis without knowing what it was.

"What?" she demanded, tossing a hand through her tousled hair, staring at him in a kind of controlled panic as she saw his shuttered face, closed off to hide his own emotions. "Is Tasha all right?"

"It's not about Tasha. It's about her new baby."

Claire's heart clutched. "Oh, no . . . Lang . . . no!"

"She's alive, as far as we know," he said, addressing her fear correctly. "But it looks as if she's been kidnapped from the hospital. She's been missing for nearly an hour."

* * *

Rita drove away from the hospital with extreme care. Extreme care.

Two reasons: one, she could not afford to be stopped, and two: she didn't have an infant car seat. She'd had to put her baby on the floor of the backseat, and the little thing was crying over every bump.

The wig she'd chosen was a light brown color in an old-fashioned "bubble" style. It made Rita look ten years older than her real age. She'd walked down the halls in her scrubs like she owned the place, and nearly had a heart attack when Carlita suddenly appeared in the hallway with another RN named Laura, who glanced Rita's way casually while Carlita, unaware, was going on about the new baby born to the woman from the cult.

Ocean Park Hospital did not have a wing devoted entirely to obstetrics. Expectant mothers were associated with doctors whose deliveries were at Seaside Hospital or Tillamook, one north of Deception Bay, one south, and Ocean Park's OB-GYN, Dr. Gallippo, was mainly with Seaside General and only came to Ocean Park when specifically requested.

For these reasons—and possibly because it was just meant to be that Rita would finally have her own baby at last!—there was no real checkpoint at Ocean Park like at other hospitals, where no one could take the baby away before it was released by the doctor in charge.

Rita had simply walked the halls, looking efficient and busy, until the moment she was assured that Tasha was finally completely alone, then she stepped into her room, swept up the sleeping child, and with the Fertility Mother looking after her, had taken the baby into the first empty room she could find, ripped off her top, slipped the child into the baby sling she wore underneath, then replaced the top. She looked pregnant herself by the time she left the room, and with her heart pounding in a wild, deafening tattoo, she walked out of the hospital unbothered.

But with all her planning, she'd forgotten the car seat. She was shocked at her own failure.

Now she had to buy the protective item, and it sent shivers down her skin. If someone should notice the baby was gone—and the news broke—and they remembered a woman buying a car seat at the local drugstore, for that's where she was headed . . . well, she couldn't think that way! The goddess had watched over her to date, even if she'd had to leave the blond bitch sleeping away in her bed, untouched, and Rita saw no reason for her luck to change now.

The drugstore was the only game in town and it had been around Deception Bay for as long as Rita could remember. Rita drove around to the back, where there were no vehicles and no activity. She had no choice but to leave the infant where she was. It would only be for a few minutes and then Rita would put the car seat in place and they would be gone. Roberto might be looking for his Wrangler, but he wasn't exactly on good terms with the police, so it could be a while before he really reported it missing.

And Cade would be Roberto's first go-to, and with him shot and probably dead . . .

She purposely shoved those thoughts aside and went inside the store. Glancing around, she was glad to see she didn't recognize the girl at the counter. Baby gear was to the back, she knew, and she walked carefully, her legs wanting to run. She grabbed up formula and a bottle and one of the two car seats they had for sale. She wanted much, much more but she couldn't afford to draw too much attention to herself. Oh, how she'd waited for this day. But these *details*.

She wondered, suddenly, the thought like a wave of cold water, if she'd made a mistake. They would find her. She should have left without taking the baby. She would be away by now and Tasha could lie all she wanted and it wouldn't matter.

But no. The baby was *hers*.

"Is that everything?" the girl at the counter asked.

"Yes." She put the money on the counter with shaking hands.

Paolo, she thought randomly. Paolo wouldn't be a bad father. If she couldn't have Rafe—or Jake at Ocean Park— maybe she could have Paolo, even though he was older?

And then she was outside, glad for the misting rain on her face. She hurried to the back of the building and the Wrangler. Quickly she opened the door. The baby was crying and Rita picked her up and cuddled her close, her gaze darting both directions. The little girl wanted to nurse, so Rita climbed in the backseat and poured the premixed formula in a bottle, holding the baby and feeding her with shaking hands.

The little girl took to the bottle well, Rita saw with satisfaction. Good. She hadn't made a mistake.

The baby fell asleep with the nipple still in her mouth. Rita gently swaddled her back up and lay her on the seat. Then she ripped the car seat box open with her bare hands. She stared at the contraption and wanted to cry. She wasn't good with these things. But there were instructions.

Painstakingly, she got the car seat in place, buckling it in. Then she put her treasure inside, adjusting the buckles.

She was a good mother, she thought with pride. A good, good mother.

But when she edged toward the highway, intending to drive south toward Tillamook, a sheriff's deputy whizzed by in the direction of the hospital, lights flashing.

They *knew*!

She couldn't be on the highway. Couldn't afford to be in view.

Because she could think of nothing else, she drove back toward the Foothillers' community. A familiar place to hide while she planned her next move.

Chapter 24

It was a melee at Ocean Park Hospital when Lang and Claire arrived together. Someone had stolen the baby from its bed inside Tasha's room while Tasha slept. Someone brazen enough, or just crazy enough, to believe they could get away with it.

And they had.

Claire knew it was Rita. Lang knew it was Rita. Hospital personnel wanted to believe it was some kind of strange mistake.

Lang marshaled Clausen for the job of finding the kidnapper and left a younger woman deputy named Dunbar at the hospital. He phoned Warren Burghsmith, still on duty at Rita's mother's house, warning him of the new development. Then he pulled Claire aside and said, "She's obsessed. She took that baby out of here under everyone's nose. Where would she go? What's she thinking?"

"She wants the baby above all else." Claire could hardly think, she was so worried. "But she left Tasha alone. That's good. That's good."

"Where the hell is she?" He was talking rhetorically, frustrated, his eyes flashing with anger. "Where *the hell is she*?"

"You've got an Amber Alert going," Claire reminded

him, more for something to say than any real reason that it needed to be stated. "Someone will find her."

"We don't know what vehicle she's in. Maybe she thumbed a ride. Maybe she stole a car. Jesus."

His cell phone rang. It was Deputy Burghsmith. "Tell me you have something," Lang answered.

"A Jeep Wrangler just drove by the Feather house really slowly with a woman at the wheel. Maybe a gawker. Couldn't see in the backseat."

"Wrangler," Lang snapped out. "There was a Wrangler parked in front of Cade's, but it wasn't there when I went inside last night. . . . Damn!"

"Want me to go after it?"

"I'll get someone there. I'll come myself!" he decided. He was off the phone and striding toward the door.

"Wait!" Claire called.

"I gotta go. I think we've got her."

"I'll come with you."

"No." He put his hands on her shoulders and stopped her as she was about to charge out the hospital doors. "Let me do my job. Stay with Tasha."

Without another word he strode out through the door and Claire gazed after him in frustration. She headed back to Tasha's room. Maybe it was a blessing that Tasha hadn't woken up again. She was bound to be exhausted, and if Catherine was right, and why wouldn't she be, this was a facet of Tasha's overall health, whether it was good or not.

While Claire waited for news, the Channel Seven team pulled up outside the hospital and Pauline Kirby began serving up special reports. When the Amber Alert went out, they'd gotten themselves a story.

Several hours later Claire, who refused to go outside and let the newspeople pounce on her, pushed aside a plate from the cafeteria with the remains of a barely nibbled hamburger and remembered her own plan to call Human

Resources and find out about Rita's employment. She dialed from her cell and was put on hold for long moments before finally getting through. The head of the department, Dale Werkken, answered her queries carefully. "You know, Dr. Norris, that I'm not allowed to give out personal information about an employee."

"Yeah, well, this employee could be the kidnapper of a baby from Ocean Park Hospital. Have you seen the news at all? Do you know about the Amber Alert?"

"That doesn't mean I should tell you. There is a protocol."

"Come on, Dale. She had to have been recommended by someone or the decision would have taken a lot longer. Who recommended her?"

"She came in and applied by herself . . ."

"And?" Claire questioned, hearing the hesitation. "Who recommended her?" she practically yelled at him.

"Paolo Avanti," he said quickly, as if that would somehow vindicate him from telling.

Claire pulled the phone from her ear and stared at it in surprise. Avanti?

What did that mean?

Checking her list of stored numbers, she put a call through to Avanti's cell. It was two thirty. He was probably in his office or patrolling Side A, maybe checking in with his favorite patient, Heyward Marsdon III.

He didn't answer and she was about to hang up, when his supercilious voice suddenly came on the line. "Hello?"

"Paolo, this is Claire."

"Claire! Are you still at Ocean Park?" He sounded extremely tense.

"Yes, I'm not sure I'll be back this afternoon. I'm waiting with Tasha, our Jane Doe, who's been unconscious since the birth."

"We've been watching the news," he said. "Any word on the kidnapper?"

"No. What you haven't heard yet, but it's bound to get out soon, is that we think the kidnapper is a nurse named Rita Feather Hawkings."

He couldn't disguise his gasp. *"Who?"*

"The recent hire at Halo Valley that you recommended for the job."

"There must be some mistake!" he sputtered. "I know of Rita, yes. We're acquaintances. And I did think she'd be good for the job, but she isn't capable, she wouldn't—"

"The sheriff's department is looking for her. I'm assuming she's not at the hospital today?"

"Um . . . no . . . I don't know." Panic ran beneath his tone.

"You'd better call and tell them what you know about her before something worse happens to that baby." When there was no response, she said, "Avanti? Paolo?" But he was gone.

She next put in a call to Lang but it went straight to voice mail. She was debating on whether to call the sheriff's department directly or find Deputy Savannah Dunbar, who was still at the hospital taking reports, when her phone rang in her hand.

It was James Freeson.

"This is Claire," she answered.

"What did you say to Avanti?" he demanded. "I heard him talking on the cell phone to you and then he stormed out of here."

"He knows the woman we think kidnapped Tasha's baby. Rita Feather Hawkings. I told him to contact the sheriff's department."

"Rita stole the baby?" he repeated sharply.

"You know her, too?"

"I know that she really *knows* Avanti well," he said in his smug way.

"Like that?" Claire said, slightly surprised.

"Claire, we need you back at the hospital. Avanti's

God knows where, and I'm going straight to Radke and bringing him up to date on all this."

"I need to tell the sheriff's department about Avanti's friendship with Rita."

"Do that. And give them my number, because I've got a few things to say as well . . ."

Lang screeched to a halt in front of the Hawkings house. Burghsmith, late thirties, tall and lean, met him on the porch. "Drove by that way," he pointed toward the north. "Turned east."

"Thanks."

He jumped back in his truck. She could be long gone. It might not even be Rita. He could be chasing ghosts. But he followed Burghsmith's directions and found himself winding back and forth through the Foothillers' community, passing by the café-cum-grocery store-cum-tavern. No Wrangler.

He drove up to Cade's house, thinking it was where the Wrangler had been parked before. Pulling into the driveway to turn around, he thought about the night before and felt a deep sadness for screwed-up Cade, who'd been undone just hearing about Rafe's injuries and then was killed himself.

Turning back into the street, he glanced toward the Blackburns'. Rita had been parked in front of their house. Quickly he reversed direction and drove to the end of the block, the nose of his truck at the end of the road, pointed across the Scotch broom–covered field where he'd chased Cade.

There was no Jeep Wrangler anywhere.

He shook his head. Rita Hawkings wasn't here. She hadn't come back to the community because it would be the first place anyone would look for her.

Throwing the truck in reverse, he put an arm around the back of the seat and started to turn his head when a light caught the corner of his eye. A light from the house across the field, turned on against the uncertain daylight of this dark day.

Angela Feather's house. Rita's aunt.

Who lived there now?

He drove out of the Foothillers' community, back onto Highway 101, and then to the side road that led to the house across the field. He pulled up to the drive and looked down the lane toward a carport.

A black Jeep Wrangler was tucked inside.

A zing ran up Lang's nerves. The muscles at the back of his neck tightened. He drove past the driveway and pulled to the side of the road, then called the sheriff's department and asked for O'Halloran. He was told the sheriff was busy and he nearly bit the administrator's head off telling her it was Langdon Stone and it was an emergency.

O'Halloran came on the phone. "Detective?" he asked, slightly miffed.

Tersely, Lang explained the situation, finishing with, "I need the name of the current homeowner, if they live there themselves, or if it's a rental."

"I'm sending backup."

Lang got out of his truck and, in a crouch, walked back to the edge of the drive. He was pretty sure striding right up to the door and saying he was with the sheriff's department wasn't going to work if Rita was inside.

As if divining his thoughts, a dark-haired woman stuck her head out of the door and looked around. Lang shrank into the tall weeds and behind a skinny pine tree, his heart beating hard and fast. He'd bet his last dollar that was Rita Feather Hawkings. He couldn't see her in this position and risked lifting his head, but she'd gone back inside.

Carefully, tramping through tall, wet field grass, he skirted the drive and came up on the north side of the house.

His Glock was tucked back in its spot at his waistband. He sure as hell hoped he didn't have to depend on it. There was a baby inside that house, and as if calling for help herself, the little girl's cries could be heard from where he was standing.

In a moment of pure reaction, he ran lightly across the driveway, tucked around the Wrangler, and let himself in through a back door that, though locked, gave when he pushed hard against it, breaking loose under pressure.

And there she was. Standing directly in front of him as he looked down the galley kitchen toward a back den. Attempting to give the crying infant a bottle. Staring at him.

Her eyes widened.

"Don't move, Rita," he ordered in a cold voice that brooked no argument. "Don't you damn well move."

"This is my baby," she said, after the longest moment of Lang's life.

"Police are on their way. Put the baby down and your hands up." He eased forward, his own hands in front of him, trying to keep her from panicking.

"You don't understand! This is *my* baby!"

"Just put her down."

"She's hungry." Rita's attention wavered and she looked down at the infant, who was trying to eat, but Rita wasn't holding the bottle correctly.

In that brief moment, he sprang forward and grabbed her upper arms. She automatically let go of the infant but Lang's body was there, keeping the baby between them. He pushed Rita to the wall and pulled the baby away. He hardly knew what he was going to do until he did it. When he stepped back, he reached around for his gun at the same moment she jumped forward, claws out, but he yelled,

"*Back off. Get back.* I have a gun, and so help me, I'll shoot you if you don't *back off*!"

His fierceness had its effect. She hesitated, looked around wildly, eyes rolling. She started screaming in frustration. "You can't take my baby! You can't take my baby!"

Lang held the child in one arm, the Glock in his other hand. He kept it steady on her. She was wild with fury. Torn between attacking him and ripping at her own hair. "She killed him!" she screamed. "She killed Rafe! And Cade! And she took my baby. Mine and Rafe's and she *doesn't care.* She's evil. She stabbed Rafe to death! And she wants everyone to think it's my fault but it's not! She cut herself." Rita made a motion across her own abdomen. "I didn't do that. She wants you to think I did, but I *didn't.* I had a knife but so did she. I went after her. I wanted my baby, but she turned on me with her knife. I stabbed her up here!" She pounded her upper chest and shoulder area. "I just wanted the baby. Yes, yes, I meant to take it. But I *didn't.* Don't you understand? I didn't. Because she came after me. She's a witch! A witch face! And Rafe was there, trying to stop her. But she kept hacking at me. Hack, hack, hack!" She stabbed at the air with a clenched fist. "But I got away. I cried all the way home because she took my baby. Mine and Rafe's. And then *she killed him*! She stabbed him to death for saving me!" Rita was crying, gulping and crying. "Don't you see? Don't you see?" She fell against the wall for support, sliding down. "I had to kill her. For Rafe. And I had to get my baby back. Don't you see? *Don't you see?*"

Before Lang could say anything, do anything more, Clausen and Burghsmith surged through the front and back doors at the same time. They stopped short upon seeing the crumpled woman crying on the floor and Lang, holding both a Glock and a crying infant, standing over her.

* * *

Lang called Claire as he drove away from the scene of Rita's capture and Claire listened to his recounting of the events in a kind of horrified disbelief. She was halfway to Halo Valley, and Lang's terse recap of what had transpired brought instant relief and a whole lot of questions.

"Thank God the baby's safe," she expelled. Then, humbly, "Thank you for saving her."

"Rita wasn't going to hurt the child, but she's definitely deluded. A candidate for the Dr. Norris treatment of care for the seriously psychotic."

"She's lying about Tasha," Claire said. Then she quickly related what had transpired in her conversation with Avanti and how she'd given the information to Sheriff O'Halloran, who was going to talk to Freeson as no one had heard from Avanti himself. "I'm on my way to Halo Valley."

"Clausen and Burghsmith have probably already talked to O'Halloran. They're on their way to the jail with Rita."

"Good. I'm glad she's caught."

"Yeah."

"You don't believe anything she said about Tasha, do you?" Claire asked anxiously. "She's obsessed. Can't take the responsibility. Wants to believe the baby's hers, and has a whole delusion about it."

"I know."

"But . . . ?"

"Rita's crazy. Really out there. But before Clausen and Burghsmith took her away, she was begging me not to give the baby back to Tasha. She said Tasha used Rafe to get away from the cult. That she got pregnant to escape. That Tasha never cared about Rafe, and that pregnancy was her way to get him to do what she wanted."

"She's transferring blame. It happens."

"She said that's why Catherine and the Colony don't want Tasha back. She's a devil. A bad seed."

"Are you seriously buying this?"

Lang sighed. "Not all of it."

"But some of it. You're buying some of it?"

"You're the doctor. You know more about this than I do. I just don't want Tasha to be a blind spot. One I didn't look at closely enough, you know?"

She did know. She'd been fooled a time or two by patients, and she'd made it a practice never to take things at face value until she had all the facts.

"I'd like to talk to Catherine again," Lang went on. "She said Natasha was afflicted with these spells. Maybe there's something more she's not telling us."

"I told Catherine I'd let her know when Tasha delivered. But I have to go to the hospital first."

"I'm heading to the department. Let's connect later and tell Catherine about Tasha and the baby together."

Claire agreed, frowning as she hung up. Catherine had already intimated Tasha would be an unfit mother. Social Services had been called to take the baby from Rita's house, and the child was now in their hands until Tasha woke up.

She thought about her last vision of Tasha, lying in bed, unaware, her clean, smooth brow and uncomplicated face, the picture of angelic peace. Rita Feather Hawkings was the villain in this piece, not Tasha.

Claire didn't see Freeson upon her return to Halo Valley. She spent the rest of the afternoon in a motherly, babysitting role because news of Tasha's disappearance and delivery, and then the kidnapping, had stirred up the residents, touching their nerves, exacerbating their own fears. Mrs. Tanaway and Mrs. Merle were in their rooms, and Maribel was circling in tight circles, muttering to herself. Donald was rubbing his jaw and looking concerned. Gibby was in his chair, asking constantly when Tasha would be home, and Thomas McAvoy was in a glaring match with Big Jenny, who was looking at him coquettishly through her lashes.

Heyward Marsdon was seated in the chair next to Gibby's, clutching his hands together, staring at the flickering images on the television while Greg, Alison, and Alphonse hovered nearby. "Dr. Avanti is usually with him if he's out of his room," Alison breathed to Claire about Heyward.

"A condition imposed to even allow him on Side A," Claire said, feeling renewed fury at the Marsdon family. Yes, they donated heavily and paid extra for the personal attention, but it didn't allow for breakdowns in staff care. Freeson was right. She'd been desperately needed back at the hospital, if for nothing else than crowd control.

With the overworked staff's care, Claire brought things under control again, and the worst of the patients' inner panic and worries were allayed by dinnertime. Freeson showed up and grudgingly helped out.

"Where's Avanti?" Claire asked him.

"With *his* doctor," Freeson said. "He's got some issues over sex that Rita tapped into, apparently. He and Rita were fornicating all over the hospital." He looked satisfied, and to Claire's questioning look, admitted, "I've been promoted to his job."

"Ah . . ."

"Don't pretend to be appalled. You're going up the ladder, too," he said.

"Did Avanti talk to the police?"

"Spilled it all to his doctor and allowed some information to be given out. He barely knew Rita. She doesn't have a cell phone and he saw her mostly at the hospital."

"How did he meet her in the first place?"

"Picked her up at that bar on the way to Salem, Vandy's, and they started seeing each other. Guess she twisted his arm for a reference. Apparently he didn't know about the baby obsession."

Lang called at six thirty. It was pitch dark and there was moisture in the air, but at least it wasn't a full-fledged rain shower. They agreed to meet at her place, and when they did, they fell into each other's arms, needing the human contact after the events of the day.

After some long kisses and desperate touches, Claire finally surfaced. "I can't think straight with you!"

Lang groaned, ran a hand through his hair, and closed his eyes for a moment. "I know. We've got miles to go before we sleep."

"Tasha still hasn't woken up," Claire worried.

"I know. Deputy Dunbar reported in when she left Ocean Park. But with Rita locked up, she's safe enough. And the baby's with Social Services, doing well."

"What if Tasha doesn't come to this time?" Claire said aloud, voicing her worst fears. "What if she stays out?"

"That's why we need to talk to Catherine. If there's something else . . ."

"Think she'll see us in the dark?"

"We'll shine the damn lights right on her."

"Let's go in my car," Claire said. "I'll let her know that if she doesn't let you in, you're going to be stuck outside the gates, just waiting."

"That oughtta scare her," he said dryly, but they headed out together.

It was the shortest time on record for the denizens of Siren Song to recognize that there was someone at their gates and hurry out to meet them. Catherine herself stepped out, wearing a red woolen cape with a hood, along with Isadora. They came together, stepping carefully over branches, rocks, and other debris that littered their walkway, and Isadora let Catherine through, locking the gate behind her. Lang and Claire, who'd come in Claire's Passat, were a bit surprised that Catherine came to them.

"Natasha's had her baby. A little girl," Claire said. "That's why we're here."

Catherine nodded. "I would like to see the child."

Claire had no idea what Catherine's intentions might be and she was feeling completely protective of Tasha's baby. "I'm not sure if that's possible right now. She's with Social Services."

Absorbing that information with a frown, Catherine said, "Then I would like to do some shopping in town. Would that be all right with you?"

"Sure," Lang said, slightly amused by her high-handedness. He held the passenger door for her. The more time they had with her, the more they might learn.

He climbed into the backseat and literally went along for the ride as Claire drove them into Deception Bay proper. This was the first time Catherine had even deigned to be within ten feet of him, and he figured it was his best, maybe only, chance to ask her a number of burning questions.

They went to the Drift In Market and Catherine picked up fresh fruit and vegetables, and a number of staples. Her garb caused a few mostly incurious second looks, but she accomplished the task without leaving any time for a discussion.

When they were walking back to the car, Lang said, "Can we step in there for a minute? Get some coffee, doughnuts?" He pointed to the Sands of Thyme bakery and Catherine, though she looked like she wanted to say no, nodded her acquiescence.

As soon as they were seated at a table, he said, "It took you long enough to claim Natasha, and now you want to see her baby. Excuse me if I'd like some kind of explanation."

Her gray eyes regarded him with a knowing look, like

he'd just lived up to her low expectations. "What do you want to know?" she asked primly, then turned to Claire, who was seated across from her, and not Lang, who'd purposely spread himself over the chair next to Claire's, sprawling, making a point of taking up room. He didn't care about her aversion to men or whatever her problem was; he was through being ignored.

Claire was looking at Lang as if she'd like to be the lead dog on this one, but again, he was through with that kind of careful dance. "I want to know about your whole tribe," he said, draping an arm over the back of Claire's chair, which earned him a cold look. "Ever since Tasha got attacked, we've been trying to figure out who she is and how to help her. You knew she was missing, yet when we finally figured out Tasha was from Siren Song, you denied it. Why?"

"There are a lot of reasons," she said.

"Name one."

"She thinks we abused her."

Lang narrowed his eyes. "Yeah? Why would she think that?"

"Because as punishment, we sometimes locked her in her room, and when she was particularly—ill—we strapped her to her bed."

"Strapped her to her bed?" he repeated. "That sounds like child abuse, all right." He turned to Claire, who was looking concerned. "Better not let her anywhere near the baby."

"I don't expect you to understand." Catherine's lips were so tight they were almost bloodless.

"Good. 'Cause I don't."

Claire said, "What do you mean by 'ill'?"

"I told you Natasha has spells. A kind of sleepwalking. Eyes open but unaware. You've seen it." Catherine was dismissive.

"She came to us in a catatonic state," Claire said. "She slips into awareness and out again."

"It's what she does," Catherine said. "But she can hurt herself and others." A shadow passed across her face and she turned to the window and squinted, as if viewing something on the far side of the street.

"So you were just happy she was gone?" Lang suggested.

"I have a duty to keep my family safe."

"By strapping them to their beds?" Lang wasn't buying any of it. "Maybe you're all as strange as the locals believe. Wanna know what we've learned?"

She finally looked his way. "I have a feeling you plan to tell me."

"Yes, I do."

And Lang did. Ignoring Claire's look of consternation, as if she felt he were bullying his way through. Again, he didn't care. He told Catherine about reading Herman Smythe's history of the cult, and about Claire meeting with the historian himself at Seagull Pointe, and about Dinah being his daughter, and possibly sister to one or more of Catherine's nieces, and about Herm's remarks about Mary's unbridled sexual desire where she took more than a few lovers. "What was the term he used?" Lang asked Claire. "Oh, yeah, she had more babies than you could count. Are any of your 'nieces' yours? And where is Mary? Is she alive? Dead?"

"You read the history," she snapped out.

"Yeah, and it ends with your birth, two years after Mary's, and a footnote about several children born at the lodge."

Catherine's brows lifted. "Nothing about the girls?"

"Either he didn't write it, or he didn't include it in the book. Whatever you're hiding, it's still safe."

"Mr. . . . ?"

"Stone. Langdon Stone."

"Mr. Stone, we've been persecuted for years. People have been frightened of us. Called us witches and Satan's daughters and worse."

"Because of your dark gifts."

Claire's head swung his way in surprise and Catherine was momentarily flummoxed.

"I forgot," Lang said. "That was in there, too."

Straightening her spine, Catherine retorted, "Our perceived extra abilities."

"And Mary? What happened to her?" he asked.

"She was forced to leave. It was better for all of us." Catherine pursed her lips and looked at Claire. "Have I sung enough for my supper, Dr. Norris?" she asked.

"I'm sorry if these questions seem intrusive," Claire said. "We want to help Tasha and the baby, and it's been difficult to understand where you stand."

"Let me be clear, then," she announced, getting to her feet. "When the child goes up for adoption, I would like to be considered as the adoptive parent."

"What?" Claire stood up, too.

"Don't think your parenting style's going to go over with Social Services," Lang stated, straightening in his chair.

"Tasha's her mother," Claire reminded them. "It's her child first."

"She doesn't want it," Catherine said tautly. "You'll find out. And when that day comes, I'll be waiting."

She sailed out of the Sands of Thyme and would say nothing else on the ride back to Siren Song.

Chapter 25

Catherine's words bothered Claire, but she didn't want to take them too seriously. There was bad blood between Catherine and Natasha, and until Tasha woke up and had a chance to speak for herself, Claire was going to give her the benefit of the doubt. But that wasn't happening anytime soon. It had been over a week since the birth of baby Beatrice, the name given to the child by Social Services. Beatrice was in the temporary care of one of the social workers themselves as they determined whether she needed foster care placement, since Tasha was not showing signs of recovery and was being transferred back to Halo Valley while they awaited an outcome.

Claire was lobbying for Dinah to become the little girl's foster parent. There was no other family member available to step in even temporarily. Rafe was dead and had no immediate living family, and Catherine and the women from the Colony were no answer, as far as Claire was concerned. Dinah was the best choice for many reasons, not the least being her willingness to bring the baby to Halo Valley to see her mother on a regular basis and try to help jostle Tasha out of her latest "spell."

After arraignment Rita remained in the Tillamook

County Jail pending trial. Her mother had gone to see her but with no money for bail and no inclination to really help, apparently, she'd just shaken her head at her daughter and complained loud and long about what a disgrace Rita was. As bad as her whore of an aunt, Angela!

Rita had chosen to hide out at the house of this spurious aunt, a house that had fallen into the hands of a local bank and was heading for foreclosure. She'd been running out of options and had hoped to squat there with the baby until some of the notoriety had died down.

She kept insisting that Tasha had killed Rafe and Cade, and that the baby was really hers.

It seemed strange, to Claire, to have Tasha back at Halo Valley, and she wondered what would end up becoming of her and Beatrice. It was a worry that followed Claire around while her world settled down from its out-of-control spin into a regular habit of seeing Lang, keeping up with Dinah, who was granted care of Beatrice on Tasha's second day at Halo Valley, and going to work.

Lang used the time to completely move into his apartment even though he spent most of his time at Claire's place, and on a Saturday night, ten days after Beatrice's birth, he brought a couple bottles of wine over for dinner and joined Dinah, Claire, and baby Bea.

"I apologize for calling you a quack's quack," he told Dinah, pouring the wine.

She was looking in the oven to the baked spinach lasagna she and Claire were making. "Apology accepted. Drop by anytime and you can hold some crystals while I chant."

"Can't wait," he said dryly, to which Claire broke into a grin, one of the first in a long, long time. He handed her a glass of Cabernet and said, "Just don't tell me you're on call."

"I'm free tonight," Claire assured him, and they drank in better spirits than they'd been in for a long while and ate the home-cooked meal, then sat around afterward, playing with little Bea.

"We can't get too attached," Claire said. "Tasha opened her eyes today."

"For the first time since Ocean Park?" Lang asked.

"That anyone noticed. Gibby says he's been talking to her. Maybe it's true, maybe it's fantasy. But there are signs that she's coming back again."

"What does that mean for the long run?" Lang asked. "You trust her with a baby?"

"Bea is hers. If Tasha becomes lucid and is physically fine, which she is, then . . ."

"I'm not going to think about it," Dinah said. "Everything's temporary. I've learned to accept." Bea started fussing and Dinah made up a bottle of formula and sat on Claire's couch, feeding the baby.

Claire thought about her own miscarriage and firmly set the memory aside. Like she told her patients, stay in the present. Dwelling on misfortunes was death to good mental health. And hoping for things that just couldn't happen was completely counterproductive, she thought sadly, her gaze on the lovely little baby.

Monday morning Claire pulled into the Halo Valley parking lot and groaned aloud to see Pauline Kirby and the Channel Seven news team camped outside the hospital.

What now?

"Dr. Norris!" Pauline called, spying Claire though she tried to enter from the far end of the medical office building. "We understand that Rita Feather Hawkings, the alleged kidnapper of one of your patient's baby, Tasha Rutledge Beeman, was involved with one of the most respected doctors at Halo Valley, Dr. Paolo Avanti."

Beeman. Claire realized that Pauline and her newshounds

must have pulled the name from the book about the Colony at the historical society, the same way Lang had learned of it. She was fairly certain, especially after all the bad press, that no one at Halo Valley had given out that information, and there was no way Catherine had granted the pushy newswoman an interview.

"Is Dr. Avanti still employed at this hospital?" Pauline thrust a microphone Claire's way.

She wanted to say, "No comment," but decided instead on the truth and answered simply, "No."

"Is Ms. Beeman part of the group known as the Colony?" Now Claire turned away from the interview. She couldn't, and wouldn't, give out information on a patient.

"Rita Feather Hawkings has also been indicted in the deaths of both Rafe Black Bear Worster and Cade Worster and the attack on Ms. Beeman. Has Ms. Beeman confirmed those accusations? How is the baby? Dr. Norris!"

Claire yanked the medical offices' door open, glad that during daylight hours it did not require a keycard and code.

"Dr. Norris!" Pauline called stridently. "There's a rumor that Heyward Marsdon the Third has been moved from the maximum security side of your hospital to the less controlled section. How does that make you feel?"

Claire racewalked down the hallway, half-expecting Pauline to follow her inside. She hurried past the first-floor receptionist and took the elevator to her office. She didn't want to talk about any part of the hospital goings-on with the press. They just never stopped digging, and sometimes they struck a sensitive nerve.

Dropping her purse on her desk, she slipped out of her coat. She hadn't planned on coming here first; she was on her way to the hospital proper. But she needed a moment or two to put herself together. Beyond Tasha and Bea and the worry about what would happen to them, she also had the Marsdon issue. She'd never told Lang that she'd accepted his apology; never explained that she'd put Marsdon and the incident behind her. It was the one subject neither of them felt compelled to address. There was enough going on as it was.

After a few moments, she locked her purse inside the closet with her coat, then closed and secured her office door and headed to the hospital.

Gibby sat in his favorite chair, hanging on with a death grip. Tasha was back and she was in the chair next to him. But something was wrong. She didn't want to talk anymore. In fact, she was really, really *mean*.

"I doan like you no more," he told her now. He crossed his arms in front of his chest, nodded and said, "Huh."

She stared at the TV but her mouth turned into a mean smile. "You are stupid," she said. "Mentally deficient."

"I'm fishent!" he tried to repeat and she turned to look at him with really scary blue eyes.

She said, "You told them about me. And now I'm their prisoner."

"No . . ."

"It's your fault."

"It not!"

"All your fault."

And then Thomas McAvoy was in front of them, standing there, really, really mean. "You're a fucking liar," he whispered to Tasha.

"Stay away from me," she snarled. "I will kill you while you sleep."

"Liar!" he roared.

And then Greg and Darlene and everyone was there and Gibby started screaming and screaming.

* * *

Claire came down the stairs at the sound of Gibby's shrieks. Once again it took a concentrated effort by most of the staff to bring things under control. Freeson, who had been in Heyward's room, strode out, looking annoyed.

He'd become more insufferable over these past few weeks. Claire was going to be happy when they hired another doctor to hopefully add more balance.

"You're going to need to stay through dinner today," Freeson said. "I have an important meeting, and I can't be here."

His goatee was already bristling, ready for a fight. Claire simply nodded. Lang had officially started with the TCSD and she thought he might be late himself.

"Good." He bustled away and Claire turned to find Tasha, who was standing by the bookcase, staring at her.

"Tasha," Claire said, encouraged. "We finally got you some acceptable clothes," she said, walking toward her. "How are you feeling?"

The blond woman just stood and waited, ignoring the dress that Claire had specifically picked out for her, her gaze faraway once more. Claire tried to engage her with talk about Beatrice, telling her that she could bring the baby to see her the next day, but Tasha was back in her own world.

Feeling slightly deflated, Claire headed back to her office, wondering if both Lang's comment that she might be faking it and Catherine's dire prediction that she wouldn't want the baby could have any merit at all.

The scream inside Tasha's head felt never ending. How had she ended up back here? Locked in. Kept from her own freedom!

She hated them.

Hated them all.

Inside her head was a black fury, a blurred buzzing

noise, the sound of her own anger. She was through pretending. Through playing their games. Through letting them rule her.

She didn't remember the birth of the baby. It seemed like somebody else had carried that child all these months. All these months of waiting! Pushing Rafe to get her free! Planning. Faking.

Her only joy was that Rita was in jail. She'd heard the news on the hospital staff's lips. Rita was rotting in a hole, caught, trapped. That, at least, had gone according to plan.

Closing her eyes, she drew a long breath, seating herself in her chair.

A moment later she came to and realized it was night. Hours later. She'd been gone into her own swirling, comforting blackness and had somehow ended up sitting in her own bed, in the stupid dress the meddling doctor had thought she would want.

Her wheelchair stood at the ready and Tasha stared at it. She dug through her mind, searching, and found there was something there. Something she'd almost forgotten.

Climbing from the bed, she picked up the cushion of the wheelchair and turned it over. From inside a slit gleamed the black hilt of a knife. Smiling, she slowly pulled it out, turning the blade over, its cold edge glinting in the light. And then a tumble of pills scattered onto the floor. McAvoy's pills. She scooped them into her hand and stared at them. During her blackout she'd found a way to acquire the items she needed for her escape.

Sometimes her mind gave her the plan when she was unaware.

Sometimes she was shown the way.

That's what happened with Nathaniel. He'd been so dull. Weak. Mentally deficient. He'd needed to be sent to the next world, so she'd taken Mary's herbs. Kept high on top of the pantry shelves. In glass jars. Forgotten. The labels nearly indecipherable.

Belladonna.

Nathaniel went into convulsions. Horrible, twisting, gasping convulsions. Tasha had watched with interest. Death had come soon and she'd left him out by the graveyard.

Catherine had guessed. Catherine had strapped her to her bed. Tasha had sworn it wasn't her. She'd cried and begged and pleaded. Catherine hadn't wanted to listen but simpleminded Lillibeth had pleaded and pleaded and finally gotten Tasha released.

Tasha had pretended. Catherine had pretended. They circled each other, each knowing, neither speaking of it.

Tasha had made love to Rafe on Nathaniel's grave. She hoped Catherine knew.

Needed her to know!

Footsteps in the hallway. Tasha squirreled the knife and pills beside her in the bed.

That meddling doctor again. Her dark eyes were all knowing, digging, burrowing, burning holes into Tasha's skin. "It's dinnertime," the doctor said. "Let me take you down."

Friendly voice. Evilness inside.

Tasha decided it was time to take a new step. "I can walk down on my own, thank you."

The doctor was so stunned she looked like she was going to pass out. Tasha hid an inward smile.

"Good," she said. "It's nice to hear your voice. Tomorrow I'll bring your baby to you."

Tasha nodded, and reluctantly, the doctor left, giving Tasha an uncertain look that meant she was beginning to suspect.

Quickly Tasha slipped the knife up the sleeve of her dress and the pills inside the side of her sock.

She was leaving tonight.

Chapter 26

"Tasha spoke to me," Claire said into the phone to Lang, unable to completely hide her surprise. "It was so unexpected. And . . . weird. I don't want to be influenced by Catherine, or Rita, but it gave me kind of a jolt."

"What did she say?"

"Basically that she was going to walk down to dinner rather than have me wheel her. I told her I would bring her baby to see her tomorrow."

"What'd she say to that?" Lang asked.

"Nothing."

Hearing something in her tone, he asked, "What are you thinking?"

"I really don't know."

"So, how long are you staying at Halo Valley?"

"Probably till just after dinner. It's just been so unsettled around here." She told him about Freeson's directive that she stick around.

"Hey, I want to see you," Lang said. "I don't feel like waiting."

A smile crossed her face. "So, what can we do about that?"

"I'm coming your way. We'll figure out the rest of the evening later."

"Okay."

She clicked off her phone, her pulse racing light and fast. She was falling for him. Oh, boy, was she falling for him.

Tasha sat at the table, trying to recall the extent of her dark dreams. Sometimes she could. Sometimes she saw Mary, her mother, hovering just beyond her reach, although that was rare. Mostly she had to rely on the clues that were left in the dream's wake. Like the knife and the pills.

Gibby was seated beside her. He'd actually pulled away when she took the empty seat next to him, alarmed. Everyone else had looked at her, too. She hadn't acted this decisive before.

His glass of unfiltered apple juice was sitting by his right hand. Tasha surreptitiously pulled the handful of pills from her sock, picked up her own glass, pretended to drink, then slipped the pills into it while she was setting the glass back down. They didn't all immediately sink, so she placed it to her lips again and made swallowing motions.

She wasn't sure what the pills were. She didn't care. Enough of them would be bad for Gibby. Might even kill him.

Maribel suddenly grabbed a dinner roll off Big Jenny's plate. A roar went up, and in the moment while everyone looked at Jenny, who lunged for Maribel, Tasha switched glasses with Gibby. Gibby glanced back at her, frowning.

With an effort she smiled, though it felt like her muscles were glued down.

"I doan like you," Gibby said.

The meddling Dr. Norris heard him and her brows raised.

Tasha gazed at Gibby blankly, as if she didn't understand.

"She is a fucking liar!" Gibby shouted.

"Shut up, moron," Thomas McAvoy snarled.

"Gibby," the doctor admonished.

She looked worried by his turnabout, but Tasha wasn't surprised. Nathaniel had been a tattletale, too. Neither of them could keep their idiotic mouths shut.

But the doctor was getting too smart. Tasha could feel the questions inside her head.

Gibby shrank back in his chair and reached for his apple juice. He drank several big gulps. Tasha saw the white edge of several pills through the glass and realized her plan wasn't going to work.

There was a roaring in her ears. They would find out what she'd done! They would lock her in a room, strap her to her bed! They would never let her out.

Her heart beat so hard her chest hurt. The edges of her dark dream crowded close, but she strained hard and pushed them back. She needed to be in control!

And then she saw that other man. The inmate who always had a guard with him. He made the hospital staff very nervous. Something wrong with him, Tasha guessed, but she had no real interest in learning what it was.

But he was watching her. With those same kind of burning eyes, like the doctor.

Burning, burning, burning.

Something had to be done.

Lang pulled up to Halo Valley Security Hospital and recognized the tension in his gut that still resided there. He had to let it go. Had to move on. As much as he'd like to piss off the Marsdons and take their sneaky end run around Heyward's incarceration to the media, he wasn't going to do it. Putting it all back in the public eye wouldn't guarantee Heyward would be put back on Side B and it sure as hell wouldn't bring his sister back. Nor would it do much for his growing relationship with Claire, either.

He'd spent the last month coming to terms with it all and had learned, in the process, just how much Claire had been a victim, too.

So, okay. Time to move on. He locked his Glock in the glove box and walked up to the sliding glass doors. The girl at the desk saw him, recognized him, and set about opening the doors.

As they slid open he stepped inside and saw that the patients were just finishing dinner.

And Heyward Marsdon sat to one side, his attention on, of all people, Tasha.

The muscles at the back of Lang's neck tightened in spite of himself.

He saw Melody in his mind's eye. Her smile. The way she was before her illness ravaged her looks and her soul.

And then Claire was coming toward him, a soft smile on her face. He took a step toward her when Heyward, seeing her, suddenly leapt up and raced toward her.

Lang moved automatically, lunging forward. He stepped between them and grabbed Heyward by his collar in one fluid movement. "Stop," he growled angrily.

Fury took over. All his warnings to himself splintered. Were obliterated.

"Wait, wait!" Claire's voice. Panicked.

Heyward sputtered, "She poisoned him. She poisoned him!"

"Shut up." Lang's teeth were gritted. He held him tight. Squeezed hard. Wanted to pop the bastard's head off.

"Stop! Stop!" Claire was there. Clawing at his arms. Freaking out. "Lang, no!"

"Let go, Claire," Lang bit out. "He's hallucinating."

"No . . . !" Heyward cried.

"No. He's on his meds! Lang, please! No!"

And then Tasha was there, flying toward them. Flying toward Heyward. Her face twisted with rage. Reaching up her sleeve.

To Lang's distinct shock she pulled a knife from her sleeve and charged Heyward, running him through his stomach.

Heyward staggered and Lang caught him.

And Tasha grabbed Claire by the hair and pressed the knife hard against her throat. "I have to kill them," she said in a hard voice. "They won't let me leave." Then to Lang, whose muscles were tense, she said, "Don't move."

Heyward gasped, blood oozing through his clothes as he pointed to the table, "She poisoned him. Gibby. I saw the pills in the glass."

"Don't talk," Tasha said to Heyward.

"Don't hurt her," he answered back, piteously.

"You talked," she said, and made a shallow cut across Claire's throat.

It was a nightmare. The same nightmare he'd imagined with Melody. Blood ran from the cut while Claire's eyes, huge and scared, silently begged him not to move.

Lang was frozen. Shackled by fear. Hearing the seconds count off in his head as Heyward sank to the ground, breathing unevenly.

Not Claire. Please, not Claire.

"Tasha," Claire said. "You can leave anytime."

"Liar."

"You don't have to stay here. We're a hospital. We've been waiting for you to get better."

"She poisoned him," Heyward murmured, clutching his stomach, his dull gaze directed toward the dining room where the patients and staff were all staring at Tasha and she was glaring back at them. "She stabbed me."

The orderly, Greg something, said loudly, "There's been a stabbing and a poisoning!"

"Shut up! Don't move," Tasha warned again. "Any of you."

Donald moaned, "Oh, dear. Oh, dear."

Gibby started crying. "It's in my apple juice!"

"Don't move or I'll kill her! You'll make me!"

Everyone froze.

Lang glanced from Gibby to Heyward to Claire, his chest tight. He saw Claire understood what Heyward had been trying to say.

"You're all looking at me like Catherine does," Tasha said, alarmed.

The blood ran in tiny rivulets down Claire's neck. Just a small wound. Flesh wound, Lang told himself. But he felt weak. Impotent. He had to do something.

Had to get the crazed woman to talk. Keep the moment from spinning into disaster.

"This isn't like you, Tasha," he said.

She laughed. "You're all so dumb. Just like all my sisters. All morons. And Catherine. But they know better now . . ."

Keep her talking, Lang told himself, pushing his fear into a deep, dark part of his soul. Keep her talking. "Rita told the truth after all. You stole Rafe from her so you could get away."

"Rafe loved me," she stated coldly. "Not Rita."

"Rafe told you about Rita's obsession over wanting a child. It gave you the idea to get pregnant."

"She couldn't have one," she gloated. "Rafe told me!"

"But you have an 'affliction.' You may not think so, but Catherine's had your number for a long time. You're the bad seed, aren't you? The secret embarrassment of the Colony."

"Shut your mouth!"

"You wanted Catherine to see you pregnant. Wanted her to see how you'd defied her again."

"Catherine shut me in my room, but I got out." Tasha was smug.

"With Rafe. But Rita followed you. She found you at the rest stop," Lang said, counting the seconds. It felt like an eternity. He didn't have his gun. Why didn't he bring his *gun*? "She attacked you, intending to take your baby. But something went wrong."

"I knew she would follow us! I wanted her to. She's crazy and jealous and she would never leave us alone unless Rafe killed her!"

"You wanted him to," Lang realized. "But it all went wrong. She got chased off. She intended to take your baby, but she didn't have a chance."

Heyward, who'd been down on his knees, had rolled to the balls of his feet. Lang sensed rather than saw the move. He wasn't sure what was in the man's mind. Knew it couldn't possibly help.

"What happened, Tasha?" Lang said. "What happened to Rafe?"

"He took Rita's knife away from her. She stabbed me! So he took her knife and said he would turn her in to the authorities. He said if she came near me, he would kill her. I was screaming at him to just do it. But Rita was shrieking like a witch. Said it was her baby! Rafe told her she was crazy. He would have killed her but she left too soon!" She inhaled through her teeth. "He said the baby and I were *his*. We were his."

"You killed him," Lang said. "Not Rita. No defensive wounds," he added. "He wouldn't fight his pregnant lover, even when she was stabbing him."

"He let Rita go, but I was his prisoner!" Tasha said intensely.

"You cut your own abdomen and blamed it on Rita."

"She was going to take my baby! She just didn't have time because of Rafe! He tried to stop me, so I stabbed him. I had to. *I had to.*"

"What about Cade?" Lang asked.

"You're just wasting time!" She started dragging Claire toward the door. "I need a driver," she stated flatly. "The rest of you stay back."

He had to keep her from taking Claire away. "Cade tried to stop you, too."

"He wanted me to call you! Wanted you to *help*!"

"And Gibby? You poisoned him with something?"

"Pills," Heyward said.

Tasha's gaze flashed on him.

It was just a moment. Not even a full second. But Lang took it, leaping forward and grabbing Tasha's arm, yanking hard, jerking the knife from Claire's throat. Tasha screamed at him, slashing wildly, slicing his arm. Blood beaded instantly but Lang didn't notice. He twisted the knife from her grasp, fighting the raging, spitting cat she'd become.

And then a body slammed into them both, breaking them apart, knocking Tasha hard to the ground, her head bouncing on the industrial carpet, her eyes rolling up.

Lang swirled around. It was Heyward. He'd hit her in a flying tackle.

And now he was on the ground, not moving, blood flowing.

"Claire?" Lang stumbled away. To Claire. The woman he loved. Who'd nearly met the same fate as Melody. "Claire!"

She'd crumpled to the floor when Lang grabbed Tasha. Now she was half-sitting, half-lying on the carpet, blood pooling around her, her eyes open and fixed.

"Claire!" He pressed his hand to her throat. Direct pressure. Not too much. Stop the bleeding, not the breathing.

The *woo-woo-woo* of an ambulance siren came rushing toward them and galvanized the rest of the staff into action. Greg knelt beside Lang. "I called 911. She said don't move, but my hand was on my phone, in my pocket. That's why I said that about the poisoning and stabbing."

"I didn't drink it!" Gibby moaned. "It tasted funny."

McAvoy said, "Those were my pills. She's a fucking thief!"

The EMTs rushed in. "Who's the poison victim?" one yelled, then they saw the prone forms of Claire, Tasha, and Heyward.

"Get another ambulance," the second one ordered.

"No poisoning," Lang said, shaking as he released Claire into their professional care. "Two stabbings. By the unconscious blond woman. The intended victim didn't drink the poison." He pulled his own phone from his pocket and called the sheriff's department.

He hadn't believed he could feel as bad as he did after Melody's death. He hadn't known he could care that much again.

And if he'd been asked, he would have denied vehemently that his pain could be over one Dr. Claire Norris.

But it was. He followed the ambulance to Ocean Park hospital and waited while Claire was rushed into surgery, pacing, praying a little, remembering his sister and Claire and Heyward and all the bad feelings. If he could take them back. If he could just please, please take them back. . . .

Then she was wheeled into recovery. He sat beside her, his hand gripping hers, his forehead down on the bed, his retinas burned with the vision of her white face, whiter bandage circling her throat, immobile form.

He ached inside. Soul-deep with misery. *Oh, please, please,* he prayed silently. *Please, don't let her die.*

He stayed beside her in recovery. Hours passed. Days. Eons. He knew it was his fault. He'd blamed her. He'd set her on this course. "I'm sorry," he whispered. "I love you, Claire."

Please, don't let her die.

"I love you."

His torture was endless, internal. Heyward had tried to save her, too.

She had to live!

And then, in the darkest moment of his soul, he felt something. Movement beneath his hand. Trembling fingers.

Slowly Lang raised his head, his blue eyes capturing her brown ones, dulled by pain, full of recognition. Joy sang through his veins. Impossible to believe. A miracle!

She opened her mouth but he put his own finger to her lips.

"Shhh."

Her fingers squeezed his. He squeezed back.

"I love you," he said brokenly. *"I love you . . ."*

Epilogue

". . . the Tillamook, the Trask, the Miami, the Wilson, and the Kilchis."

Lang sat at the end of Claire's couch, smiling down at her as she cradled a cup of herbal tea. Dinah, carrying Bea close to her chest in a blue-and-white paisley sling, had brought over a hot carafe and had just finished sharing a cup with Claire when Lang got off work. She left them, then, saying she and Bea would be right next door, sensing their need to be alone together.

"Someone's been searching the Internet," Claire said. Her voice was faint, more a case of being careful and easing around sore muscles than actual damage to her vocal center.

"Harder than you might think, given the age of my laptop," he assured her. "But if I can name all five rivers, O'Halloran seems to think I can do the job."

"That's the only reason?"

"The only one."

"Nothing to do with finding out who killed Rafe."

He reached under the covers and grabbed one of her bare feet. "Not a thing."

"Don't you dare tickle me," she warned.

"I was thinking more of a massage."

"Sure."

Lang grinned. "I called Will Tanninger at Winslow County, brought him up to date with all the little pieces he missed about the investigation. He was really interested in all the information about the Colony. Said he thought his girlfriend would want to talk to Catherine."

"Well, maybe . . ."

Lang gave her a speculative look and added, "She did come to the station, you know. Catherine. She wants to be Bea's guardian."

Claire would have shaken her head vigorously but knew better. Though she was healing well, the cut and subsequent surgery on her neck muscles and tendons damn well hurt! "Maybe Siren Song isn't the torture chamber Tasha imagined, but I don't want Bea there. I want her with Dinah."

"It'll be an uphill battle for Catherine if she wants to fight it."

"No change in Tasha?" Claire asked.

Lang shook his head.

Like Rita, Tasha had initially been taken to the county jail, but she'd fallen deep into one of her unconscious states and her breathing and pulse rate had plummeted to a dangerously low level. She'd been taken back to the hospital and was currently stabilized, but her health was uncertain.

"What'll happen to her?" Claire asked.

"If she recovers enough, a mental hospital for the criminally insane?" Lang suggested. "Locked up on Side B?"

Claire closed her eyes for a moment. Tasha would probably be confined to a single room, living her own personal hell. She said softly, "I'd love to have Bea, too."

"If something happens to Tasha, we'll adopt her," he told her seriously.

"Really?"

He nodded.

"You sound so positive."

"I'm not letting you go," he said. "And I'll do everything I know to make Bea ours. We can make it happen."

"We'll have to fight Dinah and the courts."

He shook his head, smiling gently. "She'd want us to be a family."

Claire felt tears sting behind her eyes and cursed her weakness. "Is that some kind of proposal, or am I hearing something I just want to hear?"

"I think Dr. Norris-Stone sounds great. Or just Dr. Stone. Whatever you prefer."

He leaned down and kissed her lightly, but Claire held him close, pressing her lips to his. Finally, they broke apart, grinning at each other.

"The answer's yes," she said.

"Good!" He kissed her again. A loud, smacking one this time. "I already asked my buddy, Trey, to be best man. Did I ever tell you our deal about buying each other a beer?" Claire shook her head, amused, as he told her how the day before he'd met up with Detective Curtis at Dooley's, a bar near the Portland Police Department, and as soon as Curtis walked through the door, the waitress thrust a beer in his hand, at seven A.M. "He said he'd stand up with me, but it took some convincing," Lang finished. "He, uh, remembers a few things I said about Halo Valley and Dr. Claire Norris."

"Ahh . . ."

"He then said some things about me being a jackass, and karma, and how things sometimes were meant to be. Kinda thought I was talking to Dinah for a moment."

Claire laughed. "Be careful what you wish for?"

"Something like that."

Sobering some, she asked, "Is Heyward doing okay?"

"Still at Ocean Park. Still recovering from his stomach

surgery. They say he should be okay. Of course, the Marsdons are squawking about neglect at Halo Valley, blaming everybody, threatening to pull their funding and maybe sue."

"You're kidding."

"They're a fun bunch, aren't they?" He began massaging her feet again, but when he slid a light finger over one of her soles, she yanked her foot back and gave him a warning look.

"Okay, okay." He tucked both feet back under the covers. "I put in a call to Pauline Kirby. Told her about Heyward the Third being moved from Side B to Side A at the Marsdons' insistence. Suggested maybe that wasn't what the courts had really decreed."

"Stirring up the hornets' nest."

"Heyward tried to save you," he said seriously. "He and my sister were both sick, and it was a tragedy for everyone."

Claire realized what a great admission that was. "Freeson won't like any of it, and neither will Radke," she said lightly.

"Or anyone else there, probably. The Marsdons will probably pull funding regardless."

"They've always wanted something we couldn't give them, and they held the hospital for ransom over it."

"Well, it's a whole new world order now," he said.

"Yes."

"By the way, Pauline told me she was going to kiss me the next time we met," Lang revealed.

"That woman sure is begging for a bitch slapping," Claire murmured and they both broke into laughter.

At Ocean Park hospital, Tasha opened her eyes to see herself strapped to whirring, blinking, and flashing monitors. She had no strength. It had been pulled from her by the dark forces warring within her. If she could just get up, just muster some energy, then she could leave. Get away!

The door to the room was open, but a guard in a uniform stood just outside.

Horror filled her. There was no way out. They'd blocked her escape.

No . . . ! she cried violently inside. *No, no, no!*

She was caught. Trapped.

And then the black curtain moved into her peripheral vision, smothering her, taking her down. Further and further. Lower than she'd ever gone before.

She sank beneath the darkness and didn't hear the droning buzz of the flat line or see it moving inexorably straight across the heart monitor's screen.